THE WAR AND THE FOX

Book Three of The Calatians

by Tim Susman

Argyll Productions
Dallas, Texas

THE WAR AND THE FOX

Book Three of The Calatians

by Tim Susman

Argyll Productions
Dallas, Texas

The War and the Fox
Production copyright Argyll Productions © 2019

Copyright © Tim Susman 2019

Cover and interior artwork © Laura Garabedian 2019
http://www.FairyTalesWithTails.com

Published by Argyll Productions
Dallas, Texas
www.argyllproductions.com

ISBN 978-1-61450-489-4

First Edition Trade Paperback July 2019

Typeset in Adobe Garamond Pro and Hopfer Hornbook.

CONTENTS

For Becky,
though I know it won't ever be enough

CHAPTER 1: THE FEAST OF CALATUS

According to legend, the sorcerer Calatus performed his Great Feat of Sorcery in the month of April, some year back in the 1400s, and thereby created twenty races of animal-people. So in the first week of each of the four hundred Aprils since then, the Calatians feasted and sang and danced and gave thanks for the sorcerer who had given them life. In the town of New Cambridge, Massachusetts, April brought drizzles, showers, and just about every form of rain save a full-on summer thunderstorm, but that never deterred the Feast of Calatus.

Though Kip was a fox as thick-furred as any of the New Cambridge residents, he had little trouble remaining dry even in the wettest of Aprils. He spent most of his time around fire, whether studying fire sorcery with Master Odden at Prince George's College of Sorcery in the White Tower or practicing fire spells while sitting before the fireplace at the Founders Rest Inn.

Until the previous winter, he'd lived in the White Tower's basement, but following the death of his best friend at the hands of the traitorous Master Windsor—for which Kip nonetheless blamed himself—he had been unable to sleep properly anywhere in the Tower. Coppy's gentle snoring followed no matter where he slept, he smelled the otter in places he couldn't possibly have been, and everywhere he heard the distinctive steps of Master Windsor—also impossible, as Kip had reduced the traitor to a pile of ash moments too late.

Kip and Emily had stopped Master Windsor from killing the last of the sorcerers in the American Colonies, after he'd destroyed Prince Philip's in Georgia and much of Prince George's earlier that year, but his colleague, Master Albright of King's College in London, had escaped via a quick translocation spell. They had left behind papers that tied their activities to the British Crown, which had stoked the fire of the independence movement in the Colonies. John Adams, despite failing health, had sued for reparations to the Colonies of Massachusetts Bay and Georgia for the destruction of their colleges of sorcery, but the Crown continued to insist stubbornly that the rogue sorcerers had acted alone. As far as Kip and his friends could tell, Albright hadn't even been taken into custody while the British government supposedly investigated his crimes (which included the murder of a British sorcerer). Tensions had escalated, and war was expected any day now.

Kip had studied at King's College with Master Cott, the world's foremost fire sorcerer, but last May, Odden had told Kip that he was no longer to visit London. Headmaster Patris, who bore no affection for Kip and had once insisted on his trips to London as a way to ensure his loyalty, now insisted he remain in the Colonies for the same reason.

So Kip had taken a room in the Founders Rest Inn, from where he could look up the hill and be comforted at the sight of the Tower still standing proudly atop it. His friend Malcolm O'Brien, a specialist in defensive magic, cast a protective ward over the Inn so that Kip couldn't be found by Master Albright, and Kip learned to translocate himself between the Inn and the Tower. To pay for his room, he offered Old John the innkeeper a savings in firewood by binding a burning phosphorus elemental to the inn's fireplace. Dubious at first, the old man soon grew quite attached to the cherry-red glowing lizard that capered about in the small space and engaged her in conversation. Within two months Old John had gone from reassuring his guests that she would do no harm to bringing them over to introduce them to her. When Kip dismissed her in preparation for summoning a new one, Old John bid her a solemn good-bye.

The current phosphorus elemental went by the name Ernest. He had quite a low voice and, like most of his kind, a short attention span and a cheerful demeanor. On this April morning, Kip had come from his room to find a familiar group talking to Ernest in front of the fireplace.

"Have you a favorite kind of paper?" Malcolm sat closest to the fire. A demon attack the previous year had taken his eyes and left an unsettling stretch of blank skin over the empty sockets, but he still turned his face toward whomever he was addressing. Kip and his friends were used to the young Irishman's eyeless face by now, put more at ease by the grace with which he'd accepted his fate.

"Only know one kind of paper," Ernest replied. "Thin wood." He opened and closed his mouth, which might have been called "smacking his lips" had he anything resembling lips.

"There's paper and then there's parchment," Emily Carswell, the first woman to become an apprentice sorcerer, sat next to Malcolm with her hand in his, as she often did. "And there's vellum, which is made of sheepskin."

"Never had skin." Ernest turned. "Hallo, Penfold."

Kip smiled. "Good morning, all." He sat down beside Alice Cartwright, a fox who counted herself the second female and fourth Calatian to attempt to learn sorcery. "Everybody ready for the Feast?"

"If they'll have more of those flavored breads," Malcolm said, "then aye. I've made a good deal of room in my stomach so I won't needs stop at four this time."

Emily rolled her eyes and smiled at Kip. "Are you sure it's all right for us to come with you?"

"The town belongs to the humans too," Kip said. "Some of the locals join us in the feast. It's fine."

"All right. Do tell us if you need us to leave."

Alice nodded. "We will. It will be fine except when we go talk to Father. You shouldn't be around then, I suppose."

"Good luck with that." Malcolm smiled toward the two foxes.

Kip reached out for Alice's paw. "I've gone over my arguments again and again. If this doesn't convince him…"

"Josiah Tipper from Boston arrived last night." Alice said the name as though it had gone rotten in her muzzle. "Father wanted me to come greet him, but I told him I had studying to do and I fled to the old barn."

Kip's ears went up. "Even there," he said, "I don't want you doing sorcery if I'm not around."

"I know." Alice sat up. "I took a lantern and I read through the books and memorized the binding spell again. I really think I know it." She cast him a sly grin. "At least as well as you did when you summoned three fire elementals into a basement full of dry paper."

"She makes a good point," Emily's eyes sparkled at Kip.

Kip, remembering that Master Windsor had bound the other two elementals, had to force himself to smile in return. "I'm trying to teach you to avoid the mistakes I made, not repeat them."

"Hmph." Alice smoothed down her petticoat. "Mistakes are how we learn."

"You'll have to make your own. After the Feast, perhaps we can try a summoning." Kip exhaled. "And perhaps we'll have something else to celebrate."

"I dearly hope so." Alice leaned against him and flicked her tail from side to side. "Josiah's letters are as dry as tinder."

"Tinder?" Ernest perked up. "Have you any here?"

Alice laughed. "No, but I'll bring you some next time. You'll love his letters. He scents them with jasmine."

"We'll be back this evening," Kip said, rising. "Behave yourself and don't scare Old John's customers."

"No idea what most of that means," Ernest said, "but aye, sure as the Flower."

"Malcolm," Kip asked as the Irishman rose, "can you ward us?"

"Already doing it." He cast the spell as Emily guided him around the tables and chairs of the Inn.

The foursome stepped from Ernest's warmth into a cool light rain and the grey light of morning. Despite the hour, New Cambridge bustled with activity, and today the usual crowds of tradesfolk and farmers getting their early morning bread were joined by throngs of Calatians—all the Calatians in the town as far as Kip could tell. There was Carrow Roseward the polecat; there were the Coopers, two dormice and a red squirrel with a new kit; that family of rabbits was the Lapellis.

Johnny Lapelli caught sight of Kip and hurried over to him. "Happy Feast!" the young rabbit cried out, and looked around. "Is your father coming?"

"No, he's celebrating in Peachtree." Kip embraced the rabbit and smiled. "He's about to open a shop there sometime this year, so if you fancy warmer weather, I'm certain he could find a place for you."

"Ooh." The rabbit's ears perked. "I'll ask mum. I'd love to see the world. Oh, Kip! Guess what! I'm giving one of the speeches!"

"That's marvelous. I'm sure you'll be an excellent speaker. What are you going to talk about?"

Johnny beamed at Kip's compliment. "Oh, about how we Calatians are part of this country even though we were made across the sea."

"That's a good one." The other rabbits had almost disappeared from sight, heading for the large canvas tent erected over the green in the town square. "Go on, then, and I'll listen for your speech."

"Thanks!" Johnny hopped up and hurried after his family.

"They change up the speeches every year?" Emily asked.

"Aye." Kip exchanged looks with Alice. "That one is...interesting, though."

"How so?" Malcolm stepped up level with them, no longer holding Emily's hand. Sometimes he summoned a demon to serve as his eyes, but Kip's nose did not detect the sharp tingle that announced a demon's presence to him. The Irishman was also adept at guiding himself by his hearing and his awareness of the people around him, and now his head turned shortly from side to side as he oriented himself to his surroundings.

Alice spoke up. "Usually there's a couple speeches about how we are all loyal to the Empire. There may well be some of those as well. But a speech about how we belong in this country…that sounds like rebellion."

"He could've meant," Kip gestured to the hills beyond the town, "this country, not necessarily a country separate from the Empire."

"He can claim that," Malcolm said. "But do you think that lies in his heart?"

Kip shook his head. "No."

"Nor do I." Malcolm turned as though he could see the crowd of Calatians. "'Tis a sentiment people are no longer confining to whispers. Back in New York over Christmas, well, let's just say me Ma forbad the subject from the house after the second fistfight."

"You didn't tell me you were in a fight over Christmas." Emily tightened her hand's grip on Malcolm's arm.

"Sure, and why would you assume I was in one of the fights?"

"Because I know you." She arched an eyebrow to Kip.

"Fair enough. As it happens, I wasn't, though I did hold back me Uncle Seamus to save Da from having a second eye blackened."

"What news from the Adamses?" Kip asked Emily, to forestall her making a comment about Malcolm's family.

"Were you back there again?" Alice asked.

"Yesterday, for a short time." Emily brushed the hair out of her eyes. "John Adams had a message to take to the Parliament."

"What did it say?" Malcolm asked.

"I'm not in the habit of reading the letters entrusted to me," Emily retorted.

"No, but Mr. John Adams has confided their intent to you in the past," Malcolm said.

She turned to Kip, her eyes clouding with worry so that fine lines creased her brow. "He didn't this time. But it felt like a last resort sort of message."

"The last three have," Kip said.

Emily nodded, and then said, "Yes," for Malcolm's benefit. "John Quincy believes that the King will not allow a costly war that would leave them vulnerable to the Spanish, but John and Abigail both feel that King George will try to break the rebellion quickly, as he did forty years ago."

Most of this was for Alice's benefit; she did not get to see Emily and Malcolm as often as Kip did, and he tried to insulate her from the politics of the day so they could focus on sorcery. But her sixteenth birthday had been months ago, and she displayed more maturity than that number implied.

Now her ears went back as she took in this information. She'd nearly reached Kip's height in the last year; it was easier to think of her as his betrothed (hopefully) rather than just a student.

"We're well prepared for war," Kip assured her. "The Masters have been working with the military sorcerers. Most of them have pledged to support the Colonies in any conflict."

"What about the others?" Alice asked. "The ones who haven't pledged their support."

"I don't know. Master Odden only talks in generalities."

"I expect," Emily said, "that they're simply excluded from certain conversations for now. Should open war break out, they'll likely go join the British forces."

"Likely a good number of soldiers will as well," Malcolm said.

"Perhaps not," Kip said. "There is a good deal of excitement over the idea of a country of our own—"

Alice broke in with a theatrical sigh and took Kip's paw. "Let's go find Father," she said.

That should not have been difficult even in the sea of people; the Cartwrights were one of only two fox families left in town and Kip's nose could pick them out of a crowd half a mile away. But finding them and making their way through the crowd under the tent were two very different things. He spotted the russet fur and pointed black ears quickly, but as he pulled Alice in that direction, their way was blocked by Elizabeth Asher, holding a large basket of bread rolls from which a profusion of delicious scents arose.

"Kip!" she said. "How delightful. And your friends from the College?"

"Emily and Malcolm," he said. "This is Elizabeth, who works with Mr. Scort, the baker."

"Ah, I smell cinnamon and raspberry," Malcolm cried, "so you've no need to tell me."

Only then did Elizabeth really take note of his face. Her ears went back but she kept a brave tone. "Indeed, sir," she said, slipping into a practiced recitation. "Cinnamon and raspberry, and plain sugared and blueberry as well. As you can…" Here she faltered. "They're decorated with the different types of Calatians."

"The fox one is cinnamon, as I recall." Malcolm reached for the small pouch at his waist.

Kip tapped his arm. "I'll buy the breads," he said. "I've got a little money for some work I did for Old John."

"I thought you just heated his inn in exchange for room and board?" Emily picked a blueberry bread with a squirrel decoration out of the basket, and a cinnamon fox for Malcolm.

"He needed his old oven removed and the men couldn't get to it right away, so I did it for him. It was a small thing." Kip gave Elizabeth four shillings and took two more cinnamon breads from the basket.

The warmth brought the smell of cinnamon flooding into his nose like a wave of magic, releasing memories of Feasts past: holding his mother's paw, taking a bread from his father, listening to the speeches without understanding them, giving one himself when it was the foxes' turn, receiving the blessing of Calatus and then dancing into the night.

Elizabeth thanked him and moved on with one more glance at Malcolm, her nose twitching. Kip gave one of his cinnamon breads to Alice. "I wanted to try to talk to your father before the speeches," he said, "but maybe it would be better to wait until after?"

"If we can get over there now…" Alice craned her neck to look. "It would be better to get it over with."

Her ears flicked to the side as they did when she was unsure about a spell she was learning. Kip took a bite of his bread. "All right," he said, and touched Emily's shoulder. "You'll be all right?"

"Go on," she said, "and good luck. Malcolm and I will go talk to Arthur Lean and his parents."

The Leans were black rats whose son Arthur had worked with both Emily and Malcolm. It wasn't usual for sorcerers to socialize with calyxes, but Kip approved of this change. Bringing sorcerers and Calatians together could only benefit the Colonies in the coming war.

As Alice pulled him through the crowd, he thought more about the war and his possible role in it, waving absently at the townspeople he'd grown up with. The Lapellis greeted him with smiles; Bryce Morgan, the hedgehog who spoke for the Calatians at town meetings, nodded politely; the Brocks met his eyes and turned away without another reaction.

But Bryce Morgan's son Tom and his wife Hope, who'd come down from Boston, intercepted Kip. Hope, brash and cheerful took his arm. "Master Penfold, we were hoping to find you here!"

"Oh," Kip said, "I'm not—"

Hope thrust a nine-year-old hedgehog at him. Kip cast Alice a helpless look; she returned an amused smile. "This is Charles. Charles, say hello to Master Penfold."

Charles's eyes showed white all around the dark centers as he stared up at Kip. "Hello Master Penfold," he whispered, so softly that any ears but a fox's might miss it.

"It's nice to meet you, Charles." Kip smiled, then looked up and motioned for Alice to go on. She shook her head.

"Hope." Tom pulled Charles back. "Master Penfold is busy."

"I'm not a—"

"Nonsense." Hope smiled. "It's the Feast Day. Good Master Penfold, Charles here has shown some extraordinary abilities and I wondered if you might take a moment to question him and see whether sorcery might be a path for him."

"Can we—" Kip smiled again down at the young hedgehog. "Bring him to the Founders Rest tomorrow evening?"

"I told you," Tom said. "He won't do sorcery out here in public."

"It's not about that." Kip looked up. The Cartwrights were no longer in sight. "It's only that it might take some time, and peace and quiet is better."

"Can't you simply lay your paws on him and feel whether he has the touch?" Hope asked.

Kip shook his head quickly. Alice had turned, now scanning the crowd again. "I need to talk to him, ask him to do some exercises, and even then I might not be able to tell. It wasn't until I was twelve that I was sure."

"I'll just tell you what he's done." Hope gathered herself. "He's found water. We took him out to scout a parcel of land and he said he was thirsty and wandered off and found a spring. And later he found a disused well."

"All right," Kip said. "That might or might not indicate—please do bring him to the inn, though. I am sorry, but I have to go." Alice had her paw up, gesturing him forward. "Charles, I look forward to seeing you."

He patted the young hedgehog's shoulder and moved quickly around him. As he left, Tom said, "I told you not to bother him," and Hope replied with some smugness, "He agreed to see Charles, didn't he?" and then their conversation fell away into the general murmur of the crowd.

"I suspect people ask you if their cubs are magic all the time now," Alice said. "Human children too, perhaps? Now you live in the town."

Kip shook his head. "They were the first. I don't think many people realize I live here. I keep to the inn, where it's mostly travelers that see me, and when we're having your lessons we're in John's back room or that old barn."

"More of the town appreciates you now," Alice told him. "Even my father thinks you're doing good work."

"It helps to have you whisper in his ear." Kip smiled and scanned the crowd ahead. "Where did they go? The speeches are about to start."

"They're over—" Alice pointed and then stopped. "He saw us and turned and walked in the other direction. That's Father. He doesn't want to have an argument he thinks he might lose."

"Of course he would expect this." Kip sighed. "I thought that here he wouldn't be able to avoid me as readily."

"*I* thought that with Josiah here he would be more likely to listen." Alice kept forging ahead, pulling Kip with her. "He has often said that he wanted to take the measure of him before finalizing the betrothal. Now he's here. What better time to talk to the two of you side by side? There. They're at the edge near the ale. Maybe they were just going for a drink."

Bryce Morgan climbed up onto the small dais at the front of the tent and raised his paws. "Welcome, my friends," he said.

Alice's father and suitor had stopped just ten feet from them, but now the whole crowd turned to the dais to give Mr. Morgan their attention, and Kip and Alice had to stop as well as the murmur of conversation died down.

Alice balled her paws into fists in frustration.

"Relax," Kip murmured. "We've a whole day. He knows we want to talk to him."

"Today," the hedgehog continued, "we come together to celebrate the miracle of our creation, a Great Feat of the Sorcerer Calatus who brought us forth into this world, a gift we can never repay. To his memory we dedicate this day and our lives."

"To his memory," Kip, Alice, and the rest of the crowd murmured in response.

"This year, the rabbits and squirrels and mice have prepared speeches in the honor of Calatus and our community. After that, we'll have a short prayer and then a feast in the church, since the weather is once again not so nice to be outside in, especially for those of us still in our winter coats." He pulled at the lapel of his coat and paused for the crowd to acknowledge his joke, which they did with a polite chuckle.

After that, Margaret Branch came up with a speech about all the Great Feats known in the world, and then one of the young Coopers talked about how they all knew Calatians in Boston and New York and Peachtree (making Kip think of his parents), and then Johnny Lapelli. Johnny's speech, as he'd told them, emphasized how much the Calatians loved the woods of Massachusetts and the port of New York. His family had taken a trip there to see relatives the year before and had gone to see the Great Road that ran across the ocean from New York to Bristol. They hadn't been able to stand on it, but Johnny described its path cutting through the shining waves, "with us on this side and England on the other, connected but separate." That speech got the loudest cheer of any of the three.

Looking around, Kip felt the enthusiasm of the town around him. If it does come to war—when it comes to war—he thought, there won't be many questions about the loyalty of the Calatians, at least. And he would represent them in the American forces, bringing fire magic to the army to match Master Cott's, should Britain bring him to a battle. John Quincy Adams would not be able to ignore the contributions of the Calatians then; he would have to honor his promise to grant them more rights in the new country. If the war was successful, Kip reminded himself. If not—well, he would likely not be alive to worry, in that case.

Bryce Morgan continued the applause as he returned to the dais. "Wasn't that wonderful? The future of our community is in these young people, and from those speeches I can tell it's bright. Brighter than the sky today, ha ha!" More polite chuckling, which Kip did not join this time. "The brightness of your faces more than makes up for it, though! Now, before we adjourn to the church, I just want to say a few words."

The crowd murmured briefly; this was not usual. Mr. Morgan drew himself up into every inch of his five feet and surveyed the crowd. "Nearly two years ago," he said, "our town was viciously attacked and our lives threatened." He pointed up the hill. "Over a hundred lives were lost at the College. For a year, we lived in fear without knowing who to blame. Now we know, and we live under a different kind of fear. What has not changed is that we live through this together. This day reminds us that all of us Calatians were created together in a single moment, and though our lives have taken us around the world and along many different paths, we must never forget that. We must always stand together."

The irony of this speech coming from someone who had strenuously opposed his entry into the College was not lost on Kip, but he applauded with the rest of the crowd. Mr. Morgan was as entitled to change his opinion as anyone else, or else conveniently forget it when needed for a public speaking moment.

The crowd began to disperse in clumps of twos and threes down the slick stones of Half-Moon Circle toward the church. Alice led Kip around the outside of the crowd. "There," she said.

"What?"

"Tch." She turned to him. "You're thinking about the war again."

"I'm thinking about Bryce Morgan's speech," he said, now spotting her father and the other fox a few paces ahead of Alice's mother and Corinne Lapelli. "And perhaps a little about the war."

"Don't mention the war to Father." She stopped at her mother's side and gestured for Kip to go on ahead.

"I won't." He hurried up alongside the older fox, who turned to him. "Mr. Cartwright," Kip said.

Thomas Cartwright wore an oilskin coat over a cotton tunic with blue thread trim at the collars and cuffs, and black cotton trousers. Kip's father had a similar suit for Sundays, and Kip had once thought it the finest in clothing. Now he looked at the fox next to Thomas, whose grey suit jacket and white linen shirt darkened in the rain, whose grey pants matched his jacket and whose collar bore an ivory pin in the likeness of a fox head. This was the sort of dress he'd mostly seen on the gentlemen who came to the College to discuss the prospects of war with the headmaster and the other sorcerers. Few people in New Cambridge dressed this way, Calatian or human. In fact, Kip had rarely seen a Calatian in such fancy clothes anywhere. Most of New Cambridge's Calatians farmed or sold goods, and the only other large settlement he'd visited, the Isle of Dogs, consisted of poor laborers.

Both Thomas and the other fox, presumably Josiah, turned to Kip without breaking their stride. "Penfold," Thomas said.

"Happy Feast Day."

"Happy Feast Day." The older fox looked ahead to the church. "Might we postpone this conversation until after the services?"

Kip looked back at Alice, her fur collecting rain as his own was, and then ahead at the church only a minute or two away at their current pace. "Certainly I would prefer to talk indoors," he said. "There should be a short time before the services start, and that might be sufficient."

The other fox craned his neck around Thomas. "Oh, this is Penfold, is it? I say, my good chap, don't you have a spell to keep dry?"

"Several," Kip said, "but we don't use sorcery frivolously. Mr. Cartwright, this will only take a moment of your time."

"Penfold," Thomas said, "I will listen to your argument. After the service. There will be ample time, and there is no rush in this matter." He caught Kip's look and tilted his muzzle. "Rest assured I shall not make a decision during the prayer."

So Kip nodded and hung back until Alice caught up with him. They let Mrs. Cartwright go on ahead and waited in the drizzle for Emily and Malcolm, bringing up the last of the crowd. "Did you talk to him?" Emily asked.

"No. After the service."

"All right." Emily wrapped a wet arm around him. "Good luck. Malcolm and I are going to wait in the Founders Rest until your service is over."

"You can attend," he said, amused. "Pastor Gregory is human."

"It's for you, not us." Malcolm wiped a hand through his wet hair. "We'll dry off and come by later for the food."

The church smelled strongly of wet fur from a couple hundred Calatians. Kip had grumbled about rainy days as a cub because the smells were so strong, but now he appreciated how close it made him feel to everyone, as though they were all in arm's reach rather than seated throughout the church.

Pastor Gregory led them in a short prayer in which he reminded them that the sorcerer Calatus had not created a divine spark in them but had merely moved what was created by God. Unlike the speeches of the Calatians, this prayer had not changed in all the years Kip could remember.

Nor had the response of the crowd: reverent attention from the adults while the cubs shifted and muttered, restless for the feast to begin even though many of them were still chewing on their morning breads. At the back of the church, far from the side doors, Kip couldn't smell the food that was laid out, but he remembered drier Feast days when he'd sat with his mother and father near the front, the smells of fowl and fruit and cheese filling his nose. He'd kicked the pews in front of him to distract from the droning words of the Church's Feast Day prayer.

He turned his nose toward the side, pursuing the memory, and in that moment the faintest tingle stung the inside of it. His ears shot forward and he whipped his head around to scan the crowd. Nothing untoward around him, not anywhere he could sense. Alice, who could smell demons but not with Kip's sensitivity, turned to him with worried eyes.

At the front, Pastor Gregory had begun the call and response that signaled the last part of the prayer. "May God's spirit move you."

"May God's spirit move you," Kip replied, and moved past Alice to the end of the row.

"May the Father and Son and the Holy Spirit guide our actions toward mercy and compassion."

"Do you need me to come with you?" Alice hissed, following.

The congregation chanted, "The path is hard but God is at our side."

Kip shook his head and then reconsidered. If there was danger, Alice would be safer with him than alone. As an unofficial sorcerer, she stood the risk of being captured not only by enemies, but also by allies. "Yes," he said in a low voice.

They hurried to the church's doors. Kip lost the scent there, but that was fine; he pushed the doors open and slid outside, flattening himself against the carved wood in the meager shelter of the doorway. Alice huddled beside him. "What's going on?"

"Demon," Kip said tersely. Magic came easily to his paws and lit them with a violet glow. He spoke the summoning and when Nikolon appeared before him as a nude female fox-Calatian, he bound her. "Make no move save on my order; take no action save on my order, but you may converse with me," he said. "Hello, Nik."

Nikolon inclined her head. "Greetings, Master."

"There was another demon around," Kip said quickly. "Please become invisible and survey the area within a hundred yards of this church and report back to me whatever you can discover about any demon you find."

"Yes, master." Nikolon bowed and vanished.

Alice brought her paws to her ears and smoothed them back. "Do you say that phrase every time?"

Kip nodded. "If you don't bind them properly, demons may cause mischief, or do harm. Nik is only a first level demon, so could not cause permanent harm, but her curse would nonetheless be difficult to reverse."

"Malcolm's eyes," Alice said.

"Aye." Kip took a breath.

After a moment, Alice peered around the lawn in front of the church, empty of people. "You smelled a demon?"

"Aye. It might have been Malcolm's demon, but…"

Alice folded her arms and leaned back against the church door. "How long will it take Nik?"

"Shouldn't be long," Kip replied, and even as he said that the female fox materialized before him.

"I found no other demon in the area you described, master," she said.

"Thank you." Kip hesitated. "Stay invisible and near me and tell me as soon as you detect any other magic or demon nearby."

Nikolon looked at Alice and then vanished. Alice brought her ears forward. "Why don't you have her around you all the time?"

Kip motioned her to the door. "It takes energy to keep them bound. Not so much for Nik, but…it is a drain. And when she's around, I can't distinguish between her and other demons. But mostly it's because after several hours—maybe days, I'm still not sure—the binding becomes painful to her. Nothing I have to do is so important I need to cause her pain."

They re-entered the church, where the prayer had already ended, and joined the Calatians filing toward the side room where the food awaited. "Nikolon," Kip said to the tingle in his nose, "please go tell Emily that the service is over and then return immediately to the task of watching for magic and demons around me."

Yes, master. The tingle vanished from his nose, but returned before he and Alice reached the doorway. They each collected one of the small wooden plates and went around to take food from the tables: winter apples stored for the feast, roast chicken and other fowl, greens and candied fruits, slices of cheese and bread. Cubs running around Kip's legs had piled their plates full of candied fruits and maple candies (these were no longer in evidence on any tables; apparently the cubs had swarmed them like locusts) and very little of anything else. As one mouse pup ran by him, her father grabbed her and marched her to put back some of the sugar and fruit.

Kip and Alice exchanged smiles. "Not so long ago," Alice said as they both took sensible meals of meat, bread and cheese.

"I wonder how they do the Feast on the Isle of Dogs." Kip lifted a piece of chicken to his mouth and chewed thoughtfully. "They don't have the bounty that we do."

"I'm certain Abel would allow you to visit there one day. He makes such excuses to see you."

"He invited me this year, but…"

She brushed his tail with hers. "If you want to go next year, I'd go with you."

Kip's answer was forestalled by the appearance of Emily and Malcolm at the door, Emily's hand on Malcolm's arm. He took his plate and hurried over to them.

"You haven't summoned a demon, have you?" He took Malcolm's hand and placed his plate in it.

"What's this?" Malcolm felt delicately around the plate. "Ah, lovely, Kip, thank you. No, I've not. We've been talking through a difficult bit of a warding spell."

"Can you cast one now?" Kip asked. "Just an inattention spell around the church."

"Of course." Malcolm gathered magic and cast the spell so quickly that his hands only glowed orange for a few brief seconds.

Emily shot Kip a puzzled look. "Trouble?"

"There was a demon here. I summoned one of my own and she's keeping an eye out for any demons or magic use."

"We're safe now," Malcolm said. "Nobody outside the church will think to look here."

"Inattention wards are so interesting," Alice said, impressed. Her ears perked up. "Do you really think there's danger?"

"If there was a demon here, chances are high." Kip relaxed only a little. "Malcolm's ward can be beaten if someone is concentrating on breaking it, but it's good protection."

"For someone to get through it, they would have to know it was here and physically walk into the Church," Malcolm told Alice. "It isn't simply a matter of 'concentrating on breaking it.'"

"I said it was good protection," Kip protested.

"But surely someone at the College might have sent a demon down here?" Alice asked. "To spy?"

Kip shook his head. "The sorcerers have more pressing matters on their minds. I suppose it is not out of the question, but...it seems unlikely."

Master. A sorcerer has translocated to the church yard.

Kip swore and pushed his way through the crowd of Calatians. Behind him, Emily told Alice to look after Malcolm and Malcolm retorted that he could look after himself, and then Kip reached the door and burst out into the nave of the church. A few people sat eating on the pews; their ears perked toward him as he scanned the rear of the church, behind the altar.

Is there a place where we may observe the yard without being seen? he asked Nikolon as Emily came up beside him.

After a moment, the demon replied, *Yes.*

Kip reminded himself to be precise in his language. *Where is it?*

To the left of the altar through the small wooden door. There was a pause. *Or I may show you.*

He pointed out the door to Emily and followed her. *Show me.*

Superimposed over the view of the inside of the church flashed a grey, damp yard, green tufts of grass and a few violet crocuses poking their heads out around old tombstones. Standing on one of the tombstones was a man Kip knew well, a stocky man in black robes whose face and beard dripped with water. Master Albright's hair was thinner and whiter than when Kip had last seen him over a year ago, but Kip would never forget that face, and even the sight of it by proxy had him calling magic from the earth.

"Kip," Emily said. They reached the door and she only now noticed his paws glowing violet.

"It's Albright," he said tightly. The thing to do was call fire, incinerate the man as he had narrowly missed doing a year ago. But he couldn't make himself do it in cold blood. Odden and Cott had drilled self-control into him, had thrust story upon story on him of fire sorcerers gone out of control and killed by their fellows. Even Cott, prone to the occasional ill-advised display of power, recognized the importance of restraint.

Emily swore and hurried to open the door. Kip followed her, watching as Albright stepped forward, crushing a pair of crocus flowers, and looked around uncertainly. Looking for me, Kip thought.

The small room smelled strongly of old paper and cloth and wine. At the rear, a stained window allowed Emily to look out onto the yard, but just as she did, Albright made up his mind and vanished.

"Did you see him?" Kip asked, at the same time asking Nikolon, *Did he reappear nearby?*

"For a moment," Emily said.

No.

"He's gone." Kip stared out at the crushed flower and then turned to hurry back to the others.

Emily gripped his arm. "The College," she said. "We have to warn them."

"Go," he said, and then saw Emily's apprehension. Neither of them knew what might await them, and two sets of eyes were better than one, not to mention the ability to control fire. He added, "and bring me with you. I'll tell the demon to have Alice keep everyone inside."

In the few seconds it took Emily to gather magic, he gave Nikolon her instructions and received acknowledgment. *And look for me every five minutes. If you cannot contact me, tell Alice and Malcolm to go to the Armory in Boston and alert the Army.*

Yes, Master.

Emily took hold of Kip's arm and in the blink of an eye they stood in the Great Hall of the White Tower. The background murmur of activity that Kip had always heard here was gone, the silence so absolute that he and Emily held their breaths. "It's too quiet," Emily said finally.

"The elementals." Kip pointed to the large empty fireplace where usually several phosphorus elementals lay atop one another. He lifted his nose to the air.

"Everyone's gone." Emily lifted her hands to her mouth. "Hallo!"

The word echoed in the Great Hall and then died away. They waited five, ten seconds, and still no response came.

In Emily's wide eyes Kip saw his own fear. "Everyone's gone," he said shakily.

"They might have seen Albright and fled? They might be...somewhere else?"

Kip couldn't think of where a whole school of sorcerers might have gone, and besides that, he knew as well as Emily that not all the sorcerers could translocate. It would take time for those who could to collect those who couldn't. "The air smells like...British sorcerers."

Emily sniffed. "They have a distinctive smell?"

"The soap they use." Kip avoided the stairs to the basement and walked instead to the larger staircase, ears perked. "King's College stinks of it. Let me see if—our friend is awake." He pressed his foot to the bare stone and reached down, calling the name of the spirit bound to the stones of the Tower. *Peter?*

No answer. He tried again and then set his foot on the first stair. Emily walked up beside him, her steps echoing up. "Anything?"

He shook his head. "I can't tell whether he's gone or just being quiet." He fought back the fear that Peter had somehow been unbound, kidnapped, or destroyed. He, Emily, and Master Barrett were the only ones who knew the name of the spirit in the Tower, but what they could find, someone else might also. Right now, though, he needed to find out what had happened. There would be time later for grief, if it were needed. "Let's check upstairs?"

"The library."

Together they hurried up to the second floor. The library door stood closed, but opened to their pressure. Inside, all looked as normal as though they had strolled in after a lesson looking for a reference. The only thing missing was Florian, the old librarian they had never seen the library without.

"The British must not have valued the books." Emily went to the shelves and traced a finger along the bindings. "If it was them. I suppose they have enough of their own."

"They don't have Odden's demon book. He's added so many names to it that the British don't have, and we don't have most of those names anywhere else. Without as many demons, the war will be much harder." Kip bit his lip and ran along the hall to his master's office.

Here there were signs of a struggle. Odden's chair had been pushed back from his desk, scrolls and books had spilled from one bookcase, and the great copper brazier that normally held a phosphorus elemental lay overturned on the floor. And the large volume of demon names that had been stored here for safekeeping was gone from the shelf.

Emily stopped in the doorway. "Don't you know some demon names?"

Kip searched the scattered books to make sure the volume wasn't there. "Everyone knows a few. But only a few. For the first battles, I suppose it will be fine, but once they learn what our demons can do, they can find others that will counter them. We won't have that option." Kip exhaled. "Let me try Peter again. We need to be sure of what happened."

At that moment Nikolon spoke into his head. *Master?*

Is everyone safe? Kip thought back at her.

Yes. It has been five minutes.

Thank you. I'm still safe. He paused. *Please tell Malcolm and Alice that the College is empty and Emily and I will return to them as soon as possible.*

Yes, Master.

Kip turned his attention to the stone again. *Peter?*

This time, a faint stirring. *Kip? I was hiding.*

Relief washed through him at Peter's voice. *Everyone's gone but us. What happened here?*

They came in the front door. I couldn't prevent them. When they were inside, there were a dozen of them, spiritual sorcerers and one translocational sorcerer. I woke Master Barrett, but before he could do anything they had arrived and cut off his magic. They cut off everyone's magic. Then they took them outside and they were gone. I'm sorry. I failed.

Not your fault, Kip told him. *And we're still here, and you're safe.*

I didn't act fast enough.

Did you recognize any of the sorcerers?

A pause, and then: *Yes. Master Albright. He's been here before.*

Thank you, Peter. We're going to fight and we'll get everyone back.

He relayed the story to Emily, who pursed her lips. "I'd say this is an act of war."

Kip nodded. "I'd agree." The imminence of war over the past year had weighed on him but he'd acclimated to it; the reality that now at any moment Albright might appear and abduct or kill him both terrified and excited him. Now he could join the fight. The question was— "What do we do now? There might be more clues to where they were taken."

"We have to go to Boston," Emily said. "The Armory."

"We might be able to find them, though."

"Kip. There's a war on. We need to tell the Army that there's been an attack. John Quincy Adams was very clear on that point the last time I talked to him."

"Right." And the Army would direct Kip where he could be most effective in the war. The fox cast around Odden's office for anything he could or should take with him, but the book of demon names was the most important thing by far, and that was gone. All of Kip's own books were down at the Inn. "We'll get Malcolm and Alice. Do you think the rest of the town will be safe?"

"Why wouldn't they be?"

"Some of them are calyxes."

"They can't do magic on their own, though." Emily took a bit of her hair and wound it around her finger. "Do you think Alice should come with us? They don't know she can do magic. If you tell her to keep her magic quiet…"

Kip laughed. "You try that."

"I'm serious, Kip."

"So am I." He swished his tail. The danger he felt for himself went double for Alice. As far as he knew, Albright didn't know about her, but as Emily had pointed out, there were many other sorcerers on the British side, and for them to have infiltrated the College, they had to know it very well. Even if most of the College sorcerers didn't know about Alice, that didn't mean nobody on the British side did.

"She's a girl," Emily said. "You're talking about taking her to war."

"You're going to war," he pointed out. "She's not much younger than you were when you were married to Thomas."

"I've studied sorcery for two years with, I'm sorry, skilled teachers."

He didn't bristle. "She's very talented despite my lack of skill in teaching."

"I didn't mean—" Emily shook her head. "What if something happens to her?"

"It could as easily happen here. Remember Farley?" Kip rested a paw on Emily's arm. "I've talked to her. She wants to come and fight, and I've seen for myself that she can help. Trust us."

She twisted her hair around her finger. "All right. We can't waste much more time. Let's go."

CHAPTER 2: THE MASTER COLONEL

The Boston Armory, a squat brick building that stood among several stone townhouses, buzzed with activity when Emily deposited Kip across the street from it. "I haven't been in there," she said, by way of explaining why they hadn't just appeared inside, "and besides, it's likely warded."

Kip had never experienced a ward set against him. "What does it feel like, trying to appear in a warded spot?"

Emily had gathered magic to go back for Malcolm and Alice, but paused and considered, brushing a hair out of her face with a glowing hand. "You know when you're visualizing your landing and you feel that 'yes, I can go there' feeling? If it's an inattention ward, you can't quite visualize where you're going to land. If it's a prevention ward, you can visualize it, but the spell doesn't work at all. It's rather distressing, really."

"All right." Kip gestured for her to go. "Hurry back."

Across the street, at the doorway to the Armory, two men in patchy blue and red coats stood guard with muskets, and behind them, though Kip couldn't see clearly, his ears picked up flurries of activity: footsteps and the metallic clank of weapons, both through the ground floor doorway and through upper level windows.

Master?

Nikolon. I'm fine. I'm in Boston. Is everyone safe?
They are safe. A sorcerer has appeared in the church.
Emily?
Yes.
That's fine. Thank you for your service, Nikolon. I have no more need of you.
Thank you, master.

He summoned magic and spoke the dismissal to release the demon. The movement attracted the attention of the two guards, who had not seen him appear with Emily. They cast him curious looks, and at that moment Emily reappeared with the others. Both of the guards jumped, and one started to shift his rifle to his arms, then stopped and put it back to his shoulder.

"Come on, then," Emily said, and led them across the dirty street to the ever-more apprehensive guards.

Kip took Malcolm's arm and the four of them walked to the door of the Armory. Emily approached the guards without fear and said, "Emily Carswell, adjunct to John Adams, here to report an attack on the College of Sorcery."

The two guards proved to be very young, younger than most of Kip and Emily's fellow students. "Er," one said. "Ahhh…" contributed the other.

"Either let us in," Emily said patiently, "or go fetch someone who knows who John Adams is."

"I'll go," the blond-haired of the two said, and scurried inside.

"'Adjunct' now?" Kip murmured to Emily.

She turned and flashed him a smile. "He told me to use that title in an emergency."

"I can't argue with that."

Malcolm turned to the fox. "Nor should you try, if you've not learned that lesson already."

"With Emily, or John Adams?" Kip asked.

"Either, in my experience."

"Are you a sorcerer?" The young soldier leaned around Emily to look at Malcolm and then recoiled, having not seen Malcolm's face until that moment.

"We are," Emily said. "All of us."

"All of…" He stared from her to Kip and then to Alice in her Feast Day dress, to blind Malcolm and back to Emily.

"We may not look the part," Malcolm said, "but we can toss a spell as well as anyone you've seen, I'll wager. As me ma said, judge the butcher by the cut of his meat, not the cut of his apron."

"I didn't mean…" The soldier gulped. "Any disrespect."

"None taken," Kip said. "We know we're an unusual lot."

"Though perhaps all that remains of the College," Emily pointed out.

The young man, already pale, grew paler. "All that—all that remains—?"

"Hence the urgency of our visit," Emily said calmly and pleasantly.

"Oh, aye," the young man said. "Forgive me, but they ordered us—we're not to admit anyone without—you understand, British spies—"

"Of course."

Kip stepped forward. "You're worried about British spies already?"

"Oh aye." The young man's confidence returned. "Two months ago General Hamilton told us to be vigilant. He said there would be, ah." His brow furrowed. "'Enemy agents' wanting to gather our secrets about weapons and such. That's why we must needs challenge everyone wishing to enter."

"Quite right," Emily said. "Any idea how long your companion will take?"

Kip cocked an ear as the young man turned back to the door. "They're coming now," he said.

Indeed, not fifteen seconds later, the first guard returned, red in the face, followed by a slender black man with a captain's insignia on his shoulder and a thin moustache and beard. "I'm Captain Lowell," he said. "This soldier says you're attached to John Adams?"

"Emily Carswell." Emily extended her hand. "With Kip Penfold, Malcolm O'Brien, and Alice Cartwright. We've come to report an attack on Prince George's College of Sorcery in New Cambridge."

Lowell's face twisted. "Another one? Come in, come in. Mr. Adams isn't present, but I'll take you to Master Colonel Jackson."

"Master Colonel?" Kip asked as they entered.

Lowell led them across a cold stone floor dimly lit by small, high windows. After a moment, Kip's eyes adjusted enough to see the men sitting on benches, whose whispers stopped and then picked up again as their little group passed. "His military rank is Colonel," Lowell said, "but as a sorcerer he has also earned the title of Master, so he is Master Colonel." He opened a door that led onto a stair. "Just up here."

"You're not a sorcerer, are you?" Emily asked as they climbed the stairs.

"No," Captain Lowell said. "I've neither the affinity nor the...other qualities necessary." At the top of the stairs, he turned and met Kip's eyes. "Though I will say that seeing you lot gives me hope."

"It has been anything but easy." Emily brushed down her dress and stepped aside to let Kip, Malcolm, and Alice join her in the hallway.

"But our hope is that for those that come after us," Kip said, "it will be easier, and easier still for the ones after them."

"Aye." Captain Lowell looked thoughtful. "We hope to leave our children a better world than the one our parents left us." He gestured to a closed door, thick solid oak that nonetheless allowed raised voices to leak out to Kip's ears. "Master Colonel Jackson is here."

He rapped sharply on the door. The voices stilled, and a moment later, one called loudly, "Come."

Lowell opened the door onto a room thick with the smells of burning oil and unwashed men attempting to cover their odor with perfume. Around a large table in the center of the room, six men lit by a pair of oil lamps all turned their attention to Lowell and the four sorcerers. On the windowsill behind the table, a single raven, barely a shadow against the closed shutters, also turned to examine the newcomers.

"Captain," the middle-aged man on the far side of the table said, "this is a secure meeting and hardly the place to bring visitors."

"If Madame wishes to make a donation, take her and her retinue down to the bursar," sneered the young man at his side.

"Quiet, Morgan," the middle-aged man said. He straightened, filling out a dark blue uniform that bore more decorations than any other in the room, and turned to his left, where the tallest man in the room was staring at Lowell with vague annoyance rather than the curiosity the others displayed. "Jackson, did you send for these people?"

"I did not." The tall man wore sorcerer's robes, but as he turned they flowed open to reveal a similar uniform beneath them. This had to be Colonel Jackson. "Lowell, be quick."

"Yes, sir." Lowell stood stiffly at attention. "This is Emily Carswell, Kip Penfold, Malcolm O'Brien, and Alice Cartwright. They are sorcerers and they have come with news of an attack on the College of Sorcery in New Cambridge."

"Zwounds!" Jackson clenched his fist. "Another attack? Well, if Patris hasn't been killed, he'll certainly no longer be head. What's happened, ah…" He gestured to Malcolm. "O'Brien."

Malcolm stepped forward into the light, drawing an audible gasp from the room. "Aye, I thought perhaps you'd not been able to see me properly," he said with a smile. "I'd suggest that perhaps Miss Carswell or Mr. Penfold here might be a better source for you, as they were the ones who actually saw," he did lean on that word, "what happened."

Jackson looked between Emily and Kip and couldn't seem to settle on one of them. "Well, then?" he asked impatiently.

Emily kept staring at the man who'd spoken first, and now she nudged Kip. "You start," she said.

Kip stood straight against the weight of all the military men staring at him. "I summoned a demon," he said, because he didn't like to advertise his ability to smell demon presence, "as I often do outside the College. On the Feast Day my demon alerted me that another demon had appeared in the area, but it vanished quickly. A short time later, my demon alerted me that a sorcerer had teleported to the area."

"I'd cast a ward at Kip's request," Malcolm said.

Here Colonel Jackson perked up. "What kind of ward?"

"Inattention."

"Ah, good." He waved to Kip. "Go on."

"The sorcerer was Master Albright from King's College," Kip said, fighting the anger that coiled in his chest as he thought of the murderous sorcerer. "The one behind the first attack on Prince George's."

"London was behind the attack," one of the aides said.

"They still claim Albright acted on his own volition," another said.

The middle-aged man who'd spoken first turned to that aide. "I know of no-one in these Colonies who believes that. Regardless, if Albright was about, there was danger. You are sure it was him?"

"Yes," Kip said.

"I saw him too," Emily added. She still hadn't taken her eyes from the middle-aged man.

"And then Emily took us to the College to warn them, but we were too late," and he let her tell the rest of it.

She hesitated, making Kip wonder who this decorated man was that Emily felt so intimidated by his presence. But then she spoke as clearly and confidently as ever, so he supposed it might only have been the room itself. "The College was empty when we arrived. Their book of demon names was gone."

This brought another curse from Jackson, which startled Emily before she resumed. "And then Kip…" She glanced at him; Peter's existence was secret by necessity. "He summoned back a demon who did chores for the College. It confirmed that a British sorcerer had abducted the masters."

The middle-aged man rubbed his long chin. "This is troubling."

"Troubling?" Jackson asked sharply. "It is an act of war, Philip. The raids, I grant you, there is some question, but this?"

"Do not be so quick to jump to war," Philip told him. "Once we are on that path it will take a great deal to bring us back from it."

"Yes!" Jackson pounded the table. "Victory over the tyrant George!"

Though Kip jumped at the force of the outburst—as did most in the room—he couldn't help but agree. This was war, and why did this Philip, of whom Emily seemed so in awe, hesitate?

"We all want that," Philip said, unperturbed by Jackson's vehemence, "but we must accomplish it sensibly, and that means we must declare war when the time is right. If we cannot be seen by Spain and France as a serious threat to London, then we stand no chance of winning aid from them, and to be honest, without foreign aid we are not a serious threat."

"Then you give us no chance." Jackson sneered. "It's this same caution that got many of your father's friends the gallows forty years ago."

"It's forty years too late to have that argument," Philip said, "although if you like you may take it up with Father yourself. He's due to arrive from New York tomorrow."

"I know that. He's asked for a sorcerer to bring him."

"Then save your words for—"

"You have his ear. You have seen the raids in Boston, New York, Philadelphia. Unsuccessful because we were on our guard, but now they've abducted—maybe killed—fifteen American sorcerers!"

"Again…" Philip shook his head. "This is neither the time nor the place. Lowell, please take these four to quarters on the third floor."

"Stop." With that single word, Kip could see how Jackson had risen to command. Every person in the room stiffened, froze, and turned to him, with the possible exception of Philip, but Kip couldn't tell because he was staring at the military sorcerer. "Lowell is under my command."

"As you are under mine."

"I'm under your father's." Jackson stared back at him. "In any event, do not issue orders to my adjutants, especially while I am present. As for these others, sorcerers in the American army are under my command, and so they will report to the rest of the military sorcerers on the third floor to await my orders. Lowell, take them."

"One moment," Emily said. "We haven't agreed to be part of any army. We're apprentices at the College."

"There's a war on," Jackson said. "You've just been drafted. Welcome to the American Army."

Emily argued with Captain Lowell all the way up the stairs. "He can't do that," she insisted.

"There's a war on, or hadn't you heard?" Lowell's calm demeanor cracked just a bit.

"General Hamilton said we're not yet at war."

"Major-General Hamilton," Lowell corrected her. "General Hamilton is his father."

"I haven't the patience to learn your language," Emily said. "Or the way you insist on placing people into hierarchies. Philip Hamilton said we're not at war, therefore we are not at war, and you have no authority to keep any of us here."

"You may discuss that with Master Colonel Jackson if you have the inclination," Captain Lowell said.

"She'd be the one to do it," Malcolm murmured, his hand on Kip's arm.

Alice had stayed behind them, tail tucked beneath her dress. She gave a little giggle at Malcolm's remark, and though Kip was pleased to see her ears up, here in the armory among the military men she seemed very young and frail. Had he done the right thing in bringing her along? "Don't worry," he said.

"I'm not worried for me." She smiled, ears perked. "I'm worried for them. They don't know what they're in for."

That got a smile out of him. "You've got the right of it there."

They'd gotten to the top of the stairs, Emily still arguing, Captain Lowell deflecting her salvos with practiced ease. "Fine," she said. "But I won't wait here to be kidnapped. Kip, the usual way."

And then, before Lowell could react, Emily's hands glowed lilac and she was gone.

He stared at the space where she'd been and then at Kip. "What does this mean?"

"She's gone," Kip said honestly. "I don't know where."

"Translocated," Malcolm added. "I'm guessing, mind you, but it's a thing she's been known to do and she's quite good at it."

Lowell shook his head, so Alice said, "It means using sorcery to go to another place."

This snapped him out of it. "I know what it means." He rounded on Kip again. "She said 'the usual' to you, what does that mean?"

"The usual way of communicating, I suppose." Kip saw no reason to lie. "We use a place in New Cambridge where we leave messages for each other."

Lowell gripped Kip's wrist. "Don't you go translocating."

He laughed. "You needn't worry. I'm not nearly as good at it as she is. And besides, I am—" He looked at Malcolm and Alice, got confirmation from them. "We're all eager to fight."

The man studied his muzzle and then released Kip's wrist. "Civilian sorcerers," he said with a shake of his head. "All right, the rest of the unit is here."

The rest of the unit proved to be eight other sorcerers, all men older than Kip and Malcolm, all in a restless mood. The small room they gathered in must be the private quarters of a few of them, to judge by the strong scent Kip got of unbathed men, mixed with an undertone of raven.

When Lowell left, the oldest sorcerer, who introduced himself as Captain Marsh (and whose scent pervaded the room), asked Kip what had happened, so the fox told the story again. Early on, as he described summoning a demon, the interest of the other sorcerers grew. "Ah," one said. "So this is the Calatian sorcerer."

"And a good one too," Malcolm said. "Taught me demon summoning for when I've a need for another pair of eyes."

"Why not just get a raven?" Marsh asked.

"Ah, well." Malcolm kept his cheerful demeanor. "Our Headmaster adheres quite strongly to the rule that only full sorcerers may have ravens, and I've not passed the proper tests yet."

"Despite the fact that it's his fault Malcolm's blind," Kip said. "Letting an untrained sorcerer leave the College."

Malcolm put a hand on his arm. A few of the sorcerers nodded in sympathy, but some looked uncomfortable. "Only Captain Marsh has a raven of all of us," one said, pointing to a perch in a dark corner on which a single raven stood dozing.

"And Master Colonel Jackson," Captain Marsh added.

"Anyway," Kip said, "it hasn't stopped him being a fantastic defensive sorcerer."

Alice stayed quiet, and the men didn't ask about her. But they appreciated Malcolm's ward as much as Kip's demon summoning. "Luke there is a dab hand at wards," Captain Marsh said, "but none of the others of us can do much with them."

It was a good thing Kip kept his story short, because he'd barely finished when Master Colonel Jackson entered the room, flanked by Captain Lowell. Jackson marched directly to Kip, and from his several inch height advantage, barked down, "Where's she gone? Carswell?"

"I don't know." It was difficult not to be intimidated by the man. Besides his height, his eyes bored into Kip's, unflinching, and the deep tone of his voice demanded submission. "As I told Captain Lowell."

"What men tell Captain Lowell and what they tell me are often not the same." Jackson straightened and rubbed his chin. "But you can communicate with her?"

"Aye," Kip said.

"Lowell, draft a letter telling her to return immediately and then arrange with Penfold here to take it." His eyes drifted down to Alice. "We don't have women in the army, but if they have sorcery, we can find a use for them."

"I can fight as well as anyone." Alice stepped forward.

"I'm sure when it comes to teeth and claws, you'd best any woman I know," Jackson said with a patronizing smile. "But the Army doesn't put women in harm's way."

Alice subsided, though Kip saw the unquenched rebellion in her eyes. Jackson informed the room that he would be meeting with General Hamilton soon and expected that the next day would see the official beginning of the war. "So be ready for deployment, all of you. As for you," he said to Kip and Malcolm, "you're one sorcerer short of a full unit, so your first task is to find Miss Carswell and complete your unit."

"Unit?" Malcolm said. "Begging your pardon, sir, but we're not familiar with that term, being naught but simple apprentices."

"Captain Marsh, educate them and see that they are sent properly on their way. Caldwell!" He motioned to one of the other sorcerers. "Come take me to New York. We shall see if this information may not speed up the molasses mind of General Hamilton."

The sorcerer hurried to Jackson's side with a sharp, "Yes, sir!" and they left the room together.

"Right." Captain Marsh, a short, stocky man with bright red hair and beard, came over to Kip and Malcolm and Alice. "You two have had your papers?"

"Three," Alice said indignantly.

He ignored her. "If not, you'll have to go down to the secretary on the first floor for your enlistment papers. After that you can contact the fugitive and bring her back."

"Hang on a moment," Malcolm said. "She's not a fugitive."

"She defied a direct order from Master Colonel Jackson." Marsh tried not to look at Malcolm's face.

"You've just given us enlistment instructions." Malcolm turned to Kip with uncanny accuracy. "Have I not heard that right? Me da used to say, the devil hasn't got your soul until you sign your name, and I haven't felt a pen in my fingers yet."

Marsh's already ruddy complexion reddened further, and his raven on its perch fluttered. "Go enlist and then bring back Miss Carswell," he said.

"Just a moment." Malcolm folded his arms. "If we're to join an army, should we not be given a grand speech about the cause and what our duties will be? What pay shall we receive? We must decide whether there are better ways we could serve this war."

Marsh threw up his hands. "What did you come here for, if not to enlist?"

"Emily brought us here to bring news," Malcolm said.

"You wish to fight for independence, do you not?" Marsh glared at Kip and Malcolm in turn. "This is how you must do it."

"Yes," Alice piped up.

"We've already done a good deal of fighting." Kip wanted to join the army, but Marsh's insinuation that they were valueless outside of it stung him.

"I've heard stories of your fighting, but this is a war." Marsh's eyes gleamed. "A war isn't a single sorcerer scheming to bring down a College."

"Two sorcerers," Malcolm said, "but your point is taken."

"A war," Marsh continued as if Malcolm hadn't spoken, "is an enormous enterprise and the army that fights it must be wielded as one great soldier of unified mind. Your talents will be useful, but they must be sent to the most important location and used in the most appropriate way. Do you think you can win this war all by yourself?"

"No," Kip said, ears flat at the condescension.

"Then I suggest you do your patriotic duty. The secretary is on the first floor." Marsh turned on his heel.

"That wasn't quite the rousing speech I'd hoped for," Malcolm said, "but it will have to do."

"A moment." Kip searched for any way to disrupt the smug captain. "I believe Colonel Master Jackson ordered you to educate us. What is a unit?"

"Master Colonel Jackson," Marsh corrected as he turned back, his expression remaining dark. "A unit is a trio of sorcerers, one translocational, one defensive, and one offensive. The purpose of the unit is to allow for the maximum impact on the enemy with the minimum personnel. The translocational sorcerer must be able to move two other people with him and the defensive sorcerer must be skilled in warding and defensive magic."

"Seems obvious," Malcolm murmured.

"The offensive sorcerer may be spiritual or alchemical or even physical in specialty, whatever is called for at the site of the battle." Marsh sped up his recital. "The translocational sorcerer is also responsible for retrieving orders from the commander, but secondarily to the safety of the other two. The defensive sorcerer is responsible solely for protecting himself and the offensive sorcerer. Is that sufficiently clear?"

"Perfectly," Kip said. "Thank you very much."

The sorcerer stared at him. "You should address me as 'sir.'"

"Once we've enlisted, I shall. What rank shall we all be assigned, by the by? Will we be made captains?"

"Hah!" Marsh looked down his nose. "War is an opportunity for advancement, and if you do well you may end up as a captain by the end of it. But sorcerers enter the military as lieutenants, meaning you have a commission from the government to serve and you will be able to command sergeants, corporals, and of course privates."

"Of course," Malcolm said. "And how will we be able to tell whose privates we'll be allowed to command?"

Marsh snorted. "First floor," he said, and walked away.

The only hitch with the tedium of registration was that the secretary would not give papers to Alice. "She's a woman," he said, and that was the end of it.

"I'm not going to be sent away," Alice said. "For one, I want to keep learning sorcery, and who else will teach me?"

"Don't worry." Kip had been heartened by the talk of units and the idea that he, Emily, and Malcolm could be one. "Malcolm can protect three as easily as two."

"Indeed," Malcolm said, "although I'd as soon protect four, and so let's go find our Miss Carswell."

Their meeting place was the old barn where Farley had taken Alice, but getting there was likely to be difficult without another translocational sorcerer. Over the past year, Alice had not shown an affinity for that branch of sorcery, nor for alchemical magic. Her physical magic outstripped Kip's, but he thought her real talent might lie in summoning. He'd been loath to teach her that very dangerous spell and had put it off for more than a month, but elementals and demons would prove useful in a battle.

Between the three of them, only Kip trusted his translocation enough to take himself to a spot he'd previously visited, but he couldn't take others. Summoning, though, he could do easily, so they found a room on the third floor and he and Malcolm summoned first-order demons to send to New Cambridge. First-order demons, though limited in their power, had the significant advantage that they did not require the sorcerer to perform the calyx ritual—imbibing a small amount of blood from a Calatian, termed the "calyx," whose magical qualities would increase the sorcerer's power—to successfully bind them. Kip had found that a small taste of his own blood would work for him, but he still preferred to avoid it whenever possible, and Malcolm felt the same.

Through the demons' eyes, they searched the ruined barn until they found a scrap of paper. "Peacefield, in Quincy," was all it read.

"Where's Quincy?" Malcolm asked.

"Near Boston." Kip searched his memory. "South, I believe?"

"If none of us have been there, then I suppose we could fly." Malcolm dismissed his demon but Kip kept Nikolon around.

Alice had been sitting with arms folded and ears flat, put out at not being able to see what Kip and Malcolm's demons were seeing, and now jumped up. "I can lift us if you guide me."

Before they could proceed further with that plan, shouts sounded from outside, muffled, and then the sharp retort of a gunshot.

The three of them stared at each other for a moment, and then another gunshot sounded. Kip ran outside and plunged into chaos, soldiers clogging the hallway searching for targets for their half-lifted rifles. By the time he and the others made their way to the meeting room where they'd met Captain Marsh, they were just in time to see the last of the sorcerers disappear.

"Where did they go?" Alice asked. "Where should we go?"

"The room's empty," Kip told Malcolm.

"Aye," his friend said. "Give me a moment and I'll have eyes again. Shouldn't have dismissed the blighter so soon."

"Put a ward up first." Here in the room, with men shouting outside and gunshots crashing, Kip felt vulnerable.

"Alice." Malcolm reached out a hand. She took it, and Kip took the other. The hands glowed orange for a moment and then Malcolm spoke the spell and the glow died down. "That should do," he said, "for the three of us, anyway. Now let me make the summons."

Nikolon. Show me where the gunshots are coming from.

The street outside the Armory appeared in his vision, where a row of soldiers in bright red uniforms knelt in formation and fired on the armory. Kip scanned the street around them but could not see sorcerers anywhere. Did military sorcerers wear black robes? Red uniforms? *Are there sorcerers around?* he asked.

Six on the roof of this building, Nikolon replied promptly, *three on the roof of the third house from the end across the street, and one in the stairwell of this building between the second and third floors.*

The ones on the roof might be the American sorcerers, but one in the stairwell? "What?" Kip exclaimed aloud, and at that moment shouts and curses came from the hallway outside and then stopped abruptly with several loud impacts that sounded like bodies hitting stone.

Show me the hallway outside.

Half a dozen American soldiers stood immobile against the walls to either side of the hallway. Between them strode a tall, thin man in black robes with a sharp black goatee, a sorcerer Kip didn't know. He walked quietly, peering into every room, and was only two doors down from the room they were in.

Kip pointed outside to Alice and Malcolm and said in a low whisper, "Enemy sorcerer." Alice nodded and called magic to her; Malcolm was in the midst of his summoning spell and Kip realized that in a moment the demon would appear and Malcolm would have to speak to bind it.

Can you create a light as bright as the sun just in front of the sorcerer's eyes? Kip asked Nikolon.

That seemed in line with Nikolon's abilities, and indeed the demon responded, *Yes.*

Do so when I tell you. Kip bit his lip and watched the sorcerer move down the hall. They had only seconds, and his plan was only half-formed.

"What should I do?" Alice whispered.

"Stay here," Kip said, gathering magic, and said, *Now,* to Nikolon as he jumped out into the hallway.

A bright light flashed in front of him, obscuring the face of the sorcerer. Kip used physical magic to take the rifle from the hands of one of the immobilized soldiers and swing it at the back of the sorcerer's head.

The man staggered forward but didn't fall. Kip swung the rifle again, and then another rifle flew through the air and struck the man on the temple. At that, he fell to the ground and didn't move.

Kip whirled to see Alice in the doorway, her ears back but smiling. "I told you to stay in the room," he said.

"What if you'd been hit?" she retorted. "I'd be in the room with no idea what was going on. Malcolm put a ward on us, so I was safe."

"My wards aren't completely foolproof." Malcolm came up behind her. "Especially if you jump out in front of a fellow and hit him." Kip had caught

Malcolm's orders binding his demon, and his nose tingled strongly from that one and Nikolon being both nearby.

"They'd protect me from physical magic, though." She pointed to the men around the hallway, now mobile again. "That's what he was using."

Two of the soldiers had bent to tie the arms of the sorcerer. Kip stepped forward. "That won't do any good," he said. "Keep him unconscious until Captain Marsh returns."

One of the soldiers squinted up at him. "We don't take orders from you."

"We're lieutenants, I'm told." Kip broke off, not wanting to ask the men what their rank was.

"He's telling you truth," Malcolm said. "Binding a sorcerer's hands is like taping up your mouth. Might make you feel good but does naught to stop you fighting."

The soldier's expression darkened. Kip looked around. "Where is Captain Marsh?"

Before they could answer, noises came from the stairs. One of the soldiers went to investigate, and the loudest gunshot Kip had yet heard sounded, making him flatten his ears as the rest of the soldiers dropped to alert crouches. The unfortunate soldier who'd braved the danger tottered back and then slumped against the wall.

Show me the stair, he commanded Nikolon, and there saw three red-coated soldiers, rifles at the ready, making their way up. With some concentration, he called magic and picked up the foremost one, then threw him back into the other two. They tumbled down, cursing, and landed in a pile at the bottom of the stairs.

"Go now!" he gestured to the soldiers, calling more magic and yanking the invading soldiers' rifles from them. A moment later his allies ran into Nikolon's field of vision and grabbed at the soldiers, pulling them away from each other and binding their hands behind their back.

Alice ran over to the soldier who'd been shot. Kip followed, asking Nikolon to find Captain Marsh for him. "Malcolm," he called, "can you take charge of the sorcerer?"

"Aye," Malcolm called back.

Another soldier knelt with Alice next to his wounded comrade. Alice had asked for a cloth to press to the wound, but the young man shook his head. "I fear he is beyond our help," he said.

The wounded man stared straight ahead, his breath coming in wet, shallow gasps that felt painful to Kip. He was inclined to agree with the other soldier, but Alice was not convinced. "We must put pressure on the wound," she insisted.

"Unless your friend has some healing magic," the man said, "there's naught to be done. He doesn't even hear us. Dorkay? Dorkay?"

Motion in the hallway behind Kip drew his attention. He turned expecting Captain Marsh, but the figure striding toward him was taller than Marsh and more commanding. Master Colonel Jackson took in the scene and stopped at the head of the unconscious sorcerer, with Captain Lowell and the translocational sorcerer he'd called Caldwell trailing behind him.

"What's happened here?" he snapped, staring around the hallway. "Where's Captain Marsh?"

"On the roof, sir." Kip had just received this information from Nikolon. "The Armory was attacked."

"I can see that," Jackson snapped. "Caldwell, go fetch Marsh."

Malcolm stepped up. "It appears we were attacked from the outside while this fellow took it on himself to infiltrate the building with a small group of friends." Jackson knelt to examine the captive sorcerer, so Malcolm went on. "Kip and I reconnoitered with demons, and Kip disabled the fellow with a blow to the head."

Kip wanted to interject that Alice had helped, but given Jackson's previous attitude, that didn't seem wise. She still knelt by the dying soldier, still in distress. "He'd immobilized the soldiers here, and when they were released, that one ventured the stair and got shot. So we threw the enemy soldiers down the stairs with physical magic and the rest of the men here captured them."

"Private Dorkay, sir," the soldier who'd knelt by Alice said. "He's been shot in the chest and I'm afraid there's not much to be done."

"He's died." Alice stood, and only then did Kip realize she'd been holding the soldier's hand. She came to Kip's side without another word and he put his arm over her shoulder. Her head came to rest against his side.

Caldwell reappeared with Captain Marsh. Jackson noted their appearance and stood, brushing his uniform clean of dust. "Marsh," he said. "Thank God. I've been taking testimony from Calatians and the blind here. If you please, it would be a great relief to hear the event related by a sensible man of uniform."

Kip and Malcolm both stiffened, and Malcolm looked about to speak, but thought better of it. They listened as Captain Marsh provided an account that included very little of what had transpired inside the armory but did inform them that several enemy sorcerers had been outside with a British battalion firing on the Armory. "It appears that the outside attack was largely a diversion and that they hoped to take the Armory from the inside."

"Not a bad plan." Jackson rubbed his chin. "Let's see what this fellow has to say."

He knelt by the captive sorcerer and placed a hand on his head. After a moment, the sorcerer startled awake. He stared into Jackson's face, eyes wide, and Kip could tell he was reaching for a spell to cast.

"Ah ah ah," Jackson warned him. "I've cut off your magic. Now why don't you tell me who your commander is and whether there's another attack planned."

His voice was pleasant, but Kip felt the chill behind it. The matter-of-fact way that Jackson said "cut off your magic" took him back to the panic he'd felt when similarly cut off, back in the White Tower a year ago, especially when he hadn't understood why it had happened.

"I'll tell you nothing, traitor," the sorcerer said.

"You'll tell me now or I'll dig it out of your mind, which will be considerably more painful," Jackson said with the same casual tone. "The end result will be the same."

"So you think," the sorcerer said.

"Is the Armory warded against demons?" Kip asked Malcolm quietly.

His friend replied in like tones. "Probably, but not by me."

Nikolon, please tell me if any demon other than Daravont appears inside the Armory building the instant you detect it.

Yes, Master.

Jackson lifted one hand, building a complicated spell and casting it. "Now," he said. "Tell me your attack plans."

A horrible grating noise came from the sorcerer's throat as though each word he spoke were being dragged by rusty chains. "We hoped to take the Armory unawares by attacking on two fro—"

The word cut off as though he'd been silenced by a spell. His mouth continued to work, but no more noise issued from it. His eyes fluttered and then rolled back in his head, and spittle dribbled from the corners of his mouth. A moment later he went limp.

"No!" Jackson grasped the man by his collar and stood, lifting him off the floor. The feat surprised Kip so much that he took a quick step back, worried Jackson might throw the man around the hallway. "Don't you— come back here." He slammed the man against the wall and stared into the blank eyes as though he could see the answers in there. For the space of five heartbeats thudding in Kip's ears, everyone in the hallway stood motionless as Jackson probed. Then he dropped the sorcerer to the floor.

"Nothing," he said. "Gone."

"Gone?" Captain Marsh asked, staring uneasily down at the limp robed body.

"He had a trigger set by a spiritual spell to erase his mind if pressured by another spell." Jackson turned to the three captive soldiers. "I'll wager these three don't, though they may not know anything."

Marsh knelt next to the sorcerer and put fingers to his neck. "He's still alive."

Jackson had taken a step toward the other captives, drawing even with Kip. At these words he froze. Then in one fluid motion, he spun on his heel, clapped his hand to his belt, and knelt even as he drew and stabbed downward a large hunting knife.

Kip, Malcolm and Alice jumped back, and even some of the soldiers flinched. Blood spurted from the man's neck onto the stone floor, pooling and running into the crevices between the stones. "There," Jackson said, stepping back. "Now he's alive neither in mind nor body." He looked around at the people and pointed to Alice. "Clean that up."

"Excuse me, sir," Kip said, trying not to look at the dead sorcerer or think about what this man, who was now his commander, had done. "She wasn't allowed to enlist so technically she's not under your command."

"All right, then," Jackson said, and started to say more, but Alice interrupted him.

"It's alright, Kip. I'll clean it up." She gathered magic, her paws glowing turquoise. Kip saw the slight shaking in them, but probably nobody else could.

"Here, now!" Jackson exclaimed.

Alice ignored him, casting an advanced physical magic spell. She lifted the body and collected all the blood around it in marble-sized globules that floated in a cloud around the corpse. The nearby soldiers backed away, eyes wide, but Alice stayed cool. "Where do you want it?"

Jackson raised his eyebrows. "You have some skill, that is clear. Deposit it in the room all the way down the hall to the right, just on the floor."

Alice walked down the hall, opened the door, and then guided the body through it, the blood cloud trailing behind. Kip heard the wet thump as it hit the floor, and then Alice closed the door and walked back to Kip, looking rather pleased with herself.

"Maybe we should have you enlist after all," Jackson said. "Come, I'll arrange it. Captain Lowell!"

Kip hadn't noticed Captain Lowell's return. The man stepped forward. "Yes, sir?"

"You'll be my liaison to this unit. Remain with them and I'll relay my orders to you."

Confusion creased Lowell's face. "But sir…"

"Was any of that unclear?" Jackson snapped. He pointed to Malcolm and Kip with a sweep of his fingers. "Accompany them to find their translocational sorcerer and then return here for further orders. If the British are attacking Boston there are two more places they may try, and we must be ready to defend them."

"Yes, sir." Lowell lowered his head.

Jackson gestured Alice to follow him and led her down the stairs. Lowell turned to Kip and Malcolm. "All right, then," he said, not looking nor sounding pleased. "Let's go find Miss Carswell."

CHAPTER 3: PEACEFIELD

Lowell helped immediately simply by knowing where Peacefield was. "That's John Adams' house," he said. "Down in north Braintree."

"None of us have been there," Kip said. "We'll have to take a carriage. Is it safe?"

Lowell shrugged. "As safe as can be with three sorcerers on board, I suppose."

As they descended the stairs, Malcolm hung back and whispered to Kip, "I'm keeping Dar, then, if it's dangerous."

"Right," Kip whispered back. "I'll dismiss Nik."

He did so without Lowell noticing. For the first time, he felt apprehensive about dismissing Nikolon. Rarely had he been in a situation where he might be attacked at any time, and Nikolon provided a measure of security that he was now trusting to Malcolm and his demon. At the same time, he felt that he was building a rapport with Nikolon, and part of that was not binding the demon in this world for too long. Some first-order demons remained bound at the College for months at a time, but Kip knew that being bound grew more and more painful for demons over time. He tried to limit his bindings of Nikolon to a few hours at the most.

Despite his worries, the carriage ride to Peacefield was, apart from some very bumpy roads, undisturbed by soldiers or, for that matter, conversation.

Alice, who rejoined them outside, had her hackles up because she'd been enlisted as a private and not a lieutenant, despite the fact that she was a sorcerer. Kip and Malcolm agreed that this was unjust, but they didn't want to talk about anything else in the presence of Lowell, and the captain spent the entire trip staring out the window at the sunset and darkening sky.

Kip spent most of the ride wondering if they would be able to convince Emily to come back, and also about his sudden transition from apprentice and teacher to soldier. Soon the scenarios he'd been imagining for months would become real, though almost certainly different. He knew he'd be useful, had thought he might be sent to burn shipyards or supplies, but those decisions were not his to make now.

He hadn't much choice; Master Odden was gone. Where had he been taken? Had he and the others been killed? A day ago he wouldn't have thought it likely, but Jackson's casual treatment of an enemy sorcerer's life had changed his outlook. They were at war now, and life meant less than strategy. Captain Marsh had said almost as much. Still, Jackson had only killed that sorcerer when he had no more value. Kip had to hope that the British saw reason to keep the New Cambridge masters alive.

The carriage rounded a corner and Lowell said, "Here we are." Kip and Malcolm looked out the window at a large three-story modern house, blue with white-trimmed windows and a shingled roof. A soldier standing out front shouldered his musket as they approached. "State your name and business," he called.

"Captain Lowell, Kip Penfold, Malcolm O'Brien, Alice Cartwright to see Emily Carswell," the driver said. "She's a guest of John Adams."

Footsteps, then a knock at the large door. A few moments later, the soldier returned and said, "You may disembark. The carriage can go to the stables."

So they stepped out of the carriage and walked to the open front door of Peacefield. A servant escorted them into a hallway with a carpet over a wooden floor and paintings on the walls. He asked them to wait in the sitting room and informed them that Mrs. Adams and Miss Carswell would greet them there presently.

The sitting room lived up to its name, holding a long couch and no fewer than five chairs, all with an elegantly patterned red velvet upholstery. Malcolm touched the fabric of one and murmured, "Mr. Adams' law practice has done well, it seems."

Captain Lowell remained silent, taking the chair farthest from the others and sitting at attention with his hands clasped in his lap. Kip and Alice sat together on the couch, tails overlapping, and Malcolm sat in the chair nearest Kip.

They didn't have long to admire the paintings in this room—mostly of boats and the sea, one very nice one of the fog over Boston Harbor—before

Emily hurried in, followed more slowly by an older woman in a fine blue dress, a gold necklace, and an emerald brooch.

"It's so good to see you all!" Emily said, embracing Kip, Malcolm, and Alice in turn as they stood. "This is Abigail Adams. And...who is this?"

"You remember Captain Lowell," Kip said, shaking Abigail's hand.

"Of course." Emily favored the captain with a smile, but he still didn't rise. "He escorted you here?"

"He's attached to our unit. Colonel Jackson means us to fight together."

"Well." Emily lifted her chin. "Colonel Jackson is going to be disappointed."

"Master Colonel Jackson," Lowell corrected.

"We all know about whom we're speaking," Emily said tartly.

"He's earned both ranks," the captain said, "and it's disrespectful to leave either of them out."

"Very well, then, Master Colonel Jackson is going to be disappointed, because I've been attached to Abigail Adams' diplomatic mission."

Abigail had just shaken Alice's paw. "That's correct. I'm to visit the foreign heads of state to ask for assistance in the war."

"You?" Captain Lowell exclaimed, and then snapped his mouth shut and rose to bow. "I mean no disrespect, Ma'am."

"Of course, you wonder why my husband was not chosen." Abigail clasped her hands together. "I suspect many will. John is not in the best of health and does not feel that the rigors of a prolonged journey, even a sorcerer-assisted one, would do him any good. He can consult with me as needed, since I'll have Emily to bring messages or even myself back and forth."

"Master Colonel Jackson has ordered that Miss Carswell join the 1st Sorcerers Division." Captain Lowell seemed to understand the futility of his necessary objection.

"I believe General Hamilton outranks Master Colonel Jackson," Abigail said. "We consulted with General Hamilton just a few hours ago and he agreed to this plan, as did the current leader of our American Congress."

"Your son, you mean."

Abigail smiled broadly. "We have raised an intelligent man who took many risks to assume leadership of what will, we hope, become an independent country. He has earned that position as surely as Master Colonel Jackson has earned his two titles, and he wished to ensure that his foreign emissary was one with his full trust."

"Congratulations," Kip said, embracing Emily again.

"You'll come with us, though, won't you?" she said. "Abigail will need protection."

Kip shook his head. "What good is a fire sorcerer on a diplomatic mission? Anyhow, we've enlisted already and been placed under Jackson's command. Master Colonel," he added, with an eye toward Lowell. "We'll be fighting in the battles."

"No! I did this for all of us," Emily said. "You have to get out of it somehow. We can go back to General Hamilton—"

Abigail shook her head. "The fox is correct. I have little need of a fire sorcerer and a defensive specialist when the two of them might turn the tide of many battles here. As they have already enlisted, it would create strain between the diplomatic and military offices, which for our new country must remain as harmonious as possible."

"Well," Captain Lowell said, "perhaps I was hasty in judging, Ma'am. You do have a diplomat's mind and a pleasing way with words."

"Thank you. Captain, was it? I have certainly been brash and outspoken for a good portion of my life, but I am at a stage where I see many others taking up that mantle, and I am not too late coming to the art of occasionally not speaking my entire mind. I find myself bemused at my appointment to a diplomatic position, but when one's country calls, one must answer, or else one is no patriot. Great necessities call out great virtues, or so I hope."

"When do you leave?" Malcolm took Emily's hand.

"Tomorrow," she said. "The declaration of war will happen later today and we must travel to Spain immediately to secure an audience. Oh." She clapped a hand to her mouth and turned to Abigail. "I'm so sorry."

"That information does not leave this room," Abigail said. "Is that clear to everyone?"

They all assented, and then Malcolm, who hadn't released Emily, asked, "May I stay this night and see you off?"

Again, Emily turned to Abigail. "I think that should be acceptable," the older woman said. "If it suits Master Colonel Jackson."

Captain Lowell shook his head. "My orders were to return with everyone, including Miss Carswell. I can report that she was not available, but to lose O'Brien as well?"

"You're not losing him," Emily said. "He'll be delayed a day."

"What assurance do I have that he'll return? That you won't simply take him and leave as you left yourself?"

"You have my word," Malcolm said. "I signed a document pledging my loyalty to the army of America. Emily here signed nothing and broke no pledges, and so you've no cause to consider us oath-breakers."

"We'll go back with you," Kip said. "Alice and I. Malcolm will keep his word, but if it makes you feel better to know that he won't trust us to anyone else's defense, you may have that."

"That's a true statement if ever one was uttered," Malcolm said. "So true it makes me think twice about allowing you to travel back to Boston unaccompanied."

"May we remain another hour or so?" Kip asked Lowell, "Then I can summon a demon to guard us on the return."

"Of course we would be pleased to offer you dinner," Abigail said.

Kip had not had much appetite since the battle at the Armory, but as soon as dinner was mentioned he realized that he hadn't eaten since the bread that morning; he hadn't even had time to eat at the Feast Day luncheon. "That would be lovely," he said. "We would be pleased to accept."

Captain Lowell must have been hungry as well, because he didn't argue at all, but merely said, "Thank you for your generous hospitality."

"Alice," Emily said, "did you know that Abigail has quite the collection of letters from eminent women in her study?"

"Oh?" Alice's ears didn't perk up, but she was smart enough to know when she was supposed to be interested in something. "I would quite like to see them."

"Come along then." Abigail smiled at Emily. "Dinner will be served in forty-five minutes. Will that be enough?"

"Yes, thank you."

Abigail turned to Captain Lowell. "Would you like to accompany us?"

He looked around at the people in the room and shook his head. "I think I will remain here, but I thank you for the invitation."

"He's been assigned to us," Kip said to Emily, "so he's going to stay with us. I think anything we want to say, we can say in front of him."

"He'll hear it, at any rate," Malcolm said, "and we should be aware that Master Colonel Jackson will likely hear it as well."

Captain Lowell looked sour at this but did not dispute it. Abigail took Alice with her, but as they were about to leave the room, the young vixen turned and fixed Kip with a look. "If this conversation is about whether or not I shall be allowed to fight in the war, then save your breath. My father forbad me to become a sorcerer and I did it anyway, he's forbad me to marry Kip and I shall do that anyway, and Master Colonel Jackson has allowed me to enlist. If there's to be a war and this country promises to improve the situation for the Calatians then I'm going to fight in the war, and that's the end of it."

With that, she lifted her muzzle and walked out behind Abigail. Kip and Emily looked at each other, while Malcolm chuckled. "She's left no doubt where she stands," he said.

"That was mostly what I wanted to discuss," Emily admitted. "I didn't know that she'd enlisted as well."

"And deserved it," Kip said. "I understand your worry, but she really is accomplished and smart. I would trust her over most of the human sorcerers I've met in the military so far."

Emily shook her head, taking a seat in one of the chairs. "She'll either become a hero or get herself killed, and I can't honestly say I would bet that she won't become a hero."

"There was something else I wanted to discuss," Kip said, sitting next to her. "Albright. He translocated to the church, but I don't think he'd ever been there. I believe he was homing in on me. The way you explained the wards, it sounds like he got close and knew I was nearby, but not quite where."

"Yes. You should have one of Malcolm's wards on you at all times, or a demon around."

"Both, at present," Malcolm said. "I've not lifted the ward from the Armory, just kept it around us."

"I'll summon a demon when I go back." Kip turned to Emily. "Now that we're at war and fighting…could I also translocate to Albright? How would I do that?"

"It's very much like going to a place," Emily said. "You know him, so if you could learn that magic, you could summon the essence of him—in your case I expect scent would play a large part of it—and cast the spell as if that essence were a location. I don't know if I'm explaining it well."

"Reasonably well. I imagine it takes some practice, though." Kip folded his paws together. "Could someone else read his—essence, or what have you—from my mind and do the spell?"

"If the sorcerer doing the translocation isn't the one who knows the person, then you have to involve a spiritual sorcerer to bridge the knowledge from one mind to the other. It must be an accomplished sorcerer, too. That's not trivial spiritual magic."

"Master Colonel Jackson is a spiritual sorcerer and he seemed very accomplished." Malcolm turned to Captain Lowell. "Do you think he would do it?"

Lowell looked startled at being included. "Master Colonel Jackson is indeed very accomplished. But why is Master Albright so important?"

"He orchestrated the first attacks on the Colleges here, and the failed second attacks." Kip ticked the items off on his fingers.

"And the successful third," Malcolm put in. "And he may know where the sorcerers from the College are. That would be a good group of people to recover."

"Not to mention the book of demon names, which gives Britain a strong advantage."

"If Albright can get to you," Lowell pointed out, "he must be prepared for the eventuality that you could get to him. He'll be warded as well, or protected with demons or whatever it is you do."

"But," Malcolm said, "he thinks Kip can't translocate."

"I couldn't until a couple months ago."

"So he might not be worried about it."

"He does tend to overconfidence," Kip said.

Emily placed her hand on Kip's arm. "I know you want your revenge on Albright. But in this case, the army might be correct. Until we know that he's important enough to risk a mission on…"

"One moment." Lowell rose from the seat he'd just sat down in and walked to Kip. "Revenge on Albright?"

"He killed my best friend. Well, Windsor technically killed him. And Saul. But it was under Albright's orders. And Albright did kill a master I was friends with."

Lowell walked back to his chair. "Then Master Colonel Jackson will be even more against it. Personal vendettas are not good strategy, he says."

"It's more than that. It's about recovering an advantage." Kip drew in a breath and tried another tack. "What if he planned the attack on the military sorcerers too? That…one person Master Colonel Jackson interrogated had a spiritual spell on him. It could have been Albright. What if he tries again?"

"Wait," Emily said. "They were attacked too?"

"That's where Alice fought and convinced Master Colonel Jackson to let her enlist," Kip said, and turned to Lowell.

"He is important." Lowell inclined his head. "But important enough to risk a dangerous mission to capture? His importance seems to have been his knowledge of sorcerers in America, and that knowledge has been played out."

"All the same," Malcolm said.

Lowell interrupted him. "We have spies in London. When they uncover important information and there is a target that would be useful, you may be considered for a mission. Your knowledge of Master Albright will no doubt be helpful."

"Plus Kip's been to King's College loads of times," Malcolm put in.

"Don't bother," Emily said. "It's not as though Lowell here is going to make the decisions."

The captain sat up straighter. "I have Master Colonel Jackson's ear and his trust."

"Aye," Malcolm said, "and if you could truly influence his decisions, there's no chance you'd be sitting here nursemaiding us right now, is there?"

Lowell snapped his mouth shut. "That—" He stopped again. "I understand why I was chosen for this job."

"The point is," Kip said to Emily, "I feel like Albright is instrumental in this war. If we can get to him, maybe we can't stop it, but we could find the other sorcerers, get some information. Give our side an advantage."

"It's not enough just to get to him," Emily said. "You'd need some way to contain him once you get to him, or else he'll disappear like he did last time."

Malcolm spoke up. "Master Colonel Jackson can stop magic in people."

And then they had to tell Emily about the enemy sorcerer, a story that Kip felt Jackson did not come off well in, but she sounded impressed and Captain Lowell sat up straight throughout. "He'd be the one to take along," she said. "I suppose if you're set on this, you'll have to convince him. Or find another skilled spiritual sorcerer."

"One or the other," Kip said. "But I truly believe that getting to Albright is the biggest contribution I can make to this war."

Privately, he felt that convincing Lowell would go a long way to convincing Jackson. He would have to get Malcolm and Alice to help him, especially if Lowell were to continue to work with them, and maybe together they could take that step toward capturing Albright. Here and now was not the time, however. First he would have to convince Lowell that he could be trusted, and that might take a battle or two. Kip was not afraid of fighting, but any ground conflict felt trivial compared to what he might offer the American side.

Dinner was delicious: fresh bread, spring peas, roasted chicken, and fresh greens. John Adams, a short, stout man whose words Kip had often read over the past decade, proved a garrulous host, though once or twice he lapsed into a sour mood from which Abigail rescued him. Kip thought that these moods as much as his health might have decided which of the two became the diplomat.

When the conversation turned to politics, there John's brilliance manifested itself most clearly. He spoke a little bit of the unrest of 1774 and 1775, and how the British government had made a few token concessions while using sorcerers to identify and capture the heads of the revolution. He talked about the growing strain between Britain and America since then, which he simplified down to Britain's demanding that America take on more responsibility for herself without giving her the privilege to choose where that responsibility should be placed.

"As a trivial example," he said, "consider the construction industry. In the majority of cases, local governments here have consistently preferred to build and improve roads locally. This benefits the majority of residents. Colonial governments also prefer to build roads locally. Many outside of the cities have not been improved since they were built two hundred years ago, and there are only so many sorcerers and stone-layers. But the orders of the Crown send American laborers and civil sorcerers to the west, to build roads out to areas that belong to none of the colonies, to allow trade directly from our unexplored lands to London. So our workers labor for the Crown to the detriment of America."

He continued on, explaining that the attack on the College was only the boldest of moves a London agency had made to cripple the colonies. The Crown had moved control of newspapers to London so they might control what was printed, they had appointed London loyalists into key political positions, and they had controlled the American shipbuilding industry so that the would-be country now had very few boats under their command relative to the mighty British navy.

He continued on until the servants were clearing the tables, and then Abigail said gently, "All right, John, nobody here is from the paper."

"They're about to embark on a war, Abigail. It's only right they know the history behind it."

"It's fascinating, sir," Kip put in.

"There, you see, Abigail? The young fellow hasn't had time to discover how irritating I can be." He held up three fingers. "Three dinners, young man, that's the limit. After that you'll tire of me and tell me what a bore I am."

"I doubt it very much, sir."

Abigail smiled at him. "He knows his own temperament as he knows the history of this country," she said. "Do not doubt him in one and not the other."

"I have too much respect," Kip argued.

John finished a mouthful of chicken and brandished his fork at Kip. "Respect!" he said. "Respect will win you newspaper columns and legal cases. Friends are a different matter entirely. I had the respect of the First Continental Congress, aye, and yet did they act on a single matter as I recommended? They did not. Had we acted more strategically, had we but shown our teeth to the Crown in the proper places, why, you might have been born into a free and independent America."

And how would the College have been different then, Kip wondered, but he did not voice that question. John wandered into a half-eulogy, half-excoriation of his cousin Samuel, who had taken to heart the showing of teeth but not so much the strategic part, and there Abigail stopped him. "We've a spice cake for dessert, if you can stay," she told her guests.

"That sounds lovely," Malcolm said.

Kip smiled inwardly, watching Lowell struggle to decide whether to contradict the blind sorcerer and finally keep his objections to himself. So they enjoyed a delicious spice cake and another lecture from John Adams, whom Kip would happily have listened to all night.

Finally, though, Captain Lowell stood and cleared his throat. "As much as we have appreciated your generous hospitality, we really must return to Boston. We've nearly an hour ride ahead of us."

"Of course." Abigail stood, and everyone else followed.

When they said their good-byes, Emily took Kip and Alice aside. Embracing them both, she said, "The two of you had better keep yourselves safe."

"Mr. Adams hasn't exactly been inspiring me *not* to fight," Kip said with a smile.

"Of course not." Emily sighed and turned to Alice. "I know you can fight for yourself, but Kip's got plenty of experience and if there's a question, you listen to him. He's kept me alive through some scary times."

"I will," Alice promised.

"And you," Emily said to Kip.

"I know, I know." He hugged her. "I'll keep us both out of danger as much as I can. Given that we're going into a war and all."

She glanced back toward Abigail. "With any luck, it won't last long. A few weeks of negotiation with the Spanish, a show of naval support, and once the British see we have allies, they'll choose peace over prolonged warfare. The Napoleonic wars only had battles every few months or so and then there was diplomacy just after, so let's hope you don't have to fight very much."

"If I'm allowed to learn summoning," Alice said with a pointed look at Kip, "I'll be much more useful and much safer."

"Yes." He wrapped an arm around her shoulders. "But if you hurry into summoning, it will be much more dangerous. You can watch me summon Nik again."

"I've seen it," she said. "I want to try myself."

"Luckily I have a few demon names," he said, and that reminded him of the demon book and the kidnapped sorcerers. "I hope Master Odden is all right, and Argent and Splint and all of them."

"Even Patris?" Emily raised an eyebrow.

"I don't think he should be head of the school anymore, but I don't want him killed." Kip reflected that there had been times when he might not have been able to say that honestly. "That book of demon names, though, that's an important thing. Not so much that they have it, but that we don't."

"I'm sure the military has their own book of demon names," Alice said.

"I doubt it's as big." Kip's mind wandered again. "I still don't know where Albright got the name of that demon that destroyed the college. It was so powerful, and I only found a mention of it in one old text. Does he have another source?"

"What if," Emily lowered her voice, "the kidnapping of the sorcerers wasn't targeted at them, but at getting the demon names? Nothing else was taken that we could tell."

"We didn't look at every book in the library. Who knows what things other masters might have had in their offices?"

"Master Argent didn't have anything worth taking," Emily said. "Kip, I think there was more to that attack than simply kidnapping sorcerers. Why should they risk so much for a college full of mostly old academics?"

"Barrett and Jaeger are powerful spiritual sorcerers."

"When they can be stirred from their offices. You know how spiritual sorcerers are."

"Splint—"

"I'll grant you," she interrupted, because Lowell was walking toward them with a clear eye to pulling Kip away, "that some of them were useful, but look at how much they object to your idea of capturing Albright and perhaps getting them back? Now look at it from the other side."

"What other side?" Lowell said. "Penfold, we should get back now."

"The British have more resources to spare," Kip said.

"Taking an entire school must have required a good number of sorcerers, to do it so quickly and without—leaving anyone behind."

"It was a bold stroke, one they could not have made if the College were on guard." Lowell inclined his head toward the door. "May we perhaps analyze the strategy of the attack on our return trip?"

"If you're going to talk rather than stare out the window," Alice said.

He stared down at her for a moment and then a slight smile curved his lips. "No promises," he replied, and held out a hand.

"Good-bye," Kip said to Emily as Alice took the captain's hand in her paw. "Stay safe."

"You too." They embraced, and then he followed Captain Lowell's dignified walk and Alice's attempt to match it out the door.

CHAPTER 4: THE BATTLE OF BOSTON HARBOR

Having left the Armory, the First Sorcerer's Division of the American Army commandeered a large house that had belonged to the Royal Trade Inspector, which according to Captain Marsh was a sinecure for a relative of the king and involved mostly picking choice goods to send to private families back in England. The house was not quite as big as Peacefield, but it occupied a more strategic location in the middle of the city rather than on acres of farmland and had the additional advantage that it was not visibly a military site. Marsh (who assumed command of the division when Jackson was absent) told them to be ready at all times regardless, because the British knew well the vacancy and strategic location of this house and might strike at it just to see whether the Americans had made use of it.

Kip and Alice received this information from Captain Marsh before the division left but spent the night at the Armory to wait for Malcolm. In the morning, he arrived with Emily, who embraced them all again. "I'm off to Spain," she said cheerily, and repeated her injunction for them to stay safe.

A middle-aged woman greeted Kip, Alice, and Malcolm at the door of the Trade House, slightly flushed, her greying brown hair straggling down her cheeks. "You'll be Penfold, then," she said, and ushered them in. "I'm Petunia Warrington."

"Warrington?" Kip stared. "Like…"

"Aye, I'm your Master Warrington's wife. We wives of the College volunteered here for the war."

"But," Alice said, "isn't it dangerous?"

"Quite possibly," Mrs. Warrington said with a rosy-cheeked smile. "Do come in."

They followed her inside the house, past a great room on the ground floor. "That'll be where you take your meals," she said. "I've no great talent for cooking but Harmony and Evangeline do wonders with any kind of meat. They'll feed you right. Come on, up this way."

She took them to a room on the third floor, a small room into which three cots had been crammed. It had originally been a study, perhaps a writing room, but clearly had not been used in some time. Dust lay thick on the desk, which only bore two blank pieces of paper and a dry inkwell, and the single chair in the room lay on its side on the floor. "Sorry about the dust," Mrs. Warrington said. "I'll come up here straight away I'm done with the second floor."

"No bother," Kip said. "I've cleaned up worse."

"He has," Malcolm put in. "You should have seen the basement he lived in."

"Well, thank you. I won't deny it's been a labor to get this house in shape. The mice I've chased!"

"Kip, your demon could sort out the mice, couldn't she?"

Kip gave Malcolm a laugh, and Mrs. Warrington spoke before he could. "Oh, don't trouble yourself. The mice have retreated and they'll not come back while we're around. But if they start to get into the food, I may ask for your help."

"Gladly," Kip said, and shook her hand.

When she'd left, Kip prepared to burn away the dust with a fire spell that required a good deal of concentration, but Alice stopped him. "Let me do it. I'd like the practice." She lifted the particles into a cloud, pulled the cloud together, and sent it out through the window Kip had opened.

"You have a good feel for air," Kip said. "I had thought to start you with water elementals because they're the friendliest, but maybe we could try air. I don't have any experience with them—well, only a little. I spoke to one in a memory once."

"I like air," Alice said. "It makes sense to me."

"Who doesn't like air, I'd like to know?" Malcolm said.

Over the next day, Malcolm was called to the defense of the Trade House, putting him in rotation with four other defensive specialists. When he came back to the room after a shift, he talked enthusiastically about what he'd learned from the other defensive sorcerers (Luke in particular) and what he'd been able to teach them. That was wonderful for him; Kip had hoped for something similar in the company of a new set of sorcerers, but he and Alice remained neglected or forgotten. They sat together with Malcolm at the meals, and none of the other sorcerers came over to sit with them. Captain Lowell did when Master Colonel Jackson wasn't present, but otherwise it was just the three of them.

Between meals, many of the other sorcerers gathered in the house's two large downstairs rooms, but whenever Kip and Alice walked in, the talk quieted and the gatherings broke up soon after. Kip thought that maybe all the military men were discomfited by a woman in their midst, so he ventured down to the social rooms by himself once or twice, but the outcome was the same.

Though it rankled Kip to be excluded, he reminded himself that the military was composed of fellows like Joshua Carmichael, who'd bullied Kip at school along with Farley Broadside, and that it wasn't a company he particularly desired to join. He and Alice spent the days in lessons, and Alice was so visibly happy to have his full attention that it more than made up for whatever he was missing with the military sorcerers (he told himself). Anyway, what could any of them tell him about fire sorcery?

He had been in the habit of practicing his fire spells in the stone office of the White Tower. Here in a wooden house surrounded by wooden furniture, there was no room for error. Kip's control was fine enough that he could burn the dust off a wooden desk without so much as leaving carbon black behind, and still it took him two days before he cast a fire spell in his room.

It wasn't a matter of nerve or comfort, truth be told; fire burned inside Kip and he hadn't gone more than a few days without casting a fire spell to let it out. On the third day, he found himself imagining a conflagration consuming the Trade House with him at the center of it, delighting in a fire that had promised not to harm him, and he knew that urge needed to be met. Fortunately, rain had come in that night through their open window, soaking some of Malcolm's clothes, so Kip conjured a fire for his friend to dry them off.

Alice, meanwhile, had been practicing her physical magic and pestering Kip to allow her to summon an elemental. "You can summon a phosphorus elemental," he said, "but we have to wait for a dry day outside to do it."

"You just summoned a fire here," she said.

"And I've been practicing fire sorcery for a year and a half."

"Anyway, I thought we were going to start with water elementals. Or air."

"I'd intended to take you to the water elementals in the laundry, and they're gone now. I can try to summon one, but I never have." He stood. "I suppose we can ask one of the military sorcerers."

"Or this wall," Alice suggested, standing with him. "It might be about as forthcoming."

"We could possibly go back to the College." Kip rubbed his paws together. "I could, anyway. There were a lot of books left in the library and maybe there's one on water elementals."

"Are you sure it's not dangerous?"

"No." He rubbed his whiskers back and let them spring forward again. "But I can bring Nik—my demon with me."

"I know her name," Alice said.

"Habit." Kip prepared the summoning. "Don't ever say the names of your demons in front of another sorcerer if you don't trust them completely."

"You don't trust me?"

"Shh." He grinned at her teasing and summoned Nikolon, bound her in the now-familiar way and then sent her directly to the College to see if there was any activity there of any nature, magical or otherwise. When she reported in the negative, he began the more difficult—for him—spell of translocation.

Translocation, he'd thought, would be simple, just a matter of reaching to another place and putting yourself or something else in it. It turned out that properly visualizing the real world was much harder for him than visualizing the phosphorus elemental plane, or the demon plane. He had to concentrate so hard on his destination that he couldn't yet spare the energy to bring someone else along with him.

Odden's office was by far the location he'd translocated to the most, so it was easy to send himself there again. When he appeared, he held perfectly still, partly to listen for any movement and partly because he always took a moment after a translocation to make sure he hadn't left part of his tail behind. After determining that he was both intact and alone save for Nikolon, he padded to Odden's shelves.

The office felt wrong, chilly on Kip's ears and nose in the spring weather where usually a phosphorus elemental sat happily in the brazier. He hurried through an examination of the books, the pile still strewn on the floor, and then of the notes on Odden's desk. The latter search turned up two pieces of paper with what appeared to be demon names on them (though no indication of their level), and the former revealed a book titled, *The Element Air*, which appeared promising. He took it and the paper down the hall to the library.

After a scan of the area where he'd found summoning books in the past, he found another copy of *The Element Air*, in considerably worse condition, as well as numerous copies of *The Summoner's Handbook*. He picked out one of those and then regarded the remaining two dozen shelves of books. There might be more valuable books there, but without Florian to guide him, Kip would have to spend hours looking through each title. He had books back at the Founders Rest that would be helpful, and besides he really should tell Old John he'd been conscripted.

He and Nikolon remained vigilant as he walked down the hill, but nobody disturbed him other than some chattering squirrels of the non-Calatian variety. When he reached the Founders Rest, Old John greeted him warmly and told him Ernest had been excellently well behaved. Kip fetched his books and other things from his room and then sat with John and the phosphorus elemental for a short time, explaining the war and his conscription. John said he'd keep Kip's room until someone else needed it. "Business not been too good anyway," he said, "not after what happened up hill." He jerked his thumb toward the College.

"Oh," Kip said, "you know about the kidnappings?"

"Aye," John said. "Army sorcerer came to ask if we'd seen anything. God's truth? I thought you'd been kidnapped with the rest."

Kip shook his head. "Emily, Malcolm, and I were in the feast and only went up after the others were gone. I'm trying to find out where they went."

"Ah well," John said. "Bring them back or bring a new set of sorcerers, likely as not won't make much difference to New Cambridge. They kept to themselves."

"After the attack."

"Even before. They'd come down if called but never just to sit. Never like you do. Even when you lived up there, you'd come down for a word now and then."

Kip smiled. "Often I was being punished, but I always enjoyed talking to you."

"Now this war takes you away, I reckon."

"It does." Kip gestured to Ernest. "I can come back every couple months to send him back and bring a new one."

"Ah, don't bother yourself, lad," Old John said. "Long as he don't go rampaging around and destroying my inn."

"He wouldn't," Kip said.

Ernest, who had been strolling from one side of the fireplace to the other, stopped and looked up. "I would!"

"He would," Kip amended, "but the binding won't allow him. If something happens to me, the summoning and binding will expire at the same time, and he'll go back to the Flower." That was if he died; if his magic was taken, as it had been a year or so ago, the binding would remain in effect somehow. The distinction didn't seem important to make here.

"Ah, the Flower." Ernest chewed at the stone fireplace, ineffectively.

John watched the lizard, a smile playing over his lips. Kip thought John must have had a pet once upon a time. "Fella like you," the old man said after a moment, "could wipe out the whole British fleet with a thought. Drop a bunch of these lizards on them."

"They've got sorcerers too. It's more complicated than that."

"Aye, of course it is. But take it from someone who's lived through a war." John pushed himself to his feet. "Longer it goes on, the worse it is for the people. Even those not in battle. Business here is down, food goes to the army first, every night we can't sleep for fear of hearing the enemy at our door. End it quick. Want another ale?"

"It's not really up to me," Kip laughed. He got to his feet. "And no, I'd best be on my way. I've left Alice behind and I've found most of what I came for. But…" He paused. "If you hear anything—about anything—I'd be obliged if you'd send word to the First Sorcerers Division. That's where I've been conscripted."

"First Sorcerers Division," Old John repeated. "Aye, if I'm able."

"Take care." Kip gathered his books and asked Nikolon to help him visualize the room he'd left a little while ago.

When he appeared there, Alice wasn't the only one in the room. Malcolm had his arm around her shoulder and someone behind Kip was in mid-shout. "—must have some idea!"

Jackson's voice and scent registered with Kip even as the Master Colonel changed his tone. "Oh, and here he is. Penfold, perhaps you can explain what dire emergency led you to leave your quarters without leave from your commanding officer?"

Captain Lowell flanked Jackson, his face set in a stern frown. "I—" Kip set the books down on the desk. "I went back to the College to get some books for Alice. I didn't realize…"

"You're part of the military now." Jackson stepped closer, staring down at Kip from his imposing height, and the growl in his voice pushed Kip down even farther. "Until further notice, you're restricted to the Trade House."

"But—"

"And you'll address me as 'sir' or as 'Master Colonel.' If you break discipline again, I'll remove magic from you until you're needed for battles. Is that clear?"

Kip swallowed. "Yes, sir."

Jackson turned to his captain. "Lowell."

"Yes, sir."

"You'll move up to this room. Clearly these College people need military discipline, so you'll educate them and enforce it as needed. Observe strict bedtimes and waking times."

The captain's mouth twisted, but he said, "Yes, sir," without any protest.

It wasn't until Jackson had left that Kip felt able to voice his frustration. "Where does he think I went? To cozy up to the British?" He strode to the window and threw his arms in the air, staring outside so he wouldn't be looking at all the wood in the room and thinking about how easily it would burn. "I'm the one who wants to go after them!"

"It doesn't matter where you went," Lowell explained. "You're in the Army now, and subject to the discipline of your commanding officer."

"Who is that?" Kip demanded. "You?"

"Captain Marsh. And Master Colonel Jackson over him."

"Say," Malcolm interjected, walking over to stand by Kip. "Why isn't it Master Captain Marsh?"

"Because..." Lowell turned and frowned. "Because Captain Marsh isn't a master yet."

"He's an apprentice like us?" Kip couldn't quite believe that. "He's got a raven."

Malcolm put a hand on Kip's arm. "Maybe he'd like to come for lessons with Alice."

The idea made Kip laugh, and that plus Malcolm's steadying presence beside him broke down his anger. He took a breath and then another, and then counted to ten and back (one of the exercises Cott had taught him). "He's welcome to come if he likes," he said. "As long as Master Colonel Jackson has no objection to me continuing the education of Miss Cartwright."

This last was with a glare at Captain Lowell, who remained impassive. "As long as it takes place in this room, I doubt he cares what transpires. Study and practice are how military men often pass their days. Although," he said, walking over to the desk behind which they'd moved Alice's cot, "perhaps we can give Miss Cartwright more privacy. There's a wooden screen in one of the second-floor rooms that I believe we could bring up here."

Alice protested that she had enough privacy, but only mildly, and so Kip and Lowell went to get the screen. When they'd installed it in the room, Alice spent a good deal of time sitting behind it and reading.

They all did a lot of that, including Malcolm when he wasn't contributing to the wards on the house. Kip had thought some of the other military sorcerers might want to learn fire spells, or see them demonstrated, but they remained stubbornly incurious, so he taught Alice for a couple hours each day and studied his own books while she studied the ones he'd brought her.

She pestered him to let her summon an elemental, but he worried about getting himself in further trouble with Jackson. Kip had been subject to Patris's rages when his summonings had gone wrong and he didn't wish to put either Alice or himself on the wrong side of Jackson's temper. When he'd proved himself to Jackson and earned the right to ask a favor, then perhaps he could give Alice that practice.

It was at the end of the week that he learned when he would first have the opportunity. British ships had been sighted outside Boston Harbor, and the British Army camp that had been growing north of Boston had greeted the sight with activity and excitement. An attack on the harbor was suspected. The cities of Philadelphia and New York reported similar movement.

Kip and Malcolm and Alice had talked late into the night about what it would be like to be in a battle, with a good deal of apprehension as the possibility became more real. The following morning, though, when it came to the planning of the battle, Master Colonel Jackson's calm assurance and the quiet confidence of Captains Marsh and Lowell did much to help ease their minds.

"First of all, I am to remind you of the rules of war. You are not to kill enemy soldiers directly with magic. You may harass them, you may make the going difficult or treacherous, but you are not to kill them directly."

"Yes, sir," everyone replied. Jackson's countenance remained impassive as he delivered this order, but Kip caught a glimpse of Captain Marsh's face and thought he saw a smirk before the captain composed himself.

"Now, our strategy. The Boston Neck and Charlestown Neck are of paramount importance, being the only land access from the mainland to the harbor," Jackson said over a large map in the dining room. "One unit of sorcerers will cover each. Marsh and Dapper, I want you there. One unit will be at the harbor itself to aid the soldiers should the British ships attempt an assault. Callahan, that's yours."

At a guess based on Captain Marsh's explanation, Kip had made there to be five units of sorcerers housed in the Trade House, including himself, Alice, and Malcolm, although they did not have a translocational sorcerer assigned them yet. "One unit," Jackson continued, "will remain at the Armory in case of another cowardly sneak attack. Johnston, that's yours. Now, we know the British tactics because they've been our own. They like to make the terrain difficult with elementals and harass the soldiers with demons. But they want to remain in line of sight of the battle at all times. There's nowhere above the harbor they can hide, so some will likely be on ships. They may try to take the hills overlooking the harbor, but there are fortifications there, so I'd expect them to try to appear on the roofs of harbor buildings. That's where I would send you—were I still a British officer." Jackson sneered. "Marsh and Dapper, you're defending the Necks, not soldiers. There are small customs-houses on each Neck, but they will be expecting us to use them, so I want you to dress out of uniform and pose as fishermen in a small boat off the Neck."

"Out of uniform?" Captain Marsh said, and then clapped his mouth shut. "But sir, the rules of war."

"I've discussed this with General Hamilton. We are far outmatched in this war in terms of supplies, in terms of personnel, in terms of materiel. We must scrap for every advantage we can get. This also means you cannot bring calyxes with you, so you must summon your demons at the onset of the battle and be judicious in their use."

"So who gets them?" One of the sorcerers they didn't know pointed to Kip and Alice.

Jackson frowned. "What?"

"Who gets those calyxes?"

Marsh stepped forward. "These are not calyxes. Kip Penfold and Alice

Cartwright are apprentice sorcerers."

Two other sorcerers looked at Kip as though seeing him for the first time, while those who'd met him looked down at the table. "Sorcerers? Calatians?"

"Had you not heard?" One of his fellows rounded on him. "The Calatian sorcerer who saved the College?"

"Why would I have heard about that?" But the sorcerer regarded Kip more thoughtfully. "Both of them?"

Jackson brought the flat of his hand down on the table. "You ladies may gossip later. Captain Lowell, your unit lacks a translocational sorcerer so your unit will be placed north of the Charlestown Neck and will harass the soldiers as they arrive and, God willing, harass their retreat."

Kip thought this sounded like the safest of the positions, but Lowell did not look at all happy about it. Despite this, his "yes, sir" was crisp and professional.

Later, up in the room they all now shared, Kip asked him about it. "It's a brush-off," the captain said. "Putting us out of the way of the battle. He might as well have asked us to guard this empty house."

"Someone was sent to guard the Armory," Kip said.

"Aye, because someone's attacked it and it's a known target." Lowell strode back and forth in the room. "He as much as told you that you're useless."

"Me?" Kip exclaimed.

"Without a translocational sorcerer, anyway."

"Isn't it his job to assign us one?" Malcolm asked.

"If he felt we were worth it." Lowell dragged the chair over to the window and sat there, staring moodily out.

"He's not likely to be good company," Malcolm said to Kip. "Let's go over some alchemical magic. Got your book? I want to try Sendivogius's Petrification again."

The next day dawned cloudy and cool. Kip, Alice, and Malcolm gathered with the others in the common room of the Trade House, all dressed in regular clothes. Master Colonel Jackson had his map out and small wooden counters in red and blue to show the last known positions of the British and American forces, while his raven peered down from the top of a cabinet. The red counters, for the British, lay a few miles north of the Charlestown hills, while a few blue counters guarded the hills, and the rest were clustered around the harbor and the two Necks that gave access to it. "We'd hoped for naval support, but the shipyards south of Boston haven't been able to deliver," Jackson said. "Marsh and Dapper, as you defend the Necks, look to Bunker's Hill and Dorchester Hill to make sure the soldiers are keeping them secure. If there's fighting, don't hesitate to engage."

"Yes, sir," they replied in unison.

"Callahan, the British will likely try to land ships at Noddle Island so they can fire across at the harbor. Water will be good to prevent them."

"Yes, sir."

"But first, take Lowell's unit around to Bunker's Hill. From there they should be able to see the British and aid our forces if needed."

"Yes, sir." The tall, dark-haired man eyed Kip, Malcolm, Alice, and Captain Lowell. "You lot ready?"

"I suppose," Kip said.

"Here." Lowell pressed a bag onto Alice. "These are our rations for the day. Some biscuits, some dried meats. Hold onto it."

She opened her mouth, ears flat and indignant, but took the bag and slung it over one shoulder without a word.

"I'll have to do this in two goes," Callahan said, a lilt in his voice that reminded Kip of Malcolm's, though not as strong and set in a harsher tone. "Who's first?"

"Take the Calatians," Lowell said. "O'Brien and I will follow."

"Right." Callahan seized Kip's wrist and then Alice's, and a moment later they stood atop a hill, wind blowing a light drizzle into their fur. Callahan released them and disappeared while they took stock of where they stood. Kip faced the wide Charles River and across it, the Boston Harbor. Below him on that side, amid scraggly brush and muddy soil and a few wooden buildings clustered disorganized groups of ten to fifteen men in uniforms of mottled red and blue. Most talked amongst themselves, though a few watched up the hill and some watched out to the harbor.

The sea, grey and choppy, faded out to a mist, where Kip thought he saw shadows moving but couldn't resolve them. If Nikolon were present, she'd be able to tell Kip where the ships were, but as of now they were unlikely to affect his part of the battle. Toward the harbor, he could make out more groups of blue-clad men in position around the buildings there; the British ships would be their responsibility. He didn't have to do everything.

Callahan reappeared with Malcolm and Lowell and vanished again. Kip turned to greet them and then caught footsteps coming up the hill. He and the others turned to see a stocky man, red of hair and face, hurrying toward them. "For God's sake," he called as he got closer, "do you wish to be targets? Get down here."

Kip took Malcolm's arm and guided his friend down the hill as they ran to meet the uniformed man, whose left shoulder bore what Kip had come to recognize as a lieutenant's bar (that and a captain's, which appeared on the right shoulder, were the only ones he knew with confidence). "You're the sorcerer, aye?" he asked Malcolm, and then got a better look at his face. "Strewth!"

"One of them." Malcolm smiled easily. "Don't trouble yourself, I can get around just lovely with my friends, thank you."

"Then…" The lieutenant looked at the uniformed black man, then at the two Calatians. "You're all sorcerers?"

"I'm the officer in charge." Lowell stepped forward. "Craig Lowell."

The lieutenant saluted. "Robert Murkey, sir, of Braintree. We've spotted the British but there's been no sorcery yet that we can tell."

"Good." Lowell rubbed his hands together. "Which fortification has the best view of the hill and the approaching army?"

The lieutenant looked around at the hill, up the dirt road lined with small wooden houses on either side. "Fortification's a generous word, sir. That house there, I'd say, with the red painted windows. You've got a view up to the hill and it looks out over Charlestown as well. I've got three men there but we can move them if it suits you. We're grateful for magical support."

"If there's room, they can stay." Captain Lowell took charge, and Kip was happy to let him. In all of his imagining of the war, he had simply been in the right place to work his magic. He'd never had to think about what that place might be or how to get there. Nor, for that matter, what to do. Doubt crept into his mind. There were no obvious targets in reach for him, save the British soldiers who, he guessed, would soon be charging over that hill. Their weapons perhaps? Or if they brought a cannon along?

Perhaps, he thought, Emily's negotiations had succeeded and even as they entered the small house, the Spanish fleet was on its way. The British would surrender, and no lives would be lost. He wouldn't have a chance to prove himself, but he'd take that tradeoff.

His reverie shattered as they opened the door to the small house, releasing a smell so bad that Kip had to take a step back outside. Alice gave him a quizzical look as she passed him and then hurried back out to his side. "Oh," she said, gasping, "it's horrible. I smelled it outside but I thought it wasn't going to be any worse."

"They must not be leaving the house to…" Kip breathed into his paw. "We're going to have to go in there."

"It can't be pleasant for them." Alice reached into the small bag she kept at her side and brought out two cloths. "Here. These were going to be bandages, but I think we need them now."

Kip took the cloth gratefully and folded it into his paw. Holding it to his nose, he went back inside, where Captain Lowell was talking to three men with thick beards who smelled almost as bad as the makeshift toilet they'd been using. "Sorry," the first said when he saw the foxes enter. "It's hell on us living here too, so you know."

The second, watching out the window, turned to them. "At least here we're not fighting for space with a dozen other men."

"Just the three of us. And it'll be over today one way or t'other," the first man said.

"Or tomorrow." Captain Lowell took a look out of one window. "Penfold, station yourself here. O'Brien, cast your wards."

"Alice," Kip said, "why don't you watch Malcolm cast the wards?"

"I've seen it." She gave Kip a look that said, *you know this.*

"But not," Malcolm said, "these kinds of wards. I'll tell you what I'm doing as I do it, shall I?"

Alice followed his gaze to the three soldiers, also watching. "Ah," she said. "That would be lovely."

"All right then." Malcolm said. "Now, you know the types of wards, yes?"

"Prevention, Inattention, Protection…" She chewed her lip. "There's another one, isn't there?"

"You're forgiven." Malcolm intoned a few syllables. "Stasis is the simplest one but also the easiest to forget. Stasis prevents magic from affecting a physical object. Like if you wanted to keep someone from sorcering open your lock. Or in this case, I've just cast a stasis ward on this house so that no other sorcerer can pick it up and fling it away."

"That's useful." Alice found a small rug that had been pushed into a corner and pulled it a little away from the wall. She sat cross-legged on it, the cloth still to her nose, and kept her attention on Malcolm.

"Aye, easy to hold and not so hard to learn. Even Kip's picked this one up. I reckon you could learn it easily enough if you liked."

Kip took up the station Lowell had assigned him, from which he could see the American army arrayed before him, scattered groups of men in barely better formation than on the other side of the hill, and beyond that, smears of red that he supposed were the British Army. Here he would need better eyesight, so as quietly as he could, he stepped into the other room. Captain Lowell caught his eye as he went and frowned, but Kip signaled that he'd be back in a moment and the captain nodded.

He had not yet figured out how to make Nikolon appear invisible when summoned, and he supposed that the sudden appearance of a naked Calatian vixen in the house would disturb the soldiers, who already seemed wary of Calatian sorcerers. When Nikolon appeared and Kip had bound her, he ordered her to remain invisible and to relay to him the locations of the British military units.

Back in the other room, Captain Lowell explained to the soldiers why they did not cast physical protection wards in battle. "You can easily see the effects. It is key to keep the sorcerers hidden, or the enemy sorcerers will focus their attentions on them, and most wards can be undone with vigorous attention. This is what happened at the battle of Fort Duquesne."

"Can't they just try to pick up this house?" one of the men asked.

"There are a number of houses and structures around here," Lowell responded. "They would have to pick up each one. To spot a protection ward, they could make a light rain fall and the shelter would be visible."

"Sorcerers can make it rain?" the soldier asked. He stared around at Kip, as though Kip were the only sorcerer here.

"Sometimes." Kip focused on the images Nikolon was sending him now and returned to his station at the window. "It takes a good deal of effort."

"Can they call lightning?"

"Aye," Kip said absently, looking out over a column of red-jacketed soldiers. What had appeared from a distance to be a uniform red smear over the countryside resolved into people, and more than that, the red varied from person to person: a few clean and bright uniforms, many showing stains and small tears. The soldiers bore resolute, stoic expressions, even those breathing hard from the march. Keeping Lowell's words in mind, Kip looked for the enemy sorcerer, with no luck. No doubt they had wards up just as he did.

"Why not just call lightning on the enemy?" the American soldier asked Kip.

"In a way, that's what we do with demons," he said. The great demon Farley had summoned would probably be able to curse twenty men at once, or raise a great blizzard to impede them—if Kip could control him long enough to be useful. The demon that Windsor had summoned to kill the people at the college had required even more control; he wasn't sure that anyone else save perhaps Master Odden would be able to control it. Besides, for anything more than a first-level demon, Kip would have to cut himself to taste blood, and he had no desire to do that in this house where the wound might easily fester. "But there are demons on both sides, and the more powerful, the more dangerous to the sorcerer."

"As I understand it," Lowell said, "many battles come down to demon-battles."

"I've never been in a battle." Kip gripped the windowsill, still looking over the British army. *Nikolon, are there other demons about anywhere?* he asked, while also replying, "Most sorcerers can't bind two demons at once, too."

"Kip can, though," Alice said proudly.

No, Master, Nikolon replied.

This got a startled look from Lowell. "Can you now?"

"Not any two demons," Kip said. "I have a good deal of trust in one particular demon, and we work together well enough that I can spare the energy to bind another."

"Trust?" Lowell's brow wrinkled. "I haven't heard that word used with demons ever."

"You've not heard of a Calatian sorcerer either." Malcolm finished his wards and now sat on the rug next to Alice. "Our Kip can do many surprising things. Have any of you some water?"

One of the soldiers passed over a canteen, and the room fell silent. To change the subject, Kip asked, "How long have you been stationed here?"

"This house, or the harbor?" the soldier who'd passed the canteen asked.

"Either."

"This house, five days. The harbor, ooh, must be two months now? But we were part of the British Army for some of that. Got our new kit a month ago and orders to wear it just last week. Looks a bit rough, I know, but our Captain says you can't make uniforms for a thousand men all in one week. Maybe sorcerers could, though."

Malcolm laughed. "Now there would be a better use of magic than half the spells I've seen."

"The whole house looks rough," Kip said.

The soldier nodded. "Aye, and smells it, but it's walls and a roof and we were lucky to be chosen for it. Bentley there's got an uncle high up and he dragged us along with him." Malcolm passed back the canteen, and the soldier toasted his companion.

So the rest of the army had been sleeping out of doors, and the British had marched for miles to get here. One exhausted group of men against another, and Master Colonel Jackson's sorcerers against their British counterparts to gain an advantage for their exhausted men. As Kip reflected on it, the week confined to the Trade House's shelter and regular meals didn't seem as bad anymore.

For an hour they stood there and watched, long enough that Kip began to think he should dismiss Nikolon. "Still no movement," he told Lowell, who'd asked for regular updates.

This time the captain paced away from his own window spot. "I can't tell what they're waiting for. The last of them has arrived, you said?"

Kip had said it twice, in fact, but he nodded. "Why are we waiting for them?"

The soldiers muttered agreement. "They sit there," one said. "Why not open fire on them?"

"Because they have ships coming into the harbor, perhaps," Lowell said. "It's not our place to question the generals."

Nikolon had continued to scan the army, and now Kip spotted an otter-Calatian relieving himself outside a tent. *Nikolon*, he said, *are there any other Calatians in the British Army?*

The Army had a Calatians division, he knew, but had any of his people sided with the British? "Lowell," Kip asked, and then remembered the ranks. "Sorry, Captain Lowell."

"Yes?"

"How many of the Army remained with the British?"

Nikolon answered at the same time as the captain, but Kip was gaining experience at listening to the demon while remaining attentive to the real world. *I have not seen any others.*

"A few here and there. Mostly officers, the people who own a good deal of…property. Who would have the most to lose should the government that recognizes their ownership be removed from power."

Nikolon was showing him more of the soldiers, human after human, but at the way Captain Lowell said, "Property," Kip realized that all the soldiers he was seeing were white. Most of the American Army had been white as well. "Er," he said, "What about Calatians?"

"There's one Calatian unit in the Army," Lowell said. "I don't know if any of them deserted."

"There's a Calatian on the British side." Kip pointed out the window. "In uniform but I think he's a calyx." *Nikolon, where's that otter?*

The demon returned him to the area where the otter had been. *I cannot see him.*

"Almost sure," Kip amended before Lowell could comment. "Malcolm, how can you break an inattention ward?"

"Walk into it," Malcolm said cheerfully. "I suppose you mean from a distance, though."

"Stop," Captain Lowell said. "We haven't been ordered to take any action. Surveillance is permissible, but no direct action."

"I'm only trying to break a ward that is preventing my surveillance." Kip directed Nikolon back to where they'd seen the otter, the exact spot as best he could find. "If he has a calyx, he's likely to summon something nasty."

"Take no action," Captain Lowell said. "That's an order."

Move at a walking pace back toward the camp, Kip told Nikolon. *Go back and forth until you find a tent with the otter inside it.* To Lowell, Kip said, "Very well."

Lowell stared at him until he added, "Sir," which Kip did as neutrally as he could without giving offense.

"How will we know when to attack?" Malcolm asked.

"One side or another will give orders," Captain Lowell told him. "If the British charge our position, we attack. If the generals order us to attack, we will."

Kip gave a curt nod and looked back out the window again, watching the red smears in his vision as Nikolon showed him a slow crawl back and forth across grass. There was a tent, but it didn't seem important, and Kip was going to tell Nikolon not to bother with it, but then the demon stopped.

I cannot proceed, he said.

With difficulty, Kip focused. The tent, that tent. *Can you show that tent to Malcolm?*

Yes.

Please do.

Next to him, Malcolm gave a start and then leaned back against the wall. "As I was saying, Kip, purely for speculation, if you were to try to break a ward from a distance, it requires a good line of sight to where the ward is, and then you have to feel it out. But if, for example, you were to ask me to do that right now, I'd likely have to drop the two wards I'm holding, for they require some focus to keep and if I were to cast a spell that took up my concentration, someone might easily break them while I wasn't attentive."

"The defensive sorcerer focuses only on defense," Captain Lowell said. "For just that reason. If we had sorcerers who could hold wards and attack the enemy, we wouldn't need three sorcerers to a unit."

Outside the house, the American soldiers had gotten to their feet, many looking at the ground. Kip pressed the side of his face to the window so he could see. "Something's happening."

Captain Lowell snapped to attention at his own window and then relaxed. "The ground," he said. "Standard opening tactic. It's physical magic disrupting the stability of the ground. Can you counter it?"

He spoke to Kip, but Alice responded. "I can," she said confidently, and strode to the window next to Kip to look out.

He wanted to hold her back, especially because with Nikolon's eyes he saw the British soldiers now marching toward the hill. The vulnerability of this small frail house made his fur prickle; surely any soldier with a rifle would be able to see the house and make a target of it. But no, that was what Malcolm was preventing. "They're coming," he called. "The British Army."

"I see." Captain Lowell turned back to the soldiers. "Two of you, go into the other room and guard this house against any advances."

"Yes, sir." Two of them, chosen by some method Kip wasn't privy to, got up and walked to the other room, muskets at the ready. The third kept his musket trained on the door of the house.

"Again," Captain Lowell said to Kip, "the rules of combat."

"Don't harm where avoidance suffices; don't kill where harm suffices." He appreciated that, because he'd feared he would be called on to incinerate all the men in the army, and while he could have called up that magic easily, he did not want to.

"This is hard," Alice said. Her paws had glowed and now she was manipulating the spell she'd cast. "I'm trying to put the ground back and keep it flat, but he's fighting me."

"The closer you are, the more control you have." Kip admired her concentration. "You can best him."

She was, to some extent. The men outside looked more confident in their footing and now stood their ground, waiting for the British to crest the hill. A moment later, Alice gave a short gasp. "I beat him!" She clutched Kip's arm. "He gave up! I steadied the ground!"

"Good job. We'll win this battle yet."

"He'll move on to another spell," Captain Lowell said. "Be ready."

Alice's ears went back, and Kip had to bite back a remark that of course they didn't think that this small victory had made the difference in the battle, but it was important to Alice. There would have been scant time to say anything in any event, because a man made of smoke standing a hundred feet tall came into being over the top of the hill. It gestured slowly, re-forming every time breezes pulled bits of it away, its indistinct face nevertheless showing a grimace as its hands stretched out to menace the American soldiers.

"He's called a demon!" Kip cried. "It's going to kill—"

As soon as he said it, it became clear that the demon was nothing but a distraction. The British troops appeared on either side of the smoke-man and through it, firing at the Americans and cutting a bloody swath through their ranks. There had been perhaps two hundred Americans in Kip's field of view, and in those first few seconds a quarter of them fell to the ground. The reports of gunfire echoed and echoed, so that both Alice and Kip lay their ears back, and a moment later the screams of men joined the rapid concussions.

"Well?"

Kip looked up to see Captain Lowell staring at him. The man gestured toward the window. "Do what you do!"

"What?"

"Do something! Anything!"

"Anything" for Kip led first to fire, and the first thing he could think to do was send bursts of fire down the battlefield between the British and American lines. The fire startled everyone, so it wasn't clear that it helped the Americans much, but at least it gave them time to recover, and after a few moments the British advance had halted some fifty feet from the house, though the barrage of gunfire and the screams of the men continued, setting everyone on edge.

"More smoke!" Captain Lowell yelled. "Give them cover!"

But a moment later, streams of water came pouring down the hill between the British lines, avoiding the red-coated soldiers and heading purposefully for the Americans. Where the water met Kip's fires, they went out in a puff of steam.

"Physical magic with the water," Lowell called.

"I'll get it." Alice stared out the window.

"I think they're elementals," Kip said.

"I can still lift them." Alice's paws glowed, but her magic faltered with a barrage of gunshots and she had to start over. Meanwhile, the water was eating away at the mud below the Americans, causing many to slip and fall, and some of those who fell did not get up again.

Kip sent more fire to flare up in front of a group of British soldiers that were trying to shoot from the shelter of another house up the hill. Even with Alice's help, he felt outmatched by this other military sorcerer. He hadn't the experience to know what to do besides light fires, while this sorcerer was calling demons and elementals and who knew what would be next.

Alice had managed to lift the water from the ground, but now it was in the way of the American soldiers, though at least it concealed them somewhat. Kip saw another soldier close to him fall, and then the one beyond him clutched his throat and sank to his knees. The action was strange enough to draw Kip's attention, because there was no blood on the man's uniform. His face darkened to red and then a deep purple, and then he toppled to his side. He spasmed and then lay still, bulging eyes staring at Kip.

Kip couldn't stop staring back. A moment later, a pool of water lifted from the corpse and rejoined the water Alice was levitating. Another soldier farther away touched the water and a moment later dropped his gun, choking for air.

"They're not elementals." Water elementals liked contact with people but would not drown anyone, not that way. "It's another demon," Kip cried to Lowell. "He's killing soldiers with a demon!"

"That's not the rules—"

"He's drowning them!"

Lowell shouted back, "Then stop him!"

Nikolon. Kip shifted his view and saw the tent, surrounded by grass. The soldiers that had been near it were moving away and it appeared unguarded, just another supply tent on the field. He gathered magic and translocated himself.

His feet landed in damp grass and a light drizzle tickled his ears. Something was in front of him but he couldn't quite focus on it. He closed his eyes and followed the smell of damp canvas, walking toward it until his outstretched paw touched the tent wall.

Now when he opened his eyes he could see the tent; he must be inside the ward. He gathered magic, and just as a shout rang out behind him of "Ho! Stop," he walked into the tent.

Three men in red-trimmed black robes and one otter-Calatian turned to him as he entered. He let fire loose on their robes, making the otter jump back from them, and before Kip could do anything else, one of the men had grabbed the other two and then all three were gone. Two ravens flew past him out of the tent and then all was still.

Almost all. The otter had jumped behind a small table on which sat some papers and a goblet, and cowered there, moaning in a low voice. "Please please, don't set me afire."

"Don't worry." Activity outside, someone running toward the tent. Kip hurried forward and grabbed the otter's wrist. "I'm just taking you prisoner."

His paws glowed violet as he gathered magic again and then let loose fire on the canvas of the tent, ordering it to consume only the canvas and no more.

Heat flared around them and steam hissed as the water in the canvas boiled away. The otter shrieked and hid his face in his paws. Outside, there were shouts of confusion as the men fell back, and then a bullet whistled through the tent. Kip dragged the otter down to the ground. "Where are the demon names?" he demanded.

"W-what?"

"Did the sorcerers read names off a paper? Which name did he read?"

"Aye, but—" The otter's breathing quickened. "I don't have to tell you anything, traitor."

"I'm sparing your life," Kip snapped, "and I'm trying to make a better world for all of our kind. You want to be a calyx forever?"

Another gunshot. The otter looked down at his bloody elbow. Kip said, "Give me the demon name and you'll be our prisoner. I promise no harm will come to you."

Still the otter remained stubbornly silent. Kip cursed and reached out, overturning the small table and grabbing the papers from it. They contained a map of the hill and harbor, but no list of demon names. He needed the otter's information.

"All right," he said, "I'm taking these papers back. You can give me the name and come with me, or...or I'll leave you to burn here."

He hoped dearly that the otter wouldn't call his bluff, but the Calatian remained resolute. "You do what you must," he said.

With a curse, Kip sent Nikolon back to the house where Malcolm and Alice were, to give him an anchor to translocate. He'd never tried to send another person before. "All right, now." His paws glowed purple as he seized the otter's wrist. "Just relax and you'll be safe in a moment."

"You said you'd leave me!"

Another bullet whistled past them. "I'm not leaving you," Kip said, and activated the spell.

The otter vanished. Hopefully he hadn't appeared in the middle of a wall or floor. Kip breathed in, gathered magic again—

A red-coated soldier burst through the burning wall of the tent, musket leveled at Kip. The fox reacted without thinking: he had magic in him and the fire on the tent was right there. He directed it at the man, incinerating him in a blaze of heat that flared and then went out, leaving a blackened shadow of the man who'd stood there a moment before. It wobbled and then fell with a thud.

The smell reached him while he was gathering magic to translocate himself, making him gag. He completed the spell and burst into a cacophony of gunfire and cries, the stink of the house mercifully clear of the smell of burning flesh. He staggered to the wall and breathed, trying to hold in the nausea as Alice cried out at his sudden appearance.

"Where did you go?" He registered the voice as Captain Lowell's, right beside his ear. "Who is this otter?"

"My prisoner," Kip coughed out, and those words threatened to empty his stomach, so he clamped his muzzle shut.

"You left this house without approval of your commanding officer. Where did you go?"

He didn't trust himself to answer. To his surprise, the otter spoke next. "He went to set my master on fire."

"Who's your master?"

"Master Braithwaite," the otter replied promptly.

"And Penfold killed him?"

"No." Kip drew in a breath, his stomach settling. "I set his robes afire and their translocational specialist took the three of them away."

"But not the otter."

Kip shook his head. "They left him."

Alice took his paw. "Are you all right?"

He nodded. "I—I killed a soldier. I did set him on fire—he was going to shoot me—"

Captain Lowell nodded, and for the first time, something like respect crossed his face. "Rather have you alive," he said. "That water demon is still choking our soldiers out there."

Kip turned to the otter. "Please," he said.

The otter turned away from him and stared at the floor. And then, after a moment, he said, "Khanaton."

Kip's ears perked up. He repeated the name. "Pronounced like that? You're sure?"

The otter nodded. Kip took a moment to evaluate, as Master Odden had taught him. The water demon looked to him like a second order demon, which he could probably banish without assistance from Calatian blood, and time was of the essence. So he gathered magic and spoke the dismissal spell, reaching out with the name Khanaton and finding the demon responsive. Dismissing was easier than binding, because the demon wanted to return home, so Kip mostly had to fight the binding spell, and with the sorcerer at a distance, he won that battle easily.

"It's gone!" Captain Lowell had moved to the window to watch. "The water, it's gone!"

Kip sagged back against the wall. The otter, watching him with wide eyes, said, "So you've no need for Calatian blood because of what's in you?"

"Sometimes," Kip said.

Lowell gestured at Kip. "Summon it back. Make it attack the British."

"No. You told me we're not allowed to kill soldiers. I've already—"

"They did it!" Lowell pointed outside. "We can give as good as we get!"

"No." Kip pushed himself upright. "One was enough, and I regret that. But I can…" He walked over to stand next to Lowell at the window, and called magic again. He'd never worked so many spells in quick succession and he felt now the fatigue of it, but fire was the easiest for him to work with and he knew he could do this.

Fire blossomed in the wet grass around the British soldiers. They cursed and jumped back, but patches of fire surrounded them and there was no clear ground. In a moment, their position was shrouded in steam and smoke.

The Americans, seeing their opportunity, advanced upon their blinded foes, firing upon shadows in the smoke or the noise of coughing. The cries came all from the British side now, and it was only moments before a loud horn sounded, summoning the army back over the hill.

When Nikolon showed him that the British were in full retreat from Bunker's Hill, Kip extinguished the fires and asked Alice to clear away the smoke. He sat with his back to the wall as Lowell reported that the Americans were advancing to hold the hill, and Kip watched through Nikolon as the British army pulled back, leaving trampled grass, red-coated bodies, and one charred frame of a tent from which smoke still rose.

CHAPTER 5: SPAIN

The army cleared the field around them save for a few sentry posts, but the soldiers left in the house did not seem eager to join their fellows. This was the first major battle any of them had been in, though they'd exchanged fire with British troops, and one of them had been aboard a ship that fired on a privateer.

When they'd all told their stories, Captain Lowell told them of his service in the Napoleonic Wars. There had been only two battles on the American continent, and in the battle of New Orleans in 1809, he had saved the life of his commanding officer and assisted in the capture of a crucial fortification.

"Ah," one of the soldiers said. "I thought to ask how one of you came to be a captain."

His companion nodded. "Aye, I've heard of freed slaves being made corporals or even sergeants."

"I was a sergeant at the time." If Captain Lowell felt any of the discomfort Kip did in hearing these questions, he didn't let it show. "My commander felt that my bravery and loyalty should be rewarded."

"Good for you," the first soldier said. The third remained silent, devoting his attention to cleaning his musket though he'd already cleaned it thoroughly.

Callahan appeared shortly after that, but he ignored the soldiers as if they were furniture. He brought Captain Lowell, Kip, Malcolm, and Alice to the Trade House, and that was the last Kip saw of any of the soldiers they'd shared the Battle of Boston Harbor with.

Back at the Trade House, they learned that the ships had tried to come in close enough to allow those on board to fire on the harbor, but one of the sorcerers in Callahan's unit, who had a gift with water elementals, had confounded their navigation and kept them at bay. Captain Marsh at Charlestown Neck had had much more success than Lieutenant Dapper with the Dorchester Neck unit, which had been entirely overrun. However, thanks to Kip's action and Captain Marsh's sorcery, the army at the harbor had not had to worry about its northern front and had successfully repelled the British forces back to Dorchester.

Master Colonel Jackson, in the large dining room, listened to Marsh's account of the battle and then Callahan's, acknowledging each with curt nods, but when it came to Dapper, Jackson interrupted him nearly every sentence.

"We set out in the small boat as ordered," Dapper began, "and sought a lee from the wind—"

"Did you ensure that this lee gave you the best view of the battle?" Jackson asked, his tone mild.

"As—as best we could, yes, sir." Dapper's tone wavered at the stone below his commander's bland question. "There was no activity until we heard a sharp report from one of the ships that appeared to be a signal—the same one Callahan reported."

"We've all heard Callahan's report." Jackson paced with his hands behind his back while Dapper, like the other sorcerers, remained seated, following his commanding officer with his head. "What did you do when you heard the signal?"

"We…we waited." Dapper's voice cracked and he licked his lips. "We observed smoke, a very common tactic, and so I endeavored to clear it with a mild rain."

"Rain is the least effective tactic against smoke." Jackson sounded and looked like a professor lecturing a particularly dim student. "Do you not have command of Kiva's Wind?"

"I'm more comfortable with water, sir," Dapper said.

"And why didn't you direct the rain at the British troops? Cause some mud, some slipping?"

"I—The smoke was on the American side."

The entire debrief went like this, with Jackson second-guessing Dapper at every turn, remaining mild in tone until it seemed the weight of Dapper's mistakes broke some sort of dam. Jackson slammed both hands down on the table and turned the full weight of his disdain on the unfortunate sorcerer. "You continue at every turn," he snarled, "to defend your incompetence, your hesitancy, your cowardice, even here in the presence of your fellows whose lives you endangered!"

Dapper shrank back into his chair, and even those who were not the target of the Master Colonel's ire flinched. "Meanwhile," Jackson fairly shouted, "this crew, without an able-bodied white man among them, turned back an entire British division!" He pointed at Kip and Lowell, with Malcolm and Alice behind them.

Malcolm stirred, and Kip worried he would make a whispered remark like he used to do when Patris lectured them, but his friend remained silent. "Lowell!" Jackson yelled.

"Yes, sir." Captain Lowell half-rose from his chair.

"Sit down. Tell us about Bunker's Hill."

He didn't interrupt Lowell as the captain recounted the battle. Kip's tail twitched when Lowell came to the part where Kip took his own initiative, and indeed, Lowell hesitated at that point. Then he said, "I had given Penfold considerable leeway to determine his own course of action, and through his demon, he located the main unit of sorcerers on the other side of the hill and chose to engage them."

"Highly inadvisable," Jackson said, but his voice had lost much of its anger, and he went on. "Under most circumstances. It seems, though, that Penfold takes good measure of his own abilities. Penfold, how did you best the sorcerers?"

Kip gave him a brief summary of the fight, struggling with balancing the fear that he'd done something wrong with the desire for Jackson to see his value. When it came to describing the soldier he'd incinerated, he hesitated; this was specifically forbidden. But Jackson was a spiritual sorcerer, and Kip had known some who would peer into a person's mind to see the truth of their statements. If Jackson did that, he would never miss the image and smell of the smoking body. So Kip told that part of the story and waited.

"That accounts for the calyx prisoner," Jackson said, as though Kip had stopped at the capture of the otter.

"He was helpful. What happened to him, sir?"

"He's a prisoner." Jackson gestured in the vague direction of the harbor. "We don't expect him to know much, but we have to ask."

"And after?"

Jackson wavered, and for a moment Kip thought he might slide back into furious rage. But then he laughed. "I will put you in touch with Major McLaren. So your fire abilities are as excellent as promised."

Here it was. "I know I wasn't supposed to kill soldiers directly—"

"You had no choice. And besides, they had summoned a demon to kill our boys, so I think it's only fair that we burn up one or two of theirs. I'm sorry you didn't burn up the sorcerers while you were at it. Good job, Penfold, and O'Brien, and even you, little miss."

Alice bristled, but kept her temper under control. Kip barely noticed, his shoulders sagging. He would not be punished, it seemed. Relief overwhelmed him, tinged with guilt that he tried to dispel. If Jackson did not think his action worth punishment, he should not think so either.

The Master Colonel went on to tell them that the Continental Army's next goals would be to take over the shipyards south of Boston and seize whatever ships they could, to drive the British from New York, and to defend the other ports of the Colonies: Richmond, Philadelphia, Charleston, and Savannah. "There aren't many sorcerers left in the military," he said, "so we'll be moving everyone around as we need them. You must all be ready to go at a moment's notice."

Captain Lowell asked the question that Kip was thinking, that presumably many of them were, with the possible exception of Dapper, who looked like he was still regretting every decision he'd made in the past twenty-four hours. "Sir, if we keep the British out, will that end the war?"

"It certainly puts us in a better position to negotiate," Jackson said. "I'll be honest, it looks like we lost more men than they did at the Harbor even though we won the day. If we keep that up, they'll know they can win the war by throwing more ships and more men at us. They can draw from India, from Africa, even from China, and in a matter of months could have ten thousand men at our ports."

Nobody looked particularly happy at this news. "So," Jackson said, "We've got to hurt them. Only one of us has got fire, but we've all got demons. Freeze the air so their lungs ice over when they breathe. Explode the gunpowder in their guns. Turn the ground to quicksand. You all know what your demons can do. Take as many British lives as you can. That's what'll end this war."

When they'd been dismissed, Kip followed Alice and Malcolm silently back to their room. Captain Lowell had stayed behind to ask if he still needed to watch them (he'd spoken quietly, but in range of Kip's ears as the fox paused at the bottom of the stairs), and Jackson had said, "Yes," sharply and with finality. So all four of them took turns washing up in silence and then returned to sit on their cots.

Of course Malcolm was the first to break the silence. "Is that how battles go, then?" He faced Kip, but the question was obviously addressed to Lowell. "We sorcerers throw demons and spells around and kill soldiers like toys on a chessboard while we figure out how to stop each other, and the one with the most toys left wins the battle?"

"Pawns," Captain Lowell said.

"'Pawns' the battle, then, whatever your military lingo is."

"The pieces on a chessboard are pawns. Moved about and sacrificed in service to the king."

"I never learned to play chess," Malcolm said. "Everyone talks about it as a substitute for war, that's all I know."

"Pawns are the front line soldiers on a chessboard." Lowell gestured at an imaginary board in front of him. "The sorcerers are stronger pieces behind the pawns, able to jump over them."

"I'm not asking for a lesson." Malcolm faced Lowell now, the skin over his eye sockets creased in an angry glare. "I'm asking if we're throwing away the lives of our people."

"What do you think war is?" Lowell asked. "An academic competition where demon summoning and spellcasting is judged by an impartial panel of learned masters? Grow up. This is life outside your sheltered walls. These people have chosen to risk their lives for a cause that they deem important enough to be worth that sacrifice. What difference if they die from an enemy bullet or ice in their lungs?"

"Then why not kill them directly?" Kip asked. "Why play at being civilized?"

A piece of paper appeared in front of him and fluttered to the ground. As Kip picked it up, Lowell said, "Because if we wished, two sorcerers could obliterate every soldier on the field, and then who would win the battle? Who would be left to enjoy the victory? The rules of war have been established long before our time and will persist long after. What is that, Penfold?"

"A message from Emily," he said. "She's coming here in five minutes and wants me to be with Malcolm and Alice."

Lowell folded his arms. "I will be anxious to hear what she has to say as well."

Malcolm laughed. "You're welcome to try your luck. She may decide you'd be better off walking back from New Cambridge."

"She wouldn't dare."

Malcolm turned to Kip with a grin. "Ah, he don't know our Em, does he?"

Kip smiled. "I don't think she'd send Captain Lowell to New Cambridge. But she might take all of us there."

"You're under orders not to leave."

"Ah," Malcolm said, "but Emily's not under your orders, is she?"

Kip left the two of them to walk over to Alice's wooden screen. The vixen looked up from the edge of her cot, tail curled around her hips, but didn't say anything. Kip sat on the floor beside her. "You're quiet."

"I'm all right," she said. "I think. I don't know. I keep seeing the men dying this morning but it feels like it was a bad dream. You know?"

"I know."

"What the captain says makes sense. I don't want to kill people and I don't want them to die, but if there's no other way to win a war, and…and I suppose we have to have wars or else we wouldn't be able to stop bad people like Napoleon." She tilted her head. "And King George too now?"

"And King George." Kip rested a paw on her knee. "I hope we won't have to kill many more people. Maybe Emily has good news."

She covered his paw with hers. "It was scary, but I'm glad we were doing it together. I was worried I'd disappoint you."

"Disappoint me?" Kip sat beside her on the cot. "I'm so terribly proud of you. I was scared that I wouldn't be able to protect you, but…" He saw the flash in her eyes. "I know you can protect yourself. But war is frightening."

"It is." She thought for a moment. "How long do you think you'll be able to get away with not following their orders? They seem very set on it, but Captain Lowell covered up for you this time."

"If I get results, I don't suppose they'll mind."

"Be sure you get results, then," Alice said, "because I don't want to have to do all the magic for our unit. It looks very tiring."

The faint stirring of humor lifted Kip's spirits, and to his surprise he found a smile creeping onto his muzzle. "It is that. I'll be careful. We must share the burden, after all."

Malcolm and Lowell had continued arguing in low voices that Kip had caught a little of. The gist seemed to be that Lowell could leave on his own and maybe catch a few words outside the door to make sure they weren't fleeing, or he could risk what he already knew to be Emily's mercurial temper. Lowell ceded the point, but not happily; he stalked out of the room and slammed the door behind him.

"Well argued," Kip said.

Malcolm turned and spread his hands, a grin spreading over his face. "The demon took my eyes but left my voice, and I'd much rather be blind and voiced than sighted and mute any day of the week, and twice on Sunday."

"Wouldn't you rather have both?" Alice asked.

"Aye, and I'd rather have a family fortune and a castle for all of us to live in, but life doesn't deal you the cards you want."

With a small rush of air, Emily appeared in the middle of the room, a plain traveling cloak over a formal dress. Though she'd translocated without so much as a stumble, in a way Kip hoped to emulate one day, her face was drawn and shadows lingered under her eyes.

Kip wondered if she were tired, but she caught her breath and rushed to Malcolm to embrace him. "I've missed you all. I wish you could have been with me."

"You smell different," Malcolm said into her hair, "and yet the same. And I'm quite pleased I took the time to wash."

She turned from him to Kip. "I've been from palace to ocean and I have so much to tell you."

After she released Kip, it was Alice's turn. "We were in a battle today," she told Emily.

"Alice did very well," Kip said. "I think my caution is the only thing holding her back."

"You did well, too." Alice's ears flattened in abashed pleasure. "You got rid of the British sorcerer. And Malcolm stopped them finding us."

"It sounds like it came out all right." Emily looked around at them. "You're all unharmed, and that's the most important."

"There were some tricky parts," Kip said.

"Alice, you've got nothing but that screen for privacy?" Emily asked.

The vixen smiled. "What did you have, when you lived in the basement of the Tower?"

"A door, at least." Emily smiled back. "I suppose the army isn't accustomed to having women in their midst, either."

"They will be." Alice folded her arms, her ears proudly up.

Kip smiled and turned to Emily. "What's your news?"

"Well." Emily looked around the room and then sat on the carpet in the middle of the floor. The others arrayed themselves in a loose circle. "Let me tell you."

We didn't accomplish everything we'd hoped, but this is only the first stop. Spain isn't going to weigh in on our side and end the war, but neither are they going to help the British, and all in all, after this trip I think they are slightly more favorably inclined to us. But let me start at the beginning.

Besides me and Abigail Adams, the other members of our party are Esau Plainfield, a spiritual sorcerer; Jenny Fortescue, Abigail's womanservant; Thomas Lickridge, our secretary; and Albert Dorn, who I think is a bodyguard but I'm not sure and nobody will tell me exactly what he does. Master Plainfield is along to make sure nobody ensorcels Abigail into agreeing to something she doesn't want to. I think he is also on the lookout for chances to improve our odds with a little sorcery of our own, but of course nobody will admit that.

They're all perfectly pleasant except for him. He can't stop telling stories about all the political conferences he's attended and the famous people whose minds he's snooped about in. I've tried not to listen, but I learned some terrible things about what Viceroy Middleton liked to do to dogs. Also Lickridge tried for the first three days to sit or stand next to me whenever possible until I mentioned casually that he should be careful lest he find his quill stuck in a very painful place, and now he lavishes his attentions on poor Jenny.

Master Plainfield needed to show me the Spanish Court—one reason he's part of our group is that he has been to all these places—and he's very good at that. The image was so clear that even though I'd never been to Madrid, I had no doubt I could go to this place. There's a reception room specifically for visiting sorcerers—this is common, they tell me—and Master Plainfield knew the room inside and out. Three distinctive, detailed paintings, gilt frames, the ceiling with a fresco of King Alfonso the…Sixth, I think, driving out the Moors. It's not in good taste, especially since there are Moorish sorcerers, and I wonder what they think of it? There's a carpet in bright gold and yellow that looks like it was made in Africa, though I doubt that makes up for the fresco. And the place has a different smell. Kip, I suppose you'd be able to describe it better with your words, but it smelt older and dustier somehow than the Colonies.

A Spaniard greeted us and asked our business, and Lickridge told him, and he asked us to wait. Master Plainfield advised us to make ourselves comfortable, and it was a good thing, because the Spaniard was gone almost an hour. Then he came back with a half-dozen male and female servants—two Calatians, Kip—and they took us through the palace to this very nice series of apartments and told us it would be six days before his majesty King Carlos would be able to grant an audience.

I thought that was terribly rude, but Abigail told me that they'd been counting on it. Everyone in her group would have something to do during that week—preparing, talking to lesser ministers, and so on, and really a week was a reasonable time for a diplomatic meeting. Since they would all be staying in the palace, she wanted me to make my way out to the coast where they keep their ships, learn the size of their fleet, and also learn the location so I could get back there. I had to be very discreet but we needed to know, if they did offer us aid, if they promised more than they had or significantly less than they could spare.

With Jenny's help I made myself up as a maidservant. The two of us went to talk to some of the soldiers and after two days finally convinced one to take me with him on a trip out to the harbor. Oh, don't give me that look, it was all perfectly innocent. Well, perhaps not "perfectly," but I didn't do anything untoward. I told him that my father had defected from England during the Napoleonic Wars and we had settled in Spain, but my father had just passed away and it was hard finding work in Madrid and I'd always loved the sea, and so on.

We rode for a day, and he wouldn't tell me where we were going until we arrived in Corunna. That's where Spain docks most of her armada. The soldier said he didn't know what call there might be for a maidservant there but there were women there sure enough. So after a little discussion, I shook free of him and I went down to the harbor.

There are so many ships. I thought they would be easy to count, but when I came in sight of them, they took my breath away. I counted to ten, to twenty, to fifty, and still it wasn't even half of them. I must have wandered around for an hour. After I had the feel of the place, I bought a small meal of bread and cheese and went down to the water to eat it, because it was beautiful there.

And then you won't believe what I saw. Victor Adamson, strolling along the dock as if it were one of his father's shipyards. So I left my bread and cheese and I walked down to meet him.

Yes, yes, I know, Kip, don't say it. I was startled and I couldn't imagine what he was doing there and I just had to know. I wouldn't be in any danger; I could get away with a thought and he doesn't have any magic, and he wasn't with other sorcerers. So I went up to him and he saw me coming and stopped to meet me.

"Good afternoon, Mister Adamson," I said, as if we were meeting on a Boston street.

He responded just as politely. "Miss Carswell."

I asked if he were there on behalf of his father, and he said, "In a manner of speaking," and then he asked what I was doing there. So I said I was there to take the air, that one of my friends had been to Corunna and had recommended it and I was only in for the afternoon. He wouldn't tell me how he'd gotten there, but of course it was sorcery; it had to be.

We parted without learning much more about each other's business. I returned to the Spanish court with a day to spare before our audience. Abigail told me that the meetings leading up to the royal audience had gone very well and that the Spanish were receptive to our mission. "Anything to break the power of the English, and what better than by splitting it?" she'd said to them, and her forthrightness had gone over well, it sounded.

So we were hopeful as we prepared to meet King Carlos and his advisors. And my goodness, the preparation we had to undergo! We had to be dressed in our best clothes, and we were given many instructions. Kneel when the king is announced. Don't rise until he's seated. If he stands then immediately kneel again. Don't speak unless he specifically invites you to speak, and stop as soon as he signals you to stop, even if it's in the middle of a sentence. Also, we ladies were told that while we were kneeling, he might walk close to us and even touch us and we were not to react in any way, so that was something to look forward to, let me tell you. Though in the event, he didn't touch any of us that I know of.

Oh, and we were met in a side audience room, and the Steward—he was the one who lectured us, a dour thin man named Juan—made a point of telling me that the room had no unguarded access to the royal chambers. You know, in case I should decide to jump back to it at a later date to assassinate the king. But even though it wasn't an official royal chamber, it was still gorgeously frescoed and the whole room was gilt-edged with relief molding and the chairs were velvet and gold-painted wood and the seal of the Bourbons was all over it.

We went through all of the protocol—what's that? Yes, I've heard that meeting the English King is much the same. In any event, Carlos is quite old and it was his son of the same name who did most of the talking. I believe he has an older son who tried to take over from him around the time of Napoleon and who is still around somewhere? Yes? In any event, Carlos IV, the King, was a very sweet old man but his son was much more severe. How, he wanted to know, could he count on the Americans to be loyal allies? How did he know we would engage in favored relations with Spain after winning our independence? We were rebelling against one master; how could they be sure we would not cast aside our friends once we no longer needed them?

It was a strange line of questioning, but Abigail was equal to it. He even asked why we sent an old woman to represent us, and Abigail said, "Remember that it was an old woman who first sent Cristobal Colombo to our shores, and so is it not fitting that in our time of need, we send an old woman back to Spain as our emissary?" Of course, Isabella I was only something like forty when all that happened, but it was well said nonetheless.

Still, he seemed to be pushing hard on loyalty and trustworthiness, trying to push Abigail into making a promise of some sort. She told me this afterwards; I admit I did not follow all of the subtext of the conversation at the time. I was watching Plainfield, who was watching the spiritual sorcerer of the Spanish court, both of them making sure the other wasn't manipulating any of the people there.

Abigail handled the conversations well enough that Carlos—the older one—interjected at one point in Spanish, which I understood well enough to translate as, in essence, "Oh, let's give them some ships already."

So then the son got this crafty look on his face. It reminded me of when Patris thought he'd outsmarted you, Kip, and it boded about as well. "Ships, yes," he said. "You wish some of our ships to help you counter the British advantage. Why could they not simply use sorcerers to bring their armies from place to place?"

This was another odd question but I think I read it well. Abigail asked me to address it, and I told him that moving large numbers of people via magic was so strenuous as to be not worthwhile; a good translocational sorcerer can move two other people at once, so it would either take a hundred sorcerers or a hundred hours and you'd wear out the sorcerers, and so on. Of course, you can do better with calyxes, but not very much better, and anyway I didn't want to give away too much even though the Spanish also have calyxes, I think? Yes, thank you, Kip. He was fishing to see if we had a way to move armies, because I don't think they do yet.

So anyway I told him we didn't, and he nodded and said, "Then ships. How many ships do you think you would like?"

We had talked about that, and Abigail said that we would take as many as they could spare, and we didn't think it needed to be a lot, that if we could keep the British from blockading our harbors so we could trade, that would likely be sufficient to turn the tide in our favor, so to speak.

He pressed us for a number, and Abigail said again that we didn't know, that it would depend on what they could spare. And here I started to get a little uncomfortable, because he was looking at me and I could only think of one reason he would be doing that, and that was that he knew I had already been there. And if he knew, then there was only really one way he could have.

Sure enough, after Abigail had finished her perfectly diplomatic response, Carlos the Younger turned to his father, clearly annoyed that she hadn't fallen into his trap. I expect he wanted her to say a number and then he would have said, "How do you think they knew to ask for that many?" But he said something like, "The Americans seem very earnest and trustworthy, but in fact they have brought a spy into your court, Father."

And then of course Victor came out, all smiles and unction, and told the court in perfect Spanish (Plainfield translated for me) how he'd been down at the shipyards as part of the courtesy his delegation was extending to the Spanish court, how he was lending his shipbuilding experience to help where he saw the opportunity. He'd spotted me there and he'd come back and asked if I'd been authorized to be in Corunna, which of course I had not.

Carlos the younger took up the story from then, concluding that I was a spy and that the Americans' intentions were dishonorable from the start. His father's face grew more and more angry—not angry, actually, more like disappointed—as he went on, and it was clear we weren't going to get our help from Spain.

But Abigail, God bless her, wouldn't just walk away. She said very evenly that of course it was in our interests to secure our own information about the Spanish fleet, that my orders had been to do nothing but observe and count ships, and that in fact I had done nothing but that. And then she said, "I am most curious to know what delegation comprises this young man and how close it must be to the Spanish crown to allow him to ignore all of the courtesies demanded of a foreign visitor in the presence of royalty."

Carlos the elder did look angry at that, and Carlos the younger was taken aback, clearly not having thought of this. Victor looked confused, and then the elder Carlos told us that Victor was here with an emissary of Britain to request peace with Spain while the American rebellion was being settled. We speculated later that he claimed to represent America, to show that there were some in the Colonies who didn't desire independence, but we don't know for certain. At any rate, Carlos the younger babbled something about Victor having already shown the proper courtesies, but King Carlos didn't seem impressed with that, and in the middle of it cut his son off and told us all to leave his presence, that our petitions were all denied and we should leave the Spanish court on the morrow.

Victor, belatedly, knelt, and that only highlighted that he hadn't before, and Carlos withdrew into his throne room as we all stood and left the audience chamber. So it was a disaster, and mostly my fault, but at least Abigail was sharp enough to pick up on Victor's flaw and use it to make sure our enemies got no advantage.

CHAPTER 6: THE HAND OF MASTER ALBRIGHT

When she'd finished, Kip drew in a breath. "Victor, working with the British. Not a surprise, I suppose."

Malcolm took Emily's hand. "Don't fret too much about how it turned out. Victor would have found a way to spoil the delegation somehow."

She snatched her hand away. "Very nice. You give him so much credit?"

"Nay." Malcolm reached out, and after a moment Emily sighed and took his hand back. "I meant only that he was prepared for you as you were not for him, and next time you'll be prepared for him as well and perhaps it won't go as easy for him."

"Thank you for the confidence."

While Kip was trying to think of something comforting to say, Alice stepped up to Emily. "I think you're frightfully brave, going across Spain by yourself like that and being a real spy, just like Michael Dagger in Napoleon's army. We're here fighting battles, but you might be able to end the whole war."

"Not if I keep acting this way." Emily smiled gratefully though and ran a hand through her hair. "I didn't tell Abigail that I went up to Victor. I haven't told anyone but you. I'm afraid that if she found out, she'd send me home. I told her he was there and I saw him, and she said it was simply a case of bad luck, but that next time perhaps I should be more stealthy."

"A little." Kip smiled. "But Alice is right; you did well to get to Corunna at all, and now you can go back there anytime. You become more valuable with every bit of knowledge you gain."

"Thank you all," Emily said, straightening her back. "Here, I brought you some Spanish bread. It's from this morning, really quite lovely, and I don't know how they feed you here."

"Not terribly well." Kip took one of the pieces of fragrant bread from Emily. "Oh, rosemary."

"I think so, yes."

It was as good as she'd said it was, and sitting around and eating it together reminded Kip of their early days in the College. "So," Emily said, "tell me about this battle of yours."

They took it in turns to tell her about the battle and their own parts in it. When Kip came to tell her about burning the soldier, he gave more details than he'd yet given to Alice or Malcolm. She, after all, had been one of only two witnesses when he'd burned Master Windsor to death. "He stood there brandishing the musket, and I didn't even think. There was fire, and I—I had to save myself. And a moment later the fire was—it was taking him. It wasn't like Windsor, not as hot as that fire. There was still a body, and—and the smell—the smell was terrible."

Emily took his paw gently. "This is war," she said softly. "It's terrible and yet necessary. Think of what lies at the end of the road."

"I know," Kip said, grateful for the reassurance. "But still, it's a life I took. Windsor I can justify, but…"

"We all did." Alice's voice was small but firm. "Some of the things I did might not have directly killed people, but people died all the same."

"Still." Malcolm kept the usual cheer in his voice. "The sooner we end this war, the sooner we can all stop with the necessary evils, aye?"

"Yes, good." Emily rose. "I'm not supposed to tell you where our next destination is, but—"

"Then don't," Kip said. "We'll trust that you're safe and that this time you'll be more successful."

"And you," she said, "keep fighting those battles."

Emily embraced Malcolm and then stepped back and was gone.

None of them spoke for a moment, and then Kip gave a low whistle. "I wonder when Victor went to the British side."

"Can't say you're surprised, can you?" Malcolm sat on the floor. "Little parasite attaches himself to wherever he perceives power to be. Reckon he believes the British can win this war. I wouldn't be surprised if he had something to do with the attack on the College."

"Curse it!" Kip smacked a fist into his paw. "I meant to ask Emily to try to reach Master Argent. With Plainfield, she might be able to do it."

"It doesn't sound as though Plainfield or any of them is much disposed to diverting from their mission." Malcolm crossed his arms.

"What happened to Victor this last year?" Alice asked. "I haven't heard you speak of him, and I thought that perhaps after...what happened, he might have left the school."

"No such luck." Malcolm gave a theatrical sigh. "Not as long as Patris was there, which some say was longer than he should be as well."

"Not as long as his father has money, more to the point," Kip said.

At this point Captain Lowell came back into the room, but none of the three got to their feet. "I have managed to avoid hearing inappropriate state secrets," the man said stiffly. "Mostly. I trust all is well with Miss Carswell."

"As well as can be hoped," Malcolm said cheerily. "How was the hallway? Didn't go get a bite to eat, did you?"

"I did not," Captain Lowell replied. "Though I imagine we are all hungry."

"Our friend's brought us some Spanish bread, so we're fine." Malcolm held up his last piece and ate it.

Kip had finished his and now felt slightly guilty that he didn't have some to offer Captain Lowell. Jackson's lackey he might be, but he'd also fought beside them and worked to save their lives, and he'd spared Kip a reprimand for disobeying orders.

But Captain Lowell didn't seem to mind. "Plain Boston bread will be fine," he said. "That way I don't have to wonder where this delicacy came from. Are you coming to dinner?"

"In a moment," Kip said. He did not feel that he could face cooked meat quite yet. Neither Malcolm nor Alice rose, and in fact Alice pointedly took out one of her spell books, so Captain Lowell shrugged and left the room again.

For a short time, they all sat in silence. "It was good to see Emily again," Kip said finally.

"Aye." Malcolm grinned. "And to hear and feel her too."

"Of course." Kip flicked his tail.

Alice studied her book, whiskers twitching. Kip wasn't sure she was listening, but then she said, "Emily's doing the best she can, and so are we."

"Of course. What spell are you studying?" he asked, though he was sure he knew the answer.

He was right. "Summoning," Alice said. "I really think I can master it. Can we try it now?"

"Go ahead." Malcolm sat up straighter. "I can prepare a binding in case something goes wrong."

Malcolm's senses were good, Kip had no doubt, but without sight, would his reactions be slowed? He could summon Daravont to help him see, but then he would be binding one demon already, and it had taken Kip a year to learn to hold a binding on Nikolon while summoning another demon. Of course, Alice would only be summoning an elemental, but Malcolm had had little experience with those. It had been difficult enough to get him to summon a demon.

"I don't know what air elementals can do," Kip said finally. "If it gets loose, it might just vanish out the window. Or it might pull the air out of the room to suffocate us. Or it might blow through the building and knock it down."

"You said elementals aren't usually malevolent." Alice pointed. "The book says so too."

"They're not. But sometimes they can be exuberant or unaware of what they're doing. They probably won't try to kill us, but…imagine a phosphorus elemental running around through this house. It would be a disaster."

The young vixen exhaled, then bent to her book, her ears back. She mouthed the words of the spell to herself and then said, "Were you this careful when you were learning magic?"

"No." Kip considered his words, conscious of the edge to Alice's voice. "But I didn't have anyone I trusted teaching me, and I learned how much damage a sorcerer can do. I told you about Master Cott burning that building with the man in it."

Alice shuddered. "I'm not using fire. I don't even like it that much."

"Fire's only the most spectacular example," Kip said. "Any magic can do as much harm."

"There's a reason fire sorcerers are prized in battle, though," Malcolm said.

Which reminded Kip of that morning, and he winced. Malcolm didn't see the motion, but Alice did, and her ears came up. She padded to Kip's side and put a paw on his. "You did what you had to do."

"I know," Kip said. But that didn't help the memory: the soldier had been there in one moment and gone the next, dead in an instant. He hadn't been evil like Windsor; he'd been fighting for a cause he believed to be just. He would've killed Kip given the chance, of course, wouldn't he? That was what Kip had to believe, that in that moment his choice had been to kill or be killed. That was war; that was what Captain Lowell and Master Colonel Jackson had been telling him. He knew that, but the information had yet to make it to his heart.

Alice waited a moment by his side and then said with attempted cheer, "How about some dinner, then?"

"You and Malcolm go ahead," Kip said. "I'll get something later, maybe."

"You need to eat." Malcolm got to his feet.

"Aye, but…in a bit."

Alice looked at him another moment and then walked across the room to take Malcolm's hand. "We'll bring you back something," she said, and the two of them left Kip alone with his thoughts.

Two days passed without further word from Emily or from their commanders. They saw Jackson only once, at one of the meals, with a harried-looking Callahan by his side. "He's Jackson's personal assistant now," Lowell told them. "Ferries him from meeting to meeting."

Kip would have taken that job if he were capable of it. At least then, he thought, he might have some idea of what was going on with this war. They heard scraps of information: the British ships had left Boston Harbor but anchored just offshore; the British Army was regrouping for another assault; a British force was making its way along the Road from Bristol to New York. It seemed that most of the fighting was concentrated around the northern colonies, which left Kip with the hope that his parents in Peachtree might be spared this war.

The mention of the Road in New York gave him another place to focus his attention: he'd never seen the Great Road that spanned the ocean, the closest Great Feat of sorcery to America, with the obvious exception of the Calatians themselves. What would it be like to stand on this road in the middle of the ocean, a great expanse of sea water all around him? Would it be a path of dirt? Would he be able to feel its magic? Having lived among one Great Feat his whole life and embodying part of it did not inure him to the excitement of witnessing others.

Distractions like this one slowly worked the sight and smell of the soldier he'd killed away from the forefront of his thoughts. He reminded himself often of one of the lessons Cott had taught him: that guilt for a fire sorcerer could mean paralysis and death. "We've a destructive power in us," he'd told Kip, "and sometimes despite our best efforts, that power will out. If we're to use it at all, we must make peace with that. It will happen and we must forget it as easily as we can, or it may abandon us when we need it most."

Facile words, Kip thought, from someone who'd terrified a man by burning his office around him, but it was true that that man was never in serious danger, not unless he'd run into the flames. Certainly Cott must have had incidents in his past that he hadn't shared with Kip. After all, he'd been the Empire's leading and only (to Kip's knowledge) fire sorcerer during the Napoleonic Wars. He'd never talked about war, though. Cott preferred to be left alone in his office to research fire, and Kip couldn't imagine him under orders the way Kip was now. Cott, he thought, would as soon set Jackson on fire as any enemy soldier, though he couldn't imagine his old mentor doing either.

The British soldier was dead and he was not. If he was going to be of any use to the American army, he might have to kill again. He could try his best to avoid that situation, but he would have to be ready for it. There were times, though, when he came close to wishing he had taken Emily's offer to accompany her.

Alice, forbidden to practice summoning, worked on her physical magic every day with a drive that reminded Kip of his own first year. Malcolm continued to study with the other defensive military sorcerers, learning from them and teaching them in turn. The Inattention wards, ones he had not paid particular attention to, proved useful, and he grew steadily better at them.

Often he practiced casting the wards so that Kip and Alice would not be affected by them but Captain Lowell would. This resulted in some amusement on their part, and one evening after Alice had teasingly asked him, "Where's Malcolm?" and giggled at his confusion, Lowell glared at her.

"Like it or not," he said, "we are bound together as a unit. Of course you may have your jokes on me if you like, but I would prefer it if you treated me with respect."

Malcolm dispelled the ward then. "That's fair," he said, "but come now. We know almost nothing about you. I like to get to know a fellow before we get 'bound together.'"

"My rank is all that should matter." Lowell looked around at the three of them. "This is the army, not a supper club."

"You're more than simply a captain, though." Kip sat on the chest of drawers near the window, behind Alice in one of the chairs.

Lowell rested his hand on the back of one of the chairs. For a moment he seemed about to leave the room, and then he sat down stiffly. "I was raised in Georgia and freed at the age of ten on the death of my former owner. My uncle and I came north to New York and made our fortune, and when I turned eighteen I enlisted in the Army. I've served ever since."

"What did you make your fortune in?" Kip asked.

"Carpentry. My uncle has a genius for it that sadly I did not inherit. We worked in a shop owned by a generous white man who could sell pieces to wealthy patrons who would never have bought from us directly. He gave us a very fair share of the profits and helped me acquire an education."

"My father got a spell book for me from a sympathetic master," Kip said. "That's how I first learned enough magic to get into the College. They'd never have allowed me in otherwise."

Lowell nodded. "We who found generous patrons are lucky enough to be allowed to advance a little more than others of our kind."

"It's no Greek saga," Malcolm said, "but yours is a noble story nonetheless."

"You think so?" Lowell asked, and even though Malcolm couldn't see his glare, the tone of his voice kept the Irishman quiet.

The following day as Kip practiced his translocation, the idea came to him to ask Captain Lowell if he would be a test subject for the spell. This ability seemed the most important for him to improve in, but every time he translocated Malcolm or Alice, it disrupted their equally important practices.

The captain demurred at first, but after Kip had demonstrated his ability and promised there would be no jokes played, grudgingly agreed. Only afterwards did Kip realize what a measure of trust that was, not only to allow Kip to perform spells on him, but to trust that the fox wouldn't send him to Peachtree or London or somewhere else remote that he'd never come back from. He only sent Lowell to the ground floor, the roof, and other places inside the Trade House, growing more confident with every success.

After one of those sessions, they sat on the roof together looking over the harbor in the pleasant evening breeze, and Kip thought of a possible solution to his dilemma. "Captain," he said. "I understand that I'm to come to you with—problems?"

Lowell nodded. "You may."

Kip took a breath. "I know that we're at war, and there are necessities, but...I can't stop thinking about that man I killed."

Now the captain turned to face him. "One never forgets the first time one takes a life," he said quietly. "Those are the harsh realities of war. The killing can get easier if you allow it. Whether that is a course you wish to pursue is yours to decide."

"I don't," Kip said quickly. "I wonder if you might be able to request of Master Colonel Jackson that we be used more strategically? Not in direct combat, I mean."

Lowell met Kip's eyes. "I feel the need to remind you that had you followed orders, you would not have faced that soldier. Your own recklessness put you in that position."

Kip flattened his ears. "I know. Sir."

The captain turned his gaze back out to the ocean and breathed in the salt air. "That said, I believe you may be correct that your abilities could be put to better use than incinerating single soldiers. I will make the suggestion to Master Colonel Jackson. Although," he said, "the Master Colonel is not known for his democratic style."

When their new orders came, they were not in the northern colonies— northern part of America, Kip forced himself to think. Master Colonel Jackson summoned them to a meeting in the dining room to tell them that they were being called to defend Savannah. The port, important to the British trade routes to the Caribbean, had swarmed with activity over the last week and the American command had confirmed that a fleet was heading for Savannah—they were due to arrive that day, and the short notice was because the spies had to make sure the ships were not going to Charleston.

After sunset that evening, the translocational sorcerers came to move all the units to Savannah. Though they were brought indoors, the air pressed in on Kip, warm and humid, as soon as he appeared. The air felt familiarly thick, but even more humid than he'd experienced in Peachtree, and accompanying the humidity was a thick briny smell of ocean. He, with Alice, Malcolm, and Lowell, were shown to the third floor of a modest house and into a room half the size of the one they'd had at the Trade House. Four cots lay evenly spaced on the ground and there was no screen for Alice to have privacy. There was, they found, a linen closet in the hallway which was large enough for Alice to change her clothes in when necessary, so they removed the shelves and assigned the room that purpose.

Master Colonel Jackson assembled them in the large ground floor room of this house to explain the situation in Savannah. The British had taken over a good portion of the town, including the small Calatian neighborhood, and the American forces had been attempting to dislodge them for two weeks with little success. Only one military sorcerer unit had been deployed here because it wasn't a pitched battle yet, but the ships no doubt carried reinforcements both magical and non. If the British were able to take Savannah, they would have a strong foothold in the southern part of the country.

What Jackson did not mention was that directly upriver of Savannah lay Peachtree. If Kip failed to protect Savannah, his parents would be left vulnerable. He did not think Jackson would allow him to leave the army to protect Peachtree, not when there was no college of sorcery there anymore, so he would have to do everything in his power to keep Savannah in American hands.

They had a day, maybe two, before they estimated the ships would be in range of the harbor. Even before the arrival of the ships, the Americans were at a disadvantage; many of the Royal Army here had remained loyal to the Empire and had helped hold part of Savannah for the British.

"Now," Jackson told them, "you'll be able to use calyxes here, so prepare your demon summoning and let's go out in the morning and drive them down to the docks so when the ships arrive, they'll be forced to board and go back to sea. If we keep the British on the waves, they can't occupy our land."

Murmurs of agreement from the men followed them out of the room. Kip, with Malcolm's hand on his arm, had risen to join them when Jackson said, "Penfold. A word."

Kip and Malcolm both turned, Alice and Lowell a step beyond them. "Just Penfold," Jackson said.

Malcolm lifted his hand. Alice stepped back to take it, and the three of them followed the other sorcerers out of the room.

Kip stood, his tail flicking back and forth. Jackson sat on the edge of a table, waiting until the room had cleared and the door closed behind the last of them. "I know you're not a military man, Penfold, but standing at attention before a senior officer means standing straight. In the Calatian units of the army, tails are included in standing at attention."

Kip straightened and tried to get his tail under control. "Sorry, sir. Where are the Calatian units of the army?"

Jackson shook his head. "No need to apologize. Don't worry about the Calatian units. There's one in Boston and one in New York but they work as support troops. Although the one in New York isn't there any more. The British took them."

"Took as in captured?"

The tall man inclined his head. "Some of them," he said offhandedly. "They're not available to us anymore, and that's what matters. At ease." When Kip didn't move, he said, "That means you can wag your tail, or do whatever it is you do with it."

It wasn't wagging, but Kip let his tail swing free. "What did you want to see me about, sir?"

"Firstly, I'm going to assign you a proper defensive sorcerer. Your relationship with O'Brien notwithstanding, he's crippled. A defensive sorcerer needs his sight."

"Sir, with respect…" As Kip spoke, Jackson fixed him with those piercing eyes. The fox swallowed. "Malcolm is as talented as any of the others, and he knows me better. We work together well."

The Master Colonel considered this. "I will have him cast some wards for me. If he performs to my satisfaction, I will consider your request."

"Thank you, sir." Kip relaxed only slightly.

"Now. I have special orders for you, Penfold." Jackson set his hands together, got up, and stared down at Kip. "These orders are for your ears only. You are to tell nobody else about them. Do you understand?"

"Yes, sir." The fox's heart filled with dread.

"Lowell has told me that direct combat is not to your taste. You've killed one man and he thinks you may need more time to grow accustomed to the realities of war."

I don't want to grow accustomed to it, Kip thought. "Yes, sir," he said with some hesitation.

"I've decided to place you out of the way of direct combat this time. There is another use you may serve."

"Thank you, sir," Kip said, and relaxed further. "What use?"

"I told the men that we wanted the British soldiers driven back onto the ships. That is true. But."

The malicious smile that crept onto Jackson's face did nothing to assuage Kip's dread. "It is my desire," the Master Colonel said, "that none of the British ships return to safe harbor. You are a master of fire. Once the men have boarded the ships, burn all that will burn on them."

Kip's throat had dried almost completely out. He coughed. "But sir, we are not supposed to kill directly with sorcery."

Jackson waved. "I have cannon trained on the harbor that will fire flaming cannonballs. But if there are no survivors, there will be none to speak of it. So make sure to reach every ship."

"Sir," Kip said. "That's—mass murder."

"Penfold. That's *war*." Jackson fixed him with a stare. "We are not a sovereign nation that has existed for hundreds of years with a standing army and sorceric military equal to Britain. We are building a sovereign nation out of scraps, and our only chance—our *only* chance—to win this war is to show the British that the cost to them will be devastating. Do you believe your friends the Adamses and Miss Carswell will be able to persuade a foreign power to our side? At least, in time to stop the ships that are already there at our shores?" He pointed out toward what Kip presumed was the harbor.

"But—why not let the cannonballs do the work?" Jackson stared at him until Kip added, "Sir."

Jackson kept eye contact. "The cannon do not fire quickly enough to cover the whole fleet. Their presence and noise will mask your spell. Ships with great stores of gunpowder have been known to explode under fire, and close together, whole fleets have been lost that way. It is rare, but known."

Kip remained quiet, numb. Jackson nodded and turned away from the fox for the first time. "You question the necessity of taking so many lives. You have been taught that we do not take lives with sorcery, and you took that charge seriously. Tell me." He lifted himself to sit on the table again. "Do you believe that Napoleon lost a hundred thousand soldiers at Waterloo to bullets and bayonets? That's the story. But I worked with the sorcerers there. I know how many great spells were cast and how many lives they took.

"Did we violate the conventions of war? Perhaps. Do you believe the French sorcerers restrained themselves where we did not? We create these façades that we may speak to each other as civilized men when the battles are done, but when you are surrounded by death and the weight of your country rests on your shoulders, these barriers mean no more than the words used to shape them. History is more than they write in the books. Those fine words you prize are borne on the backs of brutality."

"Yes, sir," Kip said.

"You are clear on my orders?"

"Yes, sir," Kip repeated.

"Then you are dismissed."

Jackson turned to leave the room, but Kip stayed where he was. "Sir?"

The sorcerer turned. Kip stood as straight as he could. "My parents live in Peachtree, just up the river. The site of Prince Phillip's school?"

"You haven't time to go visit, Penfold, and I can't spare a sorcerer to take you."

"No, I mean…will they be defended? They're Calatians, and many of them are calyxes."

"We have as many calyxes as we can use, and the British have an entire population across the river from their College. It would be foolish for them to risk an offensive to an otherwise useless place. It's not a tactical position."

And with that, Jackson left the room and Kip stood there alone for a long moment before returning slowly to his friends.

True to his word, Master Colonel Jackson summoned Malcolm to him immediately. Fifteen minutes later, Malcolm returned to their chambers with a smile and the news that he was to continue to serve in Kip's unit, provisionally. "It's a good job Luke taught me that distraction trick with inattention wards. They work much better when you give people something to be distracted by. Master Vendis never taught me that."

That piece of good news notwithstanding, Kip's secret orders weighed on him all that night and the next morning. This was war, he'd been told, and he was being ordered to violate the carefully laid out rules. The British would know, though, wouldn't they? Jackson knew well what had happened at Waterloo. If Kip massacred their fleet, what might the British do at the next conflict? The so-called rules of war felt like the tenuous threads of a spiderweb straining to contain a wasp. Once one strand snapped, the others could not help but follow. Would his actions here be responsible for a worse atrocity later?

Unable to confide in his friends, he wracked his brain to think of other ways he could affect the battle. "I wish Emily were here," he said at one point.

"Why?" Alice's ears went back. "You can translocate. If you want to visit your parents, go ahead."

Captain Lowell, leaning against the wall near the door, exhaled loudly and opened his mouth to speak, but Kip spoke first. "I wouldn't go without permission," he said. "And that's not the point. The point is thinking through problems."

"What problem exactly?" Malcolm stood by the open window facing the light breeze that blew across the room.

"War."

Malcolm laughed. "Ah, mucker, there's a problem I wager it'd take more than our Emily to solve. Is there a particular part of it concerning you? The 'how not to get killed' part?"

"How not to get all of you killed," Kip said.

"We can worry about that as well." Alice put her paws on her hips. "And it would be easier if I could practice."

"Right." Helping Alice would at least be something different to do. "Lowell, is there a place we could cast spells that isn't indoors, where if something goes wrong it won't be catastrophic?"

The captain's eyes narrowed. "Is there any place where a miscast spell would not be catastrophic?"

"Some less than others," Malcolm said cheerfully.

"Out in the open air." Kip picked up his annotated book. "Alice can work on elemental summoning, and I'd like Malcolm's help with what I want to do."

"And what is that?" Lowell did not unfold his arms nor look any more comfortable.

"Work on a way to end this battle sooner."

Lowell asked no more questions, only insisted that he be allowed to accompany them, and with that concession he secured permission for them to walk out to a city square some hundred yards behind the American army lines.

Kip had never been to Savannah, and though it was not as large a city as Boston, he thought the buildings were more beautiful, less austere. Where Boston matched stone to brick in elegant edifices around narrow streets, Savannah's buildings opened to the warm air, with clay-tiled roofs and medium to dark wood dominating. They walked down wide streets past barracks where American soldiers sat out front playing cards, cleaning their rifles, or just talking.

The soldiers outside the last barracks they passed weren't speaking English, and they all had skin as dark as Captain Lowell's. One of them raised a hand to him and said, "*Ho, mon ami*," and Captain Lowell responded with a salute.

"Friends of yours?" Kip asked.

"These are the *Chasseurs-Volontaires*, a regiment from Sainte Domingue." Captain Lowell raised his hand to another of them. "They came up a few months ago when we thought it likely we would be fighting the British. Master Colonel Jackson asked me to come down to help with their transition."

"Do you speak French?" Malcolm asked.

"No."

"Then why would he—"

Kip, holding Malcolm's hand to guide him, squeezed it and whispered, "They're from Sainte Domingue." When Malcolm's frown didn't clear, Kip added, "They're black."

Malcolm's face cleared, but as they walked on, an angry frown grew. Kip, searching for something else to say, breathed in the strong smell of the houses and asked, "They've been living here for months? Away from their families?"

"We can't bring their families into war," Lowell replied.

"So they just wait around until there's a fight?" Alice asked. "What if war never happened?"

"They'd go home. But it takes so long to bring people from one place to another when you have as few resources as we do. The British can use calyxes with their translocational sorcerers and move hundreds of men in a night, but then, they can also spare a hundred men here and there. We have to know where they're needed and we haven't enough sorcerers to be able to move a regiment quickly. There's another of the *Chasseurs-Volontaires* regiments in Charleston, just in case."

"It's sad that they're away from their family for so long." And then Alice looked up at Kip and saw his expression. "It's not the same for us. We can go back whenever we want."

"Not *whenever* we want," he said with a glance at Lowell, "but yes, it's different."

If the captain had heard Kip's remark and understood it, he gave no indication. "They fought for their freedom after the Napoleonic Wars, twice. First from the French, weakened, and then from the British. So when we offered them soldier's pay to come fight the British again, many enlisted happily."

"The British are soft!" called out one soldier, who'd been listening as they passed, and choruses of "soft!" and "*mou!*" rang out, followed by a song in French that Kip could not translate.

"Good on them for coming to fight for us," Malcolm said.

"They are more dedicated than many American soldiers." Lowell led them around a corner, down another street that opened into a large plaza, deserted save for two small tents at one end. The captain stopped near a stone bench and stared at them. "Go ahead and start your work," he said. "I'll take care of these people."

Malcolm took his hand from Kip's arm and listened to Lowell's receding footsteps. "What people?" he asked quietly.

Two scruffy men had emerged from the tents to confront Lowell. Kip focused his ears to hear the conversation. "There's two people in tents," he told Malcolm. "They're wearing torn clothes and they don't look terribly friendly."

"You can't pitch tents here," Lowell told them. "It's not safe."

"Don't speak to us like that," the one with the longer beard said. "Go get your master."

"My commanding officer," Lowell said evenly, "has put me in charge here. Move your tents or I'll send men to move them by force."

"How dare you," the other man said. "How dare you!"

"I've given you warning. Now, there are going to be sorcerers working in this plaza, so stay here at your own risk." With that, the captain turned to leave.

Kip gathered magic, because he didn't like the attitude of the two men, and indeed, before Lowell had taken two steps, the man with the longer beard had reached to the ground and picked up a rock the size of his fist. He wound up to throw it and Kip readied himself to catch it before it could strike the captain, but Alice stepped forward, turquoise wreathing her arms, and as the glow vanished, the tents rose up and enveloped the men.

Lowell spun at the noise, took in the scene, and then walked quickly back to Kip, Malcolm, and Alice. "Which one of you did that?" he demanded.

"Whatever it was," Malcolm said, "I'd wager it was one of the foxes, as I can't see what's happening."

"I did it," Alice said. "They were going to throw a rock at you from behind, and that's not fair."

The men had extricated themselves from the tents and now stood looking uncertainly at the group. Alice stared back at them, while Captain Lowell half-turned and then forced himself to continue staring at the two foxes. "Are they going to attack again?" he asked softly. "Do they have guns?"

"No," Kip said. "I don't think so."

After a long glare, the two men held a muttered conversation and then wrapped their possessions up and left the plaza in the opposite direction. "All right," Lowell said. "You have the plaza."

"So," Malcolm said as Kip put a paw on his shoulder, "if I may guess at your thoughts, you're thinking that to end a battle quickly, we need more power, and that means higher order demons."

"Indeed." Kip took his book out. "I don't have many names, certainly not the ones in Odden's book, but…you remember the names I copied from Cott?"

"Oh." Malcolm brightened. "Aye. I thought you were perhaps going to try summoning Farley's demon."

"No. I don't even remember the name," Kip lied. "These are all fourth order demons with fire tendencies so I'm hoping I can control them. I've managed third-order demons, and I'm pretty sure I can do a fourth, but if you're here with a banishment spell ready, that will help."

"Will it help if two of us cast it at once?" Alice asked.

"I don't think so." Kip set his book down on the bench. "But why don't you try summoning your elemental first?"

Her ears came up. "Really?"

"Of course. That's part of why we came out here. You have the spell?"

"I've memorized it." But she took her book out anyway. "I thought you might change your mind at the last minute."

"I'm sorry it's been so long." The excited swishing of her tail and her confidence made him feel even more guilty. "Go ahead, let's see what you can do. And don't forget the binding spell too."

"I know." She breathed in, gathered magic in turquoise glows around her paws. Captain Lowell watched with the fascination of someone unused to magic as Alice spoke the first words of the summoning spell.

The instructions for summoning an air elemental might as well have been in a different language for all that they made sense to Kip. Spell instructions contained some poetic flourishes often enough ("make of thy mind a ringing bell of which the only note is the destination," one of the basic translocation spells read), but the summoning for air elementals took that to a new level. It read, in part: "free upon the wings of fate cast yourself and let your body take on the lightness around you." What did that even mean? But to Alice it made sense, he hoped, and perhaps the smell and feel of the phosphorus elementals' home plane would be as baffling to her as it was familiar and comforting to Kip.

She spoke the nonsense-sounding syllables of the summoning correctly, and Kip waited with a banishment ready in case she was too successful, as he had been his first time. More likely she would not come back with anything save a better sense of how to proceed next time. Much sorcery was like that: a spell did not quite work and so you tried it differently next time, zeroing in on the most effective way over a week of practice, sometimes several. The sounds served as a way for you to tie the proper state of mind to a recital of words, the more easily to return to the state of mind when needed.

Alice looked around in disappointment. "I don't feel anything," she said.

"Nothing at all? Did you at least get close?" Kip asked. "Tell me what the spell felt like."

She had reached out, she had found a place with an "airy feeling" like the spell had said, but she hadn't been able to communicate with any of the air elementals. "The spell says to speak the language of wind," she complained, "and I don't know how to do that."

"I don't either," Kip said. "It would be nice if we had an air elemental you could talk to, but I don't even know anyone who can summon one. How about this: while Malcolm and I practice with demons, listen to the wind here and try to figure out what it's saying and how you would talk to it."

Alice nodded and sat down on the bench. Captain Lowell came over to Kip and spoke in a whisper. "Speak to the wind?" he said. "Did you just tell her that to keep her out of your way?"

Kip's ears flicked back. "Careful," he said, "she can hear what you're saying."

Lowell flinched and then settled himself, his face going neutral. "And anyway," Kip went on, "no, it's something she has to learn."

Malcolm, standing next to them, chimed in. "It took me a few tries to get the hang of demons. Tricky business, that, but thinking about it between spells helped immensely."

"I don't know how to speak to the wind, but Alice feels an affinity to it and I think she'll be able to figure it out." Kip withdrew the knife from his belt and then hesitated. "Captain, could you give us a moment of privacy?"

"I have witnessed the calyx ritual," Lowell said, "but if you prefer to perform it without my eyes…" He turned and watched Alice, who stood with her ears and nose to the wind and her eyes closed, lips fluttering.

The more Kip ventured into the world beyond New Cambridge, the more people he encountered who knew the supposedly well-kept secret of the calyx ritual. Still, it made sense for a captain attached to a sorcerer's unit to know, so he pierced his elbow and then put his mouth to the wound. When Captain Lowell turned back around, he held a strip of cloth which he offered to Kip without an emotion visible in his expression.

The captain reacted much more visibly to the parade of demons Kip summoned, who appeared in various guises: a towering man in a cloak of flame, a cloud of fiery bats, a small golden dragon only a little taller than Kip, a small sun so bright it hurt to look at. Only that last one gave him so much trouble that he had to signal Malcolm to banish it. The others strained against his control but he estimated he could hold them for ten to fifteen minutes, easily enough to wreak havoc on a battle.

After four of them, though, Kip sagged and sat heavily on the bench, his nose almost hurting from the tingling that came with those powerful demons. "No more for now," he said, panting. "Did anyone bring water? I'm parched."

"Should be." Malcolm looked toward Lowell, but the captain spread his hands and shook his head. "We'll fetch some water on the way home."

Alice had stopped to watch the demons as well, and now came over to Kip. "Can I try the summoning again? I'm quite encouraged by all those terrifying things you summoned. Air seems much less threatening now."

Kip laughed. "I've never known you to be scared of a spell yet."

"I'm scared of not being able to do it." She raised her paws until they glowed turquoise. "But I believe I will do it, if you believe I will."

"I do," he said, and sat on the ground in front of her.

She practiced the spell, again unsuccessfully, while Captain Lowell and Malcolm went in search of water. They returned shortly at a brisk pace, or at least as brisk as Lowell could manage with Malcolm, and when Kip looked up he saw another soldier trailing behind them.

Neither Malcolm nor Lowell had water with them, but that was explained when Lowell stopped and pointed the soldier to Kip. "There he is," he said. "Penfold, something has happened. There's a message for you or something like that. He's not being very clear. But we should return immediately."

"They sent a messenger." The soldier, no more than a boy of sixteen, saluted uncertainly. "It's a fox like you, but he just says the same thing over and over."

A fox like him. His father? Kip jumped to his feet, his thirst forgotten.

"Take me there."

They walked back at a brisk pace, through the encampments of the *Chasseurs-Volontaires* and then the white soldiers, past the house where the sorcerers were housed, to a large church that overlooked the harbor. As they hurried in, Kip saw on a rooftop a hundred feet past the church a sentry in a red coat standing stiffly at attention, facing the Americans.

Two guards admitted them through a small wooden door around the side. Inside the church, a low murmur of voices greeted Kip in the thick, stuffy air. Twenty men, mostly officers and three men in sorcerer's uniforms, clustered in one area that had been cleared of pews, while another dozen or so sat around a large table.

The soldier who'd come to fetch them brought Kip forward. As the crowd parted he caught the scent of another fox. Not his father, not anyone he knew. Relief drained the tension from him and he had to pause for a moment.

Captain Lowell half-turned, but Kip nodded to him and continued on forward. "Sir," Lowell said, coming up behind a stocky bearded man, "Penfold is here."

Kip recognized the bearded man as General Hamilton, but his attention flew from that flash of recognition to the figure kneeling at the center of the group. The fox, dressed in a plain tunic, stared blankly ahead into space and spoke in a low tone that Kip had to focus his ears to hear. Even before hearing the message, he could tell that something was very wrong with this person.

He caught the words, "will be repeated every day," and then Master Colonel Jackson, standing next to the fox, spoke loudly enough to cover what came next.

"Penfold, attend. This message is directed at you."

"At me?" Kip snapped his gaze up to Jackson's severe face. "What—?"

The sorcerer shook his head and pointed back down at the fox, and the other officers fell silent.

The dull-eyed fox had stopped talking, but after a moment, he started again. "This message is for Kip Penfold of the American Army, from General George Prévost. Penfold is advised that should he renounce his American affiliation and accept his birthright as a full citizen of the British Empire, he will be welcomed as a full sorcerer with all the rights and privileges accorded to him thereto. To help him make his decision, a message like this one will be repeated every day with a different Calatian until he joins the British."

Two seconds of silence and then the fox started talking again. Jackson talked over him. "He says the same thing. Won't stop, won't change his message. I took a quick look with Chavill's Small Window, but the general insisted I wait until you heard his message before going farther." He stared at Hamilton. "May I proceed?"

General Hamilton inclined his head toward Kip as the fox droned on in the background. "Penfold, you don't need to hear the message again?"

"No." Kip tried to compose himself. "Sir, you don't imagine I'll go to the British?"

"I didn't think so," Hamilton said as Jackson placed one hand between the Calatian's ears. "I am pleased to hear it confirmed from your lips. Do you know this fox?"

Kip shook his head. "He speaks like a Georgian. How many Calatians lived in Savannah, sir?"

"We believe two hundred, maybe a few more. It was not a large community compared to others."

One of the men beside Hamilton, nearly as decorated, said, "What does he hope to accomplish? To show us how little he values Calatian lives? In half a year he'll have no more messengers."

Kip's throat tightened, imagining that, and he could not have spoken even if it had been asked of him. Hamilton gave Kip a shrewd look, perhaps guessing his thoughts. "In half a year we hope this battle to be long over. But I know this General Prévost. He means to cause uncertainty among us as to one of our weapons and thereby perhaps curtail our use of him."

"The sooner we defeat the British here," Kip said, "the sooner these messages will be brought to an end. You need have no fear for my loyalty."

"Good man." Hamilton gave him an approving nod. "I know that Master Colonel Jackson has plans for you in this upcoming battle."

"It's a deep compulsion," Jackson said.

Kip looked up, startled, but Jackson had lifted his hand from the fox's head and clearly was addressing that problem. "I don't know if I can break it without breaking his mind. But I'm not sure how much of his mind is left."

"Albright," Kip said.

"What?" Hamilton turned to him.

"Master Albright, sir," the fox repeated. "He's a spiritual sorcerer and he knows me well."

"Well enough to translocate to your side?"

"Probably." Kip met Jackson's eyes. "But the sorcerers' quarters are well warded, and my friend Malcolm—Malcolm O'Brien—keeps us warded when we go out." Though, he realized, they hadn't been when they were out in the plaza this afternoon. Lowell glanced at him, perhaps realizing the same thing, but kept his mouth shut.

The general turned away from the fox to face Kip fully. "Good. I have been told of your abilities and I believe they may provide the lynchpin for this war."

"But sir." Kip felt emboldened by Hamilton's sympathy. "When is our attack planned? How many more Calatian minds will be ruined by Albright?"

"Maybe not ruined," Jackson growled. "I haven't tried Kobalt's Regrowth yet."

The other officers mostly looked at Kip as if this was the first they'd heard of a secret weapon the American Army had, but the one on the other side of Hamilton said, "If we rush into battle, we risk losing more lives than a single Calatian."

One Calatian life a day? Calatian lives were rarer than human lives by far. Kip didn't know how many Calatians fought in the Army, but it was a single regiment, and only those who had already fathered cubs were allowed to fight (having already ensured their next generation). The populations of the towns of Peachtree and New Cambridge numbered in the hundreds, the boroughs of Boston and New York a little less than that. They only numbered a few thousand total—maybe as many as five or six thousand—between the British and Spanish Empires, so he'd been told by his father. And for each of the species, the number was smaller. Legend had it there had once been twenty species, now down to nineteen, but nobody could say which was the one that had been lost. If all the foxes were killed, there would be no more.

And yet, how many human lives were worth one Calatian life? One fox? This fox looked young; he might not have fathered cubs yet. If he died, would that be one fewer fox for Kip's potential cubs to marry?

"Penfold."

Kip blinked out of his reverie to find Jackson staring at him. "Return to your quarters," he said. "There's no reason for you to witness any more of this."

Hamilton looked for a moment as though he might argue, but in the end let Captain Lowell guide Kip out of the church.

CHAPTER 7: THE BATTLE OF SAVANNAH

The following day, nobody came to tell Kip there had been another Calatian messenger, but he knew there must have been. He told Alice and Malcolm about the fox, and while Malcolm was appropriately horrified, Alice felt the impact the same way Kip had, sitting down in a chair with her tail curled tightly around her hips, her eyes wide and ears back. "Do...do you think he'll be okay?" she asked.

"If it's Albright," Kip said, "then no, I don't. I think he wiped out the fox's mind and replaced it with a message. I don't know how you could do that."

"Spiritual magic is awful." Alice buried her muzzle in her paws.

"It certainly doesn't seem to do much good to those who study it." Malcolm spoke in a subdued tone. "Haven't met one yet who's not crazy in one way or another."

"There's Master Colonel Jackson," Captain Lowell interjected.

"Aye, of course, I'd forgotten." Malcolm didn't have eyes to gesture with, but Kip felt sure that what his friend meant was that he'd forgotten that Lowell was in the room.

Kip didn't leave his quarters that day, worried about venturing outside the wards. Alice practiced her spell but still fell short of summoning an elemental. Kip suggested she try fire—there at least he could summon one for her to talk to—but she did not seem excited about it, so he let it drop.

And the following day, the sun had not yet risen before horns jolted them awake from their beds. Outside the small bedroom's thin wooden walls, wind rushed past their shutters, howling unnervingly in the dimness. In the first waking moments of disorientation, Kip thought he was back at Prince George's College and it was under attack again. Then Captain Lowell, already standing, barked crisply, "Attack. Get dressed."

They fumbled clothes on, Lowell somehow ready before Kip even had both arms through his tunic. Alice did not bother to go to her changing closet, using darkness for modesty. "Kip," she said, standing by the window pulling a uniform jacket over her gown and petticoat. "Do you think—"

"No time for that," Lowell snapped as Kip reached for his sorcerer's robe.

A moment later, a loud concussion flattened the ears of the foxes and caused Malcolm to steady himself against the wall. Seconds later, the crunch of something heavy hitting a brick wall followed. "Cannon," Lowell said, his eyes wide. "We should've been on our way down by now."

Indeed, when they arrived downstairs, the rest of the military sorcerers had already assembled and some of them been moved out. "Penfold!" Jackson roared when he spotted the fox. "To me."

Kip hurried over to him. "You remember my orders?" the sorcerer demanded.

"Yes, sir."

"The ships aren't landing, so forget about waiting. They're anchored just south of the harbor, bombarding the city. The British troops have all moved into the city, leaving the harbor clear. I'm sending you there, where you'll have a better view out to sea and they won't be firing at you. As soon as you find the ships, do it. Every moment's delay costs lives."

"Yes, sir."

"O'Brien, your defenses are ready? Good." He barely seemed to see Alice. "Then Callahan, take them."

"Can't we have sorcerers knock down—"

Kip finished his sentence on a windy pier on the harbor, the smell of the sea bursting in his nose so that he coughed in the middle of saying, "—the cannonballs?"

They stood on a long stretch of wood, choppy water splashing against the pilings below them. Nobody else that they could see stood anywhere on the pier, but behind them, just past the Customs House, a few red-coated soldiers ran toward the center of town and then were gone.

Malcolm murmured his warding spells. Kip drew his knife and poked at the wound he'd made the previous day, then put his lips to it and tasted the blood.

Alice and Lowell arrived beside him. Alice lifted her nose to the breeze, ears perked. "Kip," she said.

He held up a paw. "I need to focus on the demon," he said. "Give me a minute."

"You're warded," Malcolm told him.

Magic came strong and fast to him. He chose one of the demon names, the most biddable one from the previous day, and spoke the summoning.

"Make no move save on my order; speak no word save on my order; exert no power save on my order."

The cloud of fiery bats he'd summoned hovered in mid-air, not even flapping, which was somehow more disturbing. "There are ships out on the water firing cannons. They'll be one to two miles off the coast to the south, in range of the city proper. Find them," he ordered.

The bats disappeared. "And destroy them?" Captain Lowell asked. "You forgot to tell them to destroy them."

"One thing at a time," Kip said.

"This is war! There isn't time for 'one thing at a time'!"

As if to punctuate his point, a cannonball screamed through the air not fifty feet from them and smashed into the pier, shaking its foundations. Overhead, a cannon answered from the American side, and a second later, a flame-wreathed missile streaked overhead, reminding Kip of his mission. "Alice," Kip said tightly, keeping communication with his demon, "can you handle cannonballs as they come in?"

"There are other sorcerers handling them," Lowell said, but his eyes flicked to the impact. "They're not supposed to be landing here. That one must have missed."

"I can keep us safe here," Alice said. "I'll have a spell ready. But Kip, there's wind here."

The demon reported back to Kip that it could not find any ships, but there were other demons out there and that they had sent minor attacks against it. It had defended itself but not counter-attacked.

Show me the area of the sea where the demons are, Kip ordered, and his vision doubled. There was a stretch of ocean, choppy with the wind. He gathered magic again—

The other demons are attacking again.

Defend yourself but you need not attack them. Kip reached for fire and found it, eager as always. He sent it in a quick wave along the surface of the water and listened for it to find wood and cloth to consume. The snap and roar came, but smaller than he would have thought for a whole fleet; only two ships, perhaps only one? All those cannonballs couldn't be coming from just one ship, could they? Master Colonel Jackson had said there was a whole fleet. The fire swarmed eagerly over the one or two ships it had found and Kip pulled it back, ordering it to consume only wood, not human flesh.

"One ship and two minor demons," he said aloud. "That's all I've found so far."

"There's a fleet out there," Captain Lowell insisted.

"This feels wrong." Kip told his demon to return to them. For a battle, the air was eerily silent. If he focused his ears back, over the hiss of wind and the splashing of waves he could hear shots, but they felt as remote as the horizon. "Where are the cannonballs coming from?"

"Can't your demon see that?"

Another cannonball crashed into a building on the harbor front, a hundred feet to the other side of them. "They're attacking their own side," Lowell said. "Why not throw the cannonballs over those buildings to the American army?"

"I thought they were doing that," Malcolm said. "Isn't that why we're here?"

"They were." Lowell paced back and forth and looked out at the horizon, where a sliver of sun just showed over the water. "We should get to cover."

"Into one of those buildings?" Alice asked. "Isn't that more dangerous?"

"Being out here isn't safe now it's light. Come on."

Kip ordered his demon to show Malcolm the world around him as they hurried back into the nearest building, a warehouse next to the Customs House. Lowell bolted the door behind them as they picked their way among the empty crates scattered around the floor. Once Alice had stationed herself at the window to watch for cannonballs, Kip sent his demon to scout the battle and tell him what was happening.

"How's your control?" Malcolm asked in a low voice.

"Fine. Better than I'd expected." Kip breathed. "It's not fighting me much. I think not making it fight the other demon helped. I might bring the other one too if we're going to stay in here. I want eyes outside."

"You can't summon two demons at once, and one a fourth level," Lowell said flatly. "Don't endanger the battle."

"That one I think is a third level, not a fourth," Kip said, "and I can get the power to do it. My other demon is very easy."

He took out his knife, but as he set it to his arm, Alice turned and took a step toward him. "Let me."

"Keep an eye out for cannonballs," he said, and drove the knife into the crook of his elbow. Methodically, he cleaned the knife and then set his lips to the wound.

Another impact struck close to them; Alice whirled back to her window to watch the sky, her paws glowing turquoise as she gathered magic. Kip, too, summoned magic, holding the bat-demon while he constructed the spell to summon Nikolon.

"Are the wards being tested?" Lowell asked Malcolm while Kip spoke the summoning spell.

"A mite. Here and there. Nothing I can't handle."

When Nikolon appeared in her female Calatian form, Kip asked her to watch the area around them for any threats. Through the other demon's sight, Kip judged the battle in the city to be about even; demons thickened the air, changed the landscape, and demolished buildings, making the ground more treacherous for the soldiers and in some cases probably killing them.

"I can't tell who's winning the battle," he said, as he ordered the demon back out to sea to look for the fleet. "Where are these ships supposed to be?"

"Approaching the harbor, that's all I know," Lowell replied.

Malcolm asked, "Could they have turned and gone back to Charleston?"

The captain turned to Malcolm. "Then why attack here?"

"Diversion?"

"It's a costly diversion. If it were just the cannon..." He trailed off. "Penfold, you said the battle is engaged?"

"Yes." Kip scanned the sea through his demon's eyes, looking for anything, any telltale of a fleet. But the ocean was vast, and the wind meant that it was hard to distinguish natural whitecaps from the wake of a ship, especially if those ships were anchored. *Look for cannonballs*, he told the demon on the ocean. *See if you can determine where they're coming from.*

"Then they must mean to take the harbor."

Cannonball coming close, Nikolon warned him. "Cannonball," he repeated aloud to Alice.

She raised her paws. "I see it," she said matter-of-factly.

Kip tried hard to fight the feeling of being lost and useless. Malcolm warded them; Alice protected them from cannonballs, and what had he done to make all that worthwhile? He'd burned one ship and the cannonballs kept coming. American soldiers were being killed, and he was here trying to find ships on a seemingly endless sea.

Another idea occurred to him. *Search for the smell of men and gunpowder on the air*, he told the demon.

Another cannonball, Nikolon said. Kip passed the warning on to Alice and then Nikolon said, *That smell is out in the harbor.*

"What?" Kip ran to the window where Alice stood and scanned the harbor. It still appeared empty. He opened the window a crack and put his nose to it. Mostly he smelled the sea, but—yes, there, a faint trace of gunpowder. He wouldn't have detected it before; it had taken time to blow here once the cannon started firing. But not very much time.

Captain Lowell ran to his side and slammed the window closed. "What are you doing?"

"The ships are just north of the harbor," Kip said. "They're not missing. They're firing at *us*."

"They can't be," Captain Lowell said. "It's something else. It's—" His eyes widened. "Those soldiers running away when we first arrived. They must have seen us—It's a trap."

"My wards are breaking," Malcolm called. "Trying to hold them up, but—no, someone's close."

Captain Lowell grabbed Kip's wrist. "We have to get out of here. Out the back. Come on, now!"

"There's a man outside!" Alice called.

If there were a fight among sorcerers, the captain would be a liability. So Kip gathered magic. "Tell Master Colonel Jackson," he said, and sent Lowell back to the headquarters.

No sooner had he done that than Alice cried out. Kip spun around to see her backing away from a black-robed sorcerer, a narrow man with a pointed black beard who raised a skeletal hand to Kip immediately. "We have your friend," he said in a cultured London tone. "Your eyeless friend. If you wish him dead, by all means kill me."

Kip had already pulled magic from the earth but now stopped short of casting a spell, standing there with purple glow wreathing his black-furred paws. The British sorcerer smiled. "Good. Now I'm sure you've summoned a demon. Bring it here and dismiss it, and speak the spell out loud."

Demon, singular. He told Nikolon to go a hundred miles down the coast, not knowing what other demons these sorcerers might be employing to make sure Kip complied with their wishes. Then he brought the bat-demon back to the warehouse. He'd maintained control of it even through the surprise, but there was no time to congratulate himself on his accomplishment now.

When he'd spoken the dismissal spell, the other sorcerer nodded in satisfaction and walked over to him. "Good. Now, this won't hurt a bit. Just relax."

He reached out and Kip felt a lurch inside him. "There, you see?" the sorcerer said. "It's easier when you go along with it." He walked to the window and waved at it.

A moment later, another sorcerer appeared inside the warehouse. "All secured?"

"Aye, Penfold's taken care of. His calyx is no threat."

"Good. Let's go on with you then. The Brigadier General is waiting for you."

Was that Albright? Kip allowed himself to be taken by the paw. The world spun and he found himself in a small, dark wooden room smelling of stale rum, rope, brine, and Malcolm. His stomach wobbled; it took him a moment to realize that the floor was tilting back and forth.

"Kip?" Malcolm spoke from behind him.

"Aye. I'm here, and so is Alice." She had her ears back as she stepped close to him, and he put his arm around her.

"They took my magic away."

"Mine too." He squeezed Alice's shoulder. She looked up at him, eyeshine flashing, and he gave her a quick shake of his head. Malcolm would understand her silence. "And they made me dispel the bat demon." Again, relying on what was unsaid.

"So here we are." Malcolm sat down against the wall. "It looked like Lowell got away, anyway."

"He'll report back. Maybe we'll be rescued."

"Maybe." Kip and Alice sat together against the wall. "At least it seems they don't want to kill us right away."

His heart clenched as he said that. They'd already threatened Malcolm's life; now they had two people Kip cared about to ensure that he would do what they asked. Burn the town of Savannah? Kill American soldiers? Albright, or his superior, cared enough about Kip's abilities to send messages specifically to him, so what would they do now that they had him?

And, he wondered, now that he had no magic, what had become of Nikolon? The last time he'd been cut off from magic, the elemental he'd bound had remained bound, so perhaps the binding was intact. But when he tried to speak to Nikolon, there was no reply, and he wondered if he were only thinking the words and nobody was hearing them.

Hours went by. They spoke very little, aware that someone might be listening, though Kip's nose told him no demons were nearby. In the silence, Kip's mind spun worse and worse futures for them, beginning with Alice and Malcolm being executed and moving on to Albright casting a spiritual hold that would make him set fire to the American army. He told himself there was no use worrying until something happened; those were easy words to say but harder to feel, especially when he looked at Malcolm and Alice. Malcolm had made his own decisions, but Kip could have protected Alice better, could have forbad her from joining the army. He knew even as that thought crossed his mind that he would never have been able to stop her without irreversibly damaging their relationship, but that didn't ease any of his guilt.

And what of the men on the ships he'd spared? They'd been only decoys, probably, but what if some of them had been the ones who'd captured the three of them? If he'd completely destroyed the ship as Jackson had ordered, would they perhaps be safe now?

As if sensing his emotions, Alice reached out and took his paw in hers. "We'll be rescued," she said.

"I hope so." He squeezed her paw back.

"Course we will." Malcolm rested a hand against the wall of the cabin.

"That message from Albright," Alice said. "It seems like he wants you to think you're terribly important. Not that you aren't! But it puts a lot of pressure on you. You might be so anxious to save the day that you make a mistake."

"You mean, like I just did?"

Alice shook her head. "You didn't make a mistake. You were following orders. The people giving the orders made a mistake. And anyway, we're going to be rescued, remember?"

"I think Alice has the right of it," Malcolm said.

"She often does." The guilt didn't disappear, but became easier to bear, and Kip relaxed. "Where do you think we are? Still in Savannah?"

"Maybe New York," Alice said.

"Could be London." Malcolm rubbed his stomach. "The question growing most important to my mind is: will they feed us?"

This question became more important as the day ticked on, and when the door opened to reveal a short blond sorcerer, that was the first thing Malcolm asked. Kip stayed quiet; the shape almost resembled Victor Adamson in the light of the doorway, but a moment later he caught the scent and it was all wrong for Victor.

"You'll get food eventually," the man said. "Come on up. The Brigadier General wants you to see this."

He led them to the upper deck of what was revealed to be a British frigate, three proud masts holding sails that were partly furled. They sat in Savannah harbor amid smoking ruins of buildings, and even in the inconstant swirling wind, Kip could smell the distinctive odor of corpses through the smoke and salt air. Around them in a broad circle, twenty or thirty more ships sat at anchor, while three small ships sailed up the river.

The sorcerer brought them to the side of a red-haired man Kip had never seen before, wearing a high-ranking officer's uniform. When he saw the three prisoners, he turned and gave a cold smile. "Excellent. Thank you, Dewaite. You may remain."

Their escort nodded and took up a position behind Kip. The general continued. "We've not had the pleasure, Master Penfold. I'm Baron Stafford, the Brigadier General of His Majesty's Sorcerers in the Royal Navy. So you understand that you've been trapped by the very best, and there's no shame in that." He pointed out toward the shore. "I wanted you to see that our men have taken Savannah, and just on the other side of that building, several hundred of your fellow traitors have been taken prisoner. Your sorcerers have fled back to New York, no doubt, where we are pressing on the attack as well."

Kip said nothing. Stafford didn't look at him again, but continued to stare out at the harbor. "So you see, this war will soon be over. You can do some good still, by tipping the balance to end it even more quickly. Should you learn to use your prodigious powers properly, you might prolong the conflict by weeks or even months, causing the deaths of so many more." The general clasped his hands behind his back. "But in the end, the result will be the same. All of this will remain part of the greatest empire in the world. All of those people there, those self-styled 'Americans,' will remain citizens of the

British Empire." Now he turned to fix Kip with a steady eye. "The ones who haven't lost their lives, that is."

This was the point where the general expected a reply. Kip clasped his paws together in front of him. If Stafford thought that being faced with the top sorcerer in the Royal Navy would intimidate him, he had no idea that Kip had regularly talked with Master Colonel Jackson and John Quincy Adams, among others. So he said, "I presume that now we are inside the wards, and that's why I can see all the ships?"

Stafford blinked. "Yes. Of course."

"I wasn't sure the wards would render them invisible to demons. I had to try, though." He inclined his head. "You said this was a trap? The whole battle?"

"We sent the messenger to ensure you would be brought to Savannah at the time of our attack. I believed that your Colonel Jackson—"

"Master Colonel," Kip interrupted boldly.

Stafford looked about to strike him, but restrained himself. "Jackson would be unable to resist a tempting target of flammable wooden ships. Your fire confirmed it." He lifted his chin, smug.

"And you abandoned certain areas but left lookouts behind who could sense magic, or who would notice when they couldn't focus on part of the harbor."

"Demons riding along on cannonballs, actually. They reported to us when and where cannonballs were diverted."

Kip cursed himself. Malcolm had even told them at Bunker's Hill that enemy sorcerers could detect the effect of a ward, and none of them had thought twice about diverting the cannonballs. "Then you sent sorcerers to break our wards somehow."

Behind him, their escort—Dewaite? Dewaite—snorted. "Yes, well," Stafford said. "Your sorcerer is good, but you know, there are always ways to break wards."

"If you have sight, you mean," Malcolm said. "No need to spare my feelings, my good man. I'm well aware of my limitations."

Malcolm's cheerful smile might not have survived the withering glare he got for calling Stafford "my good man," but then again, it might have. The Brigadier General snorted. "Sight is one way. Had you been educated at King's College, you might know a few others."

"Perils of a colonial education," Malcolm said. "Along with having classmates uncouth enough to summon huge eye-stealing demons. But you know, I'm just as glad not to have sight right now."

He was not looking out across the harbor toward the smoke and the American defeat, but rather right at Baron Stafford. The latter, already a little red from his speech, flushed further and turned to Kip. "We have sorcerers who could restore those eyes, you know."

Kip stayed silent and Malcolm replied. "Ah, I'm grateful for the lie, but truly, I've come to accept my fate."

Stafford didn't say anything, but continued to look steadily at the fox. His meaning was clear: if you cooperate. His promise held no weight; demon curses remained impossible to reverse according to everything Kip had heard. Stories had survived of sorcerers who ordered demons to reverse demon curses and had ended up worse off than when they started. Master Odden had specifically told Kip that even if he summoned the same demon and ordered him to exactly reverse the curse he'd placed on Malcolm, there might be other consequences. For example, Master Petterton of Essex had been cursed with bright violet skin and had commanded the demon to reverse his condition; it turned out that the demon had placed a deadlier curse on his mind that would not take effect as long as his violet skin remained. When the demon removed the violet skin according to his command, Master Petterton lost his mind. Another Master had thought to circumvent this by ordering the demon to make him exactly as he'd been just before the curse, and the demon thus empowered had restored him to a state where he had no memory of what had happened since the curse—and also to a state in which he'd lost control of the demon, just as he had before the curse, and this time the demon changed him into an earthworm.

Kip felt very much like those old masters now, trying to outwit the British military, but they were only men, he reminded himself. He didn't reply to Stafford, but kept his eyes trained on Savannah and tried not to think of the men who'd died. What if he'd joined the battle, moved away from the harbor? He might not have been caught. British ships might not now control the harbor, might not be moving up the river.

Up the river toward Peachtree, where his parents lived. His father would tell him not to worry about what might have been, but worry about what could be. So he breathed in and out, trying to ignore the smells, and eventually Stafford said, "All right, you need more time. That's fine, we have only started to make our argument."

Kip's father's theoretical advice did not take hold well. Sorcery was supposed to give you power over the world, and yet here he stood, being told that his decision could affect the lives of thousands, caught between his convictions and his respect for life, and he had no power to escape. He should be able to forge his own decisions, but with a simple spell they had stolen his magic from him, leaving him with only guilt and a tightness in his chest. He could not bring himself to speak again.

Stafford tired of him after that and ordered them returned to the close wooden cabin. When Dewaite had shut the door, Malcolm sat down and said, "You figure they intend to feed us, or only if we betray our fellows?"

"Shh." Kip had his ear to the door. Outside, Dewaite was talking to another man, instructing him to guard the cabin. They'd lowered their voices enough to prevent any human with an ear to the door from hearing them. But even without magic, Kip's excellent hearing had taught him to pick out minute sounds from a loud background, and so he heard the other man ask Dewaite if they were going up river with the others, heard Dewaite's "no" and then Dewaite saying, "I expect they're bound for Gibraltar, but they'll go by sorcerer. Once Master Albright arrives, he'll decide what to do."

CHAPTER 8: ALICE LEARNS SHIPS

Albright was coming? Albright, the man who'd plotted the murder of hundreds, and Kip would be here without magic or any other way to fight him. His breath came in short bursts until he felt dizzy and had to lean against the door.

When Dewaite had left and their guard settled to silence, Kip stumbled across the room to Malcolm and Alice, sitting against the wall as far from the door as possible. "No demons about," he whispered, and relayed what he'd heard. "Albright is on the way. He could be here any moment."

"You think our best chance is to wait for Emily?" Malcolm asked. "If Albright wanted to kill you, you'd be dead, I expect."

"What if we're warded? They must know people will come looking for us. And Albright is a spiritual sorcerer. I'd rather not wait to see what he intends do to our minds." Kip turned to Alice. "We have to get out of here as soon as possible. You still have magic?"

She nodded, eyes bright. "Kip. There were air elementals out there. They must be using them for the ships. I listened and I could almost understand them."

His heart jumped. "Are there any about now?"

She listened. "I don't think so. They were on the upper deck, but I didn't dare talk to them there."

"Could you call them?"

"I can try." She looked around the windowless cabin and then went to the door and made soft humming sounds.

"How does she speak their language?" Malcolm asked.

"I don't know that she does." Kip kept his voice very low so that even Alice's fox ears wouldn't catch his words. "When I heard the air elementals in Forrest's memory, they sounded like words barely out of my hearing, but Forrest understood what they meant. I don't know how one learns their language, but I think one always feels like one is just about to."

Malcolm nodded. "Wonder if I could teach her a defensive spell in a few moments. Could we set our own ward against Albright?"

"Could she cast it well enough to fool him?"

Malcolm shook his head slowly. "I suppose we'd best lean on her ability to learn an elemental language, then. Better to bet on the one-legged horse than the one that isn't in the race, my da used to say."

There was a pause, and then Malcolm said, in the same soft whisper, "You reckon I'll see my da again?"

"You will," Kip said. "And I'll see mine."

Alice came back to them after a few more minutes, her ears down. "I don't think it's working," she said, "and I don't want to call any louder. I can hear the guard moving around."

"It's all right," Kip said. "We can use your physical magic. Probably the wards won't be set against that."

"If I could summon an air elemental…" Alice's ears came up. "We could escape over the side. It could surround us under the water and we could breathe there."

Kip raised an eyebrow. "You think so?"

"That was in *The Element Air*. Master LeCorbin used it to travel around Portsmouth harbor in a storm."

He recognized in Alice the same feeling he'd had when he'd rescued her from Farley, the exhilaration that all of this learning had finally conveyed the power to make a real difference in the world. Of course, then he'd been so caught up in worrying for her safety that he hadn't dwelt much on it, and afterwards he'd been punished, but in that moment, he'd saved her.

That feeling of power, what had been taken away from him; she had it now. He found it difficult to let go and allow her to take the risk, but it was necessary. She had to experience the good that her sorcery could do and the bad that could result from it.

"Let's try the summoning again," he told her. "If it doesn't work, we'll take our chances with just the physical magic. Are you ready now? Albright could be here at any time."

"Then I suppose I'd better be ready." She stood, brushing off her gown, and held her paws before her.

"Remember the spell. Think about what the wind was like and how you could almost understand it. Imagine a place with nothing but that sound, the feel of wind in your whiskers, the smell of air moving constantly."

Alice nodded, her paws glowing. She spoke the words of the spell quietly, and as she finished, the glow around her paws faded.

Kip glanced at Malcolm. The Irishman had his hands together in front of him for all the world as though he were praying. Well, that was not a bad idea, come to think of it.

A gust of air cut off his words. He lifted his head as the room filled with a spiraling wind, picking up dust and flinging it about. Malcolm cursed softly; Kip squeezed his eyes shut and folded his ears back. But Alice was... humming? He raised his ears and now perceived a murmur in the air, as though of words uttered just too softly to understand, and Alice's humming was answering.

She turned to Kip, eyes wide and ears perked despite the dust. "Her name is Poudre," she whispered, her breath halting. "She says this air tastes interesting, but the room is small and she wants to get out."

"So do we all." Kip smiled at his student. "That was very well done." The words felt inadequate to convey how proud he was of her for taking this step, a summoning he himself could not have done. And yet this was only part of the solution. She had to maintain control of the air elemental while destroying the door of the cabin, presuming it wasn't warded against physical magic.

"If Albright will be here soon, we should leave now." Alice spoke to Kip but kept looking around the cabin as though she could follow the progress of the elemental.

"Can Poudre allow us to breathe underwater? Supply us with air for a short time until we reach the other bank?"

Alice hummed her almost-words and then nodded. "She says yes."

Malcolm hissed to get Alice's attention. "Perhaps if she could supply us with air, she could also suffocate our friend on the other side of the door? Just enough to knock him out, not kill him."

After a brief conference, Alice nodded. "She—she knows exactly how to do that. I wouldn't know how to tell her. She says that she's killed people, but I asked her not to."

Kip put his ear to the door. "Be ready to break the door if he raises the alarm."

"He won't," Alice said confidently, and then made that humming noise again. The air rushing around their cabin stilled, whistling softly as it ran through the cracks around the door. One tense moment, another, and then the soft thump of a body falling to the ground.

"She says it's done," Alice whispered. "He's still breathing."

Kip stood and grasped Malcolm's hand. "Pick up the three of us first. As soon as the door is clear, we'll go down the stairs. If we can get to the bottom of the boat, could you rip the planks apart?"

She nodded. "I think so. They're just fastened with bolts and things, right? I can pull them apart. I'm pretty sure."

"If you're looking for the waterline," Malcolm said, "there's no need to go all the way to the bottom. It's right here."

He knelt next to the wall and placed his hand about two feet above the floor. "You can feel the waves hitting it if you put a hand there, or a paw, or whatever you've got."

Kip hurried to the wood and placed his paw there. At first he felt nothing and then, very faintly, he felt the ebb and flow of swells against the wood. "That's right," he said. "Can you pull apart these boards?"

Alice nodded and knelt in front of the wall. "First I'm going to have Poudre surround us with air and keep us breathing. We should probably jump into the water as soon as we can."

"Yes." Kip's heart pounded. In a moment his head was surrounded by lightly moving air, and next to him Malcolm's hissed breath told him his friend was feeling the same thing. All he could do now was watch as Alice cast the spell, held her paws out toward the boards, and closed her eyes to concentrate.

Malcolm squeezed his paw. "You'll have to tell me what's happening," he murmured.

"Nothing yet." Kip tried to breathe normally even though the thought came to him that he was maybe breathing in and out an elemental. "Wait. There's a little creaking."

"If only we'd talked to Victor about his father's business more," Malcolm said, "we'd know where to tell her to focus her energies."

"The boards are pressed together very tightly," Alice said. "It's...hard."

"I wouldn't imagine a ship would come apart easily." Malcolm squeezed Kip's paw. "Not much use to them if so, eh?"

"If I had magic, I could burn the hole," Kip said.

"Aye, and if Alice knew water we could have a water elemental, and for that matter, if we'd never been captured in the first place we wouldn't have need of any of it. Give Alice here a moment, she'll have the job done. There, I heard a larger creak."

"There's a point in the middle of the board." Alice breathed in. "It's bowing and it wants to twist."

And now Kip could see the cracks around one of the boards widening. Water sprayed in a moment later, and the creaking became a popping. "It's coming loose," he told Malcolm.

"That I can hear," his friend responded. "Make sure I don't hit my head on the boards, aye?"

Kip squeezed his hand as the first board popped free with a wave of water. "It's not big enough yet. One more."

"My feet are wet enough. Soon we'll be underwater anyway."

"Just a minute," Alice said. "It's easier now I've got the trick."

And it was barely half a minute before the second board came loose, water now flooding into the cabin. The force of the water was such that Kip had to grasp Alice's arm with his free paw. "I think you'll have to push us through the hole," he said. "There's no way we'll get through otherwise."

"All right." She closed her eyes, obviously needing to gather strength, and called magic. The three of them lifted from the ground, turned to float parallel to it, and then with a rush met the wall of water entering the ship.

Instinctively he held his breath and squeezed his eyes shut, but no water touched his ears or muzzle. He opened his eyes cautiously to see water rushing past him, cloudy with mud and silt, and on one side, dimly, the wall of wood that must be the body of the great frigate. A moment later they had left the ship behind, rushing through the water near the bottom of the riverbed. Fish scattered before them and weeds whipped across their bodies; Alice kept them low to the bottom where the silty water would hide them better.

When they reached the opposite bank, Alice stopped Kip and Malcolm and gestured that she would go to the surface and look. Before Kip could react, she was gone.

He brought his head near to Malcolm's so that their air bubbles touched. "Alice went to scout," he said.

Malcolm gave a start. "Ah, very good," he said. "All in all, I prefer traveling above water when there's a choice, you know. Next I suppose we will have to find our allies. You know, even though we're underwater, it feels good to be able to converse in normal voices without worrying about being overheard. I suppose if we needed a private conversation, we could ask Alice for the loan of an air elemental."

Kip smiled. "There are worse places to have a conversation."

"Does it bother you at all that we might be breathing in an elemental?"

"A little," the fox admitted, not voicing his other concern, that elementals were not demons and therefore not as bindable to direct orders. The air elemental was not bound to him but to Alice, and only its agreeability to her will kept it here. The murky water hovering just beyond his eyes rippled as if with sinister intent, ready to rush in and suffocate him at the least opportunity. "But it bothers me more that Albright might be arriving at any moment and would be able to find me easily if I'm not warded by then."

"Ah. I take your point."

They were moved up through the water to the shore, into a small stand of trees, where Alice's spell let go of them. Here they could see out onto the river but not be easily seen, unless someone had spotted them rising from the water. But the men of the frigate had other things to occupy their attention; the great boat listed away from them, and even as they watched, groaned upright, no doubt under a spell.

"Pity we didn't sink her," Kip muttered, and then had to tell Malcolm what he was seeing.

Alice, though as wet as the other two, beamed and wagged her sopping tail. "How do we contact Captain Lowell?" she asked.

"Can Poudre do it?" Malcolm squeezed water from his clothes.

"Maybe. We'd have to give her a scrap of paper to carry."

Kip looked at his wet clothes ruefully. "Even if we had paper and something to write with, all our paper would be useless and our ink lost in the river." He sighed. "If only I knew what had happened to Nik." In his head, he tried again to send a message out into the void. *Nikolon. If you can hear me, come and become visible. I have no more access to magic.*

He did not expect a response, but within a few seconds, a naked female fox appeared before him. "I knew you could no longer hear me, master," she said. "I awaited further instructions."

Kip breathed evenly, the relief of having Nikolon still at his disposal overwhelming his annoyance at the demon. "In the future, if you detect that I can no longer hear you, come find me." She bowed her head. "Now please go find Captain Lowell. If he's warded, find any American soldier close to the American headquarters building and ask them to bring Captain Lowell to you. When you find him, tell him where we are and remain with him until he finds a translocation sorcerer, then show that sorcerer where we are. Let them know that this is urgent. When it is done, I will dismiss you."

"Yes, master." She vanished.

Nikolon, Kip thought. *If by chance we are not here when you return, look for us on that frigate.*

There was no answer, but he hoped the message had gone through. Being without magic felt like losing a limb, or—he looked guiltily at Malcolm—his sight or hearing. That someone could just turn that off felt wrong, and yet it was the third time in his life it had happened. At least his experience with it meant he hadn't panicked this time, and Malcolm had handled it well too.

"Now what?" Alice asked. "Should I dismiss Poudre?"

"No." Kip stared out across the water. "Not unless her binding is a strain on you."

Alice shook her head. "So we wait now?"

"We also serve who only stand and wait," Malcolm murmured.

"We wait," Kip affirmed. "But be on guard. We don't know what other sorcerers might be out looking for us. I don't think there are other demons around, not right now."

Malcolm flexed his fingers. "Can't wait to have magic back again."

"I know," Kip said. "Don't worry, Master Colonel Jackson can do it."

A pop and a presence behind him. He half-turned and then the scent hit him and sent his heart racing. "Penfold," purred the familiar voice of Master Albright. "How nice to finally see you again."

A heavy hand landed on Kip's shoulder, but he only got a glimpse of the large bearded man before a powerful gust of wind rushed past him—close enough to ruffle his whiskers, but without touching him in any other way—and threw Albright back. A moment later, Alice's voice came, a little shaky, but clear, and Albright shot up into the air. He struggled rather like a fish pulled out of the water and then vanished.

Kip sat down hard on the ground. Alice's tail was puffed out and her eyes were wide. "I couldn't think of anything else to do," she said. "I told Poudre to knock him back and then suffocate him and then I shot him into the air."

Malcolm had jumped at Albright's voice and now backed into a tree. "Who was it?"

"Albright." Kip pressed a paw to his chest. "Alice, you did wonderfully."

"Do you suppose he's dead?" Alice asked in a whisper.

"I wouldn't count on it." Kip's breathing slowly returned to normal. "Any sorcerer can dismiss an elemental and he's quick enough to figure that out. Or he may have gotten away from her when he translocated. Is she still about?"

Alice lifted her nose to the sky and nodded. "I still feel her. I'll keep her ready in case he comes back."

Before she'd finished the sentence, another person popped into view beside them, but it was not the bearded Albright. Callahan, in his American army uniform, one sleeve bloody, surveyed the three of them and then rubbed at the dark shadows under his eyes. "There you are," he said. "Master Colonel's been quite worried."

Kip pushed Malcolm at Callahan. "Send the two of them back."

"Oi," Malcolm said. "We need to get you warded again."

"Albright knows this place now. He'll be back any minute. Hurry!"

Callahan, used to taking orders, grasped Malcolm's wrist and laid a hand on Alice even as she tried to get away. They vanished, and he staggered. "Been casting spells all day," he murmured. "Give us a minute."

"We may not have a minute." Kip took the other sorcerer's hand, ears flicking around, scanning the area.

"We'll take a damned minute unless you want to appear in the middle of a wall." Callahan forced himself to take deep breaths.

A rustle in the leaves behind him. Kip focused his ears in that direction and caught breathing. "He's here," he murmured to Callahan. "Go now. Now."

Physical magic gripped Kip, tried to drag him away. Callahan's eyes widened in alarm. He held tight to Kip, concentrated, and—

—they appeared two feet above the floor of the large room in the Savannah headquarters. The physical magic holding Kip vanished and he fell to the floor, weak with relief.

Back in the Trade House in Boston, magic restored, Kip had to keep his ears upright as Master Colonel Jackson spent a good deal of time explaining in front of Malcolm, Alice, and Captain Lowell how the fox's recklessness might have cost the American Army the war. Exactly what he'd done that was reckless seemed to come down to "getting captured," though Jackson also accused Kip of not burning the fleet he hadn't been able to see.

Captain Lowell had been much more deferential to Kip since his return, and during this harangue caught Kip's eye and advised him with a minute shake of his head to keep quiet. So Kip withstood it, and at the end Jackson said, "If you're going to help us win this war then you'll have to do better about carrying out my orders."

"Yes, sir," Kip said.

"Now what was so difficult about finding that fleet?"

He bit back the response of "they weren't where you said they would be," and kept his voice level. "They were warded, sir. I sent a demon out to look but it only found one ship, set as a decoy to trap me."

"We'll have to do better about breaking wards, then. O'Brien, isn't that your field?"

"Yes, sir," Malcolm said.

"Consult with Luke Tarsian. If he can't help you then we will assign him to Penfold instead of you."

"Yes, sir." Malcolm did not bring up that he had already been working with Tarsian, but his flat tone told Kip what he thought of Jackson's orders.

"Now." Jackson spoke more calmly. "Did you learn anything of interest while a prisoner?"

"I think the other sorcerers are being held at Gibraltar," Kip said. "The soldiers were asking if we were to be taken there. And I think…" He hesitated. "They talked about going up the river. I think they mean to attack Peachtree."

"There's nothing of value there," Jackson said. "Who did you meet on the ship?"

"But sir, they were sending ships up the river."

"To establish a base and cut off our land access to the city, I'm sure. Who did you talk to on the frigate?"

"Brigadier General Stafford," Kip answered. "And a sorcerer named

Dewaite."

"I don't know him." Jackson stroked his chin. "But Stafford...for him to be here, Savannah must be very important to them."

"Or Kip is," Malcolm said. "That Stafford fellow made quite the speech to him. Told him thousands of lives would be lost if he didn't join them."

"Did he now? They think highly of you. And yet you've not done much damage to them. Interesting."

Kip bit his lip. "Sir," he said. "May I have your permission to visit my parents in Peachtree and make sure they're all right in case of any British incursion?"

"No," Jackson said. "It would be a waste of your time. We may be planning for a new offensive to retake Savannah, and you will be needed for a defense of New York. The British are threatening our end of the Road."

"Sir," Captain Lowell said. "What if I accompany Penfold? He hasn't seen his parents in quite some time, and they may be concerned for his safety."

"Oh, very well." Jackson waved irritably. "But take your whole unit. From now on, Penfold, you don't go anywhere without a defensive sorcerer. Even O'Brien."

"Yes, sir." Kip kept his tail from wagging as successfully as Malcolm was keeping himself from grimacing, which was to say mostly.

Securing Jackson's permission was only the start of a frustrating process. Even though Kip could send himself to Peachtree, and potentially another person, he was not registered as a translocational sorcerer, so he wasn't allowed to officially send the others in his unit (and, he had to reluctantly admit, there was also the problem that if he sent the others into danger, they would have no way to get back). So another translocational sorcerer had to be found. Callahan had collapsed in his bed and Jackson forbad them to wake him, so after knocking on several doors, they found a younger translocational sorcerer named Broadwood, a short straw-haired man with freckles who agreed to send them even though he'd never been to Peachtree.

"Find a spiritual sorcerer to convey the destination from your mind to mine," he said. "Easy as pie."

"I can just send you there." Kip stopped and took a deep breath. "And then you can come back. Yes?"

Broadwood furrowed his brow into lines over his pale, gaunt face. "But you're not a translocational sorcerer."

"I can do it; I just can't bring a lot of people with me."

"If you're not approved, I shouldn't let you. Go find what's-his-name, Johnson, he'll do it."

Kip weighed the benefits of spending more time arguing versus trying to find Johnson and opted for the latter. By the time they did find him, Kip's frustration and anxiety had grown enough that Johnson's perfectly understandable confusion caused him to snap at the old sorcerer. Captain Lowell took over the explanation, and though Johnson clearly didn't understand the urgency, the task was (as he said) a simple one. "Think clearly of Peachtree as though you were there in this moment," he said, reaching out to put a weathered hand between Kip's ears.

Kip flattened his ears but envisioned his parents' house. "Got it," Broadwood said a moment later. "Thanks, Master."

"No worries at all. Better than rummaging around in prisoners' minds." The old man shook his head. "The important ones have charms on them that destroy their minds if I press too hard, so I'm afraid we haven't been able to learn anything." He wiped his forehead. "It's terribly disconcerting to have a mind crumble away as you're investigating it."

"Moreso for the owner of the mind, I'll wager," Malcolm said.

"Oh, no doubt, no doubt. I'm finding out more about this spell. It's devilish really. I wonder who could have laid it."

"Master Albright," Kip said.

"Oh, yes." Johnson showed no recognition. "I've heard the name but not run across his work before now. Let's hope in time I'm able to crack his spell."

When he'd left, Malcolm said, "Let's hope in time we're able to crack his head. Or burn him up."

"First things first." Kip turned to Broadwood. "Let's go."

He knew as soon as the humid evening air surrounded him that something was wrong. All the houses stood where he remembered them, but the village lay silent. His parents' scent hung in the air, as did the scent of a hundred or more other Calatians. Captain Lowell looked around uneasily, sensing the trouble as Kip did without the context to identify it.

"Wards up," he told Malcolm as soon as Broadwood arrived with the other two of their unit. "Broadwood, stay with us. We might need to leave soon."

"Take Alice and Captain Lowell first," Kip said. "Malcolm and I should stay together."

"I can fight," Alice protested. "Should I summon Poudre again?"

"It's hard to summon a particular elemental." Her question reminded Kip that he wanted to ask her about that summoning, how she had learned the air elementals' language so quickly. Later, when this situation was resolved. "They'll have gone to the river," he said.

"Should we scout around and see if anyone remains?" Malcolm asked.

My parents aren't here, Kip started to protest, but kept control enough to hold the words in. He looked to Captain Lowell, who was in charge, and the captain answered. "If there are some still here, their need is less than those who have been taken. We go to the river."

Kip didn't know whether Lowell could see the gratitude in his expression, but he gave the man a smile. He took Malcolm's arm and led them through the town to the path that led to the riverbank and the small dock.

They had just made it to the edge of town when Kip caught the scent of blood and <enstorf>, the newly dead. He stopped and peered through the evening light, spotting the light tunics of two motionless shapes lying outside one of the last cottages on this side of town. By the smell, they were dormice, not foxes, and he couldn't help them. He started forward again, but his hesitation had alerted the others, and Alice gave a small cry and ran to the bodies.

Reluctantly, Kip followed, taking Malcolm with him. "What's going on?" Malcolm asked.

"Two bodies," Kip said. "Dead no more than an hour, I'd say. I don't know them. They're dormice."

"Shot through the chest," Captain Lowell added. "They'll have died quickly, at least."

"Why shoot them?" Alice knelt beside the bodies, her nose twitching, but not touching them.

Kip had been wondering this himself, and gave voice to his only idea. "Because the British wanted all the Calatians," he said, "and they wouldn't come along."

"As a warning to the others." Lowell stared at the bodies. "To make the others more compliant. The first ones who voice any kind of resistance are shot. It's…a tactic."

"They had families," Alice said, staring down. "They weren't armed. They weren't a threat."

They weren't his parents, but they might have been. Kip's chest tightened, and then he thought, had his parents been specifically kept alive as leverage on him? Had these two been sacrificed because they weren't related to him? How much death would be laid at his feet before the war was over? "Come on," he said. "We should try to help the others if we can. We'll come back to bury these and…any others."

Alice stood without a word, her tail curled tightly around her legs, and shook a little as she composed herself and nodded. As they returned to the path, Captain Lowell extended his hand to her, and her black paw curled around his dark fingers.

At the river, Kip hurried out onto the dock and looked up and down the cool water. Evening light gave him little to work with, but he caught the sound of something moving through water not too far downstream. He could have levitated the small party, but Alice was still quiet and thinking about the dead dormice and he wanted to give her something to do. Activity was not an anodyne to grief or fear, but it could help her put those thoughts aside for a moment. "Alice," he said, "can you fly us all over the water that way? I think I hear the ship not too far off."

Her ears came up. "I hear it too," she said, and her paws glowed turquoise.

Behind Kip, Lowell cleared his throat. The fox turned to see the captain's eyebrows raised, but it took him a moment to decipher the expression. "I'm sorry, sir," he said. "You're in charge."

Lowell nodded. "Go ahead, Penfold. Your plan is sound."

"Let me call my demon, while we're casting spells," Malcolm said. "If we're to be chasing someone I'd prefer to be able to see about me. And he might be able to pierce a ward for us."

Kip fretted through the few minutes of these preparations, and when they were finally on their way, he kept his ears perked, straining to follow the faint noise. After some ten minutes of flying down the river in silence, Malcolm gestured to Alice to bring everyone together around him.

"My demon's spotted a disturbance in the water ahead, maybe five hundred feet," he whispered. "It looks like the wake of two ships."

"The third must have anchored closer to Savannah," Lowell whispered back.

Malcolm nodded. "We can break through the wards simply by flying through them."

Captain Lowell turned to Kip. "Be ready with your fire, Penfold. You may need to kill whatever sorcerers are on board before they can attack us or escape. I'll give the order. And Broadwood, be ready to effect our escape if needed."

The translocational sorcerer had spoken not at all since the bodies had been found, and even now when addressed directly only nodded. He looked ill. Kip hoped he wouldn't let them down, and hoped that he himself would be equal to the task. The idea of burning sorcerers churned his stomach, but he reminded himself that his parents were in danger. "I'm ready," he said.

Lowell nodded. "Bring us in a little higher than this," he instructed Alice. "It may be that we can escape detection for a few seconds if we are above them, and a few seconds can mean the difference between victory and defeat. And from here on out, silence."

They floated on down the river, Kip straining for any sound or smell that might indicate that their target was near. Several agonizing minutes later, he caught a waft of Calatian scent, several species, strong and rank with fear. He reached out to Captain Lowell's arm and indicated that they were close, and the Captain nodded his understanding. He gestured behind them, waiting until he'd received acknowledgment from everyone before turning back to face the twilight darkness of the river.

Around a large bend, Malcolm grabbed at Kip's robes and with urgent motions of his arms indicated the two wakes in the river below them. Before Kip could warn anyone, they were flying over the wakes and then, as though from another plane, two ships appeared below them, both sloops.

Crewmen manned the sails and rudder of both boats, but what drew Kip's eye immediately were the small groups of Calatians on the deck of each boat: three on one and two on the other, both surrounded by soldiers and facing a British military sorcerer. As he watched, the small group of two Calatians disappeared, and the sorcerer leaned on one of the soldiers near him, obviously exhausted.

In that moment, one of the crewmen happened to look up. "Americans!" he yelled. "Sorcerers!"

Kip waved to Malcolm to bring the remaining Calatians up to them, while he set fires at the stern of each boat to distract them. The sorcerers on both boats looked up.

"Kill them!" Lowell yelled to Kip.

The sorcerer who'd just translocated the two Calatians vanished. The other sent an array of light cannonballs from the deck shooting up at the small group. Malcolm and Alice were preoccupied, and Kip didn't know how good Broadwood was at physical magic, so he diverted his attention to pushing the projectiles back down at the ships. As he did, the three remaining Calatians rose from the deck, flying quickly through the air towards Broadwood.

"Fire!" screamed the sorcerer from the boat, and one soldier raised his gun and fired before Kip, taking advantage of the sorcerer's distraction, sent cannonballs into all of the soldiers. He gathered magic again and this time set fires to the wood of both ships, commanding the fire not to consume human flesh, but only the wood below them.

The people, of course, did not know the difference, and most jumped overboard. But two more gunshots sounded before one more scream cut them off, and behind Kip, Alice's voice cried out. His heart stopped for a moment, and he had time to contemplate what a foolish idiot he was before Alice said, "I'm all right," but in that space he had already turned to the other boat and spotted the soldier sighting along his rifle. Fire consumed the rifle, and this fire burned without restriction.

"Clear a place on the deck," Lowell shouted to Kip. Kip pulled the fire back from one charred portion of the nearest ship, and Lowell gestured for Alice to lower them to it. As the captain passed near Kip, he said in a lower voice, "We've no means of securing the sorcerers, so keep a close eye on them."

"They've all gone," Kip said. "I looked for the one who threw cannonballs but he'd gone too. I suppose they were all translocational."

"That's why I told you to kill them." Lowell stared pointedly at Alice, who was pressing a paw to her leg.

"She wasn't shot by a sorcerer," Kip responded. But Lowell's implication was clear and inarguable: failure to obey orders could cost lives. "I'm sorry, sir. I'll listen next time."

The man's face softened. "I know it's difficult, Penfold. You're not a soldier. But for God's sake, when we're in a battle, do try to act like one."

Kip coughed. "Yes, sir."

"I'm fine, really," Alice said. "It barely hurts."

"It will soon enough," Lowell told her.

They had nearly reached the deck, charred wood coming up to meet them, and Kip held his paw out. "Ah, Alice? The fire has burned quite a bit of the ships so let's find a good place to stand."

"Extinguish it all," Lowell ordered.

"Yes, sir."

They had reached the ships, and now Lowell called out to the soldiers swimming in the river. "We have your ships, and your sorcerers have deserted you. Surrender, you are prisoners of the American army."

Most of the soldiers managed to raise enough of their arms even while swimming to indicate surrender. One, flailing in the water, did not, and Lowell and Alice had to rescue him, for which he thanked them.

Alice was bleeding, but once Kip had found bandages on the ship and applied them to her leg, she stoutly refused to be translocated back to headquarters unless they were all going. Kip did not like this, but couldn't force her, so he stayed near her even when she told him he didn't have to be so worried.

The ships remained seaworthy enough to be sailed downriver. One of the soldiers volunteered the location of the third ship at anchor, obviously hoping for better treatment from his captors, and when they came upon it they captured it easily. That being the least damaged ship, Captain Lowell took command of it and brought his unit and all the prisoners aboard, and then ordered Alice to sink the other two.

"Easy," she said. "I know how to take ships apart now."

Her paws glowed turquoise, and a moment later the two half-burned sloops foundered and sank while the British prisoners watched the slender vixen with wide eyes.

CHAPTER 9: FRANCE

They docked a little north of Savannah, wanting to keep a presence on the river but mindful of the British fleet that controlled the harbor. Broadwood translocated them all back to the Trade House in Boston, where Master Colonel Jackson received them with loud demands to know why two badger-Calatians had appeared in the main room, as they had been unable to offer any reasonable explanation.

Captain Lowell explained the circumstances and the short battle, whereupon Jackson seized on the military importance of the river and dispatched Broadwood to take a crew of soldiers and a sorcerer unit to the sloop to hold the river, and possibly ambush the British from the weak side should the army attempt to retake Savannah.

Alice went to have her wound dressed properly while Lowell continued to brief Jackson, paying the Kip and Malcolm little attention. Kip listened long enough to hear Lowell give him a surprising amount of credit for their victory and then lapsed into his own thoughts. "There's no need to hold the river," he said to Malcolm quietly after a moment.

"You don't think Peachtree worth defending?" Malcolm asked.

"There's nothing there to defend anymore. They got what they wanted." Kip glanced at the door through which the badger-Calatians had been escorted.

"They wanted to steal the Calatians? But why? What did the ones in Peachtree have that the others in New York and Boston don't?"

"Or New Cambridge," Kip said, rubbing his whiskers.

"You don't suppose your parents were the cause?"

The fox shook his head, ears going back. "As much as they would like me to feel that important…no, they would have taken only my parents in that case. Why evacuate the whole town?"

"Why put them all onto a boat, for that matter?"

"Easier to defend a small swiftly moving boat than a whole town, if you wanted the whole town." Kip slumped back in his chair. "Maybe there was some piece of information but they didn't know who knew it?"

"About calyxes, perhaps? More calyxes there but anywhere except…"

"New Cambridge." Kip turned toward Malcolm. "What if…what if Albright wasn't looking for me, back at the church? Or not only me? What if he was looking for all the Calatians?"

Malcolm hissed a breath through his teeth. "They were all in the church."

"Which you'd warded." Kip stood quickly, the fatigue of the day burned away in a flash of worry, and strode toward Jackson and Lowell.

Both men turned to look at him. Lowell finished what he was saying and then tilted his head to acknowledge Kip. "Penfold, what is it?"

"Sir, the British targeted Peachtree and kidnapped the Calatians there for a reason. We know Albright can get to New Cambridge. Do we have soldiers there, anyone watching the town?"

Jackson frowned. "The college has already been raided. Why would we?"

"Please." A piece of paper fluttered between Kip's paws to the floor; he ignored it. "Let me talk to the Calatians who appeared here and then send someone to New Cambridge. It doesn't have to be me."

"What's that?" Jackson pointed to the paper.

"A message from Emily Carswell, I suppose," Kip said, keeping his eyes locked on Jackson's.

The Master Colonel exhaled. "Penfold, do you know how short of men we are? Why would I waste a unit guarding a town of no strategic importance?"

"You thought Peachtree was of no strategic importance, but the British sent men there and took it."

Jackson considered this, and Lowell chimed in. "He's right, sir. Perhaps it's worth a short time to question the Calatians and prepare a unit to be stationed there. Not a full fighting unit, but at least one that can come back and warn us if they're attacked."

"Yes, fine. Lowell, you coordinate the unit, bring it to me for approval. Now, once you'd secured the ships…"

Lowell went on with his briefing. Kip, relieved, stooped to pick up the paper and stepped back toward Malcolm. "Good job," Malcolm said.

"Penfold," Jackson called. "I'll see that message."

Kip held it out. "It says she's going to come visit us in ten minutes."

Jackson read it and handed it back. "Very well, then, you and O'Brien will remain here. I would like to have a word with Miss Carswell."

That was almost sure not to go well, but Kip had gotten the concession on New Cambridge and he didn't feel like arguing further. Emily could take that up with Jackson when she arrived.

Malcolm was of the same mind. "Good lad," he said softly when Kip returned to his side. "I've half a mind to summon Daravont again so I can watch the expressions."

Kip half-smiled. "Should we tell her when she arrives to come back later? I want to talk to those Calatians."

"Lowell's going to send someone to New Cambridge," Malcolm pointed out, "and Emily's not likely to stay longer than an hour. We can spare that."

"I could go to New Cambridge now."

Malcolm put a hand on Kip's shoulder. "You could also rest for the time it takes Emily to tell her story. We've been through a good deal already today, and we haven't eaten properly. There's no use you showing up half-dead on your feet." He paused. "And I promise those words are true, and not only because I wish to see her."

Kip exhaled. It was true, some time off his feet with a bit of food would be most welcome. "I'd like for Alice to be here."

"Once Emily arrives, you can go fetch her, and I wager she'll still be arguing with him," he inclined his head toward Jackson, "by the time you return."

Indeed, when Emily arrived, her first question was not to Kip, but to Master Colonel Jackson. Upon orienting herself and seeing Jackson open his mouth to address her, she snapped quickly, "Good day, sir. I presume you've been discussing important business with my friends, so can you tell me how much longer you'll be keeping them? I'm happy to wait but I must return soon."

She was learning something from being around diplomats, Kip could see. "I'll just go to see if Alice is done," he said. "If you'll excuse me?"

Jackson waved him irritably away, and as Kip left he heard the Master Colonel say, "If you have progress to report from Abigail Adams' delegation, you may tell me first."

"I only want to talk to my friends," Emily replied.

"And yet your story may be important…" And then the door closed behind him.

He found Alice still waiting for the healer, one paw holding the bandage over her leg. A bit of blood had soaked through, but the stain was a rusty red, not the bright glistening of fresh blood. "He's tending to a lot of the wounded from Savannah still," she said. "People who are much worse hurt. I'm fine. It barely even hurts anymore."

"Can you walk on it?" Kip asked, half-teasingly. "Emily's here."

Alice brightened. "Yes, of course. I told you it doesn't hurt." But when she got up, he noticed that she treated the hurt leg more gingerly, not quite favoring it but not completely confident in it either. He didn't say anything; Alice had earned the right to evaluate her own injury.

"You did wonderfully," he said as they walked down the hallway. She turned up to smile at him. "Both in Savannah—on the ship—and at the river. I haven't taught you many spells that would be useful in battle, but you've made the most of what you've learned, and gone beyond what I've taught you. When we have time, I want to hear about summoning the air elemental."

"Of course." They descended the staircase, slowly at first, and then faster as Alice gained confidence in her leg. "Is Colonel Jackson furious?"

"He was at first, but I think Captain Lowell and I—mostly Captain Lowell—have made him understand that something important is going on here."

"Good." Alice touched his arm to stop him before they went into the dining room. "You've done really well, too. We were captured and you got us to work together to get free. We got away from Albright and we rescued at least two Calatians from Peachtree. They might be able to tell us something."

"Probably they won't," Kip said, his ears flushing warm.

"Regardless, they're not in British prison or whatever happens to people captured in war. And you convinced Lowell to go there, and you told us how to get away from the ship. I think you're a much better leader than you let yourself believe."

"I'm not leading anyone. Captain Lowell is."

"But you're helping him, and when he's not there…" Alice snorted and shook her head, putting her ears back. "I'm trying to pay you a compliment."

"Sorry." Kip smiled. "Thank you."

"That's better. Now let's go in."

The tableau in the dining room made Kip stop just inside the door. Emily sat next to Jackson at the large table, with Lowell sitting on the end and Malcolm across from them. Nobody looked particularly happy, except for Malcolm chewing on some of the bread and cheese that had been brought in.

Kip and Alice sat and reached for the food without anyone uttering a word, though the slight smile he got as Malcolm turned his head told him that he'd missed a good argument indeed. Finally Emily broke the silence to say, "It's good to see you again, Alice. Master Colonel Jackson and I," and she enunciated the title so carefully that Kip knew for certain she'd said it incorrectly while he'd been gone, "have reached an agreement whereby he will remain in the room while I tell you the bulk of my story, and after that he will leave us five minutes to speak privately, as befits friends."

"Thank you, sir." Kip inclined his head toward Jackson and then folded a piece of bread around the soft cheese and ate. He swallowed and reached for more bread; his stomach seemed to have woken and realized that it had been hours since their small, simple breakfast.

"Very well," Emily said, looking at Kip and Malcolm and not at all toward Jackson. "As you know, we'd gone from Spain to France. While in Spain, of course, I met Victor Adamson, an old acquaintance of ours who seems to have allied himself with the British side, to nobody's surprise. And you also won't be surprised to learn that I encountered him again…"

I didn't have to go spy on anyone this time. Abigail told me that we already know quite a bit about the French fleet, so my job was to get to know the French sorcerers and feel out their sympathies.

France is a beautiful country, but it seems caught at the moment between two pasts. There are the extravagant kings who ruled up until Louis the Sixteenth, and then there was Napoleon and his sorcerer-based government. Louis the Eighteenth is on the throne right now, but he was put there by us—rather, by the British—and he seems as uncomfortable with this as everyone else is. When we were received, he was there, so it wasn't like with Spain at all. He didn't do much of the talking, but it didn't feel like he had other people speak for him. It was more like he didn't have anything to say and didn't want to interrupt the real decision-makers.

He received us in the palace of Versailles, which we were told they are working on restoring after it fell into disrepair under Napoleon. France doesn't have a lot of money and yet they are gilding statues and commissioning new works of art. Some of the sorcerers told me that people in Paris—all the cities, but Paris especially—are short of food, so it doesn't seem like things are going well there overall.

So there we were in the palace of the old kings while the actual king received us surrounded by the same kinds of ministers that Napoleon used. Abigail told me afterwards that it seemed to confuse even them, and that she wasn't surprised they didn't offer us any assistance because they could hardly all agree on who was to speak next, let alone on taking action as a unified country.

In any event, I didn't attend many of those meetings. I asked to talk to some of the French Masters at their Université de Sorcerie, which is in Paris proper—Versailles is south of the city. It took a day or two but at least the Université knows who is in charge, and when I told them I was part of the American diplomatic delegation, the Maître Premier—I suppose that's First

Master or maybe Prime Master literally, but it means Headmaster—invited me to come talk to the sorcerers.

So you see, none of this was spying like I'd done in Spain. I wasn't asking to talk to military sorcerers, and it was all above board and officially requested. I followed all of their protocols, and I even brought a translator along, a little weaselly man—I'm sorry, is that improper to say? A leering, oily man, then, who kept trying to touch me the whole time we were together. Really, Malcolm. I didn't let him, of course, but it was annoying all the same. I'd be having a perfectly fine conversation through him with a sorcerer and when he turned to give the answer, his hand would somehow find its way to my arm or waist. I always had to be on the lookout for it.

The Université is in a fortress called the Bastille Saint-Antoine that was formerly a prison until Napoleon freed the prisoners and offered it to his sorcerers. There's a quotation of his over the gates, something like, "as this fortress once protected our city so shall you now protect our land." They've made the interior much nicer than I imagine it was in its prison days, but it's still very close and cramped and smells of phosphorus elemental and raven all over.

Most of the French sorcerers are very like the British ones, absorbed in their own studies, and I don't think most of them even notice that there aren't many windows. Those I spoke to mostly wanted to ask me about British practices, and don't worry, I didn't give anything away about demons, which was what they really wanted to hear about. I told them very truthfully that I hadn't much experience at all. We talked about translocational magic a little, if they knew it, and they were very interested in calyxes, but I didn't tell them anything about that either.

No, Alice, there are no Calatians in most of Europe. Only Spain, outside of England. Most of the calyxes in the world are in the British Empire.

In any case, most of them were pleasant, but when I wouldn't tell them anything about calyxes they lost interest. One or two of the younger ones had another kind of interest and I quashed that quickly enough. There was one fellow, a Master Debroussard, who is a translocational sorcerer, and he thought it was wonderful that a woman had learned sorcery. He talked very seriously about adding women to the French Université. "If we act quickly, we may keep pace with or even pull ahead of Holland, Prussia, and Austria, and perhaps even Spain one day," he said. He was very kind and said I was welcome to appear in his office anytime I wanted to visit Paris. Apparently when translocational sorcerers who have ravens want to visit each other, they send the raven ahead to ask if the time is convenient, which is much nicer than pieces of paper, but I told him that we hadn't been confirmed as full masters yet and in fact that all of our masters had been kidnapped and were prisoners of war, and therefore we didn't have ravens. He offered to get me a raven, but it sounded like that would take a while and I said I would prefer that we win the war and then I could get one the proper way.

No, I don't think he was trying to get in my good graces like that. Trust me, there are enough of those kinds of men that I recognize when someone's being friendly. Master Debroussard was that, but he was far from the only one sympathetic to our cause. There's no love between the French and the British, but the sorcerers in the Université and in the military really hate the British. They still revere Napoleon, and the British not only defeated him, but humiliated him. So they said that if there's anything they can do to help, they would, but also they're bound to follow what their government says because the country's very weak right now and they know if they draw France into the war, it could be disastrous.

I told you I saw Victor again. He didn't get invited to the Université as far as I know. The British delegation wasn't foolish enough to go to France for assistance. I think they were mostly there to threaten them. Master Plainfield told me that the French sorcerers were no trouble at all, but that he had to warn Abigail twice about the British sorcerers trying to put a spiritual hold on her. It is war between us, I suppose.

Victor made his appearance after I returned to the court at Versailles. Not at our audience with the King and all the ministers, but one of the days when it was nice out and the palace had prepared a fancy luncheon to eat out in the gardens. I was talking to one of the French ministers and suddenly there he was, dressed in his fancy suit and wearing some kind of perfume he hadn't been wearing in Spain. He spoke to the minister in what sounded like perfect French, though I've no idea, and then said, "Good day, Miss Carswell," and left.

"He says you are a spy," the minister told me. "He says you were spying in Spain."

"That may be true," I said, "but I haven't been spying here. I was invited to go to the Université."

"Good," he said, and we resumed our luncheon with no more discussion of it.

It bothered me still, and even though Abigail reassured me that it hadn't changed the outcome of our mission, I felt as though I might be damaging our chances.

(Here Emily ignored a snort from Master Colonel Jackson.)

But Abigail said that the French ministers refused to help us at this moment for the same reason the sorcerers gave. France is in a precarious position, and should they enter on the side of the Americans and lose, Britain might take even more drastic measures than they did after defeating Napoleon. One minister told Abigail that they feared France might become a British territory, and even though we didn't think that likely, nor that it would last for long if it did happen, it feels very real to them.

So Abigail said that it wasn't anything I did, even though after that luncheon, a few of the French ministers refused to talk to me. Knowing that some of their sorcerers would help us given the chance is very valuable.

We made a point to talk with the French ministers about how we were going to visit Prussia next. They have the third strongest navy in Europe, even though it's farther than Spain's. Plainfield also had us keep that thought in our heads very strongly while we were in the presence of the British spiritual sorcerers. I think most spiritual sorcerers have to be very close to you to pick up your thoughts, but Plainfield is the expert so we listened to him. Only after we'd left Paris did Abigail tell us that we aren't going to Prussia next, but Holland. So we hope that Victor and his British friends will wait for us in Prussia while we take a quick audience with the Dutch King.

CHAPTER 10: THE BATTLE OF NEW CAMBRIDGE

As soon as Emily finished her story, she turned to Jackson. "May I have a few minutes with my friends now?"

He stared ahead, tapping the table, as though she hadn't spoken. Her voice remained polite but took on an edge. "Master Colonel Jackson?"

"I believed Calatians to be plentiful enough that we did not have to worry about them," he said in a low voice. "When we fought the French, our calyxes helped turn the tide. Now the British want that advantage back. They know we hold the upper hand on our own soil, but if they deprive us of calyxes…even a fire sorcerer won't be enough. They have Peachtree, Savannah, and some of our military calyxes already. Lowell, get a unit to go to New Cambridge immediately."

"We can go." Kip stood.

Emily and Malcolm stood too, Alice a moment later. "I know the town," Emily said. "I can take Captain Lowell and Malcolm."

"I'm going too," Alice said indignantly.

"You're injured—"

She cut off Captain Lowell. "That doesn't change my ability to cast spells, and it's my hometown. My parents are there."

"We'd have to find another sorcerer. You should remain—yes, Penfold?"

The fox shook his head. "We're all of us tired. Alice makes her own choices, and if she says she's capable then I believe her, and what's more, I would want her with us if I were you." He hesitated. "We could do the calyx ritual for Emily."

"I will," Emily said, "but I'd greatly prefer not to."

"Sir," Malcolm said. "I'll stand aside for Miss Cartwright. I've no family there, and besides, if there is an attack, her skills will be more useful than mine."

"Penfold must remain warded," Jackson said. "Master Albright knows him."

"I'll stay by his side," Emily promised. "I'll bring him back here at the first sign of trouble."

"And I can ward this place to allow Em to come back." Malcolm smiled at her.

"Fine." Jackson waved a hand. "Go now, and Miss Carswell, if the situation is beyond the four of you, come back immediately."

They had not changed their clothes since returning from Savannah—had all of this happened in a single day? The weariness Kip had felt while listening to Emily's story vanished as they received these instructions from Jackson.

"The church?" Kip asked Emily. "Out in front, I'd say."

"Inside would let us proceed more cautiously if there is an attack."

"Inside the doors, then." Captain Lowell and Alice moved to stand on either side of Emily. "Let's go."

Kip closed his eyes, envisioning the smell and feel of the large church doors. He reached out with magic and in a moment he was there. Emily, with Alice and Captain Lowell, stood beside him. He motioned them to silence as he and Alice strained their ears to listen for noise outside the church. While they did, Captain Lowell crept to the nearest window he could find and looked out.

No noises came to Kip, and when his eyes met Alice's she shook her head slightly. "We don't hear anything," he said.

"I don't see anything."

"But that's unusual," Kip said. "There should be people, activity. Even in the evening after sunset. There's nobody in the street?" He put his nose to the crack of the door, but all he smelled was the New Cambridge night: no gunpowder or blood, no smells of battle.

Emily gestured Captain Lowell closer and kept hold of both him and Alice. Kip cracked the church door open and peered out onto an empty street. He set his ear to the crack and still no sound came—no, wait. There was a faint sobbing sound.

"I hear something," he whispered, and pulled the door open to step out into the street.

With the church behind him and the Founder's Rest Inn off to his left, the empty White Tower (not entirely empty) a dark silhouette on the hill behind the Inn, this could be any night in New Cambridge except for the eerie stillness. He considered the Inn; Old John might be there, but the faint sobbing came from the opposite direction, toward the town.

Alice heard it now too and pointed that way. Kip nodded and confirmed his decision with Captain Lowell before they set off, the soldier and Emily following the foxes.

They walked along Half-Moon Street past empty shops, some with doors open, and as the sobbing grew clearer, so did the murmur of voices. They hurried forward along the road, the others trailing them, until they rounded the corner of the street to the square in front of the town hall.

There the human inhabitants of New Cambridge sat, knelt, or lay, while a few walked around ministering. Father Gregory, the short, stout preacher, was one of those on his feet and the first to spot Kip and Alice. His broad face broke into a relieved smile as he hurried over to them, putting a hand to the bandage across his scalp.

"Kip! Alice! How did you get here so soon? Robert left not twenty minutes ago."

"Robert?" Kip shook his head. "We came from Boston by magic. We haven't seen Robert. What happened here?"

"The British." Father Gregory's face turned grim. "Four sorcerers and maybe a half-dozen soldiers. They rounded up everyone and—"

"My parents?" Alice broke in.

"Nobody was harmed. The soldiers drove all the Calatians up the hill and left us behind here."

"Up the hill…" Kip's eyes turned to the White Tower. "If they were doing what they did on the boats, we could still save them."

Emily met his eyes. "The roof?"

"The roof. Alice, summon an air elemental and have your physical magic ready."

Alice closed her eyes, and a moment later, her paws glowed turquoise. Captain Lowell surveyed them. "We'll appear in a hidden spot?"

"The roof is out of sight if nobody's looking up," Kip said evasively, not wanting to reveal Peter's presence to Lowell. Peter's journal had had an inattention ward cast on it—he hadn't understood what it was at the time, but he did now—so he presumed that Peter could protect them in that way.

"All right. Let's assess the situation before taking action. But Penfold, if there are translocational sorcerers, you should be prepared to kill them this time. If they have any warning then they'll escape again."

Left unspoken was the truth that some of these might be the ones Kip had let escape on the boat. He summoned magic and brought fire, which was always waiting, to the forefront of his mind.

A moment later, they appeared on the roof, empty save for a pair of robins that flew away quickly as the four of them appeared. Kip perked his ears, but the movement and sharply barked orders from below were loud enough to be audible to all of them. *Peter,* he asked quickly, one paw to the stone, *can you protect us with an inattention ward here?*

A moment, and then: *Hello, Kip. Yes, that is easily done. Is something happening outside?*

Kip didn't feel any change, but he trusted Peter. *Kidnapping,* he said. *We hope to stop it.* He followed his friends to the edge of the roof and peered over.

The New Cantabrigian Calatians stood huddled in a circle, not all the town by any means, but about half of them: Kip recognized Alice's family and the Morgans at a quick glance. A moment later, it became clear what was happening: four soldiers kept guns trained on the Calatians, while two pushed a group of eight toward the waiting four sorcerers, who reached out to touch them just as the sorcerers on the boats had done before translocating those Calatians away.

This group of eight included the six Lapellis. Even at this distance, Kip recognized Bess Lapelli, an infant rabbit in her arms and two more young pups clinging to her skirt. Ahead of her, Johnny coaxed his younger sister forward.

"Move it along," a soldier said behind Bess, and Johnny turned in time to see his mother receive a hard thump from the soldier's rifle stock.

"Leave her alone!" he cried, and ran for the soldier.

Had he been a little closer, he might have closed the distance. As it was, the surprised soldier still had time to shoulder his rifle and shoot.

The loud retort that made everyone jump, including Kip and Alice. Johnny staggered back a step and then fell to the ground. His sister screamed, and the younger rabbits picked up the noise. Three sorcerers stepped up and translocated them all, leaving a hushed silence behind the screams.

Johnny twitched and clutched at his shoulder. One of the sorcerers stared down at him and then said something to the soldier, too quiet to hear. The soldier raised his rifle.

"Kill them now," Lowell said quickly.

The crack of the soldier's rifle sounded even as fire surged in Kip and he let it loose. He knew full well what he was doing, considering the lives he was saving as well as the lives he was too late to save. Letting a sorcerer escape meant they would keep threatening Calatians, again and again, and there was only one way to put that to a stop. With a thought, he reached out and became destruction, and the fire sang to him as it did his bidding.

The soldier and all four sorcerers erupted in flames, without time even to voice a cry before their bodies were consumed and charred to ash. The Calatians cried out and ran, and even the unburnt soldiers stepped back, but as they did they were lifted from the ground. The closest one to them clutched his throat and dropped his rifle.

"Stop fighting me," Alice said aloud.

"Sorry," Emily replied. "I didn't know if you could handle all of them."

One of the other soldiers, floating in the air, nonetheless attempted to sight along his gun, but a moment later he too clutched at his throat and his rifle fell, where Bryce Morgan picked it up.

Captain Lowell stepped to the edge of the roof and called in a loud, clear voice, "British soldiers! Drop your weapons immediately."

The four soldiers still holding onto their rifles dropped them and raised their hands. The other, recovering his breath, raised his hands as well.

Captain Lowell turned to the sorcerers with some satisfaction. "Can one of you convey us to the ground?"

Emily did the honors, though Alice said she could also manage it. Kip could easily have done it as well, but his attention remained on the crowd of Calatians, as much to search for familiar faces as to avoid looking at the five charred bodies that reminded him of the joy and power in the fire, how easily it had burned his enemies, how gleefully it had sung to him as it had. No wonder such power was forbidden by the rules of war (was he now a war criminal, or were they all war criminals for being party to his action?). The Calatians made a wide berth around the charred bodies, staying upwind of them, but Kip stood close and forced himself to witness what he'd done. This is part of the complicated balance of power, he told himself. The joy in being able to wield it, the ability to change the course of events for the better, and then the consequences.

He stopped at the body of Johnny Lapelli, staring sightlessly at the sky. The soldier's second shot had pierced his heart; he had likely died instantly. Looking from him back to the blackened, smoking bodies, Kip reminded himself: You did this because you made the choice to do it. It was the correct choice, and you would do it again.

At the same time, he understood more viscerally than ever Cott's dogmatic insistence on control. Letting fire loose on people could become far too easy if he allowed it. Cott, too, must have been called on to burn people during the war, and had seen in himself that same precipice Kip faced now. Cott had chosen to turn his back on the danger, but Kip still fought in a war and did not have that option yet. He would have to watch himself carefully. This time, he repeated to himself, he had done the right thing.

Captain Lowell took command of the British soldiers when they landed, distributing the rifles to three Calatians who came forward to help: Thomas Cartwright, Tom Cooper the squirrel, and Carrow Roseward the polecat, and allowing Bryce Morgan to keep his. Thomas, ears back, could not keep his eyes off his daughter as she spoke to the air with a smile and then ran forward to hug him.

"I'm so glad you're safe," she said.

"Thanks to your friends here." Thomas met Kip's eyes and gave a short nod.

"Thanks to Alice, too." Kip pointed to the soldiers. "That was her."

"What about the fire?" one of the soldiers demanded. "You burned 'em up, you ain't allowed to do that."

"I don't know what you're talking about," Captain Lowell said. "We arrived here having been warned of your sneak attack on this peaceful town just in time to see the sorcerers consumed by some kind of natural flame. Miss Cartwright, Miss Carswell, and Mister Penfold incapacitated you and brought us down here to take charge of your prisoners and return them to their homes."

"It were magical fire," the soldier insisted.

Captain Lowell stepped close to him and spoke in a low voice. "It was a natural phenomenon," he said pleasantly, "and should you continue to insist otherwise, you might attract the attention of the same natural phenomenon. Or we might, perhaps, as your sorcerers have done, erase your mind and use your body to send a message. Are your sorcerers 'allowed' to do that?"

The soldier glared at him but kept his mouth shut. Kip wanted to thank Lowell for remembering the unfortunate fox from Savannah, but the captain had enemy soldiers to contend with. Besides, Kip still shook with magical energy and the aftermath of the surge of fire, so he distracted himself by speaking to Thomas instead. "Do you know where they were meaning to send you?"

The fox shook his head. "They told us only to come up here and then they started disappearing us. Kip..." He put a paw on Kip's shoulder. "Johnny Lapelli...Matthew Porter..."

"Matthew Porter?" Josiah's father, one of the older residents of the town.

"He fell, couldn't walk...so they shot him."

Captain Lowell, listening, turned to the British soldiers. "There. Do you lot really want to talk about what you are and aren't allowed to do in war?" He gave Kip a long look of approval.

Kip returned the look with a grateful smile. "You're safe now," he assured Thomas. "And you have your daughter to thank."

"All of you," Thomas said, and turned his ears back toward the crowd, milling about and murmuring now. "Can we go back to the town?"

"I don't think that's advisable," Captain Lowell said.

"Why not stay in the Tower for now?" Kip suggested. "There should be plenty of room, and it will be easy for us to ward the Tower against future attacks." Now that they knew they were at war, Peter could keep his inattention ward active to protect those inside until an army sorcerer could be spared.

Bryce Morgan stepped forward. "I will talk to the town. For a short time, we can stay in the Tower, if someone will bring us food."

Captain Lowell said, "For as long as we need to keep you safe—"

"Excuse me," Kip said, "but I believe Old John can find someone to bring you food. I will go talk to him." He didn't want the Calatians to hear that the war would likely drag on for months, if not longer, and that they might need to live in the Tower indefinitely.

Lowell took his meaning, though his expression showed he didn't like it. "Very well. Let's move everyone into the Tower."

Emily and Alice helped, and Emily went to fetch a warding specialist to keep the Tower protected. Kip meant to set off down the hill, but Thomas pulled him aside.

"Thank you for saving us," he said in a low voice. "I have to tell you something."

"Oh…" Kip flicked his tail and looked toward Alice. "We can talk about it later."

"No, it's important." The fox lowered his voice still further. "There was a Calatian with the soldiers, one I'd never seen before. He knew everyone in the town and helped round us up."

"Who?" The crowd of townspeople walked toward the Tower. If there was a traitor among them…

"He left when we got to the hill. Another sorcerer came and got him. But he knew some sorcery, Kip. He pulled people out of their houses with spells."

Another Calatian who knew sorcery? Kip's heart pounded and then he realized who it must have been. "Was he a marmot?"

"Yes." Thomas's ears stood up. "You know him?"

"Yes, and so do you. It's Farley Broadside."

When the Calatians were safely in the Tower and Old John had agreed to send food up their way, Kip walked around to a deserted side of the Tower and laid his paw on the stone. *Peter*, he called. *I know we are under attack, but nobody who is attacking knows your name. They cannot reach you. We are strengthening your protection with wards.*

There was no answer. Kip exhaled. *I'm entrusting our people to you. You don't have to answer me, but watch over them. Keep them safe as you did me.*

He waited, and just when he was about to give up and walk away, a distant voice echoed in his head. *I will do my best.*

That's all I ask.

Emily had translocated the prisoners at Captain Lowell's request, and him along with them, so it was only her and Alice left to watch Kip walk across the lawn of the College in what little light filtered down from the moon and stars through the cloud cover. "You're thinking about something," Emily said.

Kip nodded. "They attack us here, kidnapping our people. What if we tried to help our people in their country escape? Can you take me to the Isle of Dogs?"

"Kip." Alice put a paw on his arm.

"Sorry, yes. Both of us. If you'll come."

"That's not what I mean. You haven't permission to go."

"I had permission to come here. This is part of that same mission, ensuring the safety of the Calatians for the American Army."

Alice set her paws on her hips. "You've been captured, fought in four different battles if you include our escape, and you were up before the sun this morning. Don't you think you'd best ask Master Colonel Jackson first? Put this off until tomorrow?"

"Tomorrow and tomorrow and tomorrow," Kip quoted. "I have seen enough death. One more day gives them time to do more harm. How long did it take to convince Jackson to send me here? How long will it take to convince him to send me to London, to the heart of enemy territory? How many Calatians will die in that time?"

Both Alice and Emily stood silent, the latter's face in shadow, the former's eyes glowing with reflected light. "Besides," Kip said, "I won't undertake any mission involving the Isle without getting their consent. And without that, there's no point in asking."

"All right," Alice said. "I'll go with you."

"Of course I'll take you," Emily said. "But how will you get back?"

"If I'm sending us home, where I don't have to worry about what's waiting for us, I can send us one at a time. I don't know what we'll encounter at the Isle and we might need to come back immediately." Kip turned to the vixen. "Does your family have plain clothes at your house?"

Alice nodded. "All right," he said. "There first, then London." He turned to the sky. "It'll be much later there. I'd like to get in before the sun's up."

They achieved that goal, though only by an hour or so. Emily had never been to the Isle, and the College itself was warded, but she had been to several other locations in London and one of them proved to work, a public square littered with bird and horse droppings and fouler smells, but empty of people at this time of night—morning, Kip supposed.

"We can make our way from here," he said softly to Emily. "Thank you."

"You can get past the wards?"

"People have to go in and out," he said. "Calatians go out to do work. We'll find a way."

"I'll come with you as far as the Isle." Emily yawned. "I suppose I can sleep when I get back to Abigail's."

She'd taken a hooded cloak from New Cambridge and now pulled the hood over her head as she followed the two Calatians. They kept to the shadows as best they could, especially when other people passed them in the street. At this hour, most people seemed alert for trouble of their own, and two Calatians with a third hooded figure were not the kind of trouble they were looking for, so the trio made their way unmolested. "Kip," Alice whispered at one point, "what did you mean when you said, 'keeping the Calatians safe for the American Army'?"

"Shh," he said automatically, though she'd spoken low and this narrow street was deserted. He was looking forward to seeing Abel again, and it took him a moment to parse her question and respond to it. "Only that Jackson's concern for us was because of calyxes. He treats calyxes like guns, or ammunition, I suppose. Not like people." A soft snort from behind him signaled Emily's agreement.

"He doesn't seem to treat people all that well either," Alice said. "So what do we do?"

"Now that I understand him, I can propose a strategy that he'll agree to. That's the way to get in with these people. You have to understand them and then figure out how to make the thing you want attractive to them."

"So we have to make him want to save the Calatians. How?" Alice asked.

"We'll steal some ammunition," Kip said.

They rounded a corner into a narrow alley, at the end of which they could see the bridge. Of plain stone construction, it had only knee-high blocks of stone to keep people from falling into the Thames. Upon each of the two stones nearest to Kip and Alice, a British soldier sat cradling his rifle.

Alice's nostrils flared, taking in the rank smell of the soldiers and the waste floating in the Thames River around the Isle. "We could go through the water." She held her paws around her head. "I could summon another air elemental."

"That might work." Kip looked out at the growing light in the sky over the crude cottages on the isle, a few of which now had smoke trickling from their chimneys. "If we slipped in upriver and swam down, we could surface in the shadow of the bridge there," he pointed, "behind the soldiers. If we're quiet, then with any luck we'll be in the Isle. Then we can find Abel."

"I don't think that would be so hard for you."

Kip shook his head. "The hard part will be talking him and the others into a plan."

"You have a plan?"

He grimaced. "No. But let's get in first."

Emily put a hand on Kip's shoulder. "And this is where I leave you," she said. "I'll wait here for a few minutes, but I draw the line at swimming in filth. Wave from the water if you need me."

"I hope we won't." Kip clasped her hand. "Thank you for all your help. Good luck on your next mission."

They made their way away from the smell of the Thames, through dark alleys, until Kip judged that they were far enough upriver to steal down to the bank. "What if the Isle is warded and the elemental can't move with us?" Alice asked.

"We'll surface quickly." He took her paw. "I'm not worried."

The neighborhood they stopped in smelled strongly of furnaces and forges, and now activity stirred near them, the clink of coal and the hiss of bellows, the dragging of heavy sacks back and forth. Kip and Alice hurried to the riverbank and down a muddy slope to the water.

"It's cold," she complained as she put her feet in it.

"It'll keep us awake." Kip looked around. Two boats floated nearby, only one moving, and while there were people around them, none watched that he could tell. He stood between Alice and the shore. "Face me," he said, "and keep your paws close between us as you cast the spell." It wasn't out of the question that someone on one of the boats or on the shore might know what colorful glows around the arms of a shadowy figure meant.

Alice breathed the words of the spell and the glow faded. A moment later, Kip heard the whispers of almost-words around his ears and the air acquired a different scent, cleaner and warmer than the refuse-tainted air on the Thames. Alice said a few words Kip didn't understand and then said, "All right, we can go in."

Water soaked his clothes as he waded into the river. "Are you sure?" he said, and Alice, by way of response, ducked her head underwater. So Kip followed suit, diving into the river, and found that the chilly, foul-smelling water kept its distance from him as it had in Savannah that morning. The Thames was considerably colder, and where the river mouth in Savannah had been murky and silty, this dark water held all the detritus of London: twisted bits of metal, some small and wiry enough to float; rags and bones and, half-poking out of a rotted burlap sack, the corpse of a dog.

The trick was to keep as close to the shore as they could while staying underwater so they wouldn't be spotted. They couldn't see far enough ahead to navigate properly, and it wasn't like in Savannah where it didn't matter where on the opposite bank they landed. If they missed the Isle, they would go on down the river into the English Channel and eventually they would hit Amsterdam, where at least, he supposed, Emily would be able to send them back.

A large shape loomed ahead of them; Kip tugged Alice to the left, toward the shore, as the current tried to carry them into the open water. They bumped up against old stone and felt their way along until they came to the small channel that ran between the Isle and the river bank. Here the current ran faster, so Kip held onto a jutting rock and cast a quick spell to lift himself and Alice from the water.

Keeping his back to the Isle, he strained to hold them steady in the current as they rose. When their heads broke the surface, he stopped and looked about. The sky had lightened considerably, and people moved about on the bank, but none of them looked toward the Isle, and the soldiers continued to stare outward at the city. Kip moved the two of them into the shadow of the bridge and then said, "I'm going to move us quickly into the gates. Ready?"

Alice nodded. He pushed on the spell; the two foxes rose dripping from the water, cleared the side of the bridge, and slid through the gates and along until they were concealed by the stone walls that flanked the gate.

Kip collapsed to the ground and dismissed the spell. The effort of swimming had drained him more than he'd thought. Pushing against fatigue, he managed to struggle to his feet.

Alice tugged on his wet sleeve. To their right, an otter stared at the two of them. "Strewth," he said in a voice that reminded Kip of Coppy.

"Good morning," Kip said. "I wonder if you could take us to Abel."

"Abel?"

"The fox?"

"Aye, aye." The otter scratched his head. "Ah, is he, are you expected?"

Kip smiled thinly. "I greatly doubt it."

The otter looked back at the street he'd come down, then took one uncertain step toward them. "Aye, I—yes, he's down this way."

Alice and Kip followed the otter to Abel's small wooden cottage where the fox lived with his two cubs. They knocked on the door, and when Abel opened it, the otter interposed himself between Kip and the other fox. "These foxes, Abel, they floated right in on magic and then asked to see you. Is it all right, that?"

Seeing his friend brought a rush of relief to Kip, and Abel's muzzle too broke into a broad smile. "It's more than all right, Belzer. Kip, come in, and Alice too? Let's get you out of those wet things. I'll get a fire going."

CHAPTER 11: THE ISLE OF DOGS

A bel gave them a blanket to cover themselves while their clothes dried over the fire. The warmth so relaxed Kip that he found himself dozing off in the middle of trying to explain to Abel what had happened that day. Alice had already fallen asleep slumped against Kip, so Abel told them to sleep as long as they needed.

Kip awoke to the smell of beans frying in lard, and his stomach clenched. When was the last time he'd eaten? The bread and cheese while listening to Emily's story?

"Good morning," Abel said cheerfully, holding a long-handled skillet over his fire. "I decided that as long as we were using our firewood, we should cook something."

"Is there enough for all of us?" Kip glanced toward Alice, still asleep but now curled up on the floor.

"I should hope so. I'm cooking for the whole street. This is my third batch. Aran and Arabella are taking some around to the others." He gestured to a small stack of wooden bowls. "Take one and please, take as much as you like."

Kip stifled a yawn and stood, keeping the blanket wrapped around his shoulders. Mindful that he was eating from a communal meal, he took about half of what his stomach wanted, but he knew that it would suffice and that he would be back at the Trade House for a proper meal soon enough. The thought made him fold his ears back with guilt. "I wish I'd thought to bring you food. Are they starving you?"

"No more than usual. And bringing yourself is a pleasant enough treat, as is your lovely fiancée. I suspect you bear news of a more serious nature, however."

Kip nodded. The beans, piping hot, warmed his stomach. His fur remained damp from the river and probably smellier than he thought with his nose growing accustomed to the odor, but at least he was no longer sopping wet. "Are you kept prisoner here?" he asked.

Abel inclined his head. "That rather depends on your definition of the word. We are not forbidden to leave. At the same time, when we do leave, the soldiers at the gate bombard us with questions. Where are we going? For how long? Is our errand of vital importance? We are given wooden tokens and must surrender them or risk being shut out of our home. That is enough to keep most of us here unless we have important business outside. And of course, when the sorcerers come to use us, they take us through the air. We can still load the rope and other goods we make onto barges, but now they come directly to the Isle rather than one of the docks."

"They're so worried that you might flee?"

"During the Napoleonic war, French sorcerers twice tried to steal Calatians from the Isle, at least once with the help of some of the people here." His gaze drifted beyond Kip for a moment. "Neither attempt succeeded—obviously—but they have not been forgotten."

Kip wanted to wait until Alice awoke, so rather than launch into his idea, he scraped another spoonful of beans from the bowl. "These are delicious."

"That tells me that you've not eaten much today." Aran and Arabella came back at that moment with several bowls. Kip finished his beans while Abel portioned out what was left.

When the cubs had run off with their full bowls, Abel sat cross-legged next to Kip in front of the fire and folded his paws together in his lap. "Tell me," he said.

So Kip told him about Savannah, the battle and his capture, and the British attacks on Peachtree and New Cambridge. He left out any sensitive information about American army movements, saying only that his commanding officer thought the British were trying to deprive the Americans of calyxes.

By the time he'd finished, Alice had woken and Abel had given her a bowl of beans. She devoured them as Kip concluded the story of New Cambridge.

The other fox nodded and put a paw to his chin. "They have learned that from the war with the French, perhaps. And you have come here hoping to succeed where the French failed."

"But with your full knowledge and consent," Kip said.

"Of course." Abel rubbed the tips of his fingers together, and the stump of his tail wiggled. "The war has already been hard on us. Edward Pole fainted upon his return two days ago and has not risen from his bed since, and he is the second to suffer that fate. More are sure to follow, wounded if not killed. If we could escape... How do you propose to do this?"

"I thought that perhaps we could bring sorcerers and translocate you?"

Abel nodded. "That was the French plan. We are so close to the College that magical activity is more easily spotted here, and I believe there are magical protections."

Kip considered that. "Do you think you could get a large group away from the Isle?"

"Perhaps. There is one barge captain who is more sympathetic to us than most. He could be persuaded with coin, and many of us could hide in his hold from here to the countryside above London. The calyxes, at least."

"How many is that?"

"Sixty. Plus another hundred, with their families, for they should not be made to go alone. However..." Abel held up a finger. "We have not the coin here to bribe the captain. That, and an assurance from the Americans that we will not be prisoners, would have to come before we could make a move."

"If we can procure those," Alice asked, "do you think you can convince the calyxes to come?"

Abel favored her with a smile. "For my part, the reasoning is easy, but what am I to tell them? What have the Americans to offer that is worth leaving our home? Keep in mind that if this venture succeeds, we may be forever barred from returning. And if it fails..." He smiled tightly, without humor. "There will be punishment."

"Land," Kip said. "You've visited me in New Cambridge. You've seen what is possible for Calatians in the New World. There is room for all, and the Americans have promised to treat Calatians better than the British do here."

"It's true," Alice put in. "And to prove it, the Americans are here asking for your help while the British merely captured our friends and families."

"And..." Kip took a breath. "We Calatians will be taking action to determine our own destiny."

The other fox inclined his head. "I have one last question, then. There are over a thousand Calatians here on the Isle, nearly fifteen hundred. Taking a hundred of them—knowing as you do the role of calyxes—what is to prevent the sorcerers of the College from selecting other calyxes from those left behind? Here on the Isle, the role of the calyx is no great secret, save from the cubs."

"Or," Alice said, "couldn't they just...take Calatians and use them up?"

The Calatian blood used by sorcerers could come from anyone, of course. The British seemed bent on capturing only the towns of Calatians that included calyxes, but of course they had also captured the Calatians in Savannah. As far as Kip knew, though, the two other largest neighborhoods, in New York and Boston, remained in American hands. "I don't know," he admitted.

"They could just drain us of blood," Abel said, "but thus far they have only done so accidentally. The Church has designated us as people, and therefore the sorcerers have shown us some courtesy—the bare minimum, but some."

"But if some of you escape?"

"I think all of us would have to escape before they would be pushed to breach that courtesy."

Kip rubbed his whiskers. "I know that taking a hundred Calatians would not cripple the British sorcerers, but it would at least inconvenience them. Besides which, the blow of having their calyxes stolen out from under their noses would hurt their pride and confidence, I hope. It did us, when they took Peachtree, and when they attacked New Cambridge. And last, we hope that you may be able to tell us something about their practices that could be useful to us."

"Strike them as they struck you." Abel nodded. "I can make that argument. Only those who are discontent need come along."

"The Isle is too crowded anyway," Kip said, trying to keep his tail from wagging with relief that Abel approved of his plan. This fox, after all, knew the British calyxes better than Kip ever could, and if he thought the idea was flawed then there would be no point in Kip bringing it to Colonel Jackson. "How are the others? Pierce and the Cotton brothers and the dormouse?"

"We all continue on in whatever way we can." Abel paused. "And Grinda, too."

Alice's ears perked up. "She's the wolf?" she asked Kip.

He nodded. "She distrusts sorcerers more than she trusts Calatians."

"Not without reason," Abel said mildly. "There have been many Calatians who threw their lot in with the sorcerers. One of the French plots was foiled by a fellow Calatian, in fact. This is why our little group comprises only a half-dozen and not all sixty calyxes. I can not even promise you that most will go, although they are more discontented now than a year ago."

"If all of you do not come," Kip said grimly, "it will go harder for those who remain."

Abel nodded. "That may be enough to convince them—or to stop the entire enterprise. I will do the best I can, because I believe we will be better off if it succeeds, and I trust you to see it through."

He held a paw out, and Kip clasped it. "Thank you," he said. "Thank you. I would not dare to attempt something like this if it were not led by someone I trust so greatly."

Abel's paw, warm and reassuring, squeezed his. Kip didn't want to let go, and it seemed Abel did not either, because they held each other's paw for several long seconds.

Aran and Arabella returned while they were making plans to continue meeting, and so Alice got to meet them formally, kneeling down to hug them both. "Take good care," she said, and they hugged her back, wagging their tails.

"We are at war," Kip said to Abel, "so make sure to take extra caution. You don't know which of your friends might betray you to the sorcerers."

"I am as sure of my friends as I can be, and we will keep the particulars from the others until the last moment." Abel set a paw on Kip's shoulder. "Be careful as well. You may be part of the American army, but you are still a Calatian."

"I know. I have good friends around me, and it does my heart good to know that you and I work toward the same goal." He put an arm around Alice's shoulders.

"It was lovely to see you again," Alice said.

"And you, Miss Cartwright." Abel bowed to her. "Take care, the two of you."

The wards on the Trade House were still set to allow Kip to translocate in, so he sent Alice first and then himself. When he appeared, Captain Lowell was sitting up in his dressing-gown, rubbing his eyes. "Penfold," the man said, and shot to his feet. "Where the devil have you been? We went back to New Cambridge and you weren't there. Master Colonel Jackson says he's going to take your magic, so you'd best have a good argument ready."

"Would he do that?" Alice asked.

"He has. In the Napoleonic War, there was a man who had his magic taken. He deserted again and Master Colonel Jackson had him executed."

"Executed?" Kip flattened his ears as Malcolm stirred and sat up, turning his head back and forth to focus in on sounds.

"War is not a pleasant business," Lowell said.

Alice's eyes were wide and ears as flat as Kip's, but at his gaze she shook her head, assumed a stern expression, and mouthed a mimicry of Lowell's words: *War is not a pleasant business.* The humor settled Kip and gave his tail a little wag.

He went through the broad strokes of their plan quickly. "So," he concluded, "if my friend can bribe the barge captain and get the Calatians on board, they should have several hours before their absence is noticed, perhaps a whole night."

"And then how many translocational sorcerers would it take?"

"For a hundred and sixty Calatians? I don't know. How many translocations can one sorcerer do before getting tired? The British had four for the village of New Cambridge. We might need only half that many."

"Two." Lowell rubbed his chin. "It could be done, yes. There is risk."

"There was risk in the British attack on New Cambridge. They lost four translocational sorcerers." Kip said the words with equal parts pride and revulsion, and a measure of worry that the memory did not bother him as much as the memory of killing the soldier at the battle of Boston Harbor. "But they lost nobody and captured the entire town of Peachtree."

Lowell nodded. "I am not Master Colonel Jackson, nor yet General Hamilton, but the plan seems sound to me. Do you propose to take it to them?"

"I wondered if perhaps you might accompany me," Kip said. "Master Colonel Jackson's latest impressions of me are not the best, and I would prefer that his reaction to this plan not be influenced by them."

The captain frowned. "I will accompany you if you so desire." He stood. "In the morning. Good night, you three."

Despite Lowell's dismissal of his worries, Kip felt they had been well founded. Jackson's first move upon seeing Kip was to advance on him, and without Lowell interposing himself, Kip felt sure he would have lost his magic. Lowell entreated the Master Colonel to hear Kip out, and with visible effort, Jackson restrained his anger and sat to listen.

As Kip presented the plan, Jackson directed all his questions to Lowell, even when the captain deferred them immediately to Kip. "It is an interesting thought," the Master Colonel said when Kip finished, and the fox was relieved to see that he no longer seemed to be in danger of losing his magic. "I will consult with General Hamilton and decide our best course of action."

"Sir," Lowell said. "You have said many times that we are at a disadvantage because the British have brought the fight to our shores, that they may strike at our lines of supply and our homes."

"We have that advantage," Jackson corrected him, "that our supplies are close to our troops, where they must bring them across the water. We have the advantage of desperation, because our homes are threatened. The British fight for possessions; we fight for our very lives."

"Yes, sir," Lowell said.

Jackson turned to the window and stared out at the Boston street, cobblestones glistening in the spring morning. "And yet, it would be quite the coup to strike at England on her own soil. She might reconsider this war if we could demonstrate that we could hurt her where she thinks herself safest."

"And," Kip said, "we could strike at the resource they seem to value: their calyxes."

"Yes." The Master Colonel stroked his beard. Though they had sought him out first thing in the morning, he wore his uniform, immaculately pressed, and he'd already trimmed his beard and washed, to judge from his smell. It made Kip acutely aware that he hadn't had a chance to wash or brush out his fur for days and that he still smelled of the Thames.

After another moment's pondering, not looking at either of them, Jackson said, "I suppose this idea presents enough interest that I shall discuss it with General Hamilton. He and I may be able to put enough particulars around it to make it tenable."

And that was the end of the interview. Kip and Lowell returned to their room, where Kip said, "Tenable? Tenable? We outlined the whole plan. What more does he need?"

"It may be that our plan does not fit with the American overall strategy," Lowell said. "Master Colonel Jackson has information we do not."

"It may be." Kip stalked to the window. "It may be also that he wants to take credit for our idea."

"Your idea," Captain Lowell reminded him.

"My idea." Kip sighed and paced back and forth. "I suppose if we have to wait, I'll go wash."

They waited for two days before hearing from Master Colonel Jackson, during which time they did not hear from Emily either. At least they were not confined to quarters, so they could go out (as long as they went as a group, warded by Malcolm) and see the town of Boston. Kip fretted, because he'd told Abel he would meet him again soon, and he didn't want to go back without news.

But in the afternoon of the second day, they were summoned to the first floor, where Master Colonel Jackson received them in his office. "I have consulted at length with General Hamilton," Jackson began. "We have determined that there is indeed some merit in your plan, but we have changed certain aspects of it to render it strategically more valuable."

Kip drew in a breath. "What aspects?"

Kip arrived at the plaza at what must have been four in the morning, London time. Only one other figure occupied the small open space, a fox with a stub for a tail who rose to meet him as soon as he arrived. They embraced, and Abel's smile set Kip's tail wagging. "Good news, I take it?"

Abel nodded. "Mostly. Nearly all the calyxes have agreed to come along. Grinda has not yet, but I hold out hope that we can convince her."

"She hasn't because of me, right?" When Abel nodded, slowly, Kip sighed. "Then this news won't help convince her."

"What news?"

Kip sat down on the stoop Abel had occupied, and the other fox sat next to him. "We took the plan to our superiors, and they changed it."

Abel leaned back. "How?"

"They said we would need too many translocational sorcerers. Two to transport all of you, and two to be standing by on alert in case of trouble to transport all of us back. We don't have that many to spare, it seems. They may be more conscious of the risk since I killed four British translocational sorcerers two days ago. At any rate, he doesn't want to risk more than one, and that means they want you to take the barge a little farther."

The other fox's brow lowered and his ears flattened out. "How much farther?"

"To Bristol. Well, Lechlade, just short of—"

Abel cut him off. "To the *Road*?"

Kip nodded, his own ears folded back. "They want to meet you along the Road, pick you up in an American vessel in the middle of the ocean."

"That would take days. How is this a better plan? How are we to stay safe, a hundred and fifty Calatians moving through England as traitors?"

"That's the only good part of all this." Kip put a paw on Abel's. "They want me to be one of the sorcerers who goes with you."

Abel's ears came up. "That's something, at least. But I don't understand how drawing this plan out for two extra days makes it more likely to succeed."

"It doesn't. It makes us less likely to suffer a crippling loss. But look: from Lechlade to the Road I can carry you, or between Alice and I we can. So we needn't stick to roads, and we needn't enter the Road at Eastgate. We can find a beach to the south and go out to sea, meet the Road a little bit offshore."

"That will help," Abel admitted. "I still don't like it."

"I'll keep you as safe as I can, and Malcolm will be with us to keep us hidden and warded. Alice will use air elementals to navigate and bring the Americans to the Road at exactly the right place. British ships patrol it, but Malcolm can hide our group from view." When Abel didn't speak, Kip said, "I don't fully understand what lies behind these changes either, and if any other sorcerer were entrusted with this mission, I could not recommend going through with it. But you know I will protect you to the best of my ability."

Abel nodded. "Your ability is the least of my worries in all of this. What if we are discovered on the barge? What if we are seen on the way to the Road? What if a British ship spots us on the Road, or intercepts our ship on the way to America?" He met Kip's eyes. "What if the Americans treat us as badly as the British?"

"At the worst, if you are captured," Kip said, "the British value your lives."

"Execution would fall to me and the other leaders. Well...that risk we can decide to take."

Kip didn't let his mind linger on that. "As for the Americans, that is also on my mind. I can only tell you what I have seen, which is that Calatians are treated better in America than in England. At least, better than on the Isle of Dogs."

"So have I also heard. And yet, so attached are we to our home that without the pressure of this war, I doubt more than twenty would come with me."

"And also," Kip said, "In America, Calatians may become sorcerers, as you know. Here that does not seem to be the case yet."

"No." Abel rubbed his eyes. "Alastair Cotton, cousin to the Cottons you know, did not return yesterday from the College. More and more calyxes are called every day."

"Do you know for what spells?" Kip asked.

Abel shook his head. "I gave my blood and was dismissed. I asked questions but received no answer. Thomas says he thinks they are casting spying spells to look at the positions of the armies, over and over again over all the territory of America. Whatever it is, it is killing us." He stood, and Kip hurried to join him. "I will return to the Isle and attempt to convince everyone—again—to this plan."

A new worry piled onto all the others. "Don't let them kill you."

The fox smiled. "I've survived one war already. I'll survive this one."

"See that you do."

Kip sat for a long moment after Abel left, watching the sky lighten in the east. The whole venture felt foolhardy to him now. What did he hope to accomplish? He'd started out hoping to strike a blow at the Empire, one that would weaken them enough that they would call an end to the war. Now, although Jackson and apparently Hamilton had found merit in his plan, Kip himself questioned it. There were fifteen hundred Calatians on the Isle, or more; would taking a hundred and fifty of them really make a difference?

It might, he reasoned, psychologically if nothing else. Striking at King's College was as close as Kip could get to striking a blow against Albright. He had hoped that his desire for revenge had been quenched by fighting in the war, but Albright's reappearance had only stoked the fire. The ease with which he'd stalked Kip made the fox feel powerless, and he did not like that feeling. He wanted Albright to have a taste of it.

The sun crept higher; he needed to leave. Around the corner of the building he'd been sitting in front of, he found a deep shadow from which he could translocate back. The last reason to rescue the British calyxes, and it was not a very good one, was that if he didn't do this, then he didn't know what else he could do. He only knew that if he spent the rest of the war being sent to battles, killing soldiers, seeing victories and defeats that added up to a years-long war, frustration would overwhelm him.

Perhaps this idea of his meant that he really was suited to being a military sorcerer. He shuddered and put that thought out of his mind.

CHAPTER 12: THE RESCUE

After two more meetings with Abel, one of which was cut short when Kip thought he saw someone watching them, the plan was set. Abel had convinced most of the calyxes to come, mostly by the expedient of warning them how bad the situation would be for any few who remained behind. This made Kip nervous, though not as nervous as Master Colonel Jackson's refusal to give more than the blandest, vaguest assurance that the British Calatians would not be treated as prisoners but as American people.

What made him most nervous was that he didn't understand why Jackson and Hamilton had made his plan more complicated, more prone to failure, more reliant on his unit of sorcerers for a longer time. Worrying over the cost of translocational sorcerers made some sense, and if they trusted his ability to escape any dangerous situation, he could believe that they wanted to place more of the risk on the British Calatians. Similarly, a mass evacuation would be easiest at sea, and with the Calatians unable to commandeer a boat and sail it, the Road was a logical destination. All the pieces of the plan made a sort of sense individually; it was when Kip strung one after the other that they seemed untenable.

More than once he decided to tell Abel that the whole plan was off, and every time he talked himself out of it. The British calyxes had put their faith in him, and to back out now would damage that relationship. He and Malcolm and Alice could protect the Calatians, could fight off whatever soldiers and even sorcerers the British sent against them. He would have to keep Nikolon alert for the entire time, Malcolm would have Daravont, and Alice would have air elementals. He suspected that at some level, Jackson expected him to fail, and that made him even more determined to succeed.

He did not share these misgivings with Malcolm or Alice, and only a little with Captain Lowell, because Lowell's deep faith in his commander helped Kip see that there must be more to the plan than he knew. "Only execute your part faithfully," Lowell said, "and in time you will see how you contributed to our victory."

"I wish you could come with us." The words surprised Kip even as he said them.

Lowell smiled. "As do I. But the fewer people on this mission, the better."

He meant that in two ways; fewer people in general, but also fewer humans. Kip nodded and then a trace smell made him fold his ears back. Lowell was sweating, more than he should for as cool as the room was. The captain was nervous about something. Not very nervous, not so much that Kip thought he was plotting against them, but he definitely knew something that he wasn't telling Kip, something related to the mission.

Lowell was a good soldier. Kip had to trust that whatever it was, it wasn't knowledge that would make his mission less dangerous. He believed that Lowell would tell him when everything was over. Or else…he would find out before then.

He, Alice, Malcolm, and Broadwood, who had been assigned as their translocational sorcerer for this mission, wrapped themselves in cloaks, the foxes with hoods to hide their ears. Broadwood didn't know London, so Master Colonel Jackson himself took the memory of the riverbank from Kip and showed it to Broadwood. The young man rubbed his cheeks and nodded, and a moment later the four of them stood in the chill night along the Thames River.

Malcolm had them warded within moments, and then he and Kip summoned their demons, breathing the names so Broadwood wouldn't hear. When they had been bound, Malcolm kept Daravont near them to watch out for sorcerers or other people who might interfere, and Kip took a moment to talk to Nikolon.

This mission may last three or four days, he said. *I will have need of your services for much of that time. When I can afford it, I will give you rest, but there may not be an opportunity to do so.*

Yes, master.

Kip studied the vixen's features for any sign of understanding. *Do you understand what I am saying?*

She nodded. *You are defining the length of this portion of my service.*

I'm saying I am sorry that it is to be this long. I will do what I can do make it less onerous.

Now there was a flicker on her muzzle. *You need not apologize to me. I am your servant.*

I know I need not, Kip said. *Nevertheless.*

She inclined her head. *What is my first task?*

He sent her to find the barge on the water; she found it in minutes and guided them over. Below the great red-brown sails, the deck of the barge was packed with Calatians.

Kip found space to set the four of them down near the wheel, where the tall red-bearded captain steered the ship with thick arms like corded wood and Abel watched beside him. When he saw Kip, Abel's ears snapped up and he clasped Kip's paw with a broad smile. Around them, other Calatians murmured and held out paws for Kip to touch, then withdrew so the two foxes could talk.

"Why are they on the deck?" Kip asked. "Why not in the hold? They're out in the open."

"Hold's full," grunted the captain. "Got my coin, have you?"

Kip took one of the two leather wallets he carried and placed it in the captain's hand. "Here's half. The other half when we're safely ashore at Lechlade." He showed the captain the money in the second wallet and then gathered magic and translocated it to the attic above his parents' old shop in New Cambridge, which was now deserted. "I'll retrieve it then."

The captain only raised his eyebrows at the spell, then rifled through the wallet with meaty fingers before pushing it into the pocket of his pants. "Take longer than we thought with this heavier load."

"Can the ship bear it?"

He let out a loud laugh. "Aye, she's stout and true, but I'd been told a hundred and fifty people, which is fifteen tons, and we've twice that."

"Twice that?"

Abel smiled at Kip. "More people wanted to come when they saw we were serious about this. The captain said we could bear the weight, and I couldn't leave them behind."

It made the trip more dangerous: twice the passengers meant twice the chance for someone to be seen or suffer an accident. But Kip couldn't send them back either, not if they wanted to escape the Isle. "Alice can help with the journey," he said, putting an arm around Alice's shoulders to bring her forward. "She can get you a fair wind all the way there."

"That'll help, to be sure."

"Anything else you need?"

The captain looked to either side. "Room to move my arms, that's all."

The Calatians around him drew back a little more. Abel took Kip's paw and led him to the side of the ship, the other sorcerers following except for Alice, who stayed to take the captain's direction for her air elemental. "He's kinder than he sounds," Abel said. "But he was talking about 'traitor's gold' earlier."

"Are you worried he'll turn you in?" Malcolm asked.

Abel shook his head. "He values his coin. What you're giving him is what he'd make in ten trips. He'll think it well worth it, especially if it never comes back to him, and with you hiding us from view, he suspects it won't."

"It won't." Kip indicated Malcolm. "We're well warded. Malcolm has experience and we've other protections in place." He remained vague because there was nowhere to talk privately on the boat. "As long as we're out of London by daybreak."

"You think sunlight can defeat my inattention ward?" Malcolm took a joking tone. "Why, just a moment ago you were singing my praises."

"I'd prefer fewer people around to be affected." Kip rested his paws on the railing and turned back to Abel. "Everything else went to plan?"

"There were two calyxes at the College. We waited as long as we could but they didn't come back." He sighed and looked out over the water as it rippled by. "They understood we would leave without them."

"I hope they're—" Kip stopped himself.

"If they're not dead now," Abel said, "the sorcerers will soon use them up."

"But we're getting the rest of you out." Kip's hackles rose as he sensed a presence behind him. He turned and had to look up to see the wolf glowering down.

"Hello, sorcerer," Grinda said.

"Grinda." Kip looked around her. "Did you bring your family?"

"I simply came to tell you that I am on this voyage in solidarity with my fellow calyxes, not because I trust you. Whatever a sorcerer does is for his own ends, regardless of his skin or fur."

"Kip's intentions are honorable, ma'am," Malcolm said, "and I shouldn't think that one as formidable as yourself need worry about him."

"I'm no sorcerer." Grinda growled the words and then stopped short when she got a good look at Malcolm. She recovered quickly. "But I can defend myself and mine."

"My friend thinks of his people," Malcolm went on. "It's quite inspiring. If all the Irish in London lived on an island, I'd be mounting an expedition to rescue them as well."

"He's partaken of the calyx ritual," Grinda said. "That marks him as a sorcerer."

"He never said he did," Abel put in.

"He never said he didn't, and that's near enough an admission for me." The wolf fixed Kip with a glare and then turned and made her way back through the crowd.

Kip sighed. "Not everyone will be happy. I've learned that."

Everyone around him was quiet until Abel said, softly, "If you have...I understand. You must do as they tell you, and for you to summon a demon..."

"Yes. I have," Kip said. "But only a few times. I found that for most things I can...use myself as a calyx. But it took me some time to discover that. I regret it, but I do not deny it."

He forced himself to look Abel full in the face, to see the fox's revulsion and rejection if it appeared, but Abel kept his ears up and his smile, if anything, grew. "It must have been very hard for you," he said.

"Aye. I know how it looks to you—"

"Hush." Abel patted his paw. "Let's hear no more about it."

"That's a good thought for all of us," Malcolm said in a low voice. "I'm keeping us hidden, but sound travels over water, so the quieter we are the better."

"Captain Jones said that too." Abel lowered his voice. "Sorry."

Kip nodded and indicated that he was going to go back to the wheel. Abel acknowledged with a wave but remained with Malcolm and Broadwood.

The barge had picked up speed, and in the silence the rippling of the water against the hull sounded as loud as a waterfall. At least the Calatians were keeping quiet, Kip thought, looking down over the sea of ears, rounded and pointed, perked and flat. All of these people, putting their trust in him, and so many things outside of his control. Beyond the water, the fires and gaslamps of London still burned, and anyone at one of those lights might be a sorcerer watching the water, but the barge sailed forward toward darkness and relative safety.

Kip found Alice staring up at the sail and murmuring in the language of air elementals. When she noticed Kip, her ears came up and she smiled. "They like moving," she whispered, "and don't mind pushing against things."

"Good," he whispered back, his eyes still on the shore.

"It's going to be fine. Luff will blow us to Lechlade, and you and I will get us to the Road, and Malcolm will keep us safe to the boat. The British have no idea we're here."

"I hope so." He looked again down the barge full of Calatians. "It's a long trip."

"Why don't you get some sleep?" Alice patted his arm. "I'll keep Luff company for now."

Kip slid an arm around her shoulders. "You're doing wonderfully, and I don't just mean spellcasting. You're smart and you're determined and I could not have done this without you. I just wanted you to know that."

"Of course you couldn't," Alice said, and leaned into his embrace. "But I hope you won't ever have to worry about doing things without me." She rested her muzzle against his chest.

He wanted to tell her more, how proud he was of her bravery, how scared he was that she would be hurt in this war. Being surrounded by so many Calatian families made him think about the end of the war and starting his own family, and though he would like to have her father's blessing, he saw that they would no longer need it. Alice was her own fox, in spirit and nearly in age, and if her father would not approve their marriage, she almost certainly would marry him without her father's blessing.

The barge swept past the last of the fires and the air cleared both of smoke and of the smell of refuse as they entered the cleaner waters above London. Around Kip, many of the Calatians sat on the deck or lay down, taking the chance to sleep, enough that he could see over them to Malcolm and Broadwood and Abel. Broadwood sat down, but Malcolm and Abel remained standing. Kip fought the urge to go to them, recognizing that he would be more valuable rested.

Nikolon, wake me if there is any trouble, he instructed, and lay down at Alice's feet to sleep.

Rain, not his demon, woke him after what must have been a few hours of sleep. Many of the Calatians around him stirred, stood, walked around staring at the green hills and trees on the river bank. They spoke in whispers, but Kip gathered enough fragments of conversation through the patter of rain on the river to hear that many of them had never seen countryside so green and empty. Springtime had brought flowers and an overcast sky that, with their wet fur, assured the Calatians that they were still in England. Birds wheeled about over the boat, back to shore, and back over the river again.

Malcolm had pulled his robe over his head and sat apparently asleep against the rail, and Broadwood lay on the deck beside him. And behind him, Alice stood next to the Captain, whose hands remained on the wheel as if they were part of it.

"Morning," Alice said as Kip looked up and met her eyes.

He gathered his wet tail and tried to brush the water out of it. "Everything going smoothly?"

"Aye," the captain replied. "At this rate we'll reach Lechlade before the end of the afternoon watch. Have you all food for the trip?"

"Everyone was told to bring two days' worth of food." Alice patted the small pack at her side.

Kip stood, wishing he'd brought a cloak. "We might be able to jump back and get food from Boston if anyone needs it, but I'd prefer not to."

"Why don't we have Broadwood send some people back now, while we're on the boat?" Alice asked. "I know we're supposed to meet the American boat and all that, but we've also got more people than we'd planned, and I'd wager he can get through half of them before we get to the Road."

"Not a bad thought," Kip said. "A very good one, in fact. I'll put it to him when he wakes. I don't think we can send them to the Trade House, but we should be able to send them to, ah," he glanced at the captain, "to the place where the others are."

"We'll be coming up on Windsor soon," the captain said. "Most dangerous part of the journey outside London, I daresay. Guards along the river and all, likely some sorcerers too."

"After that, then." Kip glanced toward the sleeping sorcerer. "Let us know when we're approaching, if you please."

The captain grunted, which Kip took for assent. "Weybridge," he said, pointing up ahead. On the south bank, a collection of cottages stood around three larger buildings, and resolving out of the rain was a large structure across nearly half the river.

"What's that?" he hissed, pointing ahead.

The captain raised his head. "Sudbury Lock." He raised an arm and signaled to the men manning the sail. They braced themselves and passed on the signal down the barge. "Making for the weir," the captain said to Alice. "Ready there, young miss?"

"Ready." Alice smiled at Kip. "Don't worry."

The great metal gates of the lock stood closed between stone pillars upon which men stood and waved signal flags. To the right of the lock, a small barrier separated the upper reach from the lower, over which the Thames flowed in frothy jubilation. The barge headed toward this barrier, and as it approached, Alice summoned magic and lifted the entire vessel out of the water, keeping its forward momentum so steady that when she lowered it back into the water on the other side, Kip barely felt an impact at all. He kept his eye on the men at the lock, but only once did one of them turn as though he'd heard something unusual. He looked at the sky, then the Thames, and then went back to his work.

And then they were past, and Kip relaxed. "You've done this a few times already."

"That was my fourth. Abel told me the captain had said we needed to get past the locks and that he thought you could lift the boat, and I told him I could do it, and so we did. It's much easier in the light, even with the rain."

"All right. And when you get your rest...that's all I need to do? Lift the boat, keep it moving forward, clear the weir?"

"That's all." Alice's whiskers twitched with her smile. "You can try the next one if you like. I know physical magic isn't your strong suit, but the boat is just one thing. Heavy, but simple."

"Hah." Kip smiled back and gauged the boat. "I believe I can manage it."

"Two more before Windsor," the captain said.

So Kip lifted the ship for the next lock, and though it wobbled a little upon landing, the only effect was to wake Broadwood, which was a good result anyway. The rain had not completely stopped, but had turned patchy, so there would be moments of dry weather and then a splattering squall.

As the barge approached Windsor, the whispered conversations died down as the towers of Windsor Castle came into view. King George III himself probably sat there at this moment, Kip thought, and this was closer than he'd ever been to his monarch (while Emily was off standing in the presence of kings of Spain and France and Holland).

Even in the rain, small clusters of men gathered down at the riverbank, and if Kip could see them, they might easily see the barge. But Malcolm had woken with Broadwood and stood in deep concentration at the side of the ship, keeping it concealed to the best of his ability. As the barge glided up the Thames, Kip sent Nikolon to look more closely at the men on the bank, to alert him if any were sorcerers or seemed suspicious at all.

The first group of soldiers merely lounged by the riverbank under the shelter of trees. The next group, concealed from the town of Windsor by a copse, did not look like they would have noticed the barge even without Malcolm's wards. Six soldiers in various states of undress watched while two of their fellows enjoyed the intimate attentions of two ladies. Kip ordered Nikolon to move on quickly from this one, but another of the groups of soldiers were engaged in the same pastime. Only one group swam in the Thames, and one of them noticed the ripples left by the barge.

He began to swim out to investigate. "Malcolm," Alice said under her breath.

"I see him," Malcolm said. "Give me a moment."

His hands glowed orange and he muttered some words under his breath. The swimmer pulled up in the water and stared back at the shore, directly at the soldiers and their ladies. He watched for a moment and then swam eagerly in that direction.

"A little trick Luke and I have been working on," Malcolm said. "You can invent a distraction, but it's easier to nudge them toward one that already exists."

"I'm glad you keep improving your spells," Kip said.

"Got to keep up with you lot somehow." Malcolm smiled at him and Alice.

And so they passed Windsor without incident. Once they were past, Kip had Alice curl up for a nap in the fore of the ship while he took over lifting the ship past weirs, and he instructed Broadwood and Abel to go among the

Calatians and find those amenable to being sent immediately to America. "Send them to the College," he said, "and instruct the soldiers there to house them with the New Cantabrigians pending further instructions."

Broadwood took these instructions dubiously. "I'm only here to provide swift exit for you and the others," he said. "Nothing said about sending Calatians to wherever."

"Listen," Kip told him. "We haven't a commanding officer here and I'm trying my best to make this plan work. You know the danger we run in getting these people to safety." He lowered his voice for that so as not to panic anyone nearby. "I'm not asking you to send all of them back. We have maybe five hours, according to the captain. Can you get a hundred of them there in that time?"

The sorcerer rubbed a hand through his straw-colored hair. "Forty an hour? Two every three minutes? Probably not quite that many."

"Even with the calyx ritual?" Kip hated to suggest it, but if it could save them, he had to.

"I've never done that. It's disgusting. And it doesn't matter anyway because Master Colonel Jackson gave me very direct orders. I'm to remain alert for any sign of danger, at which point I'm to take O'Brien and the young lady back to Boston." He paused. "Master Colonel Jackson said you could take yourself, but if not, I was to be available to you."

Kip had no doubt that if he were unable to take himself, Alice would be left behind, but he left that worry for another time. "They've brought double what we expected. The plan's changed."

"Then we should go back to Master Colonel Jackson and apprise him of the changes and receive his orders."

Kip sighed. "We haven't the time. Man, look at the people on this boat." Broadwood did, and the resolve in his eyes wavered. "We are responsible for them, you, me, Malcolm, and Alice. We made them a promise to take them to safety and we have to do whatever it takes to fulfill that promise."

"Yes," the young man said. "I see that, but…our orders…"

Kip saw the crack and forced his way in. "Listen: I will take full responsibility with Master Colonel Jackson. You can tell him that I claimed the authority to change your orders, since Captain Lowell isn't here."

Broadwood's eyes widened. "Have you the authority?"

Inwardly, Kip sighed. "Yes. That's what I'm telling you. In the interest of the safety of our charges and the success of the mission."

"Yes, I see." The young man scanned the full deck of the barge. "It'll take the wind from my sails, but I take your point. The fewer we have to get to the Road, the less chance of something going cockeyed."

"Right." Kip clapped him on the shoulder. "Thank you. Now let's start with the youngest and those who care for them. Abel will get some ready while you go back to the College and make sure they'll be received."

"Ah, I can't do that," Broadwood said. "I can't leave you and the others. I can see doing more than I was ordered to, but I can't shirk my duty."

"Very good. I understand. All right. I will go myself." And before the other could reply or he could reconsider, Kip called magic and an image of the Founders Rest, and he was in New Cambridge and the moon was high.

For once he was thankful for his fox's form. The sentries at the gate raised their rifles only halfway before seeing the points of his ears, and then they lowered them. "Thought you were all supposed to be inside," the one on the left said.

"I'm Kip Penfold, sorcerer," Kip said, and their eyes widened. "I'm here to tell you that there are going to be perhaps a hundred more Calatians arriving here, and you're to let them into the Tower. We will be here in a day or two to decide their disposition."

The sentries looked at each other. "Ah," the one on the left said, "Do these orders come from…"

They bore only a private's insignia. "They come from me," Kip said. "Lieutenant Penfold. I'll thank you to observe them."

They looked uncertain, but the one on the right said, "Very good, sir," and that was enough for Kip.

Sending himself back to the barge was tricky, but he keyed in on Alice and appeared next to her. After a quick embrace and explanation, he made his way to Broadwood and told him to start sending people to the Inn with instructions to climb the hill and present themselves at the gates. With that process started and little to worry about from the river, Kip dismissed Nikolon to give the demon some rest from the stress of being in this world.

The next few hours were a haze of locks, translocating, and lovely green countryside. Around the town of Oxford they worried because the shores were crowded with students, but as Malcolm observed, students at University were even more occupied with themselves than most people, and his inattention ward barely had to do any work on them at all.

A little before sunset, the captain warned that they were approaching Lechlade. Broadwood had cleared the deck of the barge enough that they could likely dock without arousing suspicion, but getting the remaining Calatians off the ship would be more difficult. Alice suggested as they floated past an empty green field that they could simply lift the boat over to that field and let everyone disembark, and this the captain flatly rejected.

So in the end, they steered toward a riverbank at an unoccupied part of the Thames that was relatively quiet. A lock was visible up the river, but the captain told them there would be no better option past this point, so Kip had to hope that Malcolm's wards would work until they got everyone to safety. The riverbank here was low and muddy in the rain, sloping up to a patchy meadow beyond which a small forest of elm trees stood with new leaves.

Abel sent his cubs to the College but refused to go himself; so too did Grinda, whose family remained on the Isle of Dogs because, she said, "I wouldn't risk some of the last of the wolves to this foolish endeavor." As she disembarked past Kip, walking the unsteady boards they had put up between the boat and the shore, she gave him a haughty look but did not say a word.

He'd hoped for some approval, having gotten them to this point without incident, but silence was better than nothing. When Abel had seen the last of the Calatians off the barge, he stepped past Kip onto the plank. "Coming?"

"As soon as I've paid the captain." Kip translocated back to his attic room, found the wallet, and came back to the barge. Malcolm was just helping Broadwood disembark as Kip walked over to the wheel and the captain leaning on it.

"Thank you for your help." Kip held the wallet out.

The captain took the wallet and counted the money inside. "Thank you for the coin."

"I hope we can count on your silence."

The man peered up at him. "I've no call to talk to anyone about aught but my cargo. Can't speak for my crew, though."

"Two days." Kip held up two fingers. "That's all we need."

The captain shrugged. "Did you bring more coin to pay them?"

After a moment of silence, Kip said, "Whatever you can do, we would appreciate," and when it became clear that there would be no response, he walked across the plank and onto the shore.

In the end, Broadwood sent over a hundred Calatians ahead to the College before fatigue overtook him. Many of them left behind the food they'd brought, so everyone had a dinner of sorts, if not quite as much as they might have liked. After consulting with Abel, Malcolm, and Alice, Kip decided it would be best to strike out for the coast during the night, when many of the Calatians had good night vision and they would be less likely to encounter anyone else. According to the maps they'd consulted, the heavily traveled road from Lechlade ran southwest to Bristol where it met Eastgate, the official beginning of the Road. They could travel south of that road and in forty miles or so they would encounter the Bristol Channel, which the Road ran down on its way to the Atlantic Ocean. From there, it would be another hundred miles along the Road before they were in the open sea where the American ship could meet them.

So, Kip calculated, one night and one day to get to the coast, and then another day during which he and Alice could fly the group of Calatians to the Road, taking turns so as not to exhaust either of them. They both could handle the weight, at least for a short period of time, but their original plan had only accounted for a hundred Calatians, and Kip was not confident in his ability to manage nearly two hundred separate people. If they had something like the boat, it would be easier, but there was no time to find nor build anything of the appropriate scale.

If they had help, though, they could levitate the Calatians for more of the journey than the ocean crossing, and perhaps speed their escape. Kip summoned Nikolon back again and asked whether the demon would be able to help levitate a number of Calatians.

All of those assembled here? Nikolon asked.

Up to that many, yes.

I don't believe so. A more powerful demon might be able to.

Thank you. Now please scout ahead and make sure we are walking toward the coast and that we are not going to cross paths with any other people or encounter a town or another road.

If a demon could lift the Calatians, that would save them a great deal of time. But a more powerful demon…Kip would need a second-order one, he'd have to use blood to summon and bind it, and most importantly, he would need to know its name. The only names he had access to were fourth-order demons he'd copied out of Cott's book while studying it, and a fourth-order demon, though he was confident he could bind it, was powerful enough that he probably couldn't hold it for ten minutes, let alone the time necessary to transport a bunch of Calatians along the Road. Unless…

Nikolon. Could a more powerful demon translocate this group of Calatians?

Not in the manner you mean, no.

That answer startled Kip. *In what manner could they translocate them?*

A demon could bring them back to the demon home, but we cannot then take them back to your world.

How do you know this?

There was a pause before the answer. *All demons have tried to break through to your world unsummoned. We are unable.*

What if I banished you without unbinding you and then summoned you again from somewhere else? Could you bring them with you?

You may try if you feel so inclined.

Would a person from my world survive unharmed in the demon world?

Who can say what you consider harm? I have never seen a person from your world in the demon world so I cannot say.

That was not very inspiring. *Perhaps another time*, Kip said.

Your course is true, Nikolon said.

Thank you.

As he walked, he reviewed his options for finding the name of a second-level demon. The Thames had disappeared behind them when he hurried to catch up to Malcolm. "How are you faring?" he asked.

"As well as someone who's spent eight hours sleeping propped up against a cold rail on a boat and now has to walk twelve more hours, all while keeping two hundred people warded." His friend smiled. "Conversation helps, though."

Kip lowered his voice. "Do you have any thoughts on where I might find the name of a second-order demon? Other than in the books that are in places we can't get to?"

Malcolm thought. "I believe Master Vendis had a few demon names scribbled down in his office. We didn't go through them very thoroughly, did we?"

"There hasn't been time." Kip sucked in a breath. "Time now, though."

"If you're sure you're of a mind to leave this lovely night and this fragrant company. I swear though we've left the Thames behind I can still smell it on my clothes."

"Didn't your ma or da say something about that?" Kip asked.

Malcolm's grin flashed white in the dim light. "Me ma and da were very silent on the subject of English rivers in my childhood. What do you want a second-order demon for?"

Kip explained, and his friend nodded thoughtfully. "The time saved is worthwhile. And it would free your attention and Alice's—well, you'll still have to manage the demon, I suppose."

"I trust myself to manage a demon more than to keep nearly two hundred people levitated."

Malcolm laughed shortly. "I don't know what I love more, that you said those words or that they make perfect sense to me. But aye, if you've a couple hours to make a study of the offices of the masters, you might well find something there of use."

"It feels presumptive to search the offices of the masters while they're not there."

"Then start with the ones who'd begrudge you the least. Vendis, Odden, Argent."

"Odden kept his demon names in the book, I know that." Kip rubbed his whiskers.

"Alternately," Malcolm said, "start with Patris and see if you can't find something to make him a bit easier to deal with when this is all over."

"Hah." Kip's ears perked. "They cleared out Windsor's office, didn't they?"

"I'd guess so. It's been a year."

"All right. I'll start with Vendis and Argent and then see what may happen after that."

He sought out Abel and Alice to tell them where he was going and to assure them that he wouldn't be gone longer than an hour, and then told

Broadwood to keep an eye on them while he was gone. The young sorcerer objected to Kip leaving enough that Kip promised to come back and check in every half hour rather than simply completing his task.

The sentries at the College were none too pleased to see him again. "Is that all that's coming in?" one demanded. "We'd like to lock the gates and not open them again every five minutes."

"There's just me," Kip said, "and I may be coming back every half hour or so. Lock the gates while I'm out."

They grumbled but let him through. He walked down the familiar path to the stately White Tower, not as decorated or ornate as the buildings he'd seen in England, but more dignified in its solitary austerity. It had been a month or more since he'd walked through the great doors in the tower to find the hall empty and the phosphorus elementals gone. Now he stepped into the Great Hall and found no phosphorus elementals, but a thick crowd of Calatians and the miasma of their combined scents.

They rushed to him with a host of questions. Nobody had told them where to sleep. Were they to sleep in the hall here? The other Calatians from upstairs hadn't known they were coming. Would there be food?

He tried to calm them. "There will be food," he said. "I'll tell Old John at the inn to send some up. I can't arrange more until we're done getting the rest of your fellows here, and that might be two more days. As for sleeping, arrange it as you would like. Would it help to have a fire in the fireplace?"

Many of the thicker-furred Calatians didn't care, but some thought a fire would be good for the children; it was chillier than in London. So Kip sparked a magical fire and showed them where the basement was, where there would be fuel and still more room to sleep, if the New Cantabrigians hadn't also taken that space. He still didn't want to go down there himself to look.

When he went upstairs to the masters' chambers, he found them similarly crowded with Calatians, many asleep but some awake and wondering what was happening downstairs. He stopped twice to explain before he arrived in Master Argent's chambers, where the Coopers had pushed two apprentice cots together and the three of them had squeezed onto the makeshift bed. Kip eased past them into the office.

At least it seemed the townspeople respected the masters' offices, or else they had been told not to enter them. Argent's had not been disturbed, and Kip found Vendis's also empty and dark.

A year and a half ago, Master Odden had set him the task of learning how to hold flame in his paw. He hadn't mastered it until recently, and he suspected that the way he'd learned to do it was not the way Odden wanted; it was an advanced technique of fire sorcery that he'd learned, where Odden had expected that a student would be able to learn it with little more than a fire spell. Holding a fire in one paw would give him better light but leave him only one paw to search with, so he kindled a magical fire in the brazier and used both paws to search, sometimes taking papers over to the brazier to examine them more closely.

A knock came at the open door. He perked his ears as a familiar voice said his name, and then a fox and hedgehog came into the office: Thomas Cartwright and Bryce Morgan. "Benjamin told us you'd come back," Thomas said. "Came to get us, actually."

"He came to get me," Bryce corrected. "And I brought Thomas along because, well, you're both foxes. What's this about bringing another hundred Calatians here from London? How long is this going to go on?"

Thomas's nostrils flared. "And why are you so wet? I haven't heard a storm outside."

Kip raised a paw. "Good evening, gentlemen. I'm sorry to intrude. These are refugees from the Isle of Dogs in London, where it has been raining all day."

"Are they to settle in New Cambridge, then? We'll be glad to have them, of course, but the town must prepare—we've never had so many come at once—"

"Mr. Morgan," Kip said. "I don't know where they'll end up settling. But we wanted to get them out of England."

"You see," Thomas said. "I told you there would be a good reason."

Whether Alice's father was defending Kip because of their common species or because he truly respected him now, Kip couldn't tell. "I know it would be wonderful to have so many more families here," he said, "but some of them may want to go to Peachtree, or New York or Boston. Some may even want to return to London when the war is over."

"But they're refugees, you said." Bryce frowned, and Thomas's ears canted toward Kip.

"They're unhappy with their treatment during the war," Kip said. "And to get them out, I had to get the support of the Army, so they may be treated as prisoners. I don't really know. I'm not supposed to be in charge of this, but Colonel Jackson didn't leave anyone else so I'm making all the decisions."

Thomas nodded. "I'll go down with Bryce and we'll welcome them and make sure everyone has some food. We've got a bit left over."

"I meant to go tell Old John," Kip said. "I'll do that before I go. You all should stay here in case there's another attack. And thank you. I'm sorry I didn't let you know beforehand."

The hedgehog smiled. "We're all in this together, aye? What else did you come back for? Can we help at all?"

Kip shook his head. "I need something to make the rest of the mission easier. We wore out our translocational sorcerer so we can't send any more people back here, and we're currently walking across England with two hundred Calatians that I presume the English Army will be looking for any minute now, depending on how long it took the sorcerers to figure out what was going on."

This alarmed both fox and hedgehog. "Will they come here looking for them?" Thomas asked.

"No. This place is warded well. And Malcolm is warding the others, and we have demons watching over them. If the sorcerers had an idea of where they were, they might be able to do something, but as it stands they shouldn't be able to find them. Still, I shouldn't be gone long. I'm just going to look through some of these offices, then I'll go down to the Inn."

"All right." Bryce disappeared, but Thomas remained behind.

Kip guessed what the older fox wanted. "Alice is with me. Well, not here, but she's with the mission."

Thomas nodded slowly. "Take care of her," he said.

"Actually." Kip smiled. "She's been sort of taking care of me. But yes, I promise no harm will come to her if it is at all within my ability to prevent it."

The fox managed a smile. "You know, I believe you."

"Could you do me a great favor?" Kip asked. "There are two fox cubs, Arabella and Aran. Their father is a very dear friend of mine. Could you make sure they are safe and well fed?"

"Arabella and Aran," Thomas repeated. "I'll gladly do that." He raised a paw and left the office.

More than the fire warmed Kip as he rummaged through Vendis's papers. It wasn't until he opened the desk and found a pile of older papers that he found what he needed: on a scrap of parchment was written the name "Valkuni" with a "2nd" scribbled next to it.

He'd taken the parchment and was about to leave when it occurred to him that he should try the summoning here to make sure that the name was a demon, that it was controllable, and that it could do what he wanted. So he closed the office door, sat down on the stone floor, and performed the summoning, ready to banish it if it turned out to be more powerful than he was prepared for.

Valkuni appeared as a great frost-blue sea serpent in a cloud of icy mist. It was indeed only a second order demon, and when Kip had bound it and asked whether it could levitate two hundred people and carry them for miles, it replied in a crackly affirmative as though talking through the breaking ice of a lake in springtime. He dismissed it and stowed the paper back in Vendis's desk after committing the name to memory.

Before leaving the Tower, he sought out Bryce Morgan again and made sure he had all he needed to make the London Calatians comfortable. That done, he walked down to the Inn so that he could bid the sentries goodnight on his way.

Old John was understandably curious about where a hundred extra

Calatians had come from, and, when he'd properly awoken, who was going to pay for the extra food. "I'm sure the Army will compensate you," Kip said.

"Aye," John growled, standing from his bed in his close, small bedroom behind the kitchen of the Inn. "I've heard that noise before. Lived through many wars, you'll recall."

In his heart, Kip knew the old man was right. Compensating the owner of an inn for food he brought to prisoners or even refugees was going to be far down on the list of priorities of an army that needed to win a war against a massive empire. The fact that John was willing to take that risk anyway, after all that he'd done for Kip over the past year, spurred the fox to go one step farther.

He laid a paw on John's arm, and when the man turned to him, said, "I will see to it that you are fairly compensated. I give you my word."

John's lined face betrayed no emotion at first, and then his lips tightened with resolve, and he straightened as though shedding a weight from his shoulders. "I would have done it anyway, but I'll do it with a glad heart now." He grasped Kip's forearm, fingers still strong over the fox's fur and slender bones. "I know how much it means, what you're doing, and I'm glad to do my part for it. There are many who have sacrificed and lost more than I will."

"Pray that those sacrifices may soon be at an end," Kip said. "Thank you, John."

"Spoken like a young pup in his first war." John smiled. "But from your lips to God's ear. Now get on with you. I'll feed your fellows."

My fellows, Kip thought as he left the Inn and gathered magic to return to his mission. Only by race, surely, though Abel and Coppy's family had other ties to him. But the thought made him smile as he returned to the cool English night.

CHAPTER 13: THE ROAD

Malcolm and Alice had kept the Calatians going at a slow pace, though many of them complained about the walking. When Kip reappeared near Alice, two otters were walking alongside her, an older female and a younger male. "But there's sorcerers here," the older one said, untroubled by Kip's appearance. "Why should we walk?"

"Ma!" The younger male gripped her arm, giving Alice and Kip a fearful look. "The sorcerers aren't ferrymen."

"They fly us across the Thames when they like." The otter stared boldly at Kip. "They appear and disappear. And these two are Calatians. Why make us walk all this way?"

"We can," Alice said. "But it takes effort."

"I'm working on doing just that. There are only four sorcerers here." Kip indicated Broadwood, still asleep and being carried by Alice. "One of them spent all yesterday sending a hundred Calatians to safety. We're doing all we can, and if you can just help us with a little bit of walking, you can sleep while we carry you to and over the water."

"We can swim," chirped the younger otter.

"This is seawater, and there's a lot of it," Kip told him. "Maybe a hundred miles."

"How much farther to the coast?" the older otter asked.

"If I can fly us, we should get there just after dawn." Kip made a quick decision. "We'll stop for a break partway through the night so people can rest and eat, and I'll try flying us then."

"All right." The otters moved away, back into the crowd.

Alice gave Kip a grateful smile. "You found a demon name?"

"Yes. And your father sends his love and worry." He looked around the crowd, two hundred Calatians trudging together up a low grass-covered hill. At least the rain had stopped. "Otherwise things have been quiet?"

"No danger, just some complaining. And a few of them tried to sing songs, but we weren't sure if we should do that. Malcolm said the less noise the better."

"I'd trust his judgment." Kip looked ahead. "Nik didn't alert me, so I didn't worry too much. Even so, I knew you could handle anything."

"Maybe not anything." Alice wagged her tail. "I can't help the rain, and it seems much nicer now it's stopped. Are the Calatians settled in the Tower? Was Father pleasant to you?"

"Very. He said he trusted me."

"Maybe he's changing his mind." Alice reached out and took Kip's paw. "I knew that once he saw you for what you are, he'd understand."

He squeezed her paw in return. "I think it was more that he saw what you can do. He is coming to see you as a young lady capable of making her own choices, not as someone whose future he has to arrange."

"Let us hope."

The peace Kip felt from that moment lasted only twenty minutes or so, until another Calatian came up to complain about the walking, but he was grateful for that small reprieve in the midst of the mission. Looking around, he noticed small things: the Calatians with better night vision, like the foxes and polecats and beavers, were helping along those with less facility to see in dim light, like the otters, and those with generally poorer eyesight that got worse at night, like mice. There might be complaining, but at the same time his people helped each other throughout, whether here or back in New Cambridge. The thought warmed and fortified him.

Malcolm's wards held up well even when Malcolm himself needed a rest, and the night was quiet out in the English countryside. Only two people, hurrying along a road, came near the group, and neither of them glanced at the crowd. Kip, alerted by Nikolon, moved to where the road crossed their path and held the Calatians back from it as the human pair walked through them, mumbling about getting to Bath before morning.

Another time they passed near a farmhouse and startled a cow that took to lowing. There was nothing the sorcerers could do about it except hurry everyone on past while watching the farmhouse for any signs of life. There, too, they remained fortunate.

How many more encounters could they risk? Kip worried about it even though Nikolon kept a vigilant eye out and Malcolm assured him that his wards would hold. When they got to the coast, there would be far more open air, there would be daylight, and they would be much more exposed.

When several more Calatians had complained about being tired and Kip judged that they were about halfway through the night, he called a stop in a large meadow near a forest. As everyone sank to the ground and broke open what remained of their provisions, Kip sat with Malcolm and Alice a little way apart from the others. "I know the ward must be a strain on you," he began, talking to Malcolm.

"It's no more than I signed up for, and a sight more interesting than holding the same ward on the same house during a battle." Malcolm's voice held less cheer than Kip was accustomed to.

"What I'd like to know," Kip said, "is whether the calyx ritual would be of use to you when we reach the shore. We'll have no cover of darkness or—"

"Aye." Malcolm rested his head in one hand. "I've thought on that. I believe I can keep the wards, though I'd like to be awake for all the time over water."

"Would the calyx ritual help?" Kip repeated.

His friend rubbed his forehead. "Are you offering yourself?"

"Or me," Alice put in. "I know what it is and I'm willing to do it."

"You're both occupied with other things." Abel walked up and sat himself between Kip and Malcolm. "I, on the other hand, have nothing to do but walk about keeping all these people comfortable and reassured as much as I can. My," he lowered his voice, "valuable blood can easily be spared."

Kip reached out, but Abel intercepted his paw and held it, his eyes steady on Kip's. "It's freely offered," he said quietly.

Malcolm took a breath. "The thing is," he said, "I've never done that. Cast a ward with enhanced…magic. I don't know how it would work exactly. We might not even need it."

"But if we do, it would be rather too late to cast in that situation," Kip said. "Why not try it here, where we have time to spare?"

Malcolm nodded. "Have we a knife?"

"I have one," Abel said. "And I can get a cup in a moment." He stood.

"And there's my last objection done away with. Yes, if all of you are so determined, try it I shall. A stitch in time saves nine, me ma used to say."

"Let's make sure nobody can see us." Kip arranged himself, Malcolm, and Alice with their backs to the main group while Abel went to fetch a cup. "You know what to expect, right, Malcolm?"

"Aye. I've done it, though not for months. Master Vendis told me I'd not need to use the ritual for much more than summoning demons, because a ward is a ward, but there's no harm in seeing if I can hold it longer or add another protection, eh?"

"That's the spirit." Kip looked over his shoulder at their charges, most of whom sat contentedly eating or rubbing their paws. The conviction seized him that he would do almost anything to keep them safe, and he understood that both Malcolm and Abel were doing the same.

When Abel returned, he saw what they'd done and seated himself in front of Kip, tail resting on the grass, hidden from the others. From a pouch at his side he produced a small knife and a cup.

Kip leaned forward to put a paw on his arm. "You understand we haven't a healer here."

"Aye. I've a length of cloth to serve as bandage."

"I can cauterize the wound as well."

"Doesn't that require a hot knife blade, though?" Abel put the knife point to the inside of his elbow, situating it over the cup he'd set on the ground.

"Not the way I do it." Kip forced himself to watch his friend's blood spill into the cup. Even though Abel had been a calyx for years and knew well how much blood was needed, after a few seconds Kip couldn't help saying, "That's enough."

Abel looked surprised, but withdrew the knife. He cleaned it and then reached for the bandage. "Cauterizing leaves a scar, does it not?"

"A healer can mend the scar."

The fox hesitated, and then extended his arm to Kip. "I'll take your offer, then."

Kip concentrated and burned the wound very lightly, enough to scarify the flesh. Abel winced but did not cry out, and when Kip sat back and dismissed the fire, the other fox probed the scar with a claw. "It hurts less than when my mother did it on my tail," he said. "Although I was only seven then, and had little to compare that pain to."

"I hope it wasn't too bad." Kip tried to see the wound, but Abel kept his paw over it. "Thank you for doing this."

"I'll do it again if need be, and need might be." The fox held the cup to Malcolm's hand, and Malcolm took it.

"Your sacrifice is appreciated," he said, braced himself, and drank. He put the cup down and said, "Now, let's see."

The glow on his arms when he called magic looked stronger to Kip, and Malcolm's indrawn breath told him his friend felt the difference as well. He murmured a series of syllables and lowered his arms to his sides as the glow faded and died.

Alice watched with wide eyes. "Did it work?"

"Oh, aye, it did." Malcolm leaned back. "The wards feel stronger. Of course, if they're not tested, we'll never know. This is the trial we defensive sorcerers must endure."

"What trial?" Alice asked.

"Our spells are rarely noticed except in failure. You there, you can lift a boat and everyone sees it, everyone oohs and aahs. But it's only when we sail past a cluster of people all staring and seeing naught but what my spell shows them that people see what I'm doing." Malcolm laughed shortly. "It's all well and good, for I know the use I am, and I know my friends do too."

"We never doubt it," Kip said.

"Of course not." Alice put a paw on Malcolm's hand and turned her eyes to Abel. "Not any of our friends."

"I'm happy to help in the success of this mission, in however small a way." Abel got to his feet. "I'm going to walk around and see if anyone else needs anything."

Kip held out a paw to Alice. "Want to come along with Abel? Let's talk to the people."

"I'd love to." She stood with him.

"I'll stay here and keep an eye on Broadwood, if you don't mind." Malcolm leaned back on his elbows. "Enjoy this fine spring night. Let me know when it's time to get on the move again."

The three foxes walked through the group, with Abel taking the lead in asking how everyone was. Kip noticed that he took the opportunity to introduce them to Kip and Alice wherever possible. "Our American cousins," he called them. They met the two otters who'd been complaining to Alice, a mother and son named Bella and Bill Sasha; they met a family of dormice named Jinx; they met another fox family named Canno, whom privately Kip thought might be related to Peter Cadno. After a dozen other introductions, they encountered Abel's conspirator friends, the other calyxes who'd agitated for action. Grinda kept to herself and they did not approach her, but Alice got to meet Pierce the otter, Callo and Charles Cotton the rabbits, and Thomas Trewel the dormouse. All of them were highly excited at the mission and kept thanking Alice for all she'd done.

After that, they went on to meet others, most resting, some talking. One small group of Calatians knelt around a beaver who was reciting passages from the Bible, all of their heads bowed in prayer.

"Are Coppy's family here?" Alice asked in a low voice as they left the prayer circle.

Kip shook his head. "They're in New Cambridge. Broadwood sent them over." He hadn't counted, but he'd seen Coppy's mother and at least two of her children go, so he assumed the others had as well.

"Good." Alice looked around. "We should depart soon."

"There's Abel. I'll need his knife."

Kip and Alice hurried over to the other fox and apprised him of their plan to depart. He produced the knife and gave it to Kip, who made sure nobody was watching and then nicked a small cut in his wrist.

"You need less than human sorcerers do?" Abel asked, watching Kip lap at the blood.

"Usually. It depends on the spell. For a second-order demon I won't need much. I might try it without any at all, but this is important and I don't want to risk anything."

The other fox nodded. "Want a cloth for a bandage?"

Kip shook his head. "It'll heal fast enough. Thank you, though." He swept fire over Abel's knife and gave it back to the other fox, then gathered magic so that his paws glowed violet. "I'll go a little ways off to summon the demon."

"Dangerous?" Abel asked.

Alice shook her head. "It's disturbing if you're not expecting it."

"Now you've warned me, I'll be expecting it," Abel said. "If you don't mind my coming along."

Kip swallowed back the impulse to tell Abel to stay. After all, he'd been so protective of Alice and had learned that she could take care of herself, and this was no more dangerous than watching a puppet show. Abel would be fine. If the demon got loose somehow, he'd be in danger whether two or twenty feet away. "All right," he said, leading them all around the other side of a stand of trees to conceal their activity. "But stay behind Alice and don't utter a word or move until I've finished the binding."

Valkuni appeared again as the serpent in the cloud of ice mist, and Kip bound it without incident, then exhaled and turned. Abel's eyes were wide, and even Alice looked surprised. "I've seen demons, once or twice," Abel said. "But…it's so strange, seeing it here in the middle of the countryside."

"Aye," Kip said. "Valkuni, make yourself invisible and speak only to me until I order you otherwise."

"Yes, master." The demon's crackly voice had barely finished speaking the words when its form faded from view.

"All right." Kip walked back to the group, and Abel and Alice fell in alongside him. "We'll have to prepare them all to be carried. The calyxes know what it's like, but not everyone may. It can be disorienting if you haven't had it done before."

"I'll get everyone together and warn them what's coming," Abel said. "And I'll enlist Thomas and the Cottons as well."

"I'll start it slowly," Kip promised, composing his order in his head. After a moment, Malcolm found them, and Kip asked if he or Alice could find any problem with his phrasing. Neither could, so when Abel finally came back and reported that everyone was ready, Kip gave Valkuni the order.

The group of Calatians rose half a foot in the air. Many oaths came, and one or two panicked and clung to each other, but on the whole they all handled it very well. The calyxes, used to being flown, helped comfort and orient the others. After a minute, people had calmed, and Kip moved them forward.

Nikolon was not much burden to Kip at all anymore, but Valkuni fought him at a low level every minute, taking a good deal of Kip's concentration. "I'll have to get us to the coast first, then rest before we go to the Road," he told Malcolm, Alice, and Abel. "I can probably hold him for a while, but I can't focus on much else while I'm doing it, not and have him keep everyone aloft."

The journey went smoothly, with the exception of one or two sheep walls that Valkuni carelessly smacked people into before Kip amended his orders. Abel made a joke about how the walls wouldn't stop sheep-Calatians, if there were such a thing, making everyone smile.

Kip and Alice and Malcolm made a small bet about whether they would see sunrise before the sea, and a side bet about whether Broadwood would wake before one or the other. Malcolm thought they were moving fast enough to reach the sea before the sun rose, but as it happened, the sun had been up for nearly an hour before the briny smell of ocean reached them.

How far away is the sea? Kip asked Nikolon.

Perhaps an hour away at your current pace.

Thank you, Kip said. *Is there a town along the shore?*

Yes. If you move to the south, you can avoid it. But there is a road that has a good deal of activity on it.

Thank you.

Forty minutes later, they crested a hill, and their long morning shadows pointed down to a small seaside town. To either side of it stretched the road that Nikolon had been talking about, a well-worn path along which several horses cantered. Beyond that stretched the shimmering blue and foaming white of the sea, and within its vast expanse, Kip saw for the first time in his life the Road, the Great Feat of sorcery that allowed people to walk from England to the New World.

It glittered on the surface of the water, far out beyond the whitecaps, a crystalline line that curved and vanished into the horizon. Just on the other side, a mere two months walk away (a little less by horse-drawn cart or barge), lay New York. The line of the Road wavered in the sunlight such that at any moment Kip thought it might vanish into the endless blue of the ocean, but no matter how long he stared, it remained.

The immensity of this Great Feat overwhelmed him. Here was a dream that Master Bolden had pulled into reality with a spell over a century ago that remained solid and real, supporting thousands of emigrants every year. A small black blotch, clearer in Nikolon's vision than his own, was probably the first of a series of small inns that had been licensed and built along the road to provide shelter for those who didn't bring their own.

Coppy had taken passage on a ship to come to the New World, but hundreds of Calatians had left England over the last hundred years to seek their fortunes, as had thousands upon thousands of humans. Kip kept staring at the beautiful ribbon snaking out over the water and his throat tightened with longing. To create something like this that would endure even beyond his death, that would enrich so many lives… "It's beautiful," he said.

"It's breathtaking." Alice floated at his side, under her own power rather than Valkuni's so that she had more autonomy. "One of two Great Feats not performed in wartime, I think you told me."

"Yes." Kip touched the fur on his paw.

"Why did it come about? What great need was there to walk to New York from here?"

She hadn't had Master Windsor's history lessons, and now Kip tried to remember. "Nobody knows. Master Bolden died soon after casting it. The official record says that he felt an overwhelming duty to please the Crown, but that could also be propaganda."

Malcolm, next to them, said, "More likely the King threatened his family. William hated the Catholics and we always thought it wasn't New York but Ireland that was on his mind when he ordered this Road. A lovely fence, and as cruel as any spike-topped iron, it is."

"A fence?" Kip turned to him.

Malcolm gestured to the north. "You know what lies that way, aye?"

"Yes." Kip blinked again at the Road. "Oh."

"Aye, 'oh.' That Road cuts off Ireland from the rest of the world. 'Oh, it's no worry,' say the Royals in Windsor. 'You can trade through our bonnie port of Bristol.' And so we do, for we must, and the British take a pretty fee for the privilege, for they can." He paused. "I suppose properly it's 'they do,' not 'we do,' for I'm an American now, but the Irish still comes up in me when I see injustice like this."

"I'd never thought of it," Kip admitted.

"And why should you? Tisn't your people they're fencing in."

"Not with this," Alice said.

Malcolm inclined his head. "Fair point, aye."

"The thing now," Kip said, "is to get all of us from here to there." He pointed out at the Road. "I'm inclined to rest here rather than risk the road and the beach and all. Can you keep us warded until we're out over the water?"

"And beyond. That calyx magic fortifies one. I understand why it's such an ingrained practice. Which doesn't mean I approve of it."

"None of us do," Kip said. "But there are times when it's necessary."

He commanded Valkuni to lower everyone, then dismissed the demon. With Abel and Alice's help, they spread the word that there would be a half hour rest before they set off again. Malcolm re-cast the wards with another dose of calyx blood, this one from Thomas Trewel.

"All right." Malcolm reached for Kip's paw. "The wards are up and strong as I can make them."

"Thank you," Kip said, clasping his friend's hand in return. "Once we get to the Road, there should be less danger."

After Kip had rested and felt capable of another binding, he summoned Valkuni and repeated his previous order. Keeping his passengers as low to the ground as he dared, he ordered the demon to move the group down the hill, across the road when there was a large enough gap, and then out over the water. The crash of surf could not drown out the gasps and exclamations of wonder at the waves below them and the thick briny smell, the small fishing boats so different from the barges on the Thames. As the coast and the town receded from view, the Calatians settled into their flight, though a cry came here and there whenever someone saw a fish swimming below them. More than one reached down to their shadows dancing on the waves, trying to touch the water or perhaps catch a fish, but Kip's attention stayed on guiding Valkuni out to the Road.

The air cooled down considerably over the water, and rushing along quickly through it made it seem cooler still. With their fur, the Calatians were all comfortable, though the foxes did put their ears back against the wind. Kip was wondering whether Malcolm was cold and if he could do anything about that when Broadwood finally woke up.

His shriek nearly broke Kip's concentration, but fortunately practice had prepared him for any distraction. He turned to ask Alice to tend to the sorcerer, only to find that she'd already propelled her way over there. She engaged him in conversation and calmed him down, much to Kip's relief. He had to keep his attention on Valkuni, barely talking to those around him and watching the glowing translucent expanse of the Road until it lay below them.

As they approached, he sent Nikolon ahead to see where there might be a large empty section where they could rest for a short time, and to his surprise, Nikolon showed him no travelers on the Road. Of course; there was a war on. Britain wouldn't allow travelers to walk to their enemy. Still, there had been rumors of British troops on the road, and even if that weren't true, there might be people who'd set out from New York before the war began. So he sent Nikolon oceanward looking for the nearest of those travelers. Malcolm's wards were good, but it would be difficult to conceal two hundred Calatians on a hundred-foot wide span in the ocean.

Nikolon traveled for more than twenty minutes before encountering a traveler, and Kip judged that enough time, so he ordered Valkuni to set all of the people down on the Road. When they were all safe, he dismissed the demon and then knelt to put his paw to the Great Feat below him.

The Road itself felt like pure magic. What glittered in the sunlight was not the Road, but the layer of salt that crystallized out of the seawater that washed up onto it. Mixed with grime from the thousands of feet that had traveled over it, the salt nonetheless sparkled in the sun.

Around him, the other Calatians gazed around with similarly rapt expressions, at the Road under their feet, at the ocean just a foot below that, back at the just-visible shore, or up at the gulls wheeling overhead. Kip took a breath of the salt air, and then something about the gulls caught his eye.

Nikolon. That black bird among the gulls, do you see it?

Yes.

Get closer to it, please. Show me what you see.

His point of view zoomed up through the air, toward the birds, and past one gull and then another, neither of which registered his presence. Then he was face to face with a raven. He kept his eye on it, gathered magic, and gripped it with a spell, bringing it down fast toward him.

Nikolon kept her view on it the whole way, from its startled look when the spell caught it to the fluttering fighting and finally resignation as Kip brought it face to face with him. "Good morning," he said pleasantly.

The raven turned its head back and forth. He held it still with the spell, forcing it to focus on him. "It's no use pretending this is just a raven. I'd like to know to whom I have the pleasure of speaking. Who was clever enough to follow us?"

"It did not take a great deal of cleverness," the raven said in a voice Kip didn't recognize. He had hoped it would be Albright, but now felt relieved that it was not. "Once we knew the calyxes were gone, there were only two places worth looking. There are ways to detect wards even if you cannot see what lies within, you know. Or, more likely, you don't, *apprentice*."

"Congratulations," Kip said. "You're too late to do anything about it." He reached out to touch the raven's wing.

"It is never too late—" The raven's voice cut off in mid-sentence as Kip sent it to the small house he'd occupied during the Battle of Boston Harbor.

"Have a nice flight back," he said mildly. Of course, the raven would be able to show the sorcerer where it was, and if he knew any basic translocation, he'd be able to go there and get it back, but Kip enjoyed having caused him some inconvenience.

That brief triumph over, he studied the Calatians still marveling over the Road. Anger flared in him at Jackson's complication of his plan. If they'd simply had two more sorcerers, they could have sent all the Calatians to New Cambridge by now.

"What was that?" Alice hurried to his side.

"A raven. We've been spotted. It seems sorcerers can detect wards, even if they can't see inside, so they found us moving out here."

"You didn't know that?"

"No," he said, "but Jackson should have. Come on, we should move them farther down the Road. The sorcerers have seen where we are."

Alice's ears flattened. She scanned the Road in either direction. "Are they coming?"

"Perhaps." Kip stopped and thought. The sorcerers must have only just found them. "But we should keep moving."

He called Valkuni again and bound him, and once again had him carry the Calatians down the Road, faster this time. They could deal with a little wind; the important thing now was to meet up with the American ship before the sorcerers caught them. He had Nikolon split his time between looking for more ravens and looking at the Road ahead for travelers and nearby ships.

They flew over a small group of weary-looking people on foot around two horses with carts, and a pair of people on horses. Twice they passed barges being towed along the Road. No ships evidenced themselves, but no British sorcerers either, so Kip felt safe stopping two more times to rest and dismiss Valkuni.

On their fourth flight, Nikolon spotted a three-masted frigate far ahead of them on the north side of the Road driving an impressive bow wave before her. Through the demon's eyes, Kip saw that the flag fluttering from the mast did resemble the one he'd been shown back in Boston at the battle; more convincingly, the men aboard the ship wore American uniforms, and he recognized Callahan, the tall translocational sorcerer from the American military sorcerers' division. No other sorcerers were visible on the boat.

At the next break, when Kip could spare the concentration, he sent Nikolon to speak to Callahan. "We're perhaps two hours away," he told the other sorcerer. "How long have you been sailing?"

"I haven't been with this ship the whole time," Callahan said. "I brought Dapper out here a few days ago, but we had a ship along the Road just in case. Dapper's been speeding it toward you, and now the other thing's done, I'm here for support."

"Other thing?"

"Oh aye, you'll find out about it soon enough." Callahan smiled.

The urgency of their plight pressed Kip past his curiosity. "You're not warded, though?"

"No. We have a few cannon to protect us. When we bring your cargo aboard, your man can handle the wards, aye?"

"Of course."

Callahan looked around Nikolon. "Any sign of the British?"

"They know about where we are." Kip told him about the raven. "I haven't seen a raven since then, but I wouldn't be surprised to see a ship come up. Watch the waves," he said, remembering the ripples on the Savannah River.

The sorcerer did not seem at all perturbed by the information. "We'll see you in two hours then. How do you plan to do it?"

"I can just lift the Calatians onto the ship." Through Nikolon, he looked around the frigate. "Is there room for two hundred aboard?"

"There will be. Broadwood and I can send back some if it's too crowded."
He gestured. "British ships rarely come north of the Road. Too much ice."

"All right," Kip said. "I'm going to get us on our way. We'll be there
soon."

When he brought his awareness back to himself, Malcolm and Alice
stood in front of him. "It looked like you were communing with your
demon," Malcolm said, "so we decided to leave you to it."

"Our ship is about two hours ahead." Kip checked the group of
Calatians, who by now had gotten used to the Road. Many of them still
wandered to the edge to sit and look out over the ocean, now unbroken by
any sign of land, but at least two-thirds of them walked about and talked and
shared food as if they were in a meadow or town square.

Kip found Abel and told him how close they were and had him gather
everyone to be transported again. Another hour with Valkuni took them
close enough that some of the Calatians (not the foxes, though) could see
the American ship from their location. Broadwood could too, well enough
to translocate himself there to greet Callahan and start making arrangements
for the Calatians. Those who could see the ship spread their excitement to
the others, and many questions circulated, mostly centered around whether
the ship would have food and drink and of what kind. Kip, still worried
that the British would intercept them, took as little rest as he dared before
summoning Valkuni again.

He had reached the point where he could distinguish sails on the
frigate with his own eyes when Nikolon warned him, *Ravens approaching,
master.*

He switched to Nikolon's point of view only for a moment, only long
enough to see two ravens wheeling around in the air. Were they inside
Malcolm's ward? It was hard to say. He asked Valkuni to hurry, but already
most of the Calatians had their eyes squeezed shut against the wind and
Kip himself couldn't keep his eyes from watering. He could see through
Nikolon's eyes, but it would be useful to have everyone alert and aware, so he
didn't dare go much faster.

Next to him, Malcolm said tersely, "Ravens," and Alice, ears perked,
looked around.

"I see them," Kip said. "I can't do anything but get us to the ship."

"Shall I blow them away?" Alice asked. "Never mind, I'll do it." She
summoned magic, and a moment later the high whispering of air elementals
cut through the hissing wind.

Kip focused on the ship, keeping the Calatians over the Road in case
something happened. Soon he would have to take them out over open water,
but not yet, not quite yet. "If you can find the ship, wherever they are…" He
let that sentence hang.

"Something's testing my wards," Malcolm said.

There was nothing Kip could do to that, or very little, except to keep moving. Then a black shape flitted back into their field of view, and Alice gasped. "They're being translocated!" she said.

And then something else happened. A dozen of the Calatians broke away from the group and flew south of the Road. *Valkuni!* Kip snapped. *Retrieve them!*

Master, my power is spread too thin. The stray Calatians slowed but kept their momentum away from the group. They comprised a beaver, an otter, a family of mice, one polecat who was reaching out to the main group, and now they were all crying out, reaching back. The Calatians over the Road reached out to them; some tried to swim through the air, to no avail.

Another dozen were pulled away, maybe more. Two foxes went in this group and Kip didn't know whether either of them was Abel. He had to watch them go, grimly set on saving the ones Valkuni could keep hold of. He still had most of them. "I'm trying to get them," Alice said next to him.

The American frigate loomed closer, ten minutes or less now. He couldn't see the British ship—but he could detect the ward, even if he didn't know what was inside. *Mark where the Calatians disappear,* he told Nikolon, *and stay over that spot.*

The stolen Calatians remained visible, paralleling the others over the water south of the Road but moving faster; the British clearly had no regard for comfort. Alice cried out in frustration. "They're too strong," she said.

"Too far." Kip gritted his teeth. If only he could get these to the frigate, keep them warded, then he could fight. "Keep those ravens out of here."

"I'm trying with physical magic. I'm sending Hoosh at the water to try to blow the British ship away, too."

"Good." As soon as the Calatians reached the British ship they would try to get another batch, he was sure. And then he took his eyes off them for a moment and when he looked back, he couldn't find them. *There, Nikolon, did you mark it?*

Yes, master. There are ripples in the water as well.

Thank you. He diverted across open water, making the Calatians gasp and hold each other as they sped toward the frigate. Sure enough, another dozen or so were wrenched away, but Valkuni had more strength spread among fewer bodies, and this time all that happened was that the dozen slowed and hung over the water as the rest reached the frigate. Kip was about to set them down when the great wooden ship burst into flame.

Men on the ship shouted; Calatians screamed above the flames that attacked the sails and sprang up from the hull, the inferno raging around them. Kip couldn't manage two demons and also devote any attention to fire, so he ordered Valkuni to set the Calatians and sorcerers on the deck and then dismissed the second-order demon. *Nikolon,* he ordered, *keep me levitated where I am right now.*

The Calatians screamed as they were dropped seemingly into the fire, but Kip knew there was only one other fire sorcerer in the world and he trusted that although Cott would consume a ship out from under the people on it, he would not burn the people alive.

I have you, master, Nikolon said as Kip pulled in magic and sucked the fire out of the frigate. The dozen Calatians last pulled away from the group, now free of Valkuni's spell, moved across the Road quickly.

"Malcolm, ward the ship," Kip called down to his friend. "Alice—"

Alice floated beside him. "I'm going to get them back," she said, and sped toward the stolen Calatians.

Take me to where the Calatians disappeared, Kip asked Nikolon, and he moved after Alice and then past the Calatians, now slowing under Alice's magic. Several hundred feet past the Road, a ship shimmered and appeared on the ocean in front of him. He'd been prepared to send fire down to it, but the sight of it took him aback. The warship below him was not a wooden frigate nor even a ship of the line, but a small, sleek vessel low to the ground and plated from stem to stern with great iron sheets. Smokestacks rather than sails jutted up from its center, but the usual array of small cannon bristled from its bow, those now the center of a flurry of activity. They fired toward the American frigate, and sailors set to reloading.

Those Kip could do something about. The gunpowder that they needed was stored in metal canisters, but as the cannon were reloaded the canisters were open, so he sent fire to the base of every cannon he could see. Loud bangs and puffs of smoke arose from each one, sending sailors staggering back with curses, some bleeding, a few falling and lying still. Kip searched for his Calatians on the deck of the boat and then he was jerked to the side and a small cannonball went whistling past him.

Thank you, Nikolon, he said, and focused on the ship. Flame could consume iron, but Cott could draw the flame out of it as easily as Kip could. Where did this ship draw its power from? It couldn't be only sorcerers pushing it through the water. The smokestacks meant that something was being burned there in the heart of the ship.

No; the stolen Calatians were his first priority. Nikolon pulled him out of the way of another cannonball, and then he spotted twenty Calatians huddled on one of the decks together. He directed Nikolon to bring him down, but then a raven flew at him, and he had to fend it off. *Can you get just those Calatians on the boat?* he asked.

Perhaps, but then it would be harder to defend you from cannonballs.

Kip cast a physical magic spell to keep himself in place and then called up fire again, eager . He would have to cripple the ship somehow so it couldn't follow once they got the Calatians away. *Let me worry about the cannonballs,* he said as he scanned the ship. It would take a lot of power to consume the iron and it might take too long, but it would occupy the sorcerers while

Nikolon rescued the Calatians, he hoped. His body thrummed with nervous energy.

A voice spoke in Kip's ear: Malcolm's demon Daravont. "Kip," it said in Malcolm's voice, "Alice made it back, but the ship is leaving. They say they can't risk waiting here. The cannon are almost in range. I can hide them, but they've ravens and we don't."

"I'll catch up," he said, his eyes lighting on the smokestacks, and at that moment Nikolon lifted the Calatians from the deck. Watching for cannonballs, Kip sought out the fire within the ship that he knew must be there somewhere, found it, and fed it twofold, threefold, fivefold.

Smoke poured from the ship and the creak of tortured metal came like a great groan from its inside. The cries of sailors rose to Kip again, and then the Calatians were pulled hard back down, two of them onto the deck of the boat and the rest into the ocean.

"Penfold!" came a voice from the deck he didn't recognize. One sorcerer stood looking up, robes flapping around him. "Leave off destroying our ship or you'll kill all your fellows there in the water."

Nikolon, lift them out!

I am trying, master, but they are being held in. He is very strong.

"Turn over the rest of the Calatians you've stolen from us or I'll kill every one of these, one at a time."

Desperate, Kip sent fire at the sorcerer, but it flared only briefly and then was sucked away. Now he saw another sorcerer, who must be Cott, kneeling beside one of the Calatians that had fallen onto the deck, a mouse that lay still.

The one who wasn't Cott sneered at Kip and pointed out into the ocean. "Just for that...you see that fox there?"

One of the Calatians floating in the water was a fox. Kip didn't think it was Abel, but as soon as he turned his attention there, the fox disappeared under the water before he could be sure.

Nikolon, help me save him!

He turned his own physical magic to the fox, combining it with Nikolon's to pull the struggling Calatian above the surface of the water. Then he lifted the fox and with some effort kept him up in the air. It was not Abel.

"Well done," the sorcerer called. "But while you were saving one, you lost another."

He gestured with a hand, and a dormouse-Calatian broke the surface of the water, hanging limply in the air with his head at an unnatural angle before falling with a splash. The others screamed and tried to swim away. With a wrench, Kip recognized the dead Calatian as Thomas Trewel.

Despair gnawed at his chest but he pushed it away. There were still many Calatians left alive that he could rescue, and if he could keep this physical sorcerer occupied, he might yet save the others. There would be time to mourn Thomas.

Help them get to the Road, please, Kip instructed Nikolon. *The farther you get from him the weaker he'll be.* A cannonball flew toward him, slower than gunpowder would propel it; he wrenched control away and sent it back toward the sorcerer, and then, letting some of the anger consume him, he took Thomas's body from the water and threw it at the sorcerer as a following shot.

The man diverted the cannonball easily but was startled by the sodden corpse and only narrowly avoided it, stumbling to the deck. Kip pressed his advantage, trying fire again only to have Cott pull it away.

"Damn you, Cott," the sorcerer cried, throwing another cannonball. "Take care of him! Use that!"

He pointed to Thomas's body. Cott turned and looked up, and Kip saw his round boyish face clearly, the petulant look he so often wore replaced by sorrow and confusion.

When he met Kip's eyes, the sorrow intensified, and Kip knew an attack was coming. But Cott, like Kip, was no military sorcerer. He threw a wall of flame at Kip, which Kip swept away easily, and then ignited the air around the fox. Kip pulled the flame back and sent it down to the boat.

A cannonball burst through the flames, headed directly for him. He didn't have time to grab it with magic so he twisted to try to avoid it, reaching out with a paw to fend it off. His paw slowed it only a little, but he got mostly out of the way before it glanced off his chest.

Pain burst through his ribs. His concentration faltered for a moment and he dropped toward the water, then kept going down even as he recovered. If they thought he was wounded or dead, they might let their guard down. *Nikolon, show me the Calatians in the water.*

They were struggling toward the Road, close to it now. They were going to make it. Kip hit the ocean, cold salt water closing over him in a shock. He pushed himself to the surface. *Show me what's on the deck of the boat.*

Cott knelt over the body of Thomas, a knife out. He hesitated, and from Nikolon's viewpoint, the horror at his situation showed plainly in his wide-eyed grimace. "I can do it without," he said.

The other sorcerer didn't let him finish. "Do it!" he yelled. "We can't let them escape."

"But—"

"Do it now or I swear I'll hold you down and drench you in his blood."

Cott shuddered and bent back to the corpse. Revulsion on his face, he plunged the blade into the dead dormouse's arm and lifted it to his mouth. Blood ran down his chin in a gruesome display. Kip, unable to close his eyes or turn away, fought against a wave of nausea.

The other sorcerer turned to stare out over the water. "I think the fox is down, but we should be sure."

"I'll send Ash." Cott straightened and wiped his mouth, leaving bloody smears on his face and hand. He stared ahead, face still twisted. "I'm ready for the frigate."

The cold of the water was nothing compared to the ice that those words brought to Kip's chest. There was only one reason Cott would need to enhance his power: he needed to be able to overcome Kip's resistance, to keep the frigate burning until it fell apart around the Americans and Calatians. And then what?

The great ironclad ship groaned again and then lifted from the water, pulling Kip toward it in the wake it created. The physical sorcerer closed his eyes, focusing as the ship came free of the water entirely and slowly moved across the Road. So that was his answer: they were going to recapture the Calatians. And what about Malcolm and Alice? Cott might not want to kill, but his companion clearly had no compunctions about that. Kip knew the wartime strategy when encountering enemy sorcerers who might translocate away: kill them immediately.

Struggling against the wave to keep himself above water, his mind and heart raced, veering toward the edge of panic until he reined himself in. It was down to him now, just him, and if he failed, he doomed his friends to death or capture. He wasn't trained for this, but there was nobody to defer to now.

A black shape swept past him. Cott cried out, "The other Calatians are escaping onto the Road."

"Let them go. We can retrieve them later," his companion said in the strained tones of someone maintaining a difficult focus. The ship had moved halfway across the Road.

Cott's raven returned, and its eyes met Kip's. Through Nikolon's eyes, he saw Cott open his mouth to speak and then hesitate. He turned to the side of the ship, staring out over the ocean to see Kip. "Get away," the raven whispered in Cott's voice.

In that moment Kip saw his chance. "I can't let you kill them," he said, and poured fire into the steel of the ship, heating it quickly.

Cott felt it and pulled the fire out, but Kip had only meant that attack as a distraction. As soon as Cott reacted, Kip sent fire to consume the other sorcerer, hot and powerful and deadly.

By the time Cott turned back to the deck; his companion's smoking, charred corpse had fallen to the deck in a spray of fiery ash, and Cott only had a moment to register that before the ship fell onto the Road, half of it still hanging off the southern edge. Sailors scurried around the ship, and the two Calatians who'd been dropped onto the deck, a mouse and an otter, took the chance to dive overboard into the ocean.

Kip flew himself to the Road and then above it, and Cott's raven followed him, shrieking. "Why did you do that? Why did you kill him?"

Fire burst around him again, an immense inferno fueled by Cott's enhanced power, but Kip was prepared and sent much of it back into the hold of the ship. The ironclad shuddered and rocked alarmingly, throwing

Cott into the railing. He clutched it as his raven flew at Kip's face and Kip had to hold it using physical magic while he dispelled the rest of Cott's inferno. The boat wasn't going to go anywhere now. Kip had won.

Below him, the otter helped the mouse up onto the Road. Kip dropped down to join them. *Nikolon, find the other Calatians along the Road.* He reached out with magic to the mouse and the otter. "I've got you now. We're going to get you out of here."

"No!" Cott howled, watching from the side, eyes wide and face bright red. "No!" He sent fire again, and again Kip drew most of it away.

The ship groaned and then shrieked as metal tore and the half hanging in the ocean shuddered and lurched. Cott lost his balance and then scrambled to his feet. "Wait there," Kip said, preparing for another fire attack. "I'll get the ship—"

His former mentor stared not at Kip and his charges, but at the Road that his ship was breaking upon, where the Calatians were escaping. He raised his hands.

Too late Kip realized that Cott wasn't forming a spell; he was casting already. The Road began to glow, first white and then yellow. The salt on it sizzled. With a curse, Kip gripped the raven in one paw and cast his physical magic spell on himself and the other two Calatians, lifting them from the heated surface of the Road. "Master Cott!" he called. "Please stop!"

Cott was beyond hearing him now. He poured fire into the Road even though Kip had lifted himself and the Calatians off it. The glow extended as far as Kip could see, and the water on either side of the Road bubbled and steamed. *Nikolon, get them off the Road!*

I have just found them.

Get them—

Cott screamed, and the raven in Kip's paws opened its beak and echoed the scream. The Road glowed unbearably bright, waves of heat emanating from it. Around the Road, the ocean steamed, and next to it, white froth bubbled up. The mouse and otter cried out and shielded their eyes, and Kip flew them higher.

How far could Cott heat the Road? Were there people at the inns, in the middle of the ocean, whose skin was blistering? Kip tried to reach into the Road to draw out the fire and encountered a surge of power unlike anything he'd ever felt. Reflexively he pulled free of it, feeling as though he'd passed out for a moment.

He still hung in the air, the mouse and otter safely alongside him, and Cott still gripped the railing of the ship, staring down at the luminescent cauldron that he'd made of the Road. How much fire must be coursing through him? His skin glowed bright red, and over the hissing and popping below them, Kip could make out Cott's voice in a strange keening moan. The raven he held opened its beak as well, but no sound emerged.

The air crackled and burned. Kip's fur stood on end. He had to do something, anything, to stop this. But what—

With a deafening crack, the Road disappeared.

The ironclad fell back into the water with a crash. Kip plummeted toward the ocean, his physical spell inexplicably gone. Wind rushed past his ears, hot, steaming; he sought magic and it exploded into him. A body's length above the water, he caught himself and reversed his fall.

Screams filled the air as the mouse and otter hit the boiling water. Squinting against the billows of steam, he found and lifted the otter, but the churning waves hid the mouse, and a moment later the screams died away. Kip pulled the otter to his side; she clung to him and he put an arm around her shoulders, holding the limp raven in the other paw. She was sobbing. "It's going to be okay," he said. "I've got you."

"I knew you would," she said, and only then did her scent filter through to him. This was Coppy's sister, either Ella or Tokka. He hugged her more tightly.

The ironclad listed dangerously to one side. Many sailors had jumped overboard, but those who remained on the ship had watched their fellows scalded and boiled in the water and now clung to the railings crying for help. Cott lay prone on the deck of the ship, unmoving, blank eyes staring out at the devastation he'd caused.

Nikolon! Kip called, speeding toward the ship. *Nikolon!*

The raven in his paw stirred as Nikolon answered. *I am sorry, master. My spell died. I have six. The rest perished.*

Six is better than none, Kip replied, though his heart sank. *Come find me.*

He looked down at the raven. If it was still alive, then Cott was too, but its movements were growing weaker and more strained. He stared down at its eyes, trying to connect. "Cott?"

"Cott?" it echoed, and stared back at him, calming. "Cott?"

Something pushed into his mind. He panicked, resisting at first, and the raven fluttered in agitation. "Calm down," he said. "Calm down. It's…"

"Cott," the raven said, and as Kip relaxed he saw himself through the raven's eyes, exactly as if it were a demon. In his paws, it settled, but he could feel strength return to it.

He'd—stolen Cott's raven? No; the raven must have been unbound at Cott's death and had sought out another soul to bind to. Cautiously, he let go, and the raven spread its wings and soared. When he tried to see through its eyes again—there, he could see what it saw.

He sent it to the railing where the sailors were clamoring. "Hold for a moment," he said, and they quieted, hearing his voice come from the raven. "I'll get you." There were a dozen of them; between himself and Nikolon they could surely lift them all over the steaming swath of ocean that a moment before had been a magical Road.

Kip landed next to Cott on the deck, the otter floating next to him (Ella, he was almost sure it was Ella, Coppy's oldest sister). "I've still got you," he told her, seeing her panic at the listing deck. "I just need to take care of this."

His former mentor had not moved; his eyes remained open and sightless. Kip checked for a heartbeat anyway, and was not surprised to find none. He closed Cott's eyes and took a moment to say a prayer for him. Cott had done so much for him, had taught him to be careful with fire, and in the end fire had consumed him anyway despite all his care. Kip's chest tightened. He'd hoped to visit Cott again after the war, to compare notes on what he'd discovered. Now he wondered if he too would end in fire, if for a fire sorcerer there was any other kind of death.

The metal of the deck was hot enough to be uncomfortable on his feet. He lifted himself back to Ella, who was sobbing quietly. Kip put his arm around her again and closed his eyes, saying a prayer for all the souls that had been lost, Cott and the Calatians and even the other sorcerer, committing their loss to God so he would not have to bear it alone.

CHAPTER 14: THE MASTER

On the American frigate, an hour later, they took stock of their losses. Kip had rescued eleven sailors from the ironclad before it sank, and seven of the stolen Calatians between himself and Nikolon. Nobody had kept close track of how many Calatians had been sent to New Cambridge, nor even how many had originally set out on the mission, but Abel estimated thirty had been lost, including those Nikolon had tried to save, the mouse Kip hadn't been able to save (one of Ella's friends named Tamrin), and several who had gone overboard from the frigate in the chaos following the destruction of the Road. One had also been crushed on board in the confusion and killed. This didn't count the injured, including the six Nikolon had rescued, who had burns of varying severity over their bodies.

Even the people looking back toward the British threat as the frigate fled had only seen parts of what had happened. But they'd all felt the thunderclap (as they described it) and the ensuing waves of heat and then water that had rocked the boat, so they understood how the Calatians could have come to be scalded. The sorcerers had known that something terrible had happened when all their magic failed in an instant, and when the Road appeared to be gone, Malcolm had sent Daravont to confirm it.

He hadn't been able to do that right away: the implosion of magic had unbound Daravont, Malcolm quickly found. He bound the demon again before it could do much mischief. "Just as you must have done with yours," he said to Kip, "and you in the middle of much more than I was."

"Yes," Kip said, "well, it had to be done." But he had not re-bound Nikolon; the demon had delivered the six Calatians to the frigate and then Kip had dismissed her. He hadn't noticed that the binding had been broken, because he hadn't asked her to do anything. Perhaps that last order had remained in force? Certainly Nikolon wasn't above cursing him if not bound properly, and had done so. But their relationship, to the extent that a person could have a relationship with a demon, had progressed since then. What he knew was that if he'd had to re-bind Nikolon, those precious few seconds would likely have meant that the six Calatians the demon had saved would have boiled alive.

That question, bothersome though it was, could wait until he had to summon her again, and perhaps after that. The larger topic of discussion on the frigate was the destruction of the Road, and the first thing Kip had to do was set the record straight. When he'd returned to the frigate with Ella Lutris and the British sailors, the first thing the sailors did upon landing was hurry to the uniformed first mate sent to greet them and cry, "That fox destroyed the Road!"

They'd seen him wreathed in fire, and a moment later the Road had glowed brightly and "exploded." It was a reasonable assumption to make, so Kip had to tell the story over and over again, and even then he wasn't sure everyone believed him. So he excused himself from the ship's crew and set about walking through the crowd of Calatians with Abel and Alice, finding any who needed the services of a healer and directing them to Callahan and Broadwood to be sent to New Cambridge.

Both the other foxes sensed Kip's need for silence and did not talk about the battle until they had gone through all the Calatians they could find (some had gone below decks to sleep). Then Alice said, "It must have been terrible," and Kip hesitated a moment before waving her and Abel toward Malcolm.

The Irishman sat in a quiet part of the deck near the middle of the three masts, and raised a hand at the sound of the three foxes settling down around him. Each fox greeted him so he would know who they were.

"Thank you kindly," Malcolm said. "How are our charges?"

"Fifteen injured," Abel said. "The sorcerers have sent them to the mainland. I hope they let you rest before you have to go home, Kip."

"Jackson will want his briefing," Kip said, but the adrenaline of the battle had long since left him and he was having trouble keeping his eyes open.

"Fifteen injured and thirty lost out of three hundred," Malcolm said. "That's not a bad loss."

The three foxes remained silent until he said, "What? Come now, I know when I've missed something."

"It's not thirty out of three hundred," Abel said. "It's thirty out of five thousand. Or six thousand perhaps."

Malcolm tilted his head. "How do you mean?"

"There are more than a thousand humans for every Calatian," Kip said. "So what would you say if we'd lost thirty thousand people on the Road?"

"Well, aye." Malcolm's voice softened. "That'd be worse."

"And worse still because there are so many different kinds and we can only mate to another of our kind," Alice added. "In fifty years there might be no more wolf-Calatians."

"There might not be any Calatians at all," Abel said darkly.

"What's that?" Malcolm turned his head. He'd dismissed his demon, so he couldn't see the expressions on the foxes' faces. If there were a way to transfer his raven to Malcolm, Kip would have done it on the spot.

"The Road was a Great Feat," Alice said quietly. "So are we."

"Everyone thought that Great Feats couldn't be undone," Kip added, though Malcolm's mouth made an 'O' and it was clear he understood. "But now we know they can, though at a price."

"But...could they unmake all of you? Or just one at a time?"

The foxes exchanged looks. "Nobody knows," Kip said. "And we'd prefer they not experiment."

"Of course." Malcolm heaved a sigh. "That's a blow, aye? Imagine if our Lord came down one day and unmade some people back into clay. Of course, it would depend on who those people were. I wouldn't be sad to see Albright gone. But we wouldn't be making those decisions. And of course," he added hurriedly, "all of you are lovely people."

Kip couldn't help a slight smile. "Let's hope it remains a theory for a long time."

"But it means we must work as hard as we can to save every one of us." Alice leaned against Kip. He put an arm around her shoulder and took strength from her confidence and support.

"To my mind," Malcolm said, "you've all done as much as could be expected, and then some. This whole operation feels cobbled together from shoestrings and bent nails and yet you've got a frigate full of London Calatians to take back to America."

Abel rested his paws on his knees and nodded to Kip. "You can't save every Calatian. Those who came along did so knowing the risk."

"I know," Kip said. "I know."

He shifted his gaze to the raven—his raven—which now sat on the rigging. From there Kip could look down on the ship and see himself and all the other Calatians moving around. The raven did have a personality of sorts, but a quiet one, and right now she—Kip knew she was a she, and that her name was Ash—clung to her bond with Kip, nudging him gently through it every few minutes to check that he were really still there. He had no idea how she had come to bond to him. In Kip's limited experience, when a sorcerer died, his bonded raven died as well. But of course, nobody else had been present at the destruction of a Great Feat.

A touch on his paw brought him back to himself. Alice said, "We lost some at Savannah, too."

"This is different." Kip leaned back and looked up through the ropes. "There were others in charge at Savannah. I was trying to go find my parents, and Captain Lowell was in charge of that expedition. This was mine, beginning to end. You all did as much—more—than I could have asked, but had I done some things differently, maybe some of those people would still be alive."

"Now, haven't you said that the plan was Jackson's?" Malcolm leaned forward and reached out a hand. "Kip, you proposed an idea, and someone else changed it and made you work under their orders. Besides which, people die in war, and nothing will change that."

Abel cleared his throat. "Losing thirty of our number is a high price. But we have been talking for years and years, and only when you arrived did we see our way clear to action. We will always be grateful to you for that, at least. And I know that you did your best to save every one. Ella Lutris is evidence of that."

"But what about Tamrin, her friend? I couldn't save her."

"Your best is all that anyone can ask," Alice said. "Do you think I'm not wondering what could have happened if I'd remained by your side? We might've stopped your Master Cott. Maybe there would still be a Road."

"I don't know if anyone could have stopped him." What if Kip hadn't killed the other sorcerer? Would Cott have been driven to madness and desperation in that moment? But if Kip hadn't killed the other sorcerer, would he have been able to stop the ironclad from catching the frigate? How many lives would have been lost?

Out beyond the railing, calm deep blue broken with specks of white stretched out to the horizon as far as they could see. The ocean had absorbed the debris of the battle as though it had never been. Nearer to them, the bow wake spread away from the ship in white ripples that faded to blue. There was something hypnotic about the movement of the waves, going up and down, traveling away and yet never really going anywhere. He could see what some of the traders from Boston meant falling in love with the sea.

And yet it was terrifying, too, to think that this ocean had swallowed an ironclad, sailors, and Calatians—not to mention the inns and other travelers along the Road—and all those were gone without a trace. What else might lie hidden in its depths? He drifted off, imagining it, and then snapped his eyes open. "Sorry. Did you ask me something?"

Abel smiled. "I asked, 'what comes next,' but it's not important. What comes next is sleep for you, obviously."

Kip yawned. "What comes next is getting all these people to America, and then finding a safe place for all of them during the war, and then finding homes for them after the war, I suppose. For me…" He eyed the bow of the ship and the horizon beyond it. "A debriefing from the Master Colonel that I expect will involve a lot of yelling, and then probably I'll be confined to quarters without magic until they need me to set fire to another British army."

"He'll recognize that you did the best you could," Alice said fiercely. "If he says a word against you, I'll—"

Kip held up a paw. "You, like me, will hold your tongue and take it. We still stand to benefit—maybe only marginally—from an American victory, and we'll do more good for our cause as useful soldiers than we will as prisoners."

"I wouldn't say anything that would get me sent to prison." Alice remained indignant. "I'd just tell him he was wrong."

He wanted so badly to be deserving of her confidence. But he couldn't help replaying the encounter in his mind, thinking of the people he could have saved if only this, if only that.

Alice took his paw. "You know that, don't you? That he'd be wrong? Look at what you mean to the people here, not just that you've saved their lives, but what an example you've been. Like Abel said, you took action. You made a difference. It's what's inspired Malcolm to keep learning spells. It—" She paused a moment, her ears flicking back to the others listening, and then she went on. "You inspire me. You haven't just taught me magic. You've shown me magic. That you care so much and risk so much when you could easily sit in Boston and be a fire sorcerer for the American army? That's why I want to marry you. Not just because you're a fox."

Her eyes gleamed in the sunlight, and the horror of the last hour receded before that brightness. Kip squeezed her paw back.

"She speaks truth," Abel said quietly.

"Thank you," he said, and reached his arms out to embrace Alice. She moved willingly into the embrace and rested her muzzle against his.

A shadow fell across them, and Kip looked up to see Callahan, the man's face lined and as weary as he felt. "Penfold," he said. "Master Colonel Jackson requests your presence in Boston."

Despite what he'd just said, Jackson was far away and Kip was very disinclined to get up, even when Alice pulled back to sit beside him. "You may tell him that I will return to Boston when all the Calatians have been sent ahead of me from this boat. My mission is not complete until they all stand on American soil."

Callahan ran a hand through his hair and squinted down. "You're refusing a direct order?"

"You said, 'requests,'" Kip said. "So it's not a direct order. My mission isn't over yet."

"You can play word games with the Master Colonel if you like, but do you expect me and Broadwood to send all the Calatians back? That'll take hours."

"Of course not." Kip closed his eyes. "You could wait until the boat reaches Boston in a month. Perhaps three weeks if Alice graces us with an elemental to speed us along."

Callahan didn't move. As an experiment, Kip shifted his view to Ash's, looking down on the deck as the tall sorcerer stalked away, and followed him around the deck to where he muttered something and vanished.

"You just said all that about being respectful," Malcolm said, though it seemed he could barely restrain himself from laughing.

"Aye, to Jackson," Kip said. "That wasn't Jackson. I don't have to be respectful to Callahan. He doesn't outrank me." He paused. "I think."

"Go ahead and sleep," Abel said. "We'll keep an eye open for you."

There didn't seem to be anywhere better to sleep, so Kip stretched out on the deck, laced his paws behind his head, and dozed.

"Penfold."

A paw rested on his shoulder, Alice's scent in his nose. Abel and Malcolm were nearby. And also, that scent, that voice. He opened his eyes.

Master Colonel Jackson stood over him, dark against the bright afternoon sky. Besides his own scent, he smelled of laundry soap, and his uniform looked clean and pressed.

Kip blinked and rubbed his eyes. "Sir?"

"Yes, Penfold, in the flesh." He paused. "Shall I be waiting long for your salute?"

Kip scrambled to his feet, lost his footing briefly with the rolling of the ship, and then braced himself against the mast and saluted.

Jackson returned the salute, a wry smile on his face. "At ease," he said. "Is there a place on this ship where we might have some privacy?"

"Er." Kip looked up at the crow's nest. "I can't think of any."

"Willoughby offered his cabin, but I quite like the fresh air. Let's go to the stern. Captain Lowell will make sure we're not disturbed."

Only then did Kip see the captain, also in a fresh uniform, standing stiffly behind Jackson. He met Kip's eyes briefly and then fell in behind the two of them as Jackson led him to a sheltered part of the stern where the wind from their passage swirled about them rather than rushing past. The smell of the sea still overwhelmed everything else for Kip, except for Jackson's scent as the Master Colonel settled himself barely a foot from Kip along the railing.

Captain Lowell positioned himself between the two of them and the rest of the ship, and Jackson said, pleasantly enough, "Now, Penfold. Debrief."

Kip took a breath and started with meeting the barge on the Thames, a night that seemed weeks ago now. He took Jackson through lifting the barge over the weirs, sending some of the Calatians back to New Cambridge, arriving at Lechlade, going back to New Cambridge himself to see that everyone was settled and finding a demon name, lifting the Calatians to the Road, finding the raven, and meeting the British ship.

At every point he expected Jackson to stop and question him, but the man merely watched him intently, nodding every time Kip paused. He did ask for further description of the ironclad, saying, "Very interesting, very interesting." When Kip reached the battle with Cott, he paused. His description wouldn't do it justice, and Jackson was a spiritual sorcerer. He could see Kip's memory.

Kip ran briefly through those events in case there was anything he wouldn't want Jackson to see, but the only thing he would want to keep private was Nikolon's behavior, and that wasn't related to the Road. Besides which, it would be nice to have someone else know for certain that he, Kip, had not in fact destroyed a Great Feat. "Sir, would you like to see the destruction of the Road?"

Jackson's mouth twitched. He parted his lips and seemed about to decline, and then stopped himself. "I…yes, I would. Thank you, Penfold."

Kip inclined his head forward, and Jackson cast a spell, a feather touch in his mind. Kip reviewed as faithfully as possible the events that led to the ironclad being stranded on the Road, his own desperation that led to him incinerating the other sorcerer, Cott's answering desperation and the sudden catastrophic disappearance of the Road.

Jackson withdrew as soon as that event happened, not even waiting to see Kip regain his magic, so he also missed Kip's communication with Nikolon. "Fascinating," he said, staring off at the sea. "Absolutely incredible."

Kip waited until Jackson's sharp eyes returned to him. "Do you think Cott was trying to destroy the Road?"

"No." The fox shook his head. "I think…he was trying to destroy one part of it, to get his ship back in the water. But also he knew the Calatians were getting onto the Road and that may have been part of it. He wanted to stop us, but he didn't want to harm us if he could avoid it. I'm sure he didn't set out to destroy the whole Road."

"Likely not, although you never know. I suppose you knew him better than I did, eh?"

Kip nodded. He swallowed against the memory of Cott's dead eyes, of the whispered "Get away" that his teacher had tried to spare him with at the end. "He would use fire to scare, but he was very aware of how easy it would be to destroy something, and he kept himself in check. He didn't have many friends because of the fire, but he wanted to be liked."

"Could he have killed you?"

"I don't think so. He wasn't a killer at heart." Kip pushed away the memory of the soldier and the sorcerers he himself had killed so far in this war.

"Tch, no. I mean, had the battle gone on longer, could he have found a way to kill you? He had the power, apparently."

"Oh. I don't know. I don't think I could have killed him. We know fire too well." Kip took a breath. He hadn't told anyone else this, but now it was irrelevant. "There was an old technique that he never taught me—I found it in one of his books. When you call up fire, you can let it know you, and then it won't turn against you. He sent fire around me and that's why the men say I was wreathed in flame right before the Road exploded."

"I wondered about that," Jackson said. "If he'd tried to consume you as you did Hadlock, it wouldn't have worked?"

Cott would never have done something like that. But Jackson didn't care about that part. So Kip shook his head, spreading a paw over his chest. "I don't think so. Nor if I'd tried it on him."

"Not something you'll have to worry about in the future, eh?" Jackson smiled.

The world felt vaster and lonelier than it had at the beginning of the day. There would be no more threats of fire, true; there would also be nowhere else to learn once the war was over, nobody else who understood what Kip's power felt like. The only fire sorcerer left in Britain or America shook his head. "No, sir."

The Master Colonel rubbed his hands together and turned to look back across the wake of the ship. "All in all, it has been a great success. I knew it would be."

"A…" Kip's ears splayed to the side. "A great success? We lost thirty Calatians."

"Acceptable losses." Jackson waved to the ocean. "We discovered that they have created a new kind of fireproof vessel, which is valuable, and you sank it, which is even more valuable. Hadlock is a middling sorcerer but a decent tactician—was, that is—and his loss will hurt them, as will the loss of their only fire sorcerer. Besides which, the destruction of the Road will unsettle them greatly." He rubbed his hands together. "It all went about as well as I had planned."

Kip stared. "Sir? I was on my own. I didn't consult you about most of what I did. If Captain Lowell had been there—"

"If Captain Lowell had been there, all that would be different is that you would have someone else to blame your shortcomings on. Don't downplay your accomplishments, Penfold. What Lowell might have done in the two places I feel you could have done better probably would not have made a great deal of difference. And depending on how you feel about the destruction of the Road, I could argue that the outcome without Lowell present tilted more in our favor."

"Our…favor? Where could I have done better?"

Jackson ticked off on his fingers. "One, you should have killed that raven as soon as they let it come close to you. Two, you should have sunk the ironclad and killed Hadlock as soon as you saw them. Finding a fire source inside it to amplify was very clever; I wager you could have done permanent damage to the ship before Cott was able to pull back the fire."

"Cott was protecting Hadlock until the end, when he was distracted. And they had the Calatians on board, or under their control. I'd have lost them."

"Perhaps. As I said, one could argue either way. They underestimated you, as I thought they would if I did not send a senior officer along, but you won't be able to count on that in the future. All in all it was quite well done. Now, why aren't you coming back to Boston? General Hamilton will want to hear your story, and we expect a British attack in the coming week."

Kip could think of nothing he wanted to do less right now than join another battle. He waved a dark brown paw at the ship. "These Calatians are my responsibility, sir, ah, until you assign them to someone else. The British could have other ships, sorcerers, ravens, and so on. I want to make sure they are safe and warded." He seized the moment to ask the other question that had been on his mind. "Sir, where will they go? The Tower isn't large enough for all of them."

The question appeared to bore Jackson. "They have tents around it, aye? They can sleep there. We will see to them presently."

"Presently? Sir, they're being fed by the generosity of—"

"Penfold." Jackson's tone sharpened, and despite his passion, Kip quieted. "My job is to win this war for America. When we win, then we will have the luxury of settling three hundred Calatian refugees."

"They won't be treated as prisoners, then?"

"Of course not. They left of their own volition."

That was the most he was going to get from Jackson, so he nodded and said, "Thank you, sir."

"Meanwhile," Jackson said, "I'll task Captain Lowell with finding someone to take charge of the Calatians here."

"Sir," Kip said. "If you leave me Callahan and Broadwood, we can have them all in New Cambridge by the day after tomorrow."

"Two of our translocators? Out of the question. You can send one at a time, can't you? You may keep Broadwood, and be back in Boston the day after tomorrow, eight in the morning on the nose."

"Yes, sir." Kip sighed. "We will manage."

"You have a boat full of calyxes," Jackson pointed out. "You can get this done." He raised a hand. "Come, Lowell, we're going back."

Kip leaned back against the railing and closed his eyes. But his ears remained perked, so he heard Captain Lowell say, "Permission to remain on the ship to brief Penfold about the other operation, sir?"

Jackson said something indistinct, and Lowell replied, "I am assigned to their unit, sir."

The reply sounded irritated, but it must have been in the affirmative, because Lowell said, "Thank you, sir," and a moment later Kip smelled him nearby on the railing.

"One more thing, Penfold," Jackson called sharply.

Kip opened his eyes to see the man's ascetic features set in a thin-lipped smile. "When people say you destroyed the Road, don't deny it too hard. Will scare the British even more if they think one of ours did it and is still alive."

"Yes, sir," Kip said, though his stomach churned. Jackson nodded and strode off to find Callahan, leaving Kip and Lowell alone.

They stood in silence while the ship cut through the water with a rhythmic rushing of waves, wood and rigging creaking above them. Finally Lowell spoke in a low voice. "Was it terrible?"

Kip nodded. "Aye. The Road was a marvel and then it was gone. For a moment it sucked magic out of the world and then magic came back. But not the Road." He paused. "It killed Cott, destroying it." His eyes traveled out to the ocean again, to the vast expanse of water that mocked any puny human or Calatian enterprise. Cott lay there somewhere in its depths while Kip sailed home on its surface.

Lowell nodded, absorbing that. "I heard you tell Master Colonel Jackson that you wished I was with you here. That means a great deal to me."

"I meant it," Kip said. "You're experienced and you've always guided us true through our battles. And…" He hesitated. "I get the impression that you care more for we Calatians as a people than perhaps some of the other officers do."

Lowell inclined his head, but said, "A free America is my first and truest pledge. But in that free America I do greatly hope that all people will be equally free."

"As do I," Kip said. "Now…what was this other operation?"

"Ah, yes, that." Lowell looked down at his hands. "We had just acquired information that the Prince George's College sorcerers were being held in Gibraltar. Thanks to you, in great part. We did some reconnaissance and determined that they were being held in the fortress. There were few other places to keep them, to be honest. So…"

Here he paused again, still not looking at Kip. The fox's tail swished against the railing, and finally he said, "So?"

"They—Master Colonel Jackson and Major General Hamilton, I believe—conceived a plan to rescue them. The operation was to be undertaken at the same time as yours, and yours was to serve as a diversion for the British sorcerers."

Kip heard the words but took a moment to fully understand them. "They told the British sorcerers about our mission?"

"No!" Now Lowell did look at him. "I don't believe so. But they were convinced that you could not sneak hundreds of Calatians out of the Isle without the sorcerers noticing, and when they noticed they would focus all their attention on you. Besides which you would be depriving them of their calyxes for a critical day or two at least."

"I see." This one piece of information answered most of his questions about Jackson's changes to his mission. Of course Jackson had wanted him to draw out the mission over days; of course he'd wanted Kip to lead the British sorcerers out into the middle of the ocean, to keep them watching him while they stealthily extracted prisoners from Gibraltar. "Did they find the Peachtree Calatians?"

Lowell shook his head. "Our mission was to extract the sorcerers, and we accomplished that. Our secondary goal was to find the book of demon names, and we accomplished that as well."

"You didn't have time to find the Calatians?" Kip searched the captain's face and saw the answer there. "It wasn't one of your priorities. But that doesn't make any sense. Why go to all this trouble to deprive the British of their calyxes if you were going to leave them the prisoners?"

"I don't know the thinking behind it. The military sorcerers seem attached to their calyxes; in many cases they travel with the sorcerers and live with them for extended periods of time. So stealing the British calyxes may take a toll on the sorcerers."

Kip had made that same argument, but now he doubted whether it would really make much difference. He focused on the fact that he'd rescued over two hundred Calatians. "It may," he allowed.

Captain Lowell put a hand on Kip's arm. "You've proven yourself a valuable asset to the American army, the more so because you're the only fire sorcerer left on either side. Besides that, this mission will be trumpeted as a great success, and you'll always know the part you played in it."

"They're going to make me out to be the destroyer of the Road," Kip said. "I don't want—" He sighed and stopped. "Tell me about the raid."

So Captain Lowell told him in some detail about the raid on Gibraltar. They'd sent several scouts ahead to find out where the boundary of the wards was, but they also had to be careful because the border of Gibraltar was heavily guarded by both British and Spanish soldiers. Lowell led a small unit, three sorcerers and one calyx, who followed the scouts in past the fortifications. But it wasn't as easy as getting into the Isle of Dogs had been; inside the outer wards were many inner spaces that were also warded, so the sorcerers had had to summon demons several times to explore the spaces.

They had only brought one calyx with them, but, Captain Lowell said, that one (a fox) had borne the calyx ritual stoically every time.

Kip gritted his teeth during that part, and Lowell moved on quickly from it to talk about the hour they'd spent creeping through the fortress, the times they'd run into guard demons and their own demons had had to do quick battle with them. "Fortunately," he said, "our demons were second order, and the guard ones are all first order out of necessity, else they couldn't be bound for long periods of time."

"Of course." Kip thought about Valkuni, how he'd fought the binding, and again about Nikolon.

"We were lucky, I think, in that they did not seem to expect us coming. Gibraltar is an odd place for a prison, being so close to Spain; if we had to guess, we would have thought them kept in the Tower of London, but Gibraltar is nearly as secure. Master Colonel Jackson said it hasn't been used as a prison before, and perhaps that's why they chose it, so those of us who'd fought in the British Army wouldn't suspect."

Kip nodded, and Lowell went on to describe the many obstacles they'd faced and how the sorcerers had overcome them. As the story went on, Kip began to understand how much Lowell's leadership must have meant to it; Jackson had given them little in the way of orders beyond "rescue the sorcerers and remain as quiet about it as possible," and Lowell had ordered the use of demons when needed, had guided their magic (in one case, he laughed at Master Johnston, who'd wanted to translocate himself into a warded area with no idea of what lay on the other side), and had kept them on track when they had to wait for half an hour for a guard to leave his post rather than attack him and risk his absence or body being discovered.

While he remained angry that the Calatians hadn't been rescued, Kip had to express his admiration. "Jackson—sorry, Master Colonel Jackson didn't seem to think that you would have made a difference in our mission here, but I believe if you'd been with me, we would have rescued all the Calatians."

Lowell smiled and lowered his head. "It's kind of you to say so."

"It's the truth." Kip lowered his voice as much as he thought he could and still have Lowell be able to hear him over the water. The crew of the ship were mostly going about their business at a distance. "You should get a promotion for this. I don't know how promotions work, but you deserve one."

"At my level, most often they are purchased, but we shall see. It would be nice to imagine that the Army is of the same mind."

Kip shook his head. "How long have you been a captain?"

Lowell's smile came humorless and crooked. "Eight years."

"Eight *years*? Is that a normal amount of time?"

"What's normal for one person may not be so for another." He pushed himself away from the railing. "And now," he said, "I believe you were going to convince poor Broadwood to send two hundred Calatians to New Cambridge."

Kip sighed and followed Lowell away from the railing. "Yes," he said. "And I must likely convince him to do the calyx ritual, and then convince some poor calyx to give him the power. How many times must we do that ritual? And how are we to keep it secret? Abel told me that most of the London Calatians know what the ritual is, but if one doesn't, it will be quite shocking to discover. Not to mention the ship's crew."

"I have some ideas on that score," Lowell said.

Lowell suggested that they secure the calyx blood in a private place and then bring it to Broadwood in a flask. Out here in the ocean air, the smell of blood from the flask dissipated quickly.

Convincing Broadwood took a good twenty minutes of arguing from Kip, and finally he told the other sorcerer that he himself had done the calyx ritual, and that if Broadwood chose not to do it, it would take him five times as long. With ill grace, the young man accepted his task.

The second problem, more surmountable, was that he needed to take a swallow before every spell. Abel rounded up all the calyxes he could, and Kip and Alice volunteered as well, but still it felt as though more blood was spilt than had been lost in the battle. Now Kip understood viscerally how the London sorcerers could literally bleed a calyx dry. In America, calyxes were mostly used for demon summoning and there was not much call to summon a number of demons in a row. But to extend one's range of perception, to try several different things while engaged in a military operation—that might require ten or twelve swallows of blood. And if a calyx were summoned several times within the week, they might well lose consciousness and even die.

Here, Abel managed the calyxes to ensure that nothing like that would happen; he forbad Callo Cotton from helping even though the rabbit insisted he was in perfect health and his sorcerer had only taken one goblet a few days ago. Broadwood, meanwhile, didn't feel well after his fifth swallow of blood and translocation spell. He had to take a long drink of wine to clear his mouth and his head.

"The first time it was worse than I thought it would be," he told Kip as the fox sat with him. "But the fifth was not nearly as bad. I hate the idea that I'm getting used to it."

"I know the feeling."

"The power is great. Ten people at a time! Once you've tried it, you wonder why you wouldn't use it all the time. Especially when you're bringing it to me in a flask and I don't have to know where it comes from. That worries me."

"London has that habit and has stopped her questions," Kip said. "Which is why we're rescuing them."

"Aye." He nodded and cleared his throat. "Imagine if the world knew we sorcerers were blood-drinkers. Myself too, now it comes to that. I thought the sorcerers who drank Calatian blood were disgusting, and I was a fellow of theirs."

"That is why we guard the secret," Kip said. "The Calatians could tell the world, but then they would lose the protection of the sorcerers."

"Of course." Broadwood's eyes widened. "You said you've done it, too, though? Does it work with—er, if you take from yourself?"

"That is how I prefer to do it now."

"It must have been worse for you." Broadwood stared out at the ocean. "If you don't think about it, though, don't you go the way of King's College, as you said it?"

"You don't think about it in the moment," Kip clarified. "Any other time, it's hard not to."

"Ah, I take your point."

They sat in silence staring out over the ocean. Kip could very easily believe that they were making no progress, just sailing the same endless water over and over again. "It's peaceful out here. I understand how some people can fall in love with the sea."

"It's boring. The clouds change but everything else looks the same. Plus I can't walk two paces without holding on to something."

"You'd get used to it." Kip sighed. "But that might be bad as well. Maybe the joy of the sea is the new places you get to at the end of the journey, even if the journey seems it will never end."

Broadwood didn't reply to that, so Kip changed his tack. "I very much appreciate all that you've done on this mission."

"You've done more than I. I missed all the interesting parts."

Kip glanced at the young man. "It sounds like you would have wanted to be there, in the range of an enemy physical sorcerer and a desperate fire one."

"I suppose not when you put it like that. But I was here when the Road was destroyed, and all my mates will ask me what it was like and what'll I say to that? 'I was on a large ship helping some Calatians get on board and then there was like a thunderclap and magic felt strange, and then a huge wave came along, and then Master Penfold came back to tell us the Road was gone.'?"

"I'm not 'Master Penfold.'"

"I don't know about that. If anyone's earned the title, you have, the work you've done."

"Thank you. I don't know what I'd get from the title."

"Well, a raven, for one."

Kip looked up at the rigging where Ash sat staring forward into the wind. "True. There is that."

The calyxes were sent back last, including Abel. Kip took him aside before they left. "I know that Wilton Blaeda is in charge of the Isle."

"But he chose to remain there."

"Aye. I don't know who the displaced Isle folk will look to, but when I come to make changes and find you a settlement, I'll come to you first, until you tell me someone else has been chosen."

Abel nodded. "It may not look the best for me to be in charge simply because I have your favor, but then…" He flicked his ears. "It has been a difficult few days. We will take a little while to settle in."

"I'm sorry for everyone who was lost."

The other fox nodded. "As am I." He exhaled. "I know you did your best, Kip. And what you did accomplish is marvelous. I never thought to leave the Isle—figured I'd die there of something or another. Now…" He waved grandly out at the ocean. "Whenever I die, at least I've seen the sea. And a few more marvelous things besides."

"Hopefully you'll die much later now." Despite Abel's forgiving words, the fox's manner had a bit of a distance to it, making Kip aware of how much he'd fallen short. They'd expected him to save everyone, had brought a hundred more people all hoping to see a new world, and he'd lost thirty of those: one out of every ten Calatians. He couldn't blame Abel at all for his disappointment.

"Yes." Abel touched his shoulder; Kip's thoughts must have been visible in his ears and voice. "It is hard, losing friends, even when so many were saved. Truly, I do not blame you."

"But some will."

"Aye, some will. Always, some will ask you for more than you did, more than you ever could. The only voices you must answer to are here." He touched Kip's chest. "And there." He pointed up to the sky, where clouds ambled across a deepening blue field toward a sinking sun.

"I am still listening to what they're saying. But I thank you. And I'll see you soon, as soon as I can."

"I'll await your visit." Abel held out a paw, and Kip took it. "Thank you again. We all owe you a debt, whether everyone realizes it or not."

He was speaking perhaps of many people, but particularly of Grinda, who remained unconvinced of Kip's heroics. She had insisted on remaining until last as well, and when Kip brought Abel back to the group, she said loudly, "Foxes conniving together again. Abel, when will you see that he's no Moses? He's a sorcerer first and last."

"I have seen more of him than you have," Abel said with a little more sharpness than usual. "Leave off."

"He brings us from one servitude to another, from British masters to so-called American. We've even had to assist in our own rescue." She held out her arm; she too had given blood. "We could easily have waited until the ship docked."

"And been in more danger."

"But we weren't consulted, were we? If the sorcerers see a shortcut, they aren't the ones bleeding for it, are they?" The wolf's muzzle, always set in a snarl, twisted even further.

"Kip did, and so did Alice," Abel pointed out.

This did not affect Grinda's argument one bit. "They should have done all the bleeding as it was their idea." And she would hear no more on the matter.

When the calyxes had been sent back to New Cambridge, Broadwood turned to Kip, Alice, and Malcolm. "Time for the three of us to go now?"

"I wouldn't say no to another five minutes of peace." Malcolm spread his arms. "With the boat empty, I can feel the wind and sun and not bump into someone every time I turn."

Kip glanced toward Willoughby, the frigate's captain, who had been thanked many times for his service and had responded that it was his duty and then added an offhanded comment about "airing out" his ship that was perhaps intended to be funny. At this moment the captain was engaged in discussion with the ship's navigator, paying them little mind. "I think we can all spend a little time recovering. The sun's very low anyway, and it will be..." He tried to remember. "Night in Boston? Or afternoon?"

"Whatever time it is there, it's pleasant here now." Malcolm sat on one of the benches that until a few hours ago had been crowded with people.

"Very much so," Alice agreed, and sat beside him.

When the sky had darkened and they were ready to go, they assembled around Broadwood. Ash flew down to land on Kip's shoulder, making Broadwood start. "Is...is that yours?"

"It seems so now." Kip reached up a finger to Ash's head, and the raven stroked her beak against it. "She was Cott's and then their bond was broken. She would have died, but...I was there. Perhaps the destruction of the Road disrupted the natural order of things and allowed us to bond."

Alice stared wide-eyed at him, and Malcolm said, "Is that a raven, Kip?"

"Yes, it is. Her name's Ash. It's a good name for a fire sorcerer's raven... I'm sorry. If I could give her to you, I would."

Malcolm laughed. "I know you would. I'd just thought I could no longer be astonished at what you can do."

Alice reached a finger up. "May I?"

Kip nodded. Ash allowed Alice to stroke her back and wings as Kip sent reassurance through their mental link.

"Well. Well." Broadwood stared at the raven a moment longer and then his face broke into a smile. "Let us go to Boston, then, Master Penfold."

After the peace of the ocean, Boston proved nearly as exhausting as the mission itself. Directly Kip returned he was ordered to clean up, given a new pressed uniform to put on, and brought before General Hamilton, Major-General Hamilton, John Quincy Adams, and several other leaders of the rebellion. These senior officers sat at the front of a stuffy courtroom that had been borrowed for this meeting because it stood in a separate building some distance from the provisional government offices. Master Colonel Jackson stood in the space in the middle of the room, and Kip and Captain Lowell had been placed in the first row of the seats on the opposite side of the room.

Lowell sat perfectly straight. Kip tried to keep his tail from twitching and his paws from scratching at the various uncomfortable seams of his uniform as Jackson gave a florid account of the resounding success of both prongs of his great plan. What kept Kip steady and silent through most of it was the idea that he would have the chance to talk to John Quincy Adams to discuss the relocation of the refugees from the Isle of Dogs. Adams had nodded courteously to Kip when he entered the room, so the fox had some hope.

Still, as the afternoon dragged on, even that hope and the sympathetic weariness on the faces of the elder and younger Hamilton couldn't make Kip feel better about the charade Jackson put on. In the hour that he spoke before the group, the Master Colonel mentioned the Calatians exactly twice, and both times he called them calyxes and talked about what their loss would mean to the British. No mention was made of the thirty lost, nor of the two hundred plus crowded into the tents and basement at the College.

What was not quite as insulting but was still enough to make Kip's hackles rise was the way he talked about Kip himself. "I deployed our fire sorcerer to distract the British, hoping to draw out some of their forces. When properly motivated, he can inflict devastating losses on the enemy, and his unique connection to the calyxes would be, I thought, excellent motivation. As it transpired, the British underestimated both his strategic ability and his power, and as a result lost an experimental fireproof ship made of iron and the great Road connecting England and America."

"When properly motivated" indeed, as though he were nothing but a complex spell that Jackson had cast. There was some discussion of the strategic benefit of the loss of the Road, but Kip missed all of it, seething over

Jackson's remarks until Lowell nudged him. He looked up to see the Master Colonel staring at him. "Yes, sir?" he said.

"With your permission, I would like to show the room the destruction of the Road as it occurred through your eyes."

The request was phrased with velvet smoothness below which Kip felt steel; it was a request only for show. "Of course, sir," he said. He had seen illusory magic before, a branch of the spiritual, but had never been part of it; still, his anger at being used and his reluctance to revisit Cott's death would have led him to refuse if he'd thought he would be allowed. So he watched as the feather touch returned and he played out the scene again, trying to distance himself from the anguish on Cott's face and the desperation in his own memory.

Jackson spun the illusion in the center of the room, a bright shimmering Road cutting between Kip and Lowell's side and the assembled officers on the other, though he could see John Quincy Adams through the ghostly image of the ironclad balanced on the Road. Patches of the ship's image showed more definition than others, the places Kip had paid close attention to either then or later. Fire burst close to Kip from Cott's spell, and everyone flinched. Cott himself showed clearest of all after that, commanding everyone's attention. "He looks unbalanced," murmured General Hamilton.

Across from Kip, the general should be looking at the back of Cott's head. Kip puzzled over this for a moment and concluded that the spell Jackson was using allowed everyone to see the same image no matter where they sat in the room; it only appeared to be projected in front of them. So everyone could see Cott overwhelmed at being the only sorcerer left in a battle, directing his power at the only inanimate object he could find, and struggling with the result. Simply touching that power had nearly knocked Kip out for a moment, a flicker in the memory that nobody remarked on. And yet Cott had endured it. This time, Kip saw not only desperation, but a certain kind of bravery in the man as well.

When the Road erupted in a bright flash and then vanished, Lowell jumped back hard enough that his chair scraped back against the floor. He was not the only one. "Bloody hell," John Quincy Adams said, the clearest amid a cloud of other oaths. He gave Kip a sympathetic look through the slowly sinking ironclad.

The image vanished. Everyone in the room stared at Kip except for Jackson, who allowed the moment to sink in before speaking again. "Some of the sailors believe the destruction of the Road to be Penfold's work, and I have encouraged that belief. If the British think we have a sorcerer on our side capable of such power, they may be more inclined to come to an agreement, especially as they no longer have a fire sorcerer."

"Or it may make them more intent on neutralizing him." General Hamilton spoke as if Kip weren't in the room. "Is he well protected?"

"He is warded at all times, as all our sorcerers are, as we are here today," Jackson said, and proceeded to talk about the rescued New Cambridge sorcerers and how they would bolster the American military effort. There was no mention of their former home and its current residents.

All the while, Captain Lowell watched Kip, and when the room's attention had shifted back to Jackson, the man reached a hand over and rested it on Kip's shoulder. Kip met his eyes and gave a short nod with a smile.

Jackson concluded his talk with no recommendations to the disposition of the refugee Calatians. Adams and the elder Hamilton did not ask about them, merely said, "Thank you," and stood.

Kip and Lowell stood respectfully as well. "Sir," Kip said, trying to attract Jackson's attention, but the tall man didn't turn. So the fox tried to catch Adams's eye, but he was deep in conversation with General Hamilton. They left the room among the others, Jackson close behind them.

Finally free to express himself, Kip let his tail loose to lash back and forth. Lowell mistook the cause of his agitation and put a hand on his shoulder again. "How many times have you had to relive that memory?"

"Only twice now since it happened."

"I pray there will be no more."

Kip tapped his head. "It lives up here, and I've no doubt I'll see it many more times."

"Not in front of an audience, though." Lowell rubbed his cheek. "I only saw the Road once, in New York. I thought it was the most marvelous thing."

"It was." Kip sent his mind back to the first steps he'd taken on it. "Walking through the ocean was…that is the correct word. It was marvelous. I didn't have the time to appreciate it when we did it, but it was incredible. It was magic that everyone could see and touch and use."

Lowell nodded. "I never got to walk on it. And now I never shall."

"There must have been a number of people drowned when it vanished," Kip said. "I haven't heard anyone talk about them."

The captain frowned. "Major General Hamilton did mention them along with the British troops that may have been lost. Travelers along the Road have to sign a book when they go across, but many people use false names and sometimes they don't list children or animals. It depends on who's in charge of the book at the time."

More people to weigh on his conscience. Kip curled his tail around his leg. "I should visit New Cambridge to see how the Calatians are doing, if I'm allowed. Do you know how the relocation plans are coming for them?"

"I'm not part of those decisions. But I have been told that you're to go back to the Trade House immediately following this meeting. I'm sorry. Perhaps once Master Colonel Jackson is back you can ask permission to go to New Cambridge again."

Anger rose again in Kip, but Captain Lowell's only fault was following his orders and it wasn't fair to take it out on him. It had to find some outlet, so he gave voice to another complaint. "He took all the credit for your work and only mentioned you once."

"As I expected."

"It doesn't bother you?"

Lowell glanced around the empty courtroom. "It's better than any alternative I could imagine."

Kip looked at the door through which all the officers had left as a question occurred to him and, immediately following, its possible answer. "Did he select you to lead the Gibraltar mission because he knew you wouldn't take credit for it?"

Lowell's humorless smile did not change. "Master Colonel Jackson chose me because he values my skill and my loyalty."

"I see." The fox felt he'd misspoken, though he still believed that he'd hit on at least part of the reason. "I can't fault that logic. I don't know a more capable officer in the army."

The smile broke, and Lowell gave a quick nod. "Let me give you a small piece of advice, from one…non-white person to another. Fight for what they're willing to give you, but don't push for too much. They can as easily kick you to the mud as draw breath, and given the least excuse, they will."

"Believe me, I know." Kip exhaled. "But how are you to find out what they're willing to give you unless you fight?"

"I have spent more than a decade struggling with that question. Should you find an answer, I hope you will share it with me."

Kip's paws twitched; he wanted to call up fire and burn something, anything. But after watching Cott again, the thought of fighting in another battle, of using fire on people, sickened him. He knew that yes, Hadlock and the soldier at Bunker's Hill and the four sorcerers at New Cambridge would have taken lives had he not stopped them, but there had to be another way. He breathed in deeply. "Have you any family in the area? Friends?"

"A small number of each. Enough to keep me sane." The smile returned, wry this time.

And as if the word "friends" had summoned it, a small paper fluttered to the ground in front of Kip.

CHAPTER 15: HOLLAND

Captain Lowell offered to leave, but Kip, wanting to cement their growing friendship, told him to remain. When Emily appeared, disheveled and slightly out of breath, he anticipated her objection. "Captain Lowell is a friend and I trust him to hear anything you have to tell us."

She remained suspicious but extended her hand. "Kip's nature is trusting, perhaps, but if you've done enough to be a friend to him then you're a friend to me as well."

He shook her hand warmly. "Penfold has proven a better friend to me than I to him thus far, but I hold out hope that I may one day return the favor."

"All right, then." Emily brushed her hair from her face and looked around. "Why are you here, and where are the others? And why are you so formally dressed?"

So Kip started to explain that they had been in a hearing about a mission and that he probably couldn't talk much about it, at which point Emily interrupted him. "Is this about you destroying the Road?"

The fox sat down in one of the chairs. "You've heard about that already."

"One of the Dutch sorcerers has a friend in King's College or something, at any rate, yes, they were all sending ravens or translocating to Bristol to see that it was indeed gone. I told them I didn't believe you would do that, but then I thought about it and I suppose if you had to, you would. But I don't see how you could, is the thing. So did you?"

Kip shook his head. "They want the British to think I did, to scare them. But I didn't. It was Cott who did it." He didn't think he would ever forget Cott's face. "It killed him."

"Well." Emily sat down, and Captain Lowell followed suit. "Perhaps you'd better tell me your story first, and then we'll fetch Malcolm and Alice."

So Kip, with an eye on Captain Lowell, told Emily most of the battle with Cott. Toward the end he called Ash to the window and opened it to let the raven in. The bird alit on his shoulder and rubbed its beak against his finger. "And this was his raven. She's mine now, it seems."

Emily half-stood. "You got a raven? How?"

"I don't know. The only thing I can think is that Cott died just after the Road disrupted all the magic in the area. Maybe their bond was disrupted before he died and then she had nobody to resume the bond with?"

"How do ravens bond?" Captain Lowell asked.

Emily spread her arms. "We don't know. We've learned so much about sorcery and there's so much yet to learn."

"War brings out extremes," Lowell said. "Courage and resourcefulness. When you're desperate…you discover things you didn't know."

"Yes," Emily said, "of course that applies to Cott destroying the Road—and Kip, I'm so sorry, I know you and he were friends of a sort—but I don't see that it applies to Kip getting a dead sorcerer's raven."

Lowell raised his eyebrows. "The raven was desperate. How often does a sorcerer die in the presence of another sorcerer who doesn't have a raven?" In the silence as Emily thought about that, he said, "I really don't know; military sorcerers don't often have ravens. Do you know?"

"I've never heard of it before." Emily put out her hand to Ash, and without Kip willing it, Ash jumped over to her. Emily ran her fingers over the raven's feathers, which Ash seemed to enjoy. "But she's lovely. Lighter than I would have thought. Can you feel this?"

"No. I mean, I might if I concentrated on it, but so far I've only seen through her eyes and spoken through her. She has her own personality, although she's being very restrained around me," Kip said. "I think she's as unsettled as I am by this whole thing."

"I should imagine." Emily held her hand out again and Ash jumped back to Kip's shoulder. "Shall we go fetch the others?"

With the window open and evening approaching, the courtroom was not at all a bad place to meet, so Kip sent Ash to have Malcolm and Alice walk over. With the permission of Emily and Lowell, he unbuttoned the shirt of his uniform to let it hang open, which was a great relief. "After all," Emily said, "you've fur and we don't, so I imagine that this warm room is even warmer for you."

Captain Lowell did not look approving of the casualness of the open shirt, but at least nodded in agreement with Emily. "They don't make uniforms for Calatians," Kip said. "My tail hangs over the waist of the pants, which is awkward, and the material is very warm."

"How do you wear pants normally?" Lowell asked.

"We have trousers with a notch for the tail and a loop and hook fastener over it. Regular trousers are easy enough for a seamstress to modify for us. But these uniforms…" He spread his paws. "You get used to it."

"Easier to get used to it than to fight for properly tailored pants?" Captain Lowell asked with an even smile.

Kip flicked his ears. "For a day, I can bear it. For the Calatian units in this army, I would fight for it."

"A noble distinction."

"Yes," Emily said, "well, that's Kip, as I expect you've come to know. It doesn't at all surprise me that he was risking his life to get Calatians out of London."

"It would have been a sight easier with you there to help." Kip again tried to hide his pleased embarrassment. "But I know you're doing important work as well."

"I do miss you all terribly," Emily said. "Especially with that dreadful Master Plainfield. Good Lord, every time I think he can't possibly have a worse story to tell, he comes up with one. I want to tell you all about them but I would hate for you to have them in your memory the way that I do, so I will refrain."

Captain Lowell didn't want to talk about his Gibraltar mission, so Kip told a little more about the rescue mission, unable to keep from mentioning the refugees and how he hoped they would find some resolution soon. He was just winding up that little speech when Malcolm and Alice arrived.

"Ash tried to bring us to the window," Malcolm said, hurrying to Emily for a hug, "and we had to explain to a guard in the street that we are allowed to be inside here. Are we warded?"

"Ah," Lowell said, "probably not anymore."

"No need to worry, I'll take care of it." Malcolm raised his hands, wreathed in flickers of orange, and spoke a few syllables. "There we are. Safe from unwanted attentions."

"Thank you," Emily said. "Now, my story isn't as exciting as yours, but I think it's still very promising."

We'd laid enough false clues about going to Prussia that I'm fairly certain Victor and his delegation went there first, but Abigail wondered to me privately whether it might not be wiser to have visited Prussia than the Netherlands. "They have a true navy," she said, "and though they were allied with Britain against Napoleon, well, so was everyone. They are an old power and could likely be persuaded to weaken Britain if it would mean they might hold on to their standing a few years longer. They haven't many colonies overseas, so pushing for colonies to become independent can only help them."

I didn't know what to say to this, but I did take messages between her and John, and John reinforced the importance of going to the Netherlands. They're a very recent monarchy, established in the wake of the Napoleonic Wars after years of being a kind of republic ruled by a few merchants, which is awfully confusing. Some of them are still getting used to being a monarchy. The King, for example, is William the First, but his father was William the Fifth, so before the monarchy he was William the Sixth, and one or two people still call him that. They've a brand new royal seal and sashes of office and all kinds of regalia that sometimes look like things that people told them a monarchy should have but didn't tell them why.

But the Dutch are fairly sensible, so they figure out a use for most everything, except the sashes of office. The nice thing about it being a recent monarchy is that the King received us himself the day we arrived and told us that he looked forward to hearing our proposal of state. He put his foreign minister at Abigail's disposal, and when we asked whether I could talk to his sorcerers, he brought a translocational master from the College to give me a tour. This master was very polite, too. "A woman sorcerer!" he said. "I shall have to tell my wife!" But after that he didn't say anything more about it.

I'm getting ahead of myself, though. The King received us in the Royal Palace in Amsterdam, a huge building that looks like the French Louvre, but topped in the center with a great bell tower. Inside it looks like a very rich person's manor house, rather like Peacefield but with more velvet all around and with older paintings, I should think. The main difference is that the French and Spanish palaces were either stuffy or drafty, and the Dutch palace was very airy. Our quarters got chilly at night, but with fires laid in they were perfectly comfortable.

To tell you more about our meeting with the King, I have to go over a little bit of the history I was told to prepare for it. The Netherlands and Britain have had an interesting relationship over the last century. In the late 1600s, of course, King William the Third—that's the great-grandfather of the current king, if you're counting, but he wasn't king of the Netherlands, he was our king, but he was still the Third—anyway, he was Dutch but married Queen Mary, and they overthrew King James because he was Catholic, so the two countries were tied rather closely together, only then there were a great number of wars and the Dutch paid for most of them, so by about a hundred years ago they couldn't afford it anymore and had to stop being so involved in war.

Now, the Glorious Revolution, where William the Third came and ruled England, that's something we learned about in history, right, Kip? That's the last war England lost to a country that didn't have calyxes.

After the Revolution, there were Calatians in Amsterdam for a good fifty years. But there weren't very many, and as I understand it, when England stopped sending them over, right around the time the Dutch stopped paying for wars, the few that were there either didn't have mates, or had children who wouldn't have mates. The sorcerers told me that the last Calatian in Amsterdam died in 1732; at any rate, none of them has ever seen one except on a visit to London.

I know, it's very sad. I hate the thought of it.

I'm getting ahead of myself again because of the sorcerers and all. William the First welcomed us in a royal audience and gave this speech himself about how much he had once loved Britain but how they had gotten too large to be accountable to anyone, and he was glad of the chance to see British people breaking away to make their own way in the world. It was a good speech; he's a better speaker than either the French or Spanish king, and we were very hopeful.

So Abigail went to talk to the ministers of state, who all seem to be bankers of one sort or another, and I went to talk to the Dutch sorcerers at the Athæneum Maleficis Artibus, which is their college of sorcery. They don't have a military branch of sorcery anymore, because they don't fight wars, so they put a lot of money into their school. It's very fancy, almost as nice as the palace. They're very close to a large public market and of course there's water all around. Kip, I don't know how you would take the smell, but there were flowers blooming all over and it was only when I was near the water that I noticed that the canals don't smell all that lovely.

Inside the school, though, it's quite fine. Mister van Demeer, the headmaster, showed me the grounds and took me around to all the offices. They have plenty of students and apprentices, and he confessed to me that he had never thought of women as students, though he knew of witches. I was about to get rather short with him—you may well imagine—when he went on to say that he would begin to ask the young men if any women in their family also showed talent. We don't know that an affinity for magic runs in the family, but as well start there as anywhere.

I was rather taken aback. After being ignored in Spain and courted in France, here were some people taking me seriously. So I told him that was a marvelous idea and gave him a few ideas about how to approach female candidates. You know, not touching them while interviewing, not asking if they plan to give up sorcery to take up knitting, asking them the same questions as the male candidates, and so on. I think that may have amused him but perhaps it will help if he actually does go through with it.

The school is close to the palace, so I stayed in our quarters in the palace, but they invited me to stay in one of the vacant offices that a master would have, and I was sorely tempted. There's a true bedroom, an office, a receiving room, and a classroom, and each master has the same suite of rooms. The better rooms are the ones on higher floors that have better views, and the older masters take those. I understand King's College is similar, Kip? Oh, the newer towers and the buildings at Prince George's that were destroyed, yes, of course.

I visited with the Athæneum two more days and talked to many of the masters there, in groups and individually, and they were all very curious about how my education had been—not as a woman, but as an American, or British subject, I suppose, as it was the same thing at the time. That's where I heard the story about the Calatians. None of them even know what the calyx ritual is anymore. I think back in the 1600s, they were still figuring it out, and nobody really thought to write it down.

Of course I didn't tell them anything about that, but I traded lessons with them, so I learned a lot about how they teach history and how they teach magic gathering. I also learned that they teach their apprentices how to suppress the light on their hands. They think that British sorcerers wait so they can keep a better eye on how their apprentices are using magic.

No, I didn't learn the technique, but it seems it's a matter of focus. They would have taught it to me if we had the time. Anyway, the third day we were there we got called back to the court and King William said that although the Dutch haven't much, they do have a fleet of merchant vessels and they have a number of banks, and if we wanted to borrow money from them they would be prepared to loan us enough to fund some mercenaries.

That was exciting. I ferried Abigail back and forth several times and brought back our financial secretary, and then this morning we heard the news that the Road had been destroyed and that it was a Calatian sorcerer who'd done it. So of course I blurted out that I know you, and then they all wanted to talk to me. I went back to the Athæneum and told them about it, and they asked me to get more information, so even though we're still negotiating, I came back here to talk to you and get the story.

"That news traveled fast," Kip said.

"There were many people in New York and Bristol who saw the Road vanish. There are spies all over and so everyone knows about it now. But they don't know the whole story," she concluded, lifting her head with a smile.

"I'd like to know Master Colonel Jackson's trick of projecting an image." Kip sighed. "Even if it meant I had to relive that moment for a third time."

"I am sorry for bringing it up." Emily leaned on the wood of her chair. "But you understand. I thought you'd undone a Great Feat."

"I understand, and I don't hold it against you," he said. "Especially if you make friends with the Dutch sorcerers."

"You can't come back with me, can you? They'd be delighted to meet you." Kip looked to Captain Lowell. The soldier spread his hands. "Who can say what is in Master Colonel Jackson's mind? You may ask, I suppose."

"May I come along if Kip goes?" Alice asked.

"I don't see why not." Emily smiled. "They're interested in one Calatian sorcerer; why not two?"

"Alice saved us in Savannah," Kip said.

This got Emily's attention. "How? Mind you, I'm not surprised."

"We saw you right after," Alice said. "Oh, of course, and then we went right to New Cambridge."

So they had to tell her the whole Savannah adventure, and this they all did in their own pieces, from Kip's account of getting captured to Alice talking about taking apart the ship and summoning her first air elemental to Malcolm's warding which kept them safe to Captain Lowell running around to all the American officers for help after Kip sent him back to the base.

"It's brilliant, all of you. I hate to think of what might have happened if you weren't quite so clever and capable, but of course you are. And you." Emily hugged Alice. "You keep showing them that we women can cast a spell as well or better than anyone."

"I will." Alice's tail wagged. "I think about that Abigail Adams line you told me quite a bit. 'Learning is not attained by chance; it must be sought for with ardor and attended to with diligence.' I try to go after every new opportunity with ardor and also diligence."

"Abigail would be proud." Emily smiled and turned to Kip. "And what happened with Peachtree?"

"We captured the ships, but not until they had already sent most of the Calatians away. We haven't found them."

"So your parents are still prisoners?" Emily put a hand on Kip's paw.

He saw on Captain Lowell's face that he'd forgotten that, but didn't pursue it. "I hope they're being treated well. I think I can be sure that they're still alive."

"We're certain that most of the Calatian prisoners are still alive," Lowell said. "And there were discussions about retrieving them. I think I know where they are."

That mission would never be undertaken, Kip knew, and to dispel the anger that thought stirred in him he diverted the conversation to Alice, to talk more about the sorcery she'd been teaching herself over the course of the war. That replaced his anger with pride and love, and a good deal of hope for their future.

CHAPTER 16: THE FATE OF THE CALATIANS

Emily stayed with them for a little longer, and then Kip took Alice and Captain Lowell back to the Trade House for dinner so that she and Malcolm could have some time alone. But she promised to return the following day to see if Kip had procured permission to come to Amsterdam, with the repeated reminder that it might be very important in securing the assistance of some of the Dutch sorcerers.

That night, finally free of the uniform, Kip lay in his bed staring at the cracks in the plaster ceiling. He'd slept for ten hours the previous night out of exhaustion, but tonight sleep would not come, no matter whether he kept his eyes open or shut. He kept seeing the Calatians packed into the basement of the White Tower, crowding the deck of the barge and later the frigate, flailing in the ocean. He thought about his parents in a stone cell in the fortress of Gibraltar. He saw the sorcerer, Master Hadlock, bursting into flame and disappearing into a cloud of ash. And he saw Cott's face, cherry red and twisted into a frenzy, and then lying with his eyes open staring at the sky.

Was that how he too might end? Had he become too careless about using his power to kill, even though he wasn't supposed to? He had tried to respect the conventions of war as much as he could and still he'd killed a half-dozen enemy sorcerers. But they'd tried to kill him as well, and those around him. If this war went on, would he find himself face to face with a fleet of ironclads, with no recourse but to use augmented power to destroy them? And would that power in turn consume him as it had Cott? His former mentor had tried to avoid killing and war had twisted him to its ends anyway; was it possible that there was no safe path, that war corrupted everything it touched all in the name of a noble goal?

On top of that, he was no longer certain that he was using this power toward a goal he believed in. The Americans had promised to treat Calatians better than did the British Empire, and maybe after the war this would be the case, but nobody seemed particularly motivated to help them now; not Master Colonel Jackson, not John Quincy Adams, none of them.

But maybe they were right. Maybe in wartime, the top priority should be to win the war, because if they lost, there would be no better treatment for Calatians, and likely all those involved would lose their lives as traitors.

If Kip wanted to approach Jackson the next day with a request to visit the Dutch sorcerers for help, it would be an opportunity for him to suggest a course of action for the Calatian refugees. Where would there be room for all of them in a place that was secure? The British plan of keeping their prisoners in Gibraltar, an unlikely spot, would have worked well had one of the soldiers on the boat not made the mistake of dropping the name in front of the prisoners.

What unlikely spot did the Americans have access to? Nothing came to mind, but perhaps Jackson himself would have an idea if Kip suggested it to him. The sorcerers at Prince George's had been exploring westward; maybe one of them could help now that they'd been recovered.

And they could help guard the Calatians, too. This would take it out of the responsibility of the Army and so it wouldn't cost Jackson anything, not even a defensive sorcerer.

Perhaps he could get to see Master Odden again. He would like to sit down and talk to him, just to tell him all the things that had happened, to go through what Cott had done. If anyone living could understand it better than Kip, Odden would be the one.

There were so many people whose welfare depended on him now—well, perhaps not depended exactly, but whose lives he could make better with a little effort. They would never know if he didn't, but he would know, and he would carry it with him as surely as he carried the face of Ella's mouse friend who had boiled to death in the Atlantic, or Thomas Trewel's dead drowned face, or his former teacher's.

He woke early, not feeling rested, but unable to get back to sleep for more than a few minutes. After breakfast, Kip discussed his idea with Captain Lowell, Malcolm, and Alice, and none of them found any fault with it. So it was just a matter of finding Master Colonel Jackson and getting time with him. He asked Lowell about it, and the soldier reminded him that since being assigned to Kip's unit, he was not privy to Jackson's comings and goings. "Check with Captain Marsh," he advised.

Captain Marsh, when Kip and Lowell went to see him, only knew that Jackson had left standing orders for them to be ready at a moment's notice. "I think we're going to New York next. The British are moving their ships and there were army movements along the Hudson River valley. He and Major-General Hamilton are scouting locations to move the army to. Good job getting rid of so many of the British translocators, by the by," he added to Kip. "The Master Colonel said that this has impeded their troop movements."

So Kip paced about the Trade House until Alice, more out of pity for him than need for herself, asked him to help her with an alchemical spell to draw water out of the air. That distracted Kip for an hour, until Emily returned to ask whether Kip could come back with her.

She appeared on the street, but the guards wouldn't let her into the Trade House, so she sent word and Kip came down to tell them she was authorized. They walked into one of the small back rooms that wasn't being used at the moment; the large dining hall was crowded with sorcerers playing cards, and some of the calyxes had joined them.

The back room, which smelled like it had been a storage closet at one time, at least had two stools they could sit on once they'd wiped them clean of dust. Emily sat and then almost immediately edged forward, half off her stool. "They're all very excited to meet you," she said. "Abigail thinks that it could really help our negotiations. They seem very willing to take Britain down a notch, and we are working out the terms of a loan, but if you come plead in person, we might also have the services of some of the sorcerers. They've got ten translocational sorcerers, and we wouldn't get all of them, but imagine just having one or two more."

"I can't go. Jackson isn't anywhere to be found and I don't know how to get in touch with him." Kip gripped the edge of the stool, imagining its wood bursting into flame. That impulse came with a burst of trepidation about abusing his power, as though the stool were alive and he had callously thought about destroying it. He let go of the wood and flattened his ears back.

"You're the hero of the Battle of the Road," Emily said. "That's what they're calling it, if you hadn't heard. You don't think you can just go on a diplomatic mission? What if Abigail asked for you specifically?"

"I expect she'd have to ask Master Colonel Jackson." He enunciated each word of the title, and then rested his muzzle in his paws. "They're so strict here. It doesn't matter what you did yesterday if you don't follow orders today. I could have magic taken away."

She wore that stubborn expression he knew so well. "From what you told me, when they sent you to London, you had a lot of freedom."

"That rescue mission—the only reason I was given so much freedom was that he hoped I would cause a great deal of destruction. He wanted me to lure the British out into the ocean and incinerate them. If I leave without permission, I'll have magic stripped until they need me for a battle, no matter what."

"That doesn't seem right."

Kip told her briefly about his conversation with Captain Lowell. "Remember, I'm a Calatian. That will always be the first part of whatever I do. Not 'the fire sorcerer,' but 'the Calatian fire sorcerer.' Not 'the hero of the battle,' but 'the Calatian hero of the battle.' Every success I have doesn't move me forward; it stops them from pushing me back."

"I know," she said.

"I'm sorry." He reached out to her. "I know you go through the same thing every day."

She nodded. "I keep believing that one day I'll do something bold enough…" She sat back on the stool and her eyes drifted up beyond Kip. "You know that they call Abigail 'the American emissary'? Not 'the woman,' not 'the lady emissary,' except when they're addressing her as 'My Lady' or something. She's earned that respect."

Kip let out a bitter laugh. "And it only took her seventy years."

"Well," Emily said, "perhaps she's shortened the time for the rest of us. As you're doing for Alice."

"And hopefully more." His tail relaxed.

Emily smiled. "Even if you can't come back, it's nice to get to see you again. I'm thankful that you're all still alive."

"How long can you stay?" Kip asked.

"Oh, I thought I would say hello to Malcolm and Alice, but I should return before too long. It's late there, and if you're not coming back, I'll get a good night's sleep and try again tomorrow. I do hope you reach Colonel Jackson. Those Dutch sorcerers are very anxious to see you."

"I do too." They rose together, but as Emily reached for the door of the room, Kip said, "Wait. One thing." She turned, and he rubbed his head. "Sorry, I'm tired. I don't know why I didn't think of this. Do you think the Dutch would give us more sorcerers, or more help, if we could send them a calyx or two?"

"I'm sure they would," Emily said, "but I wish you luck convincing the American army to give up that kind of power to another country."

"Ah, I suppose you're right." Kip opened the door for her.

"What kind of help would you ask them for?"

He followed her through. "It's stupid as I think about it. I was going to ask if they could house the refugee Calatians. Keeping them in a neutral country might be safer than anywhere here."

"They wouldn't be neutral if they agreed to that, though." Emily patted his arm. "They're safe where they are. I can't imagine a safer place."

"Not all of them are inside the Tower," Kip said. "And they're very crowded in there, and I don't know that they'll have enough food. I don't think the leaders here are worrying about them, so someone ought to."

"I will ask in a very indirect way what we might expect to get, if we were to provide a calyx to them for a limited time. Have you someone in mind who would agree to it?"

"No," he said, and stared down at the floor. "That's the other problem. I can only ask for volunteers and hope that someone is willing to make that sacrifice."

"We keep hearing that war is about sacrifice."

"Yes." Kip lowered his voice as they passed the large dining room. "I find that for the officers, war involves someone else's sacrifice."

"Of course it does," Emily said. "But you need someone to plan the battles. If General Hamilton got killed in an infantry charge, that wouldn't do the army any good."

"I don't mean that. I mean that they are looking out to make sure that they and theirs benefit from the war. When it comes to Calatians, or..." He thought of the *Chasseurs-Volontaires*. "Or any other group that aren't male British landowners, well, they don't much care what their situation is after the war."

"I believe the Adamses care more than that."

Her tone had a little chill to it, so Kip said, "Of course they do. But they are by and large the exception. Right now we are all united because we all believe we will benefit from a free and independent America. But the moment there's even a hint of someone needing more than the barest minimum..."

"They are trying to win a war." Emily sounded as though she were trying to convince herself as well as Kip. "The least distraction..." She sighed. "But I suppose it would be easy enough to simply appoint someone to take care of the housing of the Calatians, wouldn't it?"

"I would think so. But Alice and I are too important. Maybe Mr. Morgan would do it, if anyone would listen to him. It needs a human to agitate on our behalf. I can't even manage it, and I'm a sorcerer."

"John Adams has spoken in favor of Calatians in the past," Emily said. "I could approach him on your behalf."

"Let me talk to Master Colonel Jackson first." Kip paused at the base of the stairs. "He might yet do the right thing."

Emily smiled thinly. "I wish you all the luck in the world with that."

Over the course of the afternoon, Kip bothered Captain Marsh two more times, until the sorcerer snapped at him that he had no way to contact Master Colonel Jackson, and that he would likely know of Jackson's whereabouts only a very short time before Kip himself knew.

Kip resisted the urge to snap back with some difficulty; the stress of the day had worn on him, and the lack of sleep hadn't helped. He stalked back up to his room, where he created a magical fire and stared into it. There was nothing inherently bad about the fire, he reminded himself, or indeed any kind of power. Evil came from the use to which it was put. He had thought that he was justified in killing because his superiors had told him he was, because he was facing people who would have killed him. He did not doubt that he would rather have survived than not; what he was coming to doubt was that it was necessary to be in that situation at all. And yet, if he did not have Jackson's ability to strip magic from someone, what other recourse did he have against sorcerers?

It wasn't until mid-afternoon of the following day, after Emily had left disappointed from another visit, that Kip found Master Colonel Jackson, though it was actually the other way around. One of the guards came up to the room where Kip and Alice were studying spells and Malcolm was playing with Ash. "Master Colonel Jackson to see you downstairs, Penfold," he said, and then looked to Alice. "Er...he said 'the fox,' so maybe you'd best both come."

"He means me," Kip said, jumping to his feet.

Alice rose with him and followed. "I'm a fox as much as you are," she told him.

Captain Lowell, who had been reading a newspaper, stood as well. "Am I to come too?"

The guard shook his head. "He only said, 'the fox,' and you're no fox."

Kip frowned. Lowell looked as worried as he felt, but there was nothing to be done about it. So he and Alice followed the guard down to the room that served as Jackson's office when he was in the House.

Master Colonel Jackson sat behind his desk reviewing some papers and barely glanced up. "Have a seat, Penfold," he said, and Kip held one of the chairs in front of the desk for Alice, then sat in the second himself.

This attracted Jackson's attention; he looked up and said, "I didn't ask to see Miss Cartwright."

"The guard seemed confused on the matter, sir." Kip was pleased that Alice didn't get up.

"Well, well, she may stay. I suppose both of you may attend to this matter." He pulled two papers from the pile he was looking at and laid them atop the others. "We think the British are preparing for an offensive on New York, so we've been preparing for that. It likely won't happen until tomorrow at the earliest, so we'd like you to go to New Cambridge tonight."

Kip sat up straighter. "Yes, sir. Are the refugees being re-settled?"

The question confused Jackson. He shook his head quickly. "Re-settled where? They're being settled for the first time. And how did you—Oh, I see. Ha ha!" He relaxed. "You mean the ones who were already there. Yes, we have to find a solution, but in the meantime we're moving the New York and Boston Calatians to New Cambridge for safety. If the British are going to attack New York, the Calatians might be a target, and while the Boston group might be safer here, it's easier to defend them when they're all in one place."

Kip's mouth hung open. "That's—that's another thousand Calatians. They can't all stay in the College."

"Oh, it won't be a problem with the weather improving. Mainly we need to bring in food for them, you know. I have orders out to local farms, but they're sure to be restless—the Calatians, not the farms—and want to go out and get food for themselves. I want to have someone they trust explain why we have to keep them there for their own safety."

Alice had turned to stare at Kip, but he only registered her movement with his whiskers and peripheral vision, because he kept looking at Jackson's smile. The man wasn't malicious; he really was talking as though the Calatians were a store of ammunition—or, no, farm animals that needed to be protected and fed.

In the face of Kip's shock, Jackson's smile faltered. "Come now," he said. "You yourself showed me that Calatians are an important target in this war. How would you have us defend them? Leave garrisons and a defensive sorcerer warding three different areas?"

"I was going to ask about relocating the London Calatians." Kip found his voice with difficulty. "There has to be a better site. And then to add another thousand on top of them…"

"New Cambridge is where they are right now. We can find another location, but it will take time. So." Jackson fixed Kip with a stare again. "Can you go there tonight, settle the newcomers? You may bring Miss Cartwright if you wish."

"I…" Kip collected himself. "Yes, I can. Sir, I had a request for you as well. Miss Carswell tells me that the Dutch sorcerers are quite interested to meet the Calatian sorcerer who was present at the destruction of the Road, and might be more inclined to help us in the war if I visit them."

"Yes, of course." Jackson waved a hand. "A brief visit."

"And in the matter of the Calatians…Bryce Morgan was the leading citizen in New Cambridge. May I put him into a position of authority when it comes to requests from the army, and so on?"

Jackson stroked his chin. "Are there any human residents of New Cambridge you might trust to do right by the Calatians?"

"There's—"

"Marshall Winters," Alice said. "You don't think?"

"Winters would be fair," Kip allowed. "But I think it's important for the Calatians to have one of their own to voice complaints and requests to."

"Then Winters for the camp as a whole, and this Morgan fellow for the Calatians." Jackson's words carried the finality of an order.

"And perhaps a leader for the London, New York, and Boston populations? Someone they know?"

"Excellent idea." Jackson pushed the two papers across the desk at Kip. "Here are copies of the official orders in case someone questions them. I'll be back here tomorrow morning, nine sharp, expecting your report. Dismissed."

"Yes, sir." Kip stood, and Alice followed his lead.

When they left the office, she headed for the stair, but Kip stalked to the back room where he'd talked to Emily. Alice hurried after him, excusing herself as she bumped one of the other military sorcerers. When she came into the small room, Kip swung the door shut and finally gave vent to his feelings, calling magic and incinerating every speck of dust in the room, a task that required both focus and energy.

Alice jumped at the small sparks all around the room and then sniffed the chairs. "That's a quick way to clean."

Kip stomped from one end of the small room to the other. Alice backed against the door to watch. "It's terrible that they're all going to be packed into the College grounds," she said, "but he did say they would be looking for another place for them."

"And then have to move them all?" Kip kicked the wall and turned. "They'll be there until the end of the war, making requests through a human."

"I'm sorry." Alice clasped her paws together, pressed against the door. "Marshall Winters is a good person. Father trusts him."

"He is a good person." Kip calmed and came to Alice to put a paw on her shoulder. "It was a good suggestion."

"Well…we'll just have to fight well and end the war soon, then, I guess."

She smiled bravely, but her words sent Kip back to the ocean, to Cott's desperation. Again he wondered how many more people he would have to kill, or how effective a soldier he could be if he refused to kill again. "Yes," he said, and searched for reassurances that the war wouldn't last much longer.

Several of his thoughts came together in that moment and a scheme opened up in his mind. Dangerous, but the possibility it afforded if he could succeed… He turned it over in his head, considered several angles, and it remained tenable, if not completely sound. "Alice?"

"Yes?"

"If…suppose we could get the prisoners back from Gibraltar, and get all the Calatians from the Isle of Dogs, not just the calyxes."

"That's a thousand people or more. Fifteen hundred." Her eyes widened.

"Closer to two thousand, I think, with the prisoners. But suppose we could do it."

She pictured it. "The British wouldn't have any Calatians, or not nearly as many. They couldn't make strong magic."

"And we could. They'd have to surrender, wouldn't they? Emily said something about the Dutch invasion being the last war the British lost to a nation without calyxes. Well? What if they were the nation without calyxes?"

"We'd need ten more barges," Alice said. "More defensive sorcerers. It would take an entire military. Do you think Master Colonel Jackson would allow it?"

"I rather think I won't ask him," Kip said in a low voice.

Alice's ears went back. "That's dangerous."

"Yes. And quite probably the least dangerous part of this whole idea." He rubbed his whiskers. "I'll need to tell Captain Lowell, though. I'll need him to get into Gibraltar."

"He'll never go along with it if you don't tell Colonel Jackson." Alice tilted her head. "You could tell him that Colonel Jackson ordered it."

"I could," Kip said, "But I won't lie to him. If he's going to help me, he should know that he's not following any orders but mine."

"I'll help." Alice reached out to take his paw. "Whatever your plan, I'll go along with it."

Kip squeezed her paw back. "Can you help me convince about six more people?"

"I can help with Captain Lowell, anyway." Alice smiled.

"I understand all of it except why you can't tell Master Colonel Jackson, or even anyone else." Captain Lowell sat on the only chair in their room; Kip and Alice stood in front of him, and Malcolm leaned against the wall.

"Because the last time I told him a plan, he changed it and nearly got me and all the people I was trying to save killed. He doesn't care about Calatians as people. He cares about them as leverage in war."

Lowell did get stiff at that. "He cares about all the soldiers under his command, and all the people he is trying to protect."

"He cares about winning this war," Kip said. "More than the livelihood of any one person or even group of people. Listen." He put up his paws placatingly. "I'm not saying that he's a bad person. That's how a commander in war has to act. I'm sure that in peacetime, he would be working hard to find new homes for the thousand refugees he just created, as well as the thousand other ones created by the British Army." Kip was not at all sure about this. "But he can't do that now. And he can't afford to move quickly without consulting everyone else. Look at how long it took to approve the Isle of Dogs rescue, and that had to happen quickly because we had to act on the Gibraltar information."

"Yes, I see what you mean," Lowell said.

Kip went on before he could continue. "This needs to happen even more quickly. The British are reeling from the attacks on these two locations, but they won't expect us to strike again so quickly. But more importantly, because I want to be totally honest with you..." He drew in a breath. This got Lowell's attention; he inclined his head forward. "I think that if Master Colonel Jackson takes over, he'll put the Calatians at risk. Because...if I look at it from his perspective, this is what makes the most sense: get the Calatians away from the British at any cost, and if a tenth of them die, then that's fewer we have to house and feed when they arrive here." His tail lashed. "I can—I think—get them out without losing anyone. But if the plan changes and I'm made to do it without the people I want to get..."

"What if this plan works counter to some other plan Master Colonel Jackson has? That's the danger, that in doing this thing you think is the best idea, you don't see the larger picture."

"This will take one night," Kip said. "And when it's over, so will the war be. No other plans will matter."

Lowell nodded. That he didn't see a flaw in Kip's reasoning heartened the fox. But he still didn't look completely convinced. "Answer me honestly, then."

Kip braced himself. He'd promised to tell Lowell the truth, and he wouldn't put it past Lowell to have guessed the parts of his plan he hadn't revealed. The soldier met his eyes. "Are you doing this to capture the glory that was denied you from the last mission?"

That was an easy question. Malcolm got to it first. "Denied glory? He's being hailed as the Calatian sorcerer who destroyed the Road. What more glory could he wish for?"

Kip exhaled and addressed Lowell. "If you want to claim credit for it after it succeeds, I would allow it as long as all the Calatians are safe and the war ends."

Alice piped up. "The Calatians are critical to the outcome of the war and yet they have no voice in their own fate. Someone needs to look out for them."

Lowell's eyes narrowed very slightly, watching Kip as Alice spoke. He lifted a hand to his chin and rubbed it. "Well," he said, "if it will end the war..."

Kip exhaled, and Alice ran forward to hug the captain. He startled and then relaxed, hugging back and looking at Alice with a faint smile. "If I had not seen you fight in battle, I would be very concerned about Penfold bringing you on this adventure."

"I've been to the Isle," Alice said.

"I know, I know. You're the equal of any in this unit." His eyes met Kip's. "Might I have a word with Penfold in private?"

Alice stepped back. "Is it about me? Because it's not polite to make me leave a room so you can talk about me."

"No," Lowell said. "Nor is it about O'Brien. I want to talk to Penfold about a personal matter that I hope will not affect this mission, but it will be his decision."

Malcolm stepped forward from the wall as Alice came toward him. "Let's go see if we can get to the roof," he said. "I would like to feel the sea breeze."

"I can call an elemental to bring it to you." Alice's tail flicked back and forth.

When they'd left, Captain Lowell gestured for Kip to sit on the desk near him and the fox did so, resting his tail across the wood surface. The window was closed and they were far from the closed door, but Lowell spoke in a low voice. "Do you intend to commit treason?"

"No." The tip of Kip's tail twitched, but Lowell did not look angry or accusatory, merely solemn.

"It occurs to me," he continued, "that someone who could move two thousand Calatians in one night could as easily move a few thousand more."

He waited, but Kip only returned his gaze evenly, and after a moment Lowell went on. "To take people from the American army and offer their services to the highest bidder might be considered treason by some."

Kip inclined his head. "Are we not all committing treason, if you take the view of the English crown?"

"We are fighting to assert our right to self-governance against an authority that has in the past treated us…badly…" The last word trailed off, and Lowell's eyes moved to the glass of the window and the city beyond. After a moment, they came back to Kip. "I very much doubt whether General Hamilton and Master Colonel Jackson will be in the mood to discuss semantics. We will be committing treason against our superior officers."

"It is my intention first and foremost to rescue the New Cambridge and Peachtree Calatians," Kip said. "Secondly, to evacuate the Isle of Dogs. And thirdly, if all goes well and God favors our enterprise, we may find ourselves in a position to grant the American forces a decisive victory, and it will be up to the American leaders to decide whether that speedy victory is worth certain concessions to the Calatian people."

Lowell nodded and tapped the desk thoughtfully. "And if they decide that it is not? Will you approach the British with the same offer?"

"I have high hopes that everyone will be reasonable," Kip said. "And that it may be not only the Calatians who benefit from it."

When Lowell did not respond, Kip leaned forward. "You are a good man, of exceeding intelligence. Were this a just system, you should be a Lieutenant Colonel by now. Even my limited experience in the military tells me that much, and I barely understand what all these different ranks mean. But you are not, and we both know why. We are fighting this war against a crown who treated us like children, like resources to be plundered, and yet the people here in the American army are no different. If your conscience troubles you, you have only to get me into Gibraltar. Say I told you nothing of the rest of it."

"No," Lowell said. "That would be the easy way out, the coward's way. If I join this enterprise, I do it in full knowledge." He paused and looked again directly at Kip. "Would you have told me everything, had I not asked?"

Kip started to answer and then stopped, wanting to be completely honest. "I haven't told anyone else about the full extent of my idea yet. I believe that I would have told you at the same time as I told everyone else."

Lowell considered this and then nodded. "A good general tells his troops exactly what they need to know, and no more."

"But I hope," Kip said, "now that you have guessed, you will help me with the plan."

"If I choose to join…" Lowell broke off and stared out the window again. "I have served the British empire for my entire life up to a few months ago. When I was asked to serve Master Colonel Jackson, I took the decision seriously. There were officers in the Royal Army who knew me; I could have served Britain as well. But I thought about something my mother told me often, back when we were slaves. She said that our state was not right, but that it was no use to rage against it. We had seen others do that and they were punished, mutilated, or…they disappeared. She told me that I should do what my master ordered and be patient. There would be moments in my life when the Lord would put an opportunity before me to make things right, or if not all the way right, at least righter than they were. She found that moment for herself when she convinced our master to free us upon his death. I thought that this moment of revolution was my chance to do some right, and to show my loyalty to the men I'd served with."

Kip kept his ears perked but stayed silent. Lowell rubbed his hands together, looking down at the buildings and street outside. "I thought of my mother, but also of myself. By showing my loyalty, I hoped I would earn some currency in our new country. I thought, perhaps I can show my worth, and when we create something new, I'll be included in that. But I have been wondering over the last few days if I am not simply still following my master's orders."

"I know the feeling," Kip said.

Lowell looked up, still thoughtful, and his face settled into a smile. "You saved me from capture at the expense of yourself. I suppose the least I owe you in return is a second in command. I never thought the Almighty would put a second opportunity before me, but He does work in mysterious ways, we're told."

He extended a hand, and Kip took it with a wash of relief that made him glad he was sitting down. "Tell me," he said, smiling, "do generals tell their troops when they're terrified?"

"Almost never." Lowell matched his smile. "But sometimes they tell a trusted captain. At least, that's what I hear."

As they talked through the details of the plan, Kip was pleased that Lowell found many of his ideas sound. He proposed improvements in many places, demanded they review every step even when Kip thought they were settled, and thereby found more flaws to fix. When finally he declared himself satisfied, Kip could hardly believe he'd been considering going ahead with his original plan. Lowell accepted his thanks with modest demurral.

The only part of the plan the captain didn't want to know was where Kip intended to send the Calatians. "The fewer people who know, the better," he said. "As long as the location is secure."

"As secure as I can imagine," Kip said.

After nearly an hour, Malcolm and Alice came back in, announcing themselves with a cheery, "Hallo, we're back," from Alice. She closed the door behind them and eyed Kip and Lowell, still sitting on the desk by the window. "It's nearly time for dinner. Have you worked out whatever it is you're working out?"

"Very nearly," Kip said. "It's complicated. Captain Lowell has been very helpful. I think we have to start with Emily tomorrow, and then Captain Lowell can go with her while I go to New Cambridge."

"Go where with her?" Alice asked. "And where are Malcolm and I going?"

"You to New Cambridge," Captain Lowell said. "I'll need O'Brien with me."

Malcolm turned his head from one side to the other. "Why, it seems I've been enlisted into the army all over again."

"We need you to keep Lowell and Emily safe in Gibraltar," Kip said. "I don't trust anyone else to do it. And I need Alice to come with me to talk to the Calatians in New Cambridge."

"When do we go to the Isle of Dogs?" Alice asked.

"Last of all." Kip and Lowell had gone back and forth on this. Lowell thought that as this was the least certain part of the plan, it should go first so that if it failed, the rest could be aborted. Kip understood that logic, but argued that they would move fast enough that even if they were discovered in the midst of the evacuation, they could probably hold off the British long enough to complete it. In that case, it would be best if the rest of the Calatians had already been moved so that even if he and Emily were captured, Malcolm and Alice and Lowell could move ahead with negotiations.

Malcolm addressed Lowell. "How certain are you of this plan?"

Lowell gave Kip a slight smile. "More certain than I am that the war will end in a year otherwise. More certain than I am that the war will end in our favor otherwise. I have no confidence that any of the other great powers of Europe will risk anything to throw in with a ragged band of insurgents, not unless we demonstrate more mettle than we have thus far."

"The friendliest reception we've received to date is an offer to loan us money to buy mercenaries and perhaps some ships," Kip said. "And the help of some sorcerers, which we should not discount, but the British sorcerers are very good. Better than we are, all told."

"Because there's more of them," Malcolm said. "If fewer translocators, now."

"Yes." Captain Lowell nodded. "They will likely be more cautious with their offensives, but all that will do is drag out the war for months and years. They sit safely in London and until we capture the entire British fleet or army, it costs them little to continue to harass us."

"But the war is on our soil, destroying our towns." Alice's ears came up, her muzzle set in determination. "It was so strange seeing New Cambridge half-empty, all the people's houses gone because they can't live there, and then we were sailing up the Thames and there were people playing in the river, taking their produce to market on the road, as if they didn't even know there was a war. Maybe they didn't." She gestured out to the street. "What will be left after months or years?"

"Exactly," Lowell said.

Dinner was difficult to get through. The other sorcerers wanted to talk about when they would be going to New York, while Kip could barely eat because his stomach kept turning over when he thought of all the risks they were going to take the next day. He'd gotten the Calatians all the way up the Thames, he reminded himself, and that was in a way more complicated than what he intended now. It certainly had taken longer. But tomorrow's enterprise had far higher stakes, and if just one part of it failed...all the British would need was a handful of Calatians.

No; he'd talked through that part with Lowell. There were undoubtedly Calatians scattered across England, and perhaps the College could even find them quickly enough to be of use. But if the Americans had an effectively inexhaustible resource plus the rescued sorcerers from Prince George's College, the scales of sorcery would tip decisively toward the New World.

And yet Kip kept seeing Master Albright calmly kidnapping Calatians off the streets of Edinburgh or Birmingham, taking them to be prisoners in the College, unwilling participants in the ritual for as long as it took to defeat

Kip and the Americans. And then? Kill them outright, or merely wipe their memories? More innocent lives laid at his feet.

Lowell had talked through this possibility with him, reasoning that many other innocent lives would be saved (how many Calatians from the Isle had already died in the course of this war?). He felt that the overwhelming odds would induce London to a peace rather than scrape out an extra two weeks of fighting, and that in either case, the Americans with the allies they hoped to gain in the course of this operation could begin taking the war to England.

All of it sounded logical and perfectly sound when talking it out, but whenever Kip was alone, fears and doubts crept in again. Lowell had never seen Albright's cruelty in action; the man had orchestrated the destruction of two colleges full of sorcerers to ensure London's continued primacy in the world.

CHAPTER 17: AN END TO THE WAR

Emily arrived the next morning as expected. "Well?" she asked Kip. "Have you permission to come?"

He clasped his paws together and looked her in the eye. "You, ah, you said you wished you could have come with us on our Thames adventure," he said. "Did you mean it?"

Malcolm, Alice, and Lowell all watched Emily, who registered their attention and then raised her eyebrows to Kip. "What are you planning?"

"An end to the war," he said.

She studied him for a moment and then looked around the room again. "If all of you are part of it, then I won't be left out. What do I need to do?"

They explained her part briefly, and she followed along with quick nods of her head. "How are we going to pay the Dutch sorcerers? I don't think they'll be willing to do this just for a chance to talk to you."

Kip tapped his own chest, making Ash, who had been dozing on his shoulder, jump. "We're offering them us. Well, not us specifically, but Calatians. Calyxes."

"Ohhhhh." Emily raised her eyebrows. "That would work. Yes, it would indeed." She turned to Lowell. "You approve of this plan?"

"I admit to being a touch uneasy about giving the Dutch such a powerful weapon," he said, "but Penfold has argued persuasively that the Calatians should be allowed to control their own fates, and also that 'treason' is a term reserved for people on the losing side of a war. I have judged this cause and this risk worthwhile."

"Well put." Emily folded her arms. "Then yes, I can do all that. You're not worried about the Dutch sorcerers knowing where we're sending everyone?"

"I can't think of a way around it," Kip said, "and nor can Captain Lowell. We'll have to trust that what we're offering them, contingent on their cooperation, will be enough to dissuade them from betraying us."

"I believe it should be," Emily said. "You didn't see their faces when I said I knew you, Kip."

Kip's ears folded back, and he looked down at the floor. "Well," he said, "if they will help us then I will be just as glad to meet them."

"Right." Emily turned to Lowell. "You'll be coming with me?"

"Aye," he and Malcolm replied at the same time.

"But first," Kip said, "let's you and I go to the place."

Emily blinked. "The place? I thought we were sending them all to New Cambridge."

Kip shook his head as Captain Lowell said, "Take O'Brien as well. You should be warded at all times."

"Oh, ah, I see." Malcolm smiled. "Take O'Brien, whether he likes it or not."

Emily reached out to take his hand. "Do you like it?"

"As it happens, I do. Very much so."

"All right then. Stop complaining about it."

He laughed and pulled magic into his arms so they glowed orange, then cast his spell. "Right. We're all three warded and ready to go."

Kip leaned up to Emily's ear and whispered, "The cabin where Windsor took us."

She startled. "Seriously?"

"To start with."

"It'll be—"

"Captain Lowell thinks that the fewer people who know the place we're going, the better, so let's just go and have the discussion there. Can you get us all three there?"

She nodded. "Of course."

And a moment later they stood on the floor of a cabin, the door open to a cool fall night outside with the sharp scent of eucalyptus. Ash, fluttering from Kip's shoulder, flew outside immediately.

Below the eucalyptus, though, the smell of <*yora-storf*>, year-old death, lingered in the cabin despite the open door and windows. The memory of Windsor's scream as Kip's fire consumed him returned, and he remembered thinking at the time that he never wanted to be pushed to that point again. The pile of ash had long since blown away, now indistinguishable from the dust and dirt that coated the floor, the table where Windsor's papers had lain with their royal seal indicating the king's approval, and the bench where Coppy had lain and bled out his last. Patris and Kip and Emily had removed everything they could without any outside help so that nobody else would know where this remote Australian cabin was located.

"Kind of fitting in a way that we're using this place," Emily said. "Don't you think?"

Kip nodded. "I don't want to use this cabin, though."

"Too small, for one thing," Malcolm said, reaching his arms out. "I can feel the air hitting the wall."

"I wanted to pick a location we could see easily from here. Ideally a ridge that we could send people down the other side of, so they aren't visible from here, but..." He moved to the doorway.

By the dim light of the cloud-covered moon, Kip looked out over a field of low scrub. Behind the cabin, some distance away, the tall trees that gave off the eucalyptus smell loomed dark, and before him, a dirt path wound through the scrub.

An impact on his shoulder made him jump, but it was only Ash, beak open in a silent laugh at Kip's reaction. He tapped the bird's beak affectionately and then beckoned the others forward. Alert for any noise or danger, they walked about a quarter mile until they rounded a bend and looked down on a gentle slope, at the base of which lay a shimmering inlet. The wider end gave onto a larger bay, and the smell of salt told them that this was ocean and not a lake. "There," Kip said. "Can you see the area down there, the little valley?"

"Barely," Emily said. "But I can see this place. You say there's room down there for thousands of Calatians?"

"Yes."

Behind them, Malcolm said, "You should get yourself a demon, Em. They're grand for seeing in the dark. Dar can see the bay as clear as day."

"I have quite enough to worry about," Emily said.

Kip cleared his throat. "I wanted to ask you two one last time if you're sure you want to help with this. I know we've been through a lot together, but not all of it's been by choice. If you help me—help us—you might be called race traitors."

"Kip," Emily said, "I'd sooner betray my race than a friend."

"Aye." Malcolm moved to put a hand on Kip's shoulder. "You should know better than to ask."

He looked back at the cabin. "It's just that I'm terrified of something going wrong. If I'm captured, imprisoned, even killed...I brought it on myself. But here I'm pulling all of you into it with me. And you're not even Calatians. Alice, Bryce—if he agrees—they stand to benefit if we can negotiate terms. But—"

"We benefit by the war being over," Emily said.

"And what's more," Malcolm added, "we benefit from your situation improving. Everyone benefits. Why, you're only asking to be treated the same as everyone else, to be given the same chances, and if Calatians can do it, then perhaps so can women, and all of our friends who aren't white-skinned." He gave a dry chuckle. "And when that's all been done and settled, mayhap they'll even get around to the Irish."

"I shouldn't have come to the cabin," Kip said. "I can't get the smell out of my nose now."

Emily put her arm all the way around his shoulders. "What happened here—neither of us could have done more than we did. But we're not being pulled into it at the last minute. We're setting the terms now. If someone else comes in, we'll be ready for them. Eh, Mal?"

"More than." Malcolm cracked his knuckles. "Let that Albright try something."

"All right." Kip exhaled through his nose, trying to replace the <yora-storf> with calming eucalyptus.

"It will work, Kip." Emily sounded as confident as he wanted to feel. "It's well thought out and as long as everyone does their part, there won't be much time for anyone to respond."

He nodded. "Promise me something, both of you." They watched him steadily from the near-darkness. "If things go bad, keep yourselves safe. If anything happened to one of you—"

"Only if you promise the same," Malcolm said.

Kip thought of Alice, of Abel. "I'll do the best I can," he said. "But as I said, if something happens, I brought it on myself."

"That won't be much consolation to us if you're gone at the end of it." Malcolm squeezed his shoulder and let go. "But we're all of us bound to be who we are, in the end. Me ma…" He coughed and smiled. "Me ma used to say, if the Lord wanted you to be different then He wouldn't have made you the way you are."

"What I think he's trying to say," Emily said, "is that we appreciate how much you care for other people, but also try to take care of yourself."

"We'll all sit down at the end of this together." Kip smiled. "Succeed or fail."

"God willing." Malcolm turned to Emily. "Best get us back to Boston now."

"I'll go directly to New Cambridge," Kip said. "Send Alice along and I'll see you there in a few hours, hopefully."

He embraced them both and then stepped back. Emily took Malcolm by the arm and a moment later, they vanished.

Under the dim cloudy light, he picked his way down the path to the water and looked around. Night birds called, and a few things that were not birds flew overhead—giant bats? He could send Ash up there, but the raven did not seem inclined to go investigate, so Kip let her sit on his shoulder. The smells here contained different plants, different animals: an alien world. But the soft, warm sand felt welcoming to his feet, and the water warmer than he expected.

He reached a finger up to stroke Ash's beak, and she rubbed back. "I suppose I brought you into this without asking as well," he said. "But we're a team now, aren't we?"

She gave a croak, soft and contented. Kip looked through her eyes to see if the view would be very different.

Ravens' eyes did not have the light-gathering capability that foxes' eyes did, so her view was darker than what he was seeing, but sharper at a distance. She could see down to the land around the inlet, see the small coves and the flat grass on the softly rolling hills that surrounded the water. The land looked welcoming enough. "We complement each other, I see," he said to Ash, and brought his sight back to himself.

There was room enough. Soon, if things went well, this inlet would be crowded with Calatians—most of the Calatians in the world. He couldn't imagine it, but he hoped he would get to see it.

He waited outside the Founders Rest Inn, not wanting to talk to Old John for fear of giving something away, until Alice appeared near him. "Emily and Captain Lowell and Malcolm went off to—"

"Shh." He put a finger to his lips.

She looked around, and then looked indignant. "I wasn't going to say where, only that they're on their way."

"All right." Kip looked up the hill. "Then let's be on ours."

A dark-haired man showing a little bit of stomach on his physique had come out of the guard house and was talking with one of the guards when they approached. Kip recognized him as one of the military sorcerers maintaining the wards and greeted him. "Oh, Penfold," the sorcerer said. "What are you doing here?"

"Orders of Colonel Jackson. Master Colonel Jackson," he corrected as Alice nudged him. "I'm to talk to the newly arrived refugees and settle them down, tell them we'll be moving them along very soon."

"Oh, will we?" The man shook his head. "All right, let him in, he's one of ours."

"I know." The other guard moved to open the gate. "Was in and out of here the other night, wasn't he?"

Kip acknowledged him and turned back to the sorcerer as the gates creaked open. "Any attempt on the wards?"

"Nay. Britain's licking her wounds and leaving us be for the moment. Reckon they didn't think our Master Colonel was such the strategist, eh?"

"I suppose not." Kip smiled thinly.

"Say." The sorcerer peered at Ash. "That your raven?"

"She is now," Kip said, and walked on into the College.

The smell of Calatians reached him even outside on the lawn. The large tents where he'd practiced spells and eaten meals now held perhaps two hundred Calatians each, crowded together on top of each other. Another fifty or so wandered around the grounds, and Kip thought he saw some over in the orchard. He wanted to tell them to be respectful of the trees, but he had more urgent business.

Alice went off to get Bryce Morgan, while Kip found Abel and asked him which of the Calatians from the Isle would be considered most in charge. "Wilton Blaeda, but he's still on the Isle." The fox put a paw to his muzzle. "Mmm, I suppose of the people that came with us, probably Grinda. I think she's in the basement telling stories to the children. I'll go get her."

Kip's whiskers twitched at that. He'd hoped that he wouldn't have to confront Grinda again, but maybe it was for the best. If he could convince her, he could convince anyone.

The tents held most of the Boston and New York Calatians, so Kip went there next. By the time he'd located a middle-aged vixen from Boston and an older rat from New York willing to represent their communities, Abel and Grinda had joined Alice and Bryce Morgan around the back of the tower, out of sight of the gates. Alice's father had also come along, and Kip supposed he had as much right to be there as anyone, so he didn't object. "Gentlemen and ladies," he said, "I need to speak to you in private, so Alice is going to take you all up to the roof. I wanted to warn you so you won't be alarmed when we lift off. You will all be perfectly safe. Are you ready?"

They murmured among themselves, except for Grinda, who stared silently at Kip, and Thomas Cartwright, ears up, who stood beside his daughter. Alice gathered magic, and at the glow on her arms, the murmurs grew louder. Then she cast the spell, and everyone startled as they were lifted from the ground. Kip remained calm, tail swishing as Alice lifted the group of them to the roof, over the parapet, and down onto the warm stone.

When she released the spell, the Calatians took a few steps in different directions. The rat from New York walked to the edge and looked down as though he couldn't believe they'd actually been lifted to the roof. Bryce Morgan, more used to sorcery, said, "All right, Penfold, what's going on?"

Kip stepped back to face the group, Alice at his right side. Abel stood off to the left, between Kip and the others, and having the two other foxes flanking him reassured Kip. "I'm here," he said in a low voice, "to ask all of you to take a small risk to advance the position of Calatians everywhere.

"The American army has decided that we are a resource in need of guarding, but won't spare more than a single guard to do it, and as a result we find ourselves crowded two, maybe three thousand strong into this space meant to hold two hundred.

"The British crown thinks us valuable enough to attack our settlements in Savannah and Peachtree, and disposable enough to kill us when we try to escape, as they did on the Road." Grinda and Abel looked down at the memory. "We are reckoned valuable in the whole and disposable in the individual—unless the individual happens to be a fire sorcerer." He gathered magic and conjured a fire in the space between sentences, which caused the Boston vixen and New York rat to step back. "Or an air sorcerer."

Alice summoned an air elemental and sent it through the group, ruffling fur and causing the Calatians to look around nervously. Kip went on. "We have an opportunity here, when their need of us is greatest, to show them that we matter, each and every one of us. We have an opportunity to be people to them, not just reserves of magical ammunition to be bled dry and then discarded." Abel looked alarmed at this, and Kip remembered that not everyone here was a calyx or even knew the calyx ritual. He hoped his words would stand as metaphor. "One of my most trusted friends has accompanied a diplomatic mission to foreign countries and has secured a promise from another country's sorcerers to help us move the Calatians." He gestured around the Tower. "All of us."

Grinda spoke for the first time. "One of your human friends, no doubt."

"Yes," Kip said. "But I trust her completely."

The wolf folded her arms. "And what price do these sorcerers ask?"

Kip took a breath and looked back at her steadily. "They want a small group of Calatians to settle in their country and join them as calyxes."

"I knew it!" Grinda barked sharply. "He pretends to be so concerned with the welfare of 'his people,' but he's a sorcerer through and through. He sells us out just as surely as the Americans or British do."

"Penfold—" Bryce Morgan began.

Kip held up a paw. "I don't like this bargain, but it's better than any we've ever had."

"It's still a violation." Grinda growled.

"It's a contract on our terms." Kip tried to remain calm. "They have never used calyxes. We can tell them how best to use our help. Limit the number of consecutive days a calyx can be used. Require healing, require comfortable housing for us and our families."

"Until they talk to their British and American friends and realize that they don't need to do any of that."

Kip breathed in, but Alice stepped forward before he could respond. "Maybe they will," she said. "Maybe it will all go back to the way it was. But if we don't do this then it definitely won't change. And it's the chance to grow a community in another country. Britain won't let us go abroad to other countries; this could grow our numbers worldwide. Isn't that what we talk about at the Feast? Growing our families and keeping our communities strong?" She stopped and took a breath. Everyone's eyes were on her. "And even if it does all go back to the way it was, the way it is now…" She took Kip's paw. "At least we'll have done it. At least we'll have tried. And Calatians in the future will remember this, will know that it's possible. That's something they can't ever take away."

The roof fell silent. Kip squeezed Alice's paw. After a moment, Grinda spoke, but the snarl was gone from her voice. "Pretty words," she said. "From another sorcerer, and another fox."

"That's my daughter," Thomas said sharply. "She's speaking what's in her heart, not parroting someone else's words."

"I suppose you're very proud of her," Grinda said. "But—"

"I am." He looked directly at Alice. "More so than I've ever been in my life. I believe her, and Kip Penfold, and whatever they need, I will do my best to provide."

Alice made a small choking sound, and when Kip looked down, she was smiling and her eyes were bright. He gave her paw another squeeze and then let go. "There will be some danger," he said. "I'd be lying if I said otherwise, and you wouldn't believe me. We are defying two great human powers and there are still many things that could go wrong."

"Of course there's danger," Bryce said. "We know that. Tell us what you need from us."

"Thank you." Kip rubbed his foot on the warm stone. "All of us must undertake this together. The more we have, the better our chance of success, and any left behind here at the Tower will still be in danger. I need all of you to go to your communities and tell them that we're striking a blow for our people, and convince them all to go along."

The New York rat laughed. "Oh, is that all? Get a bunch of New Yorkers to agree on something?"

"We'll do what we can," Abel said, with a look at Grinda. "Tell us what happens next."

Kip nodded gratefully. "The other sorcerers will be here in a few hours. They are rescuing the Calatians taken prisoner from Savannah and Peachtree. If something goes wrong with that and they don't appear, then…none of this will work anyway. But if they do, and I believe they will, they will translocate all of you to a safe location, where you will be warded and hidden. We will do it inside the Tower, and we'll need everyone to come in small groups so as not to alert the guards. Alice and I will be here in case there's a problem. It should take two hours to get everyone. And—I'm sorry about this—anyone who can volunteer to be a calyx should do so. We will need the sorcerers at their fullest power to move everyone quickly, and the longer it takes, the more risk of being caught.

"Once you're in the safe location—"

"Bring food," Alice interrupted.

"Yes, bring a day's worth of food," Kip went on. "I hope we won't need that much, but there isn't a whole lot to eat there. We can send provisions along if we need to. But once you're there, I would like a leader from each community to accompany me back to Boston. We will talk to the American leaders and inform them that we can give them the power to end the war—if they concede certain rights to us."

"What rights?" the Boston vixen asked.

"That's why I want you all there," Kip said. "All I know is that I want a place where we can be left alone. I don't think we can stop being calyxes; that's the reason we're valuable." Grinda didn't like that, but didn't interrupt him. "But we can put limits on it. We can make sure that only those who volunteer and understand will participate. We can ensure that Calatians with an affinity for magic can be trained as sorcerers."

"What about owning land?" Bryce Morgan asked.

"What about punishing people who cut off tails?" Grinda growled, making the American Calatians look at her tail while Abel stood very still.

"All of that," Kip said.

"And why America? Why not approach Britain too? Play them off against each other, see which one gives us more?" the wolf asked.

"I believe there's more chance of getting what we want in a newly-formed country than in asking an old empire to change," Kip said. "But I know there will be some who favor the British side, especially among the Isle. I hope Abel and I may convince them to stand together as Calatians."

"We had some Calatians who favor the British side," the Boston vixen said. "Not many. They went and joined the Royal Army, or tried." The New York rat nodded in agreement.

"So because the Isle is in the minority, we lose." The wolf sniffed.

At least she wasn't snarling at him anymore. He opened his mouth to answer, but Abel spoke before he could. "America, if she forces peace, can dictate terms of peace for those of us who must go back to London."

"Yes." Kip nodded. "That should be included in any talks."

"And how do we know the humans will keep their word?" This was the rat again. "They've lied to us over and over. What if they make us promises and then punish us for rebelling?"

"If we help them win the war," Kip said, "we're not rebelling. Nor are we traitors."

"Except us British," Grinda pointed out.

"And who is there to call us 'traitor' except those who would be coming along with us?" Abel asked. "When we go back to the Isle, we'll all be complicit."

"The sorcerers…"

Abel laughed. "So now you care what the sorcerers think? Will you be going to tea with them?"

Grinda scowled. Kip held up a paw. "She brings up a good point. The Calatians the world over will have to live with sorcerers. We hope that as a result of this war, there will be more freedom of movement. Isle Calatians will be freer to move to America, or perhaps to Holland. If anyone finds the London sorcerers particularly intolerable, they may seek their fortunes elsewhere."

The wolf stared at him levelly and then said, "We have freedom now," but she said it quietly and did not seem to require an answer.

Kip waited for any other questions. When none came, he asked Alice to return herself and the leaders to the ground, explaining that he would stay on the roof to watch for Emily's arrival with the other sorcerers. Ash took off and wheeled around, then headed to the forest in search of food while Kip went to one of the parapets and leaned over it, one paw pressed to the ancient stone.

Did you hear that? he asked into the stone.

The breeze fluttered against his tunic. The sun came out from behind a cloud and warmed his fur. The stone of the parapet remained cool to his touch.

After several seconds, Peter replied. *I heard.*

We are a small people up against the might of an empire. Any help would be most useful.

What can I do?

You're a spiritual sorcerer, the only one I can trust. Kip paused. *I know you're bound to this building, but can you maybe teach me a useful spell? I learned how to break spiritual holds.*

I don't know what could be useful.

Maybe… Kip looked down at the guards. *If the guards come and find an empty building, you could cast a spiritual hold on them? I don't know. But I needed to ask.* His fingers traced the cracks of the stone. *Anything you can think of that might help…*

Peter paused again, a long pause. *How long before you need to leave?*

Kip squinted up at the sun. Emily and Lowell would be in Gibraltar by now, hopefully, if not collecting the last of the Dutch sorcerers. They had hoped to be back in New Cambridge by one in the afternoon, and then five more hours to translocate all the Calatians here (assuming everyone could be convinced) plus the military calyxes before he would leave for the Isle. *Seven hours, perhaps eight,* he said.

It might be enough. Peter's voice came faintly and then strengthened. *After…what happened last year, I became frustrated with my prison. I withdrew for a few months and thought it would be best if I did not talk to anyone again.*

Kip fidgeted, understanding this sentiment all too well. He'd had his friends to help him through that time, and though he had once or twice asked Peter to talk, he hadn't thought that Peter might feel as guilty as he himself did. After all, Peter's entire purpose was to protect the Tower and the people in it.

But that is lonely. And at the end of it I thought that I could devise a way whereby I might leave the Tower, in case anyone needed my help again. And then I failed to protect the Masters against a direct invasion. What if I leave the Tower and fail again?

You could leave the Tower? Kip tried to restrain his excitement. *I can see how dangerous that might be. But I promise you that if you're in my care, I will do all I can to protect you.*

The ensuing silence went on long enough that Kip sat down with his back against a parapet and his paw resting on the stone of the roof. *I felt like I'd failed too,* he said. *I lost my best friend because I wasn't quite smart enough, wasn't quite fast enough. But if this works…it could change the world. And you could help us succeed.*

The fault wasn't yours. Master Windsor conducted his treachery here under my supervision.

Kip closed his eyes. *There is fault enough to go around, but I believe the main fault rests with Master Windsor and Master Albright. They cast the spells that killed our friends and colleagues.*

Peter digested that for a moment. *What if my spell doesn't work? What if I'm unbound forever?*

I don't know, Kip said. *Could you be summoned like a demon? Could you be dismissed?*

And then where would I go?

Kip leaned his head back against the stone. *Where does anyone go? That's for each of us to discover in our own time.*

I'm scared.

I know. I am too. For myself and for everyone. Kip looked up at the clouds moving across the sky. *If we succeed, though,* he went on, *it could be wonderful. We could have a college where Calatians are welcome to learn sorcery. Think about the classmates you might have had. That I might have had.*

Peter's voice grew stronger again. *That does sound lovely.*

You're a Calatian as much as I am. And I want you to come with us, wherever we end up. I don't think they will let us have this school, Kip said. *But imagine if you could come live with us and protect all those new Calatian students.*

I failed to protect—

You'd be with me, with Emily. We would help you be more effective.

Silence. Kip took a breath. *If we could help you leave the Tower, you could help us make that dream real.*

He breathed in the warm spring air. The stone beneath his paws seemed to tremble with the weight of the decision. And finally Peter said, *Yes. Let me explain the spell to you.*

The spell as Peter envisioned it would focus his being into one small part of the Tower, which could then be lifted away from it. Kip only needed to be there to see if it worked, and to take the piece if it did. He searched the roof for loose rocks; there was a great deal of debris gathered in the corners, but all the pieces of stone were either the size of his thumb—too small—or the two pieces larger than his foot.

In the end, Peter advised him to cut a piece of the right size away, which had the added advantage that it could be set right up against the Tower until it needed to be pulled away—and then put back if needed. Kip had no cutting tools but could send a thin line of fire through a section of stone, and given enough concentration, he could burn the stone.

He was afraid of hurting Peter, but the spirit encouraged him again to go ahead, and so, careful and determined to get it right the first time, he cut away a segment of stone that could fit inside the palm of his paw. The act of destroying the Tower even in such a small way felt transgressive, but he kept telling himself that this was what Peter wanted.

The palm-sized stone came away from the Tower, heavy, but not too heavy. He could keep it in his trouser pocket and thereby keep Peter nearby. Having a spiritual sorcerer at his side as an ally would shore up his confidence greatly; he had asked Emily whether one of the Dutch spiritual sorcerers could join them, but she didn't know whether any would.

As the morning went on into afternoon, Peter worked on perfecting his spell. His theory was sound, but whether it was his own fear holding him back or some problem with the spell, he hadn't managed to cast it successfully by the time the sun reached its zenith. Shortly after that, the gates opened to admit a cart full of food, so Kip left the stone on the parapet he'd cut it from and lowered himself to the ground to see how his allies fared.

In the Great Hall, a group of some thirty Calatians milled about. Alice and the New York rat walked quickly up to Kip when he entered. Both started to talk, but the rat talked more loudly and Alice, ears flat, let him go on. "Most of our people like your idea, or at least we could talk them into it," he said, and jerked his thumb over his shoulder. "This lot are scared or angry, and some of them want to talk to you, and some of them claim they just won't budge."

"I've convinced several of them." Alice spared a quick angry glance at the rat. "These need to hear it from you."

"All right," Kip said. "Let me go talk to them."

So he spent the next half hour making his way through the crowd. To the ones who worried that it was too dangerous, he assured them that he was taking most of the risk. "As the instigator," he said, "if we're stopped or this doesn't work, it will all fall on me."

"But we're going along," a dormouse said. "We're collaborators."

"There's safety in numbers. They won't blame all of you when they can publicly blame me. But," he added, "the only way this can work is if we all go along. If some of you stay behind then we've already failed."

"So you've put us in a position where we either go along with you or we bear responsibility for your death by hanging," another fox said. "Shouldn't you have asked us before you put these plans in place?"

"I had to move quickly," Kip said. "This chance wouldn't wait for days. And I am still asking you. You have the choice. If you don't want to come along, there are places in the Tower where you can hide, or we could send you back to…New York?" He guessed from the accent. "And you can hide there, claim you were missed."

"If you want to be a coward," the rat said.

"It's their choice." Kip spread his paws. "I won't think less of you."

"I will, though." The rat glared at the stubborn fox. "This thing he's doing is taking a chance to make life better for all of us, permanently, and if you don't have the courage to join us in the risk, you shouldn't reap the reward."

"I know how you feel," the fox snapped back. "I have a family to think of. If I'd wanted to fight the humans for better conditions, I would've joined the Shakers a few years back, and been dumped in the East River with them as well."

The rat said, "That was different!"

"How?" the fox asked.

"We have something they need," Kip answered. "We have a chance to force them to listen. I heard about the Shakers, and I hated what happened to them. Tell me, did you refuse to follow them because you truly believed we don't deserve better? Or because you thought they would fail?"

The fox's ears went back at Kip's words and he looked down. Kip pressed on. "We all have families, now or in the future. We're doing this so they can grow up in a better world. I believe in that world. I've seen that when properly motivated, humans can treat us almost as equals. But they won't bestow equality on us. We have to take it.

"If your cub shows promises of magic," he said, lifting his arms and gathering magic so that the violet glow flickered along his black fur, "would you want them to be allowed to learn to use it? Should you own the land you live on, the building where you run your business?"

All of the Calatians in the room watched them silently. The fox raised his head slowly. "Is this possible?"

"I believe it is." Kip extended his paw. "But I need all of you to help--we all need to work together to achieve it."

The fox took a breath. "All right," he said. "All right." He reached out and grasped Kip's paw.

There would be others, Kip knew; there always were. But he prayed that the fox and the others listening would spread the message of hope. More than anything, he prayed that the hope he had extended to them was not false.

He joined them for lunch, eating sparingly because there was not enough food to go around (there never was, he was told, but everyone made sure that the cubs were fed). More than a few Calatians came up to Kip in private and asked if this adventure would mean they would be fed, and he said that he hoped it would mean the end of the war and a return to a better life all around—including more food.

Toward the end of the meal, the New York rat brought another group of Calatians to Kip. "Give 'em the 'equality' speech again," he said. "Go on, you lot. Listen to this, it'll convince you."

Kip tried to remember what he'd said, but in the end he spoke off the cuff as he had before. It made the same impression, and then one of the Calatians ran to get another group who'd been feeling doubts and Kip had to say the words all over again.

By the time he got back to the roof, he was fighting the mixed emotions of being grateful that he could inspire people and feeling intense pressure not to let them down. He lifted himself over the roof and to his surprise found Emily standing there flanked by a dozen men in black robes, most of them middle-aged and white, but one with tan skin and another with skin as dark as Captain Lowell's. All of them had ravens on their shoulders, one asleep, the others looking around curiously.

"Hallo," Emily said. "We were just about to come looking for you."

The sorcerers behind Emily stared at Kip, and one asked in accented English, "Is that him?"

"Hello," Kip said. "Yes, I'm Kip Penfold."

He called Ash to him; she soared over from one of the parapets to land on his shoulder. Emily walked up and put her hand out for Ash to rub her beak against. "Captain Lowell went back to the Trade House to wait for you there," she said. "Everything went swimmingly at Gibraltar. Your parents are fine. Hungry, but fine. Malcolm relieved the sorcerer at the gate and took charge of the ward, so he let it down just long enough for us to get through."

"Is he—the other defensive sorcerer—going back to Boston?"

"Malcolm knows him a little, enough to know that when we told him the Founders Rest had some excellent ale, he would go down there right away." She paused. "I asked about the spiritual sorcerers, but it sounds like nobody likes them very much. At least, none of these masters would go ask any of them to join us, and I didn't have time. I'm sorry. I can go back now if you like."

"I think I have a solution," Kip said. "You're more valuable here, and we're all ready, so we should start to go."

"All right." Emily smiled. "Just show us where to go."

He tried to slow the beating of his heart, with a little success. "Everyone's inside the Tower. I'll take you."

The Dutch sorcerers followed them, but once they were inside the Tower, they crowded around Kip, asking for the story of the Battle of the Road. He told them while they translocated the Calatians, because while they could do ten at a time with a calyx's blood, they had to rest in between. Abel set up the calyxes in Master Splint's room and collected their blood in flasks to take down so that it wouldn't be visible to the other Calatians. Like Broadwood, the sorcerers reacted at first with revulsion, and one refused to participate in the ritual until he'd seen all his fellows drink the blood and marvel at the power.

When Kip had told the story of the Road, he cautioned the sorcerers that the calyx ritual must be kept secret. "Of course," said the tan-skinned one, the most loquacious of them. "Master O'Brien told us and Master—Mistress—Carswell told us as well, and we are not stupid. If people heard of this, we might be hunted down as demon-worshippers. This explains at least in part why the ritual was not handed down."

"And us as demons," Kip said.

"Yes. The drink is revolting, but what it can do for us…we would work twice as long and hard as this for the chance to have this power at our disposal."

Kip looked around anxiously, but Grinda was not in earshot, thankfully. "It's not just the power," he said. "These are people providing the power for you, and the ritual must always be undertaken with respect, or else you end up with conditions like this, disaffected people."

"Of course, of course," the master said. "We have nothing but respect for your people. Our older masters were taught by their masters that the best age of Dutch sorcery was when your people lived alongside us, and we want to bring that age back." His eyes glowed.

"I hope that your golden age may also be one for us," Kip said. "It's my pleasure to help you, and you will always have our deepest gratitude for helping us."

And then Peter said into his head, *I have it, I think,* and Kip excused himself to return to the roof.

Clouds had covered the sun, but the day remained warm and humid and the stone of the Tower had soaked up enough heat to warm Kip's feet as he landed. He hurried to the small piece he'd carved away and rested his fingertips on it. *Are you here?*

Peter's voice came to him, small but certain. *Yes.*

Kip took a breath and lifted the stone away from the Tower. He levitated himself from the roof and hung in the air, the breeze ruffling his fur. *And now?*

The stone in his paw felt as warm as if the sun were still shining on it. *I am here.*

You did it! Kip pressed the stone between two paws. *You came up with a new spell.*

It is…not likely to be useful to anyone save myself. Peter sounded amused. *But I am pleased that it worked.*

It's going to be useful to a lot of people. Kip held up the piece of stone, marveling at how extraordinary it could be while looking so unremarkable. *May I take you with me now?*

Yes. Peter hesitated. *May I cast a spell to see through your eyes? I promise I will not touch any other part of your mind. My perception is limited to what is around me, and I have not…seen…in two hundred years.*

Of course. Kip lowered himself back to the roof and slid the stone into his trouser pocket.

He felt nothing different, but a moment later Peter said, *Oh. It has been a long time since I saw the Tower from the outside.*

Kip climbed over the side and lowered himself slowly to the ground, being sure to take in the entirety of the Tower as he did. *It looks older*, Peter said. *But still in good repair.*

You've kept it very safe.

Maybe I…am I wrong to leave it?

You can return, Kip said. *It's only for a day. And there will be nobody in it to protect.*

His feet touched the grass outside the Tower. *Yes*, Peter said. *I suppose you are right.*

But he stayed silent after that as Kip returned to the Tower to see how the translocations were going.

Their main worry was that the guards would notice the movements of the Calatians and come inside to investigate, but they were not very curious, and Malcolm was there to keep their attention off of the College. Once all the Calatians in the outdoor tents had been moved, they moved the ones still in the Tower. The Dutch sorcerers, though showing signs of fatigue, remained game, and more than once one of them told Kip it was a pleasure to "put a finger in the eye of Great Britain," an expression they'd all doubtless shared at the beginning of the day.

When the last group had been sent, the sun low in the sky, Kip convened the leaders, Bryce Morgan and Thomas Cartwright and the vixen and rat. "There are over two thousand Calatians there now," he said, "and about to be two thousand more, God willing. We need you all to go and keep everyone calm. The weather is pleasant there—" Kip hoped it wasn't going to rain; that would make everything more difficult. "And once we get all the Calatians off the Isle, it will probably take us several hours, if not a day, to reach an agreement. We'll bring food as we can, but if you need to forage, send only people who have never met a sorcerer. That's very important. If they stray outside the wards, then a sorcerer who knows them will be able to translocate to their side, and they will be trying as soon as they notice that everyone is gone. All right? I'm going to send Ash with Malcolm, so if any of you have a problem, Malcolm will be able to let me know right away."

The rat and vixen looked at each other and then nodded. Thomas cleared his throat. "What about my daughter?"

"I'm going to go with you," Alice said sourly, ears back, "while Kip goes to the Isle alone."

"The other people need protecting as well, and there are many more of them. Malcolm will have wards up, but he's only one sorcerer and there isn't another one there. If there's rain, or wind, maybe your air elementals can help ease it. Keeping them comfortable is important too." He smiled. "I wouldn't trust just anyone with it."

"I know you're only saying that to make me feel better about you sending me out of danger." Alice's ears didn't come back up.

"If I could send you out of danger, I would." Kip sighed. "I don't think there is such a place now."

That, oddly, seemed to make her feel better. "If I'm going, may I at least take Ash? Then I'll know if you're in trouble."

"Yes, all right." Kip called the raven to him, opening the great doors for her to glide in and settle on Alice's shoulder.

Alice reached up to stroke the raven's head. "I'll take care of her."

"I'll check in every now and then."

She tilted her muzzle up and kissed him on the side of his muzzle. "Good luck," she said. "I know you'll do this."

"I couldn't do it without all of you." Kip kissed her back. "And especially you. Be safe. When this is over I'm looking forward to spending more time with you."

"When we're not fighting battles," Alice said.

"Or learning spells. Just...being ourselves."

With her smile lingering in his memory, he left the Tower and went to get Malcolm. The tents and the Tower sounded so quiet to him that he could not imagine that the guards were not suspicious, but they merely nodded at him and didn't even seem curious that no other sorcerer came to take Malcolm's place.

Only he and Emily and the Dutch sorcerers remained in the Great Hall, and Kip was about to return to Boston when his ears caught the click of claws on the stairs leading up to the Masters' rooms. He snapped his head up as Abel walked down into the hall.

"I thought you'd gone with the others," Kip said.

The other fox shook his head and smiled. "I'm going with you to the Isle. I know I haven't any magic, but I know all the residents."

"Abel," Kip said, "that's exactly the problem. We are going to be taking some of these people against their will. Maybe many of them. You're part of their community; do you really want to throw your lot in with us?"

Abel looked around the Great Hall. "Seems to me I've already done that," he said with a smile. "Besides, I know which ones can be swayed and which can't, and what's more, I can find some people to help us go around so it's not all human sorcerers with one fox."

Kip looked at Emily. "It makes sense to me," she said. "But it's your decision."

"Besides," Abel said. "Are you going to bleed for these sorcerers all night? I haven't given any yet so I'm ready." He held up a bag that clinked, full of flasks. "And I have some that we haven't used yet."

"All right, all right." Kip reached out and took the other fox's paw. "But at the first sign of trouble, I'm sending you away."

"That's fair." Abel smiled and squeezed his fingers.

In Boston, Captain Lowell accompanied Kip to the military calyxes. Lowell told them they were being sent to New York, and then Kip sent them to Australia. The deception was necessary; as soldiers, they could be executed if they deserted.

"Everything went well?" Lowell asked as they returned to Kip's chambers.

"So far." Kip looked around the small room. "Thank you again for your help."

"I want to see us succeed."

The "us" made Kip's tail wag for a moment. "The hardest part is coming up, but we have more help. Where do you think you can be most useful?"

Lowell looked around the room. "Here, I think. In case someone questions your absence. But you'll come get me when it's over?"

"I can. I don't need to. You can stay here and—"

The soldier held up a hand. "I told you. I'm part of this. I'm not afraid for them to know it. Now go finish this."

A knock came at the door, and then Captain Marsh's voice. "Lowell?"

"Go," Lowell said in a whisper, and Kip went. One more piece of the plan done, the last and most dangerous to go.

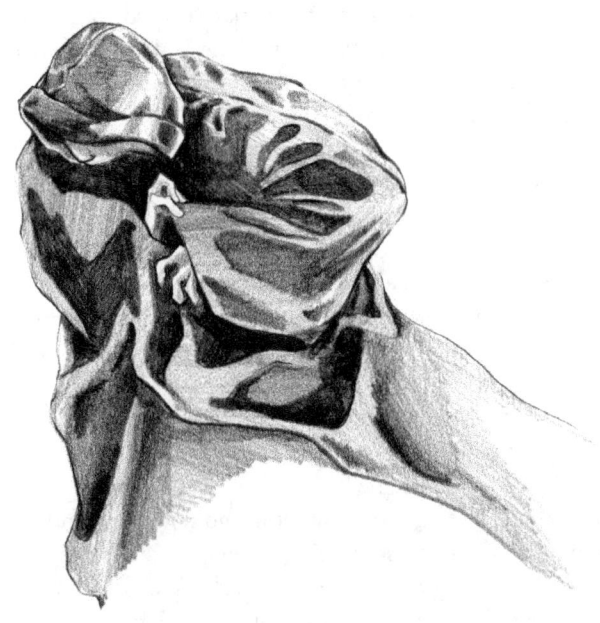

CHAPTER 18: THE RESCUE OF THE ISLE

Barges taking rope from the Isle of Dogs now received their cargo at a dock upriver so that they didn't have to enter the warded Isle. Abel and Kip planned to join one of the crews loading a barge and return with them hopefully unnoticed. Once they were on the Isle, Kip would send Nikolon to find the sorcerer maintaining the ward once they were on the Isle. If the demon could take Peter to him, Peter could cast a spiritual hold that would trick the sorcerer into dropping the wards long enough for Emily and the Dutch sorcerers to translocate in.

Peter was confident that he could do it, and Kip trusted Nikolon to find the sorcerer. Getting onto the Isle with Abel would be the hard part; one extra fox might pass unnoticed, but two could arouse suspicion. Still, it was hard to argue that the British fox's help wouldn't be well worth the extra risk.

So Kip brought them to London and they dressed in worn clothes, and Abel had Kip rub paws full of street dust into his fur so he would have a London smell. Thus disguised, they made their way down to the dock where one of the barges was loading, away from the Isle. Abel had guessed when the loading would start, hoping to be able to join the crew as they began, but when they came in sight of the dock, the carts that had brought the rope stood half-empty and a dozen Calatians carried coils onto the waiting barge.

"We could wait until they're done," Abel whispered. "They'll load the carts with food to bring back to the Isle and then we can walk along with them. No sense in exposing ourselves too early."

The human dockmaster and ship's crew leaned over the railing of the ship, not helping, just drinking from flasks and laughing when one of the Calatians tripped. "They can't tell us apart," Kip whispered. "Look, there's a fox in the group already."

"So they'll notice if two more show up."

"We'll say we were late." Kip sighed. "The faster they load, the faster we can start."

Abel looked keenly at him. "You hate sitting by and not helping, even when it's the smarter course of action."

"That is also probably true."

The other fox sighed. "I suppose you're right. They don't even usually count the crew. All right, but let me go down first and join in. If after a few minutes nobody says anything, then you can come join me." When Kip opened his mouth to argue, ears back, Abel said, "You can watch me the whole time. If anything goes wrong, there's no wards, right? I'm safer here than I'll be anytime after."

This, Kip had to admit, was true, so he watched with trepidation as Abel joined one of his fellows at the cart. There was a short greeting and then the fox shouldered the other end of a coil of rope and walked up to the ship.

None of the humans noticed an extra fox. Abel returned to the cart, took another load, and returned again, and this time he looked toward Kip and beckoned. The badger next to him looked suspiciously in the direction Abel had gestured, but the fox spoke to him and he calmed down as soon as Kip came into view.

When Kip reached them, the badger gave a short nod. "Welcome, then. Grab a coil."

And that was all. None of the others remarked on his presence; none of the humans spoke to him or said anything, apart from one who called out, "That's a pretty tail, that is."

For a moment Kip panicked. Abel had lost his tail, and so had the other fox in the crew. His own full tail stood out; had he put himself in danger?

"Probably a girl, Royce," another voice said. "You want to take her to quarters?"

"Ain't no girl," the first voice said. "Just a lucky fellow."

"All right, ain't no girl," the other replied. "You want to take him to quarters?"

This got an epithet and a blow in reply, and a reprimand from an authoritative voice, reminding them that the Calatians were there to load the ship and not to be a diversion. After that, they finished loading without any more disruption.

Kip itched to get back to the Isle, but first they had to pick up the crates of vegetables and meat that had been sitting waiting for them. By the look of it, many of them had been out for more than a day, and some of them had clearly been picked through already, but nobody commented on this to the dockmaster. They loaded each crate onto the cart without complaint and then climbed up into the carts.

Abel guided Kip to the last cart, where they rode behind the badger who'd greeted them earlier. Kip hid his tail under a cloth as best he could. "So," the badger said in a low voice, "you're back for some more mischief."

"Ever the fox's lot," Abel replied lightly. "Can we count on your help?"

"Depends."

"We're taking the Isle out for a picnic. Lovely place by the sea, warm, lots of other Calatians there to meet. Just for a day or two, while our Penfold here tries to put an end to the war and the suffering."

The badger grunted. "All by himself?"

"With a few well-chosen friends. They want to go start their own country where Calatians might be treated better, a sort of latter-day Promised Land, as it were. And for those of us back on the Isle, we may look to them for a better future ourselves."

"Huh." The badger said not another word. Kip opened his mouth to speak, but Abel raised a paw and shook his head, so they rode on in silence to the Isle.

Two guards searched each cart as it passed them. Most carts got no more than a cursory look, but the guards stopped Kip and Abel's. "Foxes," one said. "We was told to watch for foxes."

Kip's chest tightened, but Abel remained outwardly relaxed, and he tried to follow the other fox's lead. The badger, in front, addressed the guards. "These are Abel and Andrew," he said. "They went out with me, they come back in with me."

"You." The guard gestured to Abel. "Where you live, on the Isle?"

"Millet Road," Abel answered promptly.

The guard turned to Kip. "And you?"

Kip tried his best to imitate Abel's accent. "Same house," he said. "I'm his brother, aren't I?"

The guards retreated to confer, and though they whispered, Kip's ears caught their words. He fingered Peter's stone, making sure Peter was ready to ensorcel the guards if needed. "We was told to look for a fox…but just one fox…he don't look like a sorcerer…we could go get Seamus and Rob, they were here when the carts left…ay, no, they'll be asleep or drunk by now… what about Master Godwin? we were told to find him…ay, and do you know where he is? no, nor do I…stuck up snot…"

Finally they waved the badger through, and Kip and Abel leaned back and relaxed as the cart rattled over the bridge and into the Isle.

The carts stopped at the only place on the Isle with room for all of them: the plaza where a stone column commemorated the Calatians who'd died in the Blackstone bakery fire. The horses stamped as they were guided into the small space, standing still as the Calatians leapt down to unload the crates.

A crowd stood around the plaza, ready to take the food as soon as it was unloaded. Abel climbed down and helped Kip down from the cart. "Go ahead to my house," he said. "You can find it?" Kip nodded. "All right. I'll start getting people ready and I'll send them there."

"Thank you." Kip held the other fox's paw. "This is going to work."

Abel smiled brightly and then leaned forward to kiss the side of Kip's muzzle, the side Alice had also kissed. "For luck," he said. "Go."

Kip touched the side of his muzzle where the warmth from both kisses still lingered and then went, hurrying through the streets until he reached Abel's empty house. Inside, he summoned Nikolon and bound her, then told her quickly that he was involved in a dangerous enterprise again. "But hopefully the last one," he said. "You have helped me greatly and I pray you may do so again."

The demon vixen inclined her head. "I await your orders, master," she said.

Kip took the stone from his pocket. "First, find the defensive sorcerer keeping a ward over this island. He will be human and not one of the guards and you should be able to feel the spell coming from him. Bring this stone into contact with his skin and hold it there for fifteen seconds. When that is done, leave the stone and go to Emily, who is waiting with several other sorcerers at St. Paul's church. Tell Emily that the Isle is open, and then return here to me. Is all of that clear?"

"Yes, master."

"If any part of those orders fails, come back to me right away and tell me."

"Yes, master."

Good luck, Peter, he said, and held the stone out to Nikolon.

The first Calatians arrived before Emily did. These were the eager ones, impatient to leave, carrying small sacks of food with them. They crowded into the small house, mice and rabbits and a hedgehog, asking Kip excited questions about where they were going, how the war was going, if they could come to America when it was over.

He fielded their questions and asked them to keep their distance from him as the sorcerers had to arrive in the house. It soon became clear there would be no room for another dozen people inside, so Kip moved outside into the street where Calatians continued to pester him. Fortunately, Abel returned with a polecat and drew the crowd away a minute before Emily and the dozen sorcerers appeared in the street around Kip.

"How goes it?" Emily asked.

"Well." Kip took a flask from Abel and gave it to one of the sorcerers. "Start with all the people in that house."

"I'll come in with you," Abel said, and accompanied the sorcerer into the house.

"How will we do this?" asked another of the sorcerers.

"Each of you will go house to house, working our way across the Isle," Kip said. "We will meet on the docks when we finish, hopefully in two hours. And if you run into any trouble, have them come find me or—"

"No need." Abel came out of the house leading five people: two of the mice, two rabbits, and the hedgehog. "These people will try to explain what's happening and keep everyone calm. I'll go with another of you, and Kip can go with Emily. Thomas."

The polecat who'd arrived with Abel stepped forward. Abel rested a paw on his shoulder. "This is Thomas Pole, one of the Isle's leaders. He will go with another of you and will select another Isle resident to accompany each sorcerer. I hope this will help accomplish our task quickly."

"And what do we do for calyxes?" the tan-skinned sorcerer asked.

"Use the flasks." Abel passed his bag around. "Use it sparingly. Fill them only in empty houses."

"Most houses," Kip said, "should have enough people that you can send them in one or two tries, and then rest in the time it takes to go to the next house. There are a dozen of us so you each need to send only a hundred and fifty or so."

Each of the Calatians chose a sorcerer and took a flask. When all the flasks had been given out, they were short three, so Kip, Abel, and Thomas took cups from Abel's house and made sure they had knives.

Emily did not like this. "It was bad enough when I didn't know them," she told Kip, eyeing the cup and knife.

"I'll do it where you can't see it," he said. "But we need to do this quickly." When she still hesitated, he put a paw on her shoulder. "I am asking much of you. The least I can do is give more of myself."

"All right, stop talking." She shook free. "I suppose that's the best way to do it."

The next hours passed in a blur of houses and scents, beavers and foxes and otters and mice, polecats and squirrels and one more family of wolves. "You're in danger from the war," Kip told them. "We're here to send you somewhere safe."

In about half the houses, this was enough. A few wanted to know more, and he told them the sorcerers at King's College planned to use more calyxes to death in the war, that he was trying to end the war and keep them out of danger. Some had to be woken from sleep, and some objected; if they took too long Kip sent them without their permission, though he hated doing it and knew they would hate him for it.

The decision weighed on him as he went through the town, so that it was nice when once in a while someone recognized him. "Master Penfold," an older hedgehog said. "I knew you'd come to save us."

He held on to these words as he watched Emily send an angry mouse with her husband and two sons to Australia. "I'm sorry," he told the next house, less angry and more stubborn. "I'll bring you back as soon as possible, I promise." And off they went.

Halfway through, he sent his perception to Ash to see how everyone was settling in. Alice was trying her best to accommodate all the arriving Calatians, but people were squabbling over the best places to sleep. The earlier arrivals had taken the sandy spots near the water, and many of the Calatians from the Isle had started to range away from the inlet, despite Alice and Malcolm's warnings. Alice had twice given Malcolm blood to strengthen his ward. Bryce and the other leaders were doing their best to keep an uneasy peace, and there was nothing Kip could do from where he was.

The sight of a vast sea of Calatians cheered him, and also reminded him of how vulnerable they were. The last part of this would have to go as quickly as possible, even if he had to wake up John Quincy Adams and the other leaders once they got back to America.

They had almost reached the docks. He listed the remaining steps on the Isle: send Emily and Abel and the Dutch sorcerers away, collect Peter. *Nikolon, be ready to bring the stone back to me. Soon now.*

Yes, master.

The sorcerer is still untroubled?

He is pleasuring himself. With this came a picture of a portly man with unkempt hair and a very distracted look on his face.

All right. I don't need to see more. And Kip went on to the next house with Emily.

It seemed a full day later, but the moon was only halfway up the sky when they came to the end of their street and the stiff breeze from the Thames cut across them. Three of the other pairs already stood out on the plaza, huddled together, and as Kip and Emily walked out, another sorcerer and Calatian joined them.

"Anyone have problems?" Kip asked.

Nobody had, although one of the pairs had seen a cloaked figure running between houses, and the Calatian, a mouse, hadn't recognized it. "Thought it might be a mouse," he said, "but wasn't any I knew."

"We'll keep an eye out," Kip said. "All of you send the Calatians on, and go back home. We will come get you when we need your services for—I hope—the last time."

Six more sorcerers emerged with their Calatians, including Thomas Pole and Abel, and all of them left the dock except for Abel, who refused to go until the last two pairs had returned. Kip argued quietly with him, hoping that the others would return while the argument was going on. They did not, and his fur prickled with worry.

Nikolon, Kip said, *please go find the last two sorcerers and their Calatians.*

There was no response. Now his hackles stood up. "Get out of here," he told Emily and Abel. "Something's wrong."

"But—"

"Take him!" he yelled at Emily, pushing the other fox against her. "Go! I'll follow."

Abel vanished, but Emily didn't, staring stubbornly at him. "You're the most important part of this now," she said. "I'm staying until you leave, and for God's sake, why are you still here?"

"I need to get—" Peter. "One more thing. It's vitally important."

"What?"

"Not here. After."

She searched his eyes. "All right. Where is it?"

The picture Nikolon had sent of the sorcerer had been in a house somewhere. It must be near the Isle, probably one of the houses facing it along the Thames. "Near here, but I'm not sure where, and Nik isn't answering me. I might have to summon her again—"

Emily wasn't moving. A shadow emerged from the houses behind her, and he lunged toward Emily to send her away, but a hand seized his arm from behind and he felt a now-familiar blankness as magic was ripped away from him.

"Well, Penfold," Master Albright's voice said, "you have been busy."

CHAPTER 19: THE BATTLE OF THE ISLE

Kip's ears flattened as he turned to see the very satisfied smile on Master Albright's face. "Stealing away the entire Isle, are you? Well, most of them. I admit we were a step behind you—again—but I think you will find there were a few who hid from you, and my young apprentice's lackey there has probably rendered a few more incapable of leaving."

The shadow from the houses came into sharper focus: a marmot, but one from whom all the fur had been shaved, whose head and snout were a mottled canvas of nicks and scars and whose triumphant smile looked crooked and terrible and, worst of all, familiar. "Farley," Kip said.

"Aye." Master Albright avoided looking at Farley even as the shaved marmot reached a furless finger up to brush Emily's cheek. "Still with magic, still useful here and there, and with an ever-larger hate for the people he now finds himself—"

"I ain't no animal," Farley growled. "Victor's going to cure me."

"Once the war is over." Albright spoke as if to a child insisting on a treat. "Which we must accomplish soon, and I think your help here will be invaluable. Cott was reluctant, you know, and a bit on his guard around me. I might have you to thank for that."

"Or maybe you shouldn't have murdered Master Gugin." The longer he kept Albright talking, the more time he had to come up with a solution. "I suppose that would put everyone on their guard around you."

"You would be surprised." Albright narrowed his eyes. "You realize that you were responsible for that, don't you? That you made him dangerous enough to be eliminated?"

"Why?" Kip asked. "Because of Azelart?" He deliberately misspoke the name.

"Have a care, Penfold. You walk a knife's edge between useful and dangerous yourself."

"Victor needs him to fix me!" Farley stepped forward, dropping his paw from Emily.

"Yes, yes." Albright drew in a breath. "Now, let's speak reasonably, Penfold. We need not be enemies, you know."

"You're going to hand me over to Victor to do experiments on and we need not be enemies?"

"Adamson's experiments need not be fatal, nor even more than a mild inconvenience."

"To you."

Albright frowned. "I can have the rodent silence you if you are unable to let me finish my proposition." Kip clamped his muzzle shut, mind still working furiously. "Perhaps, despite David Windsor's history lessons, you have forgotten where you stand in the world. The British Empire traces its roots back for three quarters of a millennium. This island has withstood invasion, division, revolution, and competition, and we remain the greatest power in the world. I was raised on stories of Cromwell and William the Conqueror and Alfred the Great. I have advised Nelson and Wellington and seen us push back the greatest powers the world can muster against us. This trans-oceanic civil unrest will not bring down my Empire, but without my intervention here, you may have the capacity to weaken it. The Holy Roman Empire lasted hundreds of years. I believe this Empire can endure even longer, and I will give my life and as many other lives as necessary to ensure that it will."

He stood tall, seeming to look down at them from the summit of history. "Now. You and Miss Carswell here are extraordinarily capable sorcerers. David Windsor believed so, and though I doubted him at the time, further events have proven him right beyond even my considerable capacity for doubt. Therefore. If you two will forswear your allegiance to the rebels and join the British Empire into which you were, after all, born, the Empire that has sustained you and nourished you and to whom all your accomplishments owe a debt…if you will return to her, then I can promise you a full royal pardon for your rebellion. In addition, you and Miss Carswell, yes, and O'Brien if you like, will be made full and recognized sorcerers of King's College with the right to work and teach anywhere in the Empire. Here, or New Cambridge, or Peachtree, when it reopens. In addition," he held up a finger, "we will open one of those colleges to women and Calatians. My interest is in sustaining the British Empire, and you have made it abundantly clear that ignoring a full half of the potential sorcerers in our midst is a fool's game."

While he was talking, Kip tried to find Ash in his consciousness. The link felt blank, but he spoke along it anyway, trying to get the raven to tell Alice that he and Emily had been captured and to be alert for enemies coming in. He could not see whether the message had been delivered, but he hoped that, like Nikolon in Savannah, Ash could hear him but not relay anything back.

Albright waited for his response at the end of that speech. Kip came back to himself. "And if we refuse?"

"Oh, then I will find where you've sent all these Calatians, and you and I will go there and you will believe that your dearest friends are under attack. You will set fire to all of them."

Kip gaped. He had gathered most of the Calatians in the world in one place, a place he'd thought safe, but of course their safety was in being spread out. Lowell, being human, would not have seen this flaw, but Kip should have. "You—you—"

"Ha ha!" Albright put a hand to his chest. "You should see your expression! My simple fox, of course I would not destroy the Calatians. They're far too useful. But see what horrors you believe of me? You still do not understand that I value the Empire above all. No, if you refuse, you and Miss Carswell will be put on trial for treason and likely executed, while we find the inhabitants of the Isle and crush the rebellion. The Calatians will no doubt suffer from having to wait until we find them—have they food for a week or a month?—and the continuing war will cost both your Americans and your British hundreds or thousands of lives.

"If you join us, however, I suspect that well-placed conflagrations in the cities of Boston and New York will lead to an American surrender before long, and we can have our Calatians back in their homes in a day."

Kip registered the words, but his mind kept working on a plan. He almost had it; he just had to think of a way to get Albright to the defensive sorcerer. Weren't foxes supposed to be cunning in all the stories? "Minus the ones you've let Farley kill." Albright started to respond, but Kip forestalled him. "Why did you not have Cott set those fires in New York or Boston?"

"For one thing, you would have been whisked there in moments to remove them. For another, as I've said, Cott was suspicious of me, and for as much as he loved fire, he spent a lifetime learning to restrain his deep desire to use it."

"He was a good man," Kip said. "Better than you know, better than you deserved."

"Yes, I see his influence in this plan of yours. He would have approved. Which is no doubt why you have failed."

"Why don't you just go into my mind and find out where the Calatians are?" Kip hoped that Albright would interpret this bravado as evidence of a trap.

"Ha ha!" This laugh held much less humor. "We will get there, once I'm certain you're of no further use to me. By now I'm sure that Jackson has figured out my little trick of protecting minds against spiritual intrusion, so I will have to be nimble and extract the information before his spell renders your mind worthless. I prefer not to do it now and leave you useless to the British cause. Now look, I understand that this is a large decision to make, but really, we have very little time left."

"You've left out one of our allies," Kip said. "Your Master Godwin."

He prayed he'd heard the name right, and apparently he had, because Albright's smile vanished. "Godwin? What's this?"

"How do you think we got in here? I suppose you didn't notice that the wards were down for a short time."

"A-ha!" Farley barked. "That's why you couldn't come back in here the normal way."

"Stay here," Albright ordered him. "We'll soon see to the truth of this." He gripped Kip's arm, and a moment later they stood in a dark room lit only by the dim light filtering through a window. In front of the window sat Master Godwin just as Nikolon had shown Kip, breathing rather heavily. The air stank of his recent activity.

"Godwin!" Albright snapped.

The sorcerer fairly jumped out of his chair, hastily arranging his robes, and in the process sending a chunk of stone tumbling to the floor about three feet from where Kip stood. "M-master! I was—my attention had not—I—"

Albright wrinkled his nose. "What have—never mind. Penfold here has told me of the part you played in tonight's events."

"What—what part?"

Kip took two steps toward the window, pointing out even as his bare foot landed on the stone. "From there we signaled him," he said, and in his mind said, *Peter?*

Kip! I could not see through your eyes anymore and I feared you had been—

"Signaled?" Godwin turned to Kip and then back to Albright. "Sir, I—"

Yes, I know. I'm cut off from magic; can you reverse it?

Albright frowned at Kip. "Have you lied to me?"

Yes.

"Of course not." He tested his link with Ash, and he could see through the raven's eyes again. "This is our ally."

Thank you. Can you cut someone off from magic?

Godwin stared at Kip and then turned back to Albright. "I swear to you,

I have never seen this fox before."

Yes.

"How would you know?" Kip demanded, spreading his arms to show his dirty tunic. "How could you tell me from any other fox?"

Be ready to do so the moment Albright touches you.

"I—I haven't spoken to any fox?" Godwin appeared disoriented and bewildered. "I don't understand what's happening."

I am ready.

"Oh no?" Kip bent to pick up the piece of stone and moved deliberately to be nearer to Albright. "Then what is this, if not a message telling you that we were ready?"

He held the stone out, prepared to toss it to Albright, but as he'd hoped, the sorcerer seized it himself. He turned it over and back. "I see no message."

"And yet," Kip said, "there is one there."

He gathered magic. The moment the purple glow lit his arms, Albright's eyes widened. He dropped the stone and his hand shot out to Kip's shoulder, but nothing happened. Kip reached out to Godwin and sent him to the roof of Lord Winter's Tower at King's College.

Albright stared at the stone on the floor, and then lifted his gaze up to the fox. "If you do this," he said, "you are driving a knife into the back of the greatest empire the world has yet seen. She will survive, bloodied and weakened, make no mistake. And she will not forget."

"Your empire is built on the backs of me and those like me," Kip answered. "We aren't driving a knife into her; we are standing straight like men, and if she is thrown from our backs, let her stand among us rather than atop us."

"You think the Americans will treat you any better?"

"We shall see." Kip reached down to pick up Peter's stone.

Albright followed the motion, his eyes lingering on the stone. "You will have to teach me that trick sometime."

Kip gathered magic again. "Not in a thousand lifetimes," he said, and reached out to send Albright to Australia.

He told Alice through Ash to take Albright into custody, that he was without magic and would not be a danger as long as she didn't listen to anything he said. Then he returned to the Isle, immobilized Farley with a physical magic spell, and had Peter remove his magic as well.

Emily sank to her knees when released. "That brute," she growled, and before Kip could stop her, her hands and arms glowed lavender, and she'd barely touched Farley when he disappeared.

A splash sounded from the middle of the Thames. "You'd best let him move again," Emily said, "if you prefer he doesn't drown. It's all the same to me."

Kip cursed and removed the physical magic spell. "I don't want to kill anyone, even him. Where is he?" He went to the edge of the dock and perked his ears to the splashing sounds. There wasn't just Farley, though; there were a few boats going by and other noises, and the sound of one person swimming did not stand out, even over water.

"If you still care, let's go find the sorcerers and Calatians he's undoubtedly murdered and then you can feel better about letting him drown."

"He should pay for his crimes," Kip said, but he couldn't make out Farley at this distance and didn't want to spend more time looking for him.

"He will. But for now, we have a plan to finish." Emily held out her hand. "Boston? Or New York?"

"Boston first." Kip took Emily's hand. "But let us go to John Adams, not Master Colonel Jackson."

"I was about to suggest the same." She smiled at him and gripped his paw tightly, and a moment later, they were there.

CHAPTER 20: THE BARGAIN

John Adams had retired to bed only fifteen minutes before, so he was not yet asleep when they arrived and requested an urgent audience. He grasped the situation quickly from Emily's story and, impassively enough that Kip could not tell whether he approved or not, told them where to find his son and the rest of the rebellion leaders.

Kip told his story to John Quincy Adams, Alexander Lawrence, and Samuel Bayard. At the end of it, they all nodded, and then looked at each other. Adams spoke first, carefully. "As I understand it, then, you have deprived the British of their Calatians. But you have also taken the American Calatians? Are we to understand that there will be conditions for their return? And have you also offered their return to the British?"

Bayard spoke more coldly. "Aye, are you playing both sides off against each other?"

"No," Kip said quickly. "I've only come to you. I don't want to go back to the Empire—to Britain."

This relaxed them. "All right, then," Lawrence said. "What do you ask? If it be within reason, I see little impediment. We all wish an end to this war and a beginning to our country, and we'd promised better treatment for your people anyway."

"I—" Kip had thought only to ask for a college of sorcery, and remembered that he had several more experienced Calatians to consult. "I will gather our leaders and we can sit down for a proper negotiation. But we also want a quick end to the war."

Bayard yawned. "Is this negotiation to be tonight?"

"We would greatly prefer it," Kip said.

"We will be much better rested in the morning," Lawrence put in.

Emily, who had remained quiet until then, coughed. "You may wait until morning if you like," she said, "but we have promised calyxes to the Dutch sorcerers, and once they receive them, they will have calyxes and nobody else in the world will. I presume they will then be willing to sell their services."

"And besides," Kip said, "we are anxious to return the Calatians to their homes as soon as possible. For that to happen we have to agree to terms with you, and then you have to agree to peace with the British."

"Yes." Adams rubbed his eyes. "Go fetch your leaders and return here. We will bring a secretary to draft the agreement and one or two other people if that is agreeable to you."

"Of course," Kip said, and held out his paw for Emily to bring him to Australia.

They gathered Bryce Morgan, the rat from New York, the vixen from Boston, Wilton Blaeda, an old polecat from the Isle, and then Kip had to go find the Peachtree Calatians. He had not seen his parents since the war started and found them in a small huddle with some others he recognized from Peachtree.

When they saw him, they leapt up and embraced him. "Kip!" his mother said. "Emily told us you were behind this. It's so dangerous."

"I know," he said. "But the hard part is over. I hope."

His father smiled. "We've heard a few stories about you already. I don't believe that you destroyed the Great Road."

"No," Kip said, "but I was there when it happened."

The smile vanished. "The Road is really gone?"

"Yes. But that's a story for another time. Who would you say could speak for the Calatians of Peachtree?"

His father walked him over to a pine marten whom he introduced as Richard Branch, an older fellow with some grey on his muzzle but a bright, alert expression. Richard listened carefully to Kip's explanation and then gravely agreed to represent Peachtree. He suggested that the Calatian leaders convene before being taken to the meeting so that they could present a unified front on their requests, so they walked together over to where the others sat in a small circle on the sand.

There were disagreements between them, from what Kip could tell, but they were minor. He and Emily put in that they wanted to continue to study sorcery, and Bryce waved a paw, saying, "That's just a starting point."

Wanting to go back to his parents and to find Alice and Abel, Kip said, "I don't suppose you need me anymore, then. I'll just—"

He stopped because all of them had turned to stare at him. "Don't need you?" the rat said.

"Kip." Bryce put a paw on his arm. "We'll handle the negotiations, but—you've got to be there. You're the one who started all of this."

"Me?" He looked around and saw everyone's agreement. "But I—all I did was—"

"All you did," Wilton Blaeda said gently, "was gather Calatians from all over the world and get them to agree to work together toward a common goal."

"I dragged many of them here against their will."

"Aye, well." The polecat smiled and scooped up a paw full of sand. "That is the way of things." He nodded toward the grains of sand sifting through his fingers. "You can never grasp everyone at once, but to lift as many as you did, Penfold, is remarkable."

Richard Branch spoke up. "We have no true leader, but to the humans, you are the most prominent among us."

"Not to mention," said the rat from New York, "we got to have you there in case they try some sorcery on us. That's what I meant, anyway."

"All right," Kip said, "but if I'm coming, then so is Emily. She did as much as I did to make this happen."

"Of course she's staying." Bryce seemed surprised that Kip would have expected otherwise. "All that aside, it gives us a stronger position if we don't appear to just be a group of Calatians."

So Kip and Emily stayed and listened as the five leaders discussed what they might ask for in exchange for their services. Wilton Blaeda, the most conservative, worried that anything agreed to by the Americans would not necessarily carry over to Britain. The rat from New York wanted to have an entire territory run by Calatians, which sounded impossibly ambitious to Kip, but the others came around to the idea. "We should at least propose it and then see what they come back with," Bryce said. "If we don't ask for it, we'll never know."

All the while, Kip thought about their praises of him. What had he done, really, except take a bold action to help his people? He was hardly the only one to suffer, much less the one who'd suffered most. He had the power and the access to power to take action, otherwise someone else surely would have done something like this years ago, decades ago.

Those thoughts led him to recalling the fight with Albright and then Nikolon, and he worried about the demon. What had happened to her?

So he excused himself for a moment to walk a few feet away—there was really nowhere to have full privacy, not with the air full of Calatian scent and murmuring conversation and a hundred pairs of eyes on him. But he found a spot where he could sit quietly. *Nikolon, please come if you can hear me.*

The nude female Calatian appeared before him, provoking gasps, so he ordered Nikolon to clothe herself and then asked her what had happened.

"I was prevented from communicating with you by a spiritual magic spell." She wrapped her arms around herself. "Then the spell was removed. I made sure you were not in danger and waited for your orders."

Emily came up behind Kip. "They're ready," she said, and smiled at the demon. "Hello, Nik. Kip and I have to go to Boston."

The demon inclined her head. "Shall I accompany you as well, master?"

"Please, but remain invisible. If there is any hostile action taken against any of us, protect Emily and myself first, but if you cannot save us then go to the Dutch sorcerers and tell them they may come here and rescue as many Calatians as they can. What they do after that is their choice." He glanced in Emily's direction, and she nodded. "We hope the leaders will negotiate in good faith, but—"

"But they probably won't." Emily folded her arms.

The meeting took place in a large room in a house called "Mount Morris," a house that belonged to an officer of the Royal Navy named Henry Gage Morris, who was considered to have forfeited it when he remained with the British side. On one side sat the five Calatian leaders with Kip and Emily (and the less visible Nikolon and Peter) behind them, and on the other sat the three Revolution leaders along with General Alexander Hamilton and Master Colonel Jackson. Between the two sides sat two secretaries, one human and one rabbit-Calatian, each with an inkwell, several pens, and small stacks of paper.

The appearance of Master Colonel Jackson had been more of a disappointment than a surprise to Kip. Of course it made sense for the rebellion's foremost sorcerer to attend, but he'd hoped they would view these negotiations as purely political. So he stationed himself behind Bryce Morgan, who by general acclaim had been appointed the spokesperson of the Calatian side.

As a precaution against spiritual sorcery, the five Calatians had agreed to allow Peter to blur their memories of Australia enough to make them useless for anyone spying on their mind. Emily kept Peter with her, Kip had Nikolon monitoring him, and they had requested that a prevention ward, negating any spellcasting, be placed on the meeting room. There was always the danger that the defensive sorcerer, under the command of Master

Colonel Jackson, had allowed some loopholes in the ward, so even after testing it and finding it secure, they remained vigilant.

The first hour of the negotiations was spent in introductions, writing down everyone's names and stations, and each side discussing the precautions they'd taken against sorcery from the other. Kip was especially pleased to see that this discussion calmed down Jackson, who had entered the room looking as though he would personally capture and interrogate all the upstart Calatians.

When they moved on to business, the first item broached by the Americans was the calyxes and when they would be able to resume their duties. Master Colonel Jackson seemed especially to press on the point of whether calyxes would now want to be paid for their services, asking that several times even when first Bryce and then Wilton Blaeda said that that was not part of their negotiations.

As a part of this, Kip brought up the question of Captain Lowell. Jackson's scowl when Lowell's name was mentioned told the fox that Jackson had found out Lowell's part in their plan. He insisted that as part of the settlement that Captain Lowell would not be charged with any crimes. Nobody but Jackson cared particularly about this, but they had to listen to him rant about loyalty for a good five minutes, punctuated with several blows of his fist to the table. He still commanded attention, but Kip found that the pounding of his fist had lost much of the force it had. The Calatians stayed politely attentive during the rant, while most of the American politicians made no attempt to hide their boredom. When Jackson ran out of energy, John Quincy Adams asked if he was finished, and Jackson sat without another word. Adams turned back to the Calatians and said, "Done."

Once that had been settled, they moved on to the meat of the Calatians' demands. Bryce presented them in a list: strictly enforced laws preventing violence against Calatians, acceptance for Calatian and women sorcerers, and a territory governed by Calatians. Kip's only intervention in the forming of this list had been to argue that the point should say "acceptance for any candidate for sorcerer," but Bryce felt that Calatians should argue for Calatians, and in fact only Kip reminding him about Emily and Alice got him to grudgingly include women.

The first two passed without much argument, though Jackson grumbled about female candidates in a way that reminded Kip of the arguments the masters at Prince George's had made against Emily's acceptance. It was when it came to territory that the discussion grew more spirited. Jackson stood firmly against it, but fortunately, he seemed to have the least influence on that side. "A territory for Calatians?" he said. "Are we humans to be excluded from this? Will we also have a territory where the animals of the forest are allowed to govern themselves in accordance with their laws? If the Calatians have any civilization, it is entirely due to their upbringing among good God-fearing men."

"Clearly that is false," Adams said.

"Is it?" Jackson rounded on him. "I suppose that in your law offices you only encounter the best exemplars."

"Not so." Adams remained mild in the face of Jackson's scorn. "In fact, I encounter many scoundrels, usually of the human variety. I have often seen them go on to great success in a military career." Jackson sputtered, and Adams went on. "But if the Calatians have indeed learned civilization from men, one has only to look at their town of New Cambridge or the Dorchester community to see that they have learned well. They have at least earned the chance to prove themselves apart from us."

"I have seen them in the battlefield, and I know how helpless they are without direction or instruction."

"Maybe," the Boston vixen said, "because they've been beaten down over a lifetime and taught not to make a move without a human approving."

"Besides," the New York rat said, "I believe we're here because a Calatian outsmarted you all."

Jackson turned very red and shouted, "Only with tools I gave him!"

"That's enough." Adams turned. "This is no longer productive."

"I'm trying to help," Jackson snarled, but sat down in his chair, glaring at Kip, who tried to ignore him.

A short time later, Wilton Blaeda began to argue against the territory as well. "After all," he said, "we in England would not benefit from that. And how would we govern without humans?"

This alarmed Bryce, who said softly, "We discussed this."

Now Kip paid attention to Jackson, whose face had resumed his normal color. He no longer glared at Kip or at anyone, but stared at the table with concentration—as if casting a spell.

Kip glanced at Emily, holding Peter, but she had also noticed Blaeda's change in attitude and discreetly brought the stone to the polecat's shoulder. So Kip tapped Bryce and told him that Jackson had tried to influence the negotiations. Wilton blinked, looking as though he'd dozed off for a moment, and turned to Bryce to apologize.

The hedgehog listened to both Thomas and Kip, and then addressed Adams. "We would like to request the removal of Master Colonel Jackson. He's trying to affect the negotiations via sorcery."

This caused a great commotion on the other side, as Bayard protested, Lawrence rounded on Jackson, and Jackson stood to defend himself. "They toss about accusations, even though there are wards here," he cried. "That one resents me!"

He pointed at Kip, and the fox half-stood himself before Bryce reached back to push him into his chair. "You may replace him with another spiritual sorcerer if you like, but we will not continue with him present."

"That will cause a delay of an hour." Adams rubbed his eyes.

"How," General Hamilton said, "if we promise that Master Colonel Jackson will limit his activities to monitoring for sorcery from your side? You have shown that you can detect his spells; if he tries one again we will eject him and continue without a spiritual sorcerer."

"What if they accuse me without cause?" Jackson snapped, taking his seat slowly.

"Did they?" Hamilton asked sharply, and Jackson made no answer.

The negotiations resumed, and whether it was because of Jackson's actions or not, Kip was surprised to find that the idea of a Calatian territory was not rejected out of hand. Lawrence spoke in favor of it, while Adams and Bayard worried about how that territory would be treated by the others in the new country.

"I don't suppose it would be too much trouble to carve off a piece of land for the Calatians," Adams said finally.

"With our own representation in the new government?" Bryce asked, to confirm. "We're fighting a war to stop being colonies and we'd prefer not to be immediately re-settled in one."

"Yes, with representation. Where did you have in mind?"

"We would like an area where Calatians have already settled," Bryce said. "Something like New Cambridge."

"Out of the question," Jackson blustered. "We're not giving you the college. You see? They won't ask for payment; they want to run the whole enterprise."

"New Cambridge would present a number of difficulties," Adams said smoothly. "Where else have you considered?"

"You're not getting any part of Boston or New York," Bayard put in.

"That doesn't leave us many options." The hedgehog looked aggrieved, though Kip knew they had never expected a place in one of the cities.

"You could start a new settlement in some of the territory to the west, if we get some of it ceded from Britain," Lawrence suggested. "New Orleans, perhaps."

"There's Peachtree." Bryce spoke doubtfully. "But we would also want to include Savannah, to have a port."

"That's what they've wanted all along," Jackson said. "The rebuilt college."

"Giving you territory that's been settled for decades has a number of problems," Adams said. "What if we go farther west? The Connecticut territory has established a shipping port on Lake Erie called Cleveland. You would have access to the St. Lawrence."

Kip enjoyed the idea of living in Peachtree, but Richard Branch had said that the summers were terribly hot and muggy, and that he would prefer a more northern climate. So after some more discussion, including at least some mention of the natives already living in that area, they tentatively agreed on the settlement of Cleveland and a territory surrounding it.

The topic of Calatians being sorcerers came up again then because Jackson insisted on a school that would not have to take them, and Prince George's was the most likely candidate for that. Lawrence suggested the new Prince Philip's, but Richard Branch countered by asking why the school might not be located in the new Calatian territory, and there followed a long discussion that ended with them deciding that this issue didn't need to be resolved at this meeting.

By this time it was nearly three in the morning. The secretaries drafted an agreement giving the Calatians a land to call their own, and as the Calatians and humans shook hands with paws, Kip hung back with Emily. She passed Peter's stone back to him and they talked about the meeting in low voices until John Quincy Adams sought them out.

Kip expected the revolution's leader to be angry, but the tall man smiled down at him and grasped his paw warmly. "I knew that when I approached you to join our cause that I was on the right path. I had no idea how right. And Miss Carswell..." He shook her hand as well. "You have been an inspiration."

"Thank you." Emily brushed hair out of her face.

"Mother speaks very highly of you."

This brought a flush to Emily's cheeks. "It's been my great pleasure to work with her."

"I am..." Kip's tired brain was not producing usable words. "Very honored to have been part of this."

"Part of this?" Adams laughed. "Mister Penfold—Master Penfold, I daresay—you have caused this, at least."

General Hamilton joined them and also wanted to shake Kip's paw and Emily's hand. "I have every confidence that our American troops would have won the day, but I also believe it would have taken many years. With your assistance, I believe we can negotiate a peace within the week."

"Within the week?" Emily's eyebrows shot up.

Hamilton held up a weathered hand and his lined face creased into a smile. "Have no fear. While negotiations go on, we will provide food for your Calatians. We can't return the British ones until a peace is declared."

"Will they be allowed to live here if they choose?" Kip asked.

"Of course!" Hamilton's smile grew wider. "As far as I'm concerned, this country will need every citizen's contribution, and the more citizens the better. If you do indeed settle Cleveland, that will strengthen our claim to that land."

"And the idea of a new school," Adams added, "is a very interesting one. England, after all, has only the one college of sorcery, and our new country might soon boast three."

The idea of starting a new territory and a new school felt dizzying to Kip. But in the midst of it, Peter spoke to him. *I would be proud to guard a school of Calatians.* And he felt in that moment, as Peter's words gave the future school reality, that everything he'd done had been worthwhile.

CHAPTER 21: THE PROMISE

In the end there were changes, as there always were. From what Kip gleaned, the "Cleveland solution" drew worry from some because it would be on a border with Britain's Canada, and possibly also with the northern extent of the Louisiana territory, depending on where the peace negotiations drew the border. This, some people felt, would afford the Calatian territory the option to turn and ally with Britain in future conflicts, and they had already shown their independence once. Why not give them Savannah and Peachtree, and keep them surrounded by America? Ports along the Atlantic were numerous, but Cleveland might be the gateway to the western territories and could become an important city. The counterargument was that the Peachtree and Savannah land already had owners who would need to be compensated if their land were given to the Calatians.

This argument took place against the backdrop of peace negotiations with Britain. When Britain agreed to cede some of the Louisiana territory to the new country, new land became available to landowners in Georgia, and thereby the largest objection to the "Peachtree solution" fell away. So the Calatians were granted a territory initially called East Georgia, a small piece of land between the Savannah and Ogeechee Rivers, bounded to the west by an arbitrary line about halfway from Savannah to Augusta.

Peace with Britain took nearly a week to settle, and Kip and Emily were present for some of it, though not all. They met the British foreign minister, Lord Castlereagh, an austere man with a sharp nose and a calm, deep voice, at a meeting to determine the fate of Master Albright. The Americans insisted he remain their prisoner for his crimes against the two schools of sorcery. Castlereagh fought surprisingly hard against this, arguing that Albright's crimes had been committed against what was at the time part of Britain and therefore he should stand trial there. It wasn't until Kip mentioned the letters Master Patris had found between Albright and the British government that Castlereagh finally relented, asking only that a British representative from King's College be allowed to interview Albright privately.

Kip also argued that Farley Broadside should be an American prisoner, but that case was even harder to argue and was abandoned almost immediately. True, he had murdered two Dutch sorcerers and several Calatians—when Kip and Abel were allowed to return to the Isle with British officers, they found the bodies of the sorcerers, their Calatians, and the families they had been transporting when Farley discovered them—but none of those victims were American, and the attacks had been on British soil. The question of Victor's experiments that Farley had alluded to met with blank stares and polite deferrals from everyone on the British side, so Kip would have to wait and see what Albright said about them when he was questioned.

He didn't have the chance to supervise the relocation of all the Calatians back to their homes, but he did visit the Australian site when he could. The American Calatians were allowed to return to New Cambridge and Peachtree first, and then Boston and New York and Savannah, this last proving a more popular destination when news of the Calatian territory spread. With only the Isle of Dogs Calatians left, for the most part, the smell of a couple thousand people all living and relieving themselves in the same small area was better than it could have been, though still very bad.

Any time Kip walked through the camp, he heard his name cursed, but many more times Calatians of all species came up to him wanting to hold his paw, say a short thank-you, or simply touch his shirt. He remained as polite as he could, trying not to let the negative outweigh the positive.

When he could, he spent time with Alice and Abel, who had joined a small camp of foxes that included Kip's parents and the Cartwrights. On the last evening, Kip brought two roasted geese from New York and the dozen or so foxes sat around tearing off pieces and eating them. Kip's mother Ada sat with Abel's cubs Arabella and Aran, wiping their muzzles with napkins when the goose fat smeared across their fur; Abel sat between them and Kip, and on Kip's other side, Alice sat with her parents. Emily and Malcolm and Kip's father Max completed the circle. Ash gobbled scraps happily when they were tossed to her, and hopped around the circle to eye the ground when they weren't.

"So, Max," Abel said when the geese had been devoured and Arabella and Aran were chewing on the great leg bones, "I have been wondering how you raised Kip here to be the sort of fox who grows up to create a territory made for Calatians as if by magic. I would very much like to apply those same techniques to my little ones."

Max laughed and took Ada's paw. "I don't know that I have any great secret to impart to you. Most of it came from inside him."

"You got me a spell book," Kip reminded him, his ears warm.

"That I did, that I did." Max leaned back and looked up at the sky. "I suppose you could say that I encouraged you to think of the world as not having limits."

"And that led to him envisioning a Calatian territory." Abel rested a paw on Kip's knee. "Aran, Arabella, do you hear this? No limits."

"First of all," Kip said, "I'm right here. Please don't talk about me as though I'm away in—"

"New York?" Alice asked, her eyes glinting.

"London?" Emily offered. "New Cambridge?"

Kip mock-growled at all of them. "It's been very tiring. I'm glad it's almost over."

"Aye," Malcolm said. "What a burden, being tasked with the creation of something new."

"You could help a little. After all, you're all coming to Prince Philip's with me."

"Only once you've thought of a new name," Malcolm said lazily.

"As it happens…" Kip cleared his throat. "Um."

Emily leaned forward with interest. "You've thought of one?"

"I don't know if they'll let me name it, but…" He stared down at his paws. The idea seemed so right in his head and yet it would not come off his tongue.

"Ha." Max smiled. "They'll let you do whatever you like to it. Build an immense castle, put a statue of yourself out front. What do you want to call it?"

"The, ah." He rubbed his eyes. "The Lutris School of Sorcery."

The circle grew quiet. Alice set her paw on Kip's, but it was Malcolm who spoke first. "That's the best name I've yet heard proposed, and if anyone gainsays it, they'll have to go through me to get to you."

"No fighting," Emily told him, but her tone was soft. "It's lovely, Kip."

"Aye," Abel said. "You know Ella Lutris wants to come to Peachtree? I believe she would love it as well."

"Thank you," Kip said. "I haven't told anyone because—"

Alice squeezed his paw. "It's perfect." To her parents, who looked slightly puzzled, she said, "Coppy was his friend, who Windsor killed. He worked at the perfume shop."

"All of our friend," Malcolm said as the Cartwrights nodded.

"We all lost people in the war." Kip nodded to Abel. "The ones Farley killed, and the ones lost by the Road. Even Saul and the others lost in the initial attacks. What right do I have to elevate one?"

"You've earned it," Thomas Cartwright said.

"Aye, so." Malcolm leaned forward. "You said, 'first of all,' and usually when one says that, there's a second thing, and you've not gotten to that yet, but I'm curious about it, because we haven't had much of a chance to hear from you since this whole thing started. So what was the second thing?"

"Oh, the second thing." Kip held out his paw. "About the Calatian territory. Two years ago—it seems like much longer—Master Odden told me if I wanted to be his apprentice, I had to learn to hold fire in my paw. Simple, right? But I could never do it. I summoned phosphorus elementals and that was good enough for him. Master Cott wouldn't tell me how to do it either, and I didn't understand why, but then, when—at the Road—he did—well, I figured it out." Violet flickered up his arms and fire blossomed naturally, small and contained, sitting in his paw.

"You burned your paw over and over," Emily said. She tilted her head. "What's the secret? Or are you not allowed to tell us?"

Kip smiled. "Now I can simply tell the fire not to burn me." He moved his other paw through it. "But that's beyond what I could have learned as a student. No, the secret is..." He remembered Cott's spell, the fire surrounding him but not touching him. "The secret is that you create the fire, but it's not part of you. Holding it in your paw doesn't mean you have to touch it. Fire doesn't have to be attached to something." He dropped his paw and the fire remained hovering in the air.

Alice lay her ears back. "That's not a secret. That's a trick!"

"Of sorts. But it's important. That a creation can be let go to exist by itself? It's a hard thing to learn."

"Any parent knows that," Max murmured.

"Of a certain age." Abel glanced fondly at his cubs.

"And I was thinking about—about when that happened with Cott, and—well, I couldn't stop thinking about it. And then Master Colonel Jackson..." He nodded as Emily made a face. "They were cramming all the Calatians into the Tower, the College, and I just thought, why can't we float free? Why do we have to be attached to anything?"

"And here we are," Abel said. "Proud residents of East Georgia."

Kip dismissed the fire and turned, ears perking. "You're going to come to America?"

"If you'll have me." Abel gestured. "And the cubs. We'll have some business on the Isle to take care of, but—"

Alice leaned across Kip, her ears just as perked, smiling. "We'd love to have you."

"Arabella," Abel called. "Aran." The cubs looked up. "Would you like to come to America? And stay with the Penfolds, all of them?"

They looked up at Ada. "Yes," they chorused, and went back to licking goose bones.

"That's settled, then." Abel smiled.

Thomas Cartwright cleared his throat. "'The Penfolds,' is it now?"

Alice's ears went back. "I'm going to marry Kip, Father. He's asked me."

"Yes, I'd gathered that." Thomas put an arm around his wife's shoulders. "Laurel and I have discussed it and we will not object. Not because our minds have changed at all, but because we have finally recognized the futility of telling our daughter what she may or may not do."

"Kip's a hero!" Alice protested.

"Yes," her mother said, "and heroes do not always make good husbands."

"She's not wrong." Kip curled his tail around Alice.

"Hush." Alice elbowed his side. "Maybe heroes don't make good husbands for some wives, but you're perfect for this one. Besides, you have to teach me enough sorcery that I can teach the next class of Calatian cubs. I'm tired of being the only female Calatian sorcerer." She looked toward Arabella, but the young vixen didn't look back, still occupied with a goose bone.

Kip smiled and addressed the Cartwrights. "She's something of a hero herself, you know. She saved us at Savannah, she helped me get onto the Isle, and we couldn't have made that first rescue without her. She's as capable as any sorcerer I've worked with."

Laurel looked uneasy, but said, "In that case, when you are both off being heroes, you can leave your cubs with their grandparents."

"Are you coming to Peachtree, then?" Kip asked.

Laurel said, "Yes," at the same moment as Thomas said, "We haven't really discussed it," and then they both laughed.

"It'll be a place for foxes," Kip said, leaning back himself. "And all Calatians." He had always thought of the Calatians who'd come after him as nameless, generic people, and often when he said he wanted to make the world better for the next Calatians, he had been mostly thinking that he wanted to make it better for himself right now, this very minute. But Laurel saying that he and Alice would have cubs, like Bryce saying that the Calatians could have their own territory and Peter saying he would guard a Calatian school, had spoken that vision into existence. Now he felt a great warmth in him, imagining having cubs of his own in a world in which they would grow up believing that they could be anything, next to a sorcerer's college whose gates would stand wide open.

EPILOGUE

Captain Lowell knew the men guarding the Tower, and so he got Kip through the gates and into the college area. "The masters are deciding the headmaster position over in Boston," he said, "but they were moved in yesterday."

"I can't believe Patris won't be headmaster anymore," Kip said. "Do you know who will be?"

Lowell hesitated. "I heard Master Colonel Jackson say that he was hoping to retire from the military. I don't know whether they would accept him, but…he has rarely failed to get anything he wants."

Kip shuddered, disturbing Ash, who croaked and re-settled herself on his shoulder. Jackson running the college? And he'd thought Patris was bad. But maybe it wouldn't come to pass. And all the more reason for his mission this evening.

As they walked along the stone path, amid the torn-up grass and the smells that thankfully had been muted by a recent rain, Kip said, "We're going to ban slavery in East Georgia."

Lowell gave a faint smile. "You haven't come up with a better name for your territory?"

"That's not so high up on the list," Kip said. "But I thought you'd like to know. And I think they'll all approve my suggestion that you come work with our army."

"I thank you for that," Lowell said. "I will have to decide whether I would rather be limited in my advancement because I'm not white, or because I'm not a Calatian."

"You wouldn't—" Kip stopped, tail swishing.

"Being human in a Calatian-run territory would be challenging," Lowell said. "And I haven't a particular skill like sorcery, like your friends who are needed at your school."

"You do, though. You're an excellent soldier. Most of our people with military training haven't risen to your level. And we don't want to bring in someone like Jackson—"

"Master Colonel Jackson."

Kip raised his eyebrows, and Lowell scowled. "He's earned the title."

"Anyway. I think we can both agree that he would be a terrible leader of a Calatian army. But you—people know the part you played. We wouldn't have East Georgia if not for you." When Lowell remained silent, the fox went on. "Besides, I can't imagine you're very welcome in the American army."

"No, that is true." Lowell sighed. "But I must decide whether I want to continue with my military career or join one of the anti-slavery movements in the South. As the new country forms, the laws we put in place will have a long reach into the future. I am glad there will be no slavery in East Georgia, but…there are many other places."

They had reached the great doors. "I hope you will continue to visit us, whatever your choice," Kip said. "It has been my great pleasure to get to know you." He opened the door and gestured Lowell through.

"And the same pleasure has been mine, Master Penfold." Lowell preceded him into the Great Hall.

Four phosphorus elementals lay sprawled around the fireplace, emanating warmth, and one raised its head as Kip and Lowell went by. "Hallo there," Kip said out of reflex, but these elementals were all newly-summoned, bright and glowing, and he'd never talked to them before.

Still, this one tilted its head, as if trying to work something out. Maybe it had been summoned previously and remembered Kip. The effort was too much, though; it lay its head back down and closed those ember-bright eyes.

No tingle touched Kip's nose, so no demons were about. The fox paused at the top of the basement stairs. This might be the last time he had the chance to see the room where he and Coppy and Emily had once lived. The Tower was being cleaned, but the smells of thousands of Calatians still lingered, and he was unlikely to be able to catch Coppy's scent anymore. "One moment," he said, and walked down the stairs, Lowell following behind.

The door had been left open. The semi-circle they'd cleared in the floor for Neddy, the first elemental Kip had summoned, was no longer visible, as the entire floor had been cleared and all the old, moldering papers pushed and stacked to the side. Emily's little room at the back had been used as a toilet; Kip could smell that from here. But the stone walls, the smell of dust and age underlying it all, everything felt familiar and yet distant.

Lowell came up behind him. "Are you going to go in?"

Kip shook his head. "I only wanted to see it. This is where—this is where they put us when Coppy and I started here. And Emily, too." He pointed. "She stayed in the back, we slept in the main room."

Lowell sniffed, but didn't say anything else. Kip leaned against the door. "I wanted to be a sorcerer so badly. Coppy did, too, but—he wanted to go back to the Isle and help people. I just wanted it for its own sake, at the beginning. I was obsessed with creating a Great Feat."

A hand rested on the shoulder that wasn't occupied by a raven. "It seems to me that you have done that," Lowell said. "Not in the traditional way, but…this Calatian territory will endure, and I doubt anyone will be able to replicate what you've done."

Kip nodded. "Malcolm said that too. 'Sorcery is just imposing your will on the world,' he said, 'and what have you done if not that?'" He sighed. "I wish Coppy could have seen it."

"I didn't know Coppy." Lowell's hand squeezed Kip's shoulder briefly and then released it. "But I wager he'd be proud of you."

It bothered Kip that Coppy was distant enough now that his memory didn't evoke throat-tightening emotion; it was an ache rather than a wound. But the thought of Coppy leaning back and smiling over these last few months of Kip's life and where they'd led brought a smile to Kip's muzzle as well. "He'd hate that I was naming a school for him," he said.

"I understand a little more why you are, now," Lowell replied. "I wish I'd had the chance to meet him."

"He'd have liked you," Kip said, and turned around. "He liked everybody."

They walked back up the stairs in silence and crossed the Great Hall to the stairs going up. "We had classes here." Kip gestured as they walked. "And private lessons up where we're going, in the masters' offices. It was—well, magical. Learning sorcery meant so much."

"It gave you a key to unlock your chains," Lowell said quietly as they climbed the stairs. "Even if you didn't know it at the time. And now you're unlocking someone else's."

"If the book is back here now."

Fortunately, it was, the thick tome sitting on Odden's desk. Lowell stopped at the door to stand guard while Kip hurried to the book and opened it. It took him only a moment to find the page he wanted, and with his finger on it, Kip summoned and bound Nikolon.

"I have wanted to ask you something," he said. "When the Road was destroyed, you were unbound. But you continued to carry out my instructions." Nikolon watched him, unblinking. "Why?"

"Because you asked me to."

"But you were no longer bound." Nikolon's expression did not waver. "Were you?"

"I do not believe so."

"So you completed my instructions because you wished to?"

"Yes."

"All right. Well. I wanted to thank you. Come over here to look at this book." Kip pointed down to the page with the entry that read: "NIKOLON: First-order demon. Physical magic. Good for beginners."

The vixen walked over and stared down at the book. "I see it, master."

Kip called magic and told the fire to very precisely burn the ink out of the book, and maybe a very little bit of the paper. Nikolon watched as her name vanished from the book. "There," Kip said. "Nobody can put it back now. If I find it elsewhere, I'll do the same again. And I promise I will summon you no longer."

The vixen kept staring down at the paper. Kip couldn't read her emotion. "Unless you want to be summoned, uh, I mean, you always seemed like you wouldn't like it…"

"Your summonses have not been particularly onerous," Nikolon said. "If you are in need, I would not object. But if you are not, then I also enjoy peace."

"Thank you. If I am in great need—well, you know, there are lots of other names." Looking at the book, thinking that each one of those names represented another demon like Nikolon, that statement made Kip uneasy.

Nikolon didn't take her eyes from the book. "Why do you do this?"

"Because you served me well. And you carried out my orders when unbound, and you didn't curse me when you had the chance."

"Thank you, Master Penfold," the vixen said.

As he spoke the dismissal spell, Nikolon stood straight, her tail swishing as though it were a normal Calatian tail. "Curses take many forms," she said in a soft voice, and then she was gone.

SNEAK PREVIEW: THE REVOLUTION AND THE FOX

Astute readers will have noticed that although the war is over, several questions remain unanswered. I know that the trilogy is the classic form of fantasy, and back when I planned out The Calatians, the two-book series did grow into a trilogy. But it didn't stop growing, and the originally conceived second book that became the third is now the fourth.

The Revolution and the Fox is planned for release in summer 2020, but immediately following, you can read the first chapter to get an idea of where the story is going.

Thanks as always for picking up this book and following my stories. I'm deeply grateful that in this busy, stressful world, you chose to give Kip and his friends some of your attention.

CHAPTER ONE

Kip stomped into Emily's office brandishing a small bound pamphlet, his fox's ears flat back against his head, his tail all bristled out despite his efforts to control it. "Have you seen this?" he asked, and threw the pamphlet down on her desk.

Emily finished adding a column of numbers and then pushed the ledger aside to look at the pamphlet. "'The Softest Fur,'" she read from the cover. "Is this supposed to be you and me?"

"Yes." Kip stared down as she flipped to the first page and read. "Abel brought it back from London. It's—embarrassing."

"Oh, I don't know. 'His claws traced the milky-white her breast.' Apart from the hideous grammar, it's actually not bad." She set the pamphlet down and slid open one of the drawers of her desk. "Have you seen the one about me and Abigail Adams?"

Kip's ears came back up as she handed him another pamphlet, smaller than the one he'd brought. "'The Comfort of a Beast'? Am I in this too?"

"I think that's meant to be 'breast,'" Emily said. "My former husband gave it to me when he came to one of Abigail's lectures."

"Did he write it?" Kip searched the pamphlet for an author's name but found none.

"Honestly, it's too inventive for Thomas. Besides, whoever wrote it, I don't think he's seen a woman's body ever. He has a very curious idea of where things are and how they work." She picked up 'The Softest Fur' again. "Does this one have sorcery in it?"

"Yes," Kip said. "But they have no idea how it works." He gave her pamphlet back to her. "You may keep that one too, if you like."

Emily slid both into the drawer and closed it. "I shouldn't let it worry you. Thomas wanted me to be embarrassed and it quite took the wind from his sails when I accepted the thing cheerfully. It's a sign of respect. Not everyone gets made into the subject of a penny dreadful, you know."

"I'd rather they respect me another way." Kip slumped into the chair on the other side of her desk. The warm breeze from the window brought scents of flowers from the peach trees that had given the town outside the school its name. Usually he enjoyed the sweet smell as a reminder of the territory owned by Calatians, but today he was more than usually aware of how precarious their school and that territory were.

Emily pulled the ledger back toward her. "Did you come up here just to show me that? I've got several more pages of numbers before I can officially tell you that we're in danger of running out of money."

"I know that." Kip craned his neck to look at the figures. "No, I came to tell you that Alice is expecting, so she won't be coming with us to the

Exposition of Sorcery."

"Oh!" Emily brightened. "Congratulations. Are you nervous at all?"

He shook his head. "I'm anxious to get back to Amsterdam. I know not all the Calatians there like me, but—what?"

Emily was glaring at him. "I meant, are you nervous about her health, or about becoming a father?"

"Her health will be fine," Kip said. "She's eighteen and as healthy as can be. I do want to try to convince a healer to come teach at the school, which I hope to do at the Exposition. As for becoming a father..." He smiled tightly. "I will be the best father I can, but Abel will be there, and my father and mother, and Aran and Arabella, so Alice and I will have plenty of help."

"Better you than me. This tedious work gives me a new respect for our disgraced Master Patris. I'd never be able to do it and then tend to an infant as well."

"What, Malcolm wouldn't help?"

Emily looked up over the rim of her spectacles. "My dear Irishman has many excellent qualities, but progressive ideas about the responsibilities of child care are sadly not among them."

"I suppose nobody's been reminding you every day about your duty to produce offspring."

"No, Mother gave up on me when I ran off to become a sorcerer, which she equates with becoming a man." Emily tapped the ledger. "And if she could see me now, she would be even more convinced of that. Speaking of... we should discuss how we intend to approach nobles at Amsterdam, now we're both going."

Kip nodded. "Can we just tell them we need money to keep going?"

"Abigail says that it's not wise to confess how much you need money. It puts them off."

"How does one approach them, then?"

"You talk about how you'd like to do more for the students, but sadly, you haven't got quite enough, and while you don't need their money, it would certainly help. And unfortunately we will probably have to offer sorcery in exchange for money."

"That doesn't feel right." Kip got up and swung his tail back and forth.

"What, selling sorcery for money? You did as much with Old John."

"That was different." He stopped and stared past Emily, as though they were in New Cambridge and he could see down the hill to the Founders Rest Inn. "I was doing work, little jobs, and John was giving me a place to live. What sorcery could I do that would be worth the amount we need? These moneyed people should be contributing because they want to invest in American sorcerers and help make us great."

"They've got the New Cambridge school for that." Emily made a face. "I guarantee you that Master Colonel Jackson, the great hero of the

Revolutionary War, has no trouble getting his friends to contribute."

Kip paced. "I asked Bryce again about money yesterday. He said that until we get a harvest this fall, we won't have much money to spare, but after that the East Georgia government might be able to contribute a little."

"That'll help. But it doesn't sound hopeful to keep us going."

The fox shook his head. "And with no promises from our country, even though we helped end the war—"

"The position that East Georgia was our reward is a not unreasonable one." Emily smiled.

"I know, I know." Kip heaved a sigh and walked over to Emily's window, looking out over the town of Peachtree. Already the memory of the village when he'd first come to visit his parents felt distant before the large, sprawling town below him. "The school went up quickly and we're all established here, and I have to admit that it's been more peaceful than I'd imagined possible."

"Then don't worry. Come with me to Amsterdam."

He lowered his head, looking inward now. "Do you think Victor will be there?"

"It's a place only for those who can do sorcery," Emily said. "Of course he will find a way in. And so what if he is?"

"We haven't heard anything about him in two years."

"I know."

"It's Victor. I know he's up to something."

"Kip."

The fox turned from the window. Emily had turned sympathetic eyes on him. "We all know who he is and what he is. Have the Pierces reported anything back from the Isle?"

"No," he admitted.

"Until they do—"

"But they won't see all the things going on at the college, only what calyxes are allowed—"

"I know." She held up a hand. "We've been through this. They're the best eyes we have right now."

"At least they're still speaking to me."

Emily clucked. "Don't worry about the Amsterdam Calatians not liking you. They've acclimated. At least, Charles Cotton says he quite looks forward to seeing you again. Every time I see him, he can't stop talking about how luxurious his house is."

"It wasn't the housing," Kip said. "They missed their community. We took volunteers, but they have a small group to start with, just fifty, so there could only be four different species, and people had to leave their friends. Charles may be able to see the bigger picture, but to many people, they lost the life they knew."

"For a better one."

"It's not all about how nice your house is, it seems." Kip brought his ears up. "It's for the best, though, and that's something to remember."

"I still think you should go see them, but we can work out details later." Emily waved at her ledger. "Now, if you don't mind, I do need to finish this."

Kip leaned back against the window. "Malcolm's not going to the Exposition, is he? I don't mind sharing a room there with you if it would save the school some money. We've done it before."

She raised an eyebrow and pulled out the drawer from her desk, where the pamphlet he'd brought in still lay. "Have you forgotten this so quickly?"

"Oh." His ears flattened, and he shook his head. "You're right."

"Besides," she said, closing the drawer, "I rather suspect Alice will want some privacy even from me."

"Alice isn't going." Kip went on in the face of Emily's growing smile. "She's pregnant. She can't. What?"

"Oh," Emily said, "I was just wondering whether I could summon a demon to follow you home so I could watch you try to tell her that."

When Kip arrived back at the house he shared with Alice, Abel, Aran, and Arabella, he called Alice's name from the foyer just inside the front door. "In here," she replied from the main bedroom upstairs.

The house, newly built by Calatians from the town in the past year, followed an open floor plan for the warmer climate and its Calatian residents. The foyer led directly to the wide staircase, and to the left and right, large open doorways led to the dining room and parlor, respectively. Both the great oak table in the dining room and the plush blue chairs of the parlor sat silent to Kip's ears as he walked up the stairs and to the main bedroom.

When he walked in, she held up two gowns. "Which one do you think is better? I like the blue one because it's more comfortable, but the yellow one goes better with my fur and also I think it's more formal. Oh, but the blue one would look better under a purple robe."

"I like the blue one," Arabella announced from a chair beside the bed, swinging her legs and tail. I like patterns better than flowers."

"I do too, but the flowers are more elegant, and there are only a few of them." Alice weighed them and looked again at Kip.

He smiled and shook his head. "There's no point in asking you not to go, is there?"

"None."

"You're—"

He gestured at her midsection, but she cut him off before he could say it. "Yes, I am, and what of it? It'll be months still until that slows me down. After that, yes, there will be a long time where I won't be able to travel or go anywhere interesting. But that time hasn't started yet, and I'm not about to allow it to start now."

Arabella frowned, looking between them. "What's going to slow you down?"

"Remember, you're going to have a new sister or brother?" Alice asked. They had talked, the three of them, about whether to call Alice's cub a "step-sibling," and Kip and Alice had both told Abel that they wanted their cubs to be considered full siblings to Aran and Arabella.

"Ohhh." Arabella put a paw over her own stomach. "It makes you slow?"

Kip walked over to the gowns and touched the yellow one. "When Aran was little and you carried him around, didn't you have to go slower? And be careful with him?"

Arabella looked back to Alice. "Oh, I see."

"I'm not carrying around anything like Aran's weight yet," Alice said, "and it's only a week in Amsterdam. Emily will send me right back if there's any trouble. Besides," she added, "there's more likely to be healers there than here."

"All right, all right." Kip smiled.

"Speaking of…" Alice paused. "Do you think you might ask one of the sorcerers there about your dream?"

"I'm done with that." He pulled the sleeve of the yellow gown up. "I like the pattern on this one better. Where's Abel? Have you told him we're going?"

"Not officially, but I'm sure he's worked it out."

"Daddy's out in the garden," Arabella said.

"Do you want time with him tonight?" Alice asked. "I don't mind. I'll be busy packing, and we'll be together over in Amsterdam."

"Thank you," Kip said. "I know it's out of turn, but I think so, if that's all right."

"It's fine. Ara, darling, would you fetch my petticoats from the chest there?"

Down the stairs and behind them led Kip to the back door, which opened onto a wide porch. Beyond that lay the garden, only now starting to show results of the planting they'd done a month ago. Abel and Aran knelt in the dirt, pulling weeds from between the small shoots.

"Is that a weed?" Aran asked as Kip approached them.

"I don't think so." Abel examined it. "But we can wait until Mrs. Pole comes around tomorrow and we'll ask her." He saw Kip and stood, smiling, ears perked. "We'll learn in another year," he said, "and I wager Aran will be a better gardener than any of us."

The nine-year-old cub wagged his tail and showed Kip the weeds he'd pulled. "That's wonderful," Kip said. "Our plants will grow tall and strong for sure."

"And have lots of strawberries!" Aran said.

"The strawberries are over there." Abel pointed. "They should be ready in another month or two."

The cub clapped his paws, sending pieces of weed scattering over the ground. Kip laughed. "I hope they're as good as the ones we got from Savannah last year."

"They will be." Aran touched his nose. "The plants smell sweet."

"Go take a look at them." Abel gave the cub a pat on the shoulders.

Aran needed no more encouragement; he ran along the garden to the shady patch of ground where the dark green strawberry plants spread their leaves. Abel and Kip watched him, and then Abel said, "Alice was packing for Amsterdam. I presume you couldn't talk her out of it?"

Kip shook his head. "She pointed out that there would be better healers there anyway."

"Hopefully not for long."

"That's part of the idea." Kip smiled.

Abel looked at him for a long moment. "Maybe someone there can explain your dream?"

"If I feel the need to be laughed at in Amsterdam as I was in Boston, I'll ask." Kip smiled. "I'm sorry. I know you mean well."

Abel looked neither offended nor amused. "It's not an ordinary dream. You've said that."

"I know. Maybe you're right. Maybe there will be someone there who can help."

"All right." The other fox met his eyes. "It's a lot of weight you're carrying. Can I help with any of it?"

Kip draped an arm over his shoulders. "You can look after Aran and Arabella, and help with Alice's cub when it arrives."

"That I can do." Abel answered Kip's smile with one of his own.

"And keep talking to the Isle Calatians. If you can find us two more students as good as Jorey, that'll be a great start to the next class."

"I can do that as well. Jorey himself will be the best ambassador, though. Take him back to the Isle to show them what he's learned."

"Maybe we'll stop there on the way back." Kip squeezed Abel and then dropped his arm.

Aran had finished inspecting the strawberries and now ran back to them, into his father's arms. "They look healthy," he announced.

"Good." Kip reached down to rub between his ears; he flattened them and smiled. "I'll be gone for a few days and I'm counting on you to keep them looking healthy until I get back."

"You're taking Jorey with you?" Abel asked.

"We're taking all three of the students," Kip said. "Emily thinks it'll be good for them, and it'll show people that we're a real school. We won't tell them that three is the entire class."

"I imagine Master Argent will be pleased to have a break." Abel smiled. "Whenever he comes to dinner, he looks as though he's been trying to chase them all around the town."

"I wouldn't be surprised. I only have them for one class and they're exhausting. I don't know how he manages every morning. In our classes with Patris, we were so quiet. Is it something we're doing wrong?"

"They're not afraid of you." Abel gave a slight smile.

"I'm not afraid of you," Aran echoed. "I think you're a very nice second father."

"That's good." Kip crouched down to be at the cub's level. "Because you're a smart, wonderful little fox, and I love you very much."

Aran detached himself from Abel to go hug Kip. "Do you think I'll be magic too one day?"

"We'll see." Kip had watched, but neither he nor Abel nor Alice had seen any sign that Aran or Arabella had any more access to magic than their father. "Maybe in a couple years we'll play some games and see how you do."

"Good." His little tail wagged.

Kip let go and stood. "I suppose I should get ready to go, too."

"Come on, Aran," Abel said. "Let's help your second father pack."

ACKNOWLEDGMENTS

I've never written a full war book before. This was a learning experience that could not have happened without contributions from a number of people.

This year, I launched a Patreon to support my writing (*https://www. patreon.com/timsusman*), and serialized this book through it (if you want to get to the fourth book more quickly, that will also be serialized on my Patreon, and more stories when these are done). Patrons as of this writing include: Furlia, wolfeye, tav fox, Shader, Pinemarten Avatar, and John Hawley. Thanks to them for their support!

Camielle Adams and PJ Wolf read an early version of this manuscript and gave me helpful feedback.

My fellow Unreliable Narrators Ryan Campbell, David Cowan, and Watts Martin all provided valuable feedback that helped shape this book (a comment from that group after reading The Tower and the Fox is largely responsible for the existence of this book). Some of the Happy Little Comets writing group, specifically Alisa Alering, James Brady, M. Milks, Dayna Smith, Brooke Wonders, and Becky Wright, either contributed to the brainstorming and plotting or provided critique or both (you have them to thank for the survival of Master Albright into this volume). Malcolm Cross proved an essential resource for 19th century warfare and life in general and pushed me to improve my prose.

Laura Garabedian worked around a strenuous and busy schedule to deliver her usual fantastic artwork both on the cover and the interiors. Mark and Grant from Argyll have been fantastic publishers, and I'll always be indebted to them for believing in this series.

And Mark, Jack, and Kobalt continue to be the best family a writer could ask for. Their constant love and support make these books possible.

ABOUT THE AUTHOR

Tim Susman started a novel in college and didn't finish one until almost twenty years later. In that time, he earned a degree in Zoology, worked with Jane Goodall, co-founded Sofawolf Press, and moved to California. He has attended Clarion in 2011 (arooo Narwolves!) and published short stories in Apex, Lightspeed, and ROAR, among others. He has also published many more novels and short stories under the name Kyell Gold and has won several awards for his fiction under both names. You can find out more about his stories at *timsusman.wordpress.com* and *www.kyellgold.com*, and follow him on Twitter at @WriterFox.

ABOUT THE ARTIST

My childhood was spent moving, changing locations and school environments. My constant companions became a dragon's horde of fantasy novels and my animals. This connection to creatures through the lens of fantasy has always been a touchstone for my work.

Through the years, I've experimented with many different media, wandering many paths. Now I've settled into the twin focuses of watercolor and oils. I find the dichotomy of their approach refreshing, and each time my hands move from one to the other I approach my work with new ideas and a cleaner view of where I should go.

Art is a way for my to communicate my love of the natural world and the fantasy I see within it. I think that the creation of a narrative around wildlife and fantastical animals can lead people to see the world and the many lives encompassed within it with more compassion and joy, returning the wonder of childlike curiosity to their lives.

I enjoy employing abstract backgrounds with minutely detailed subjects. The duality of the abstract work with small areas of focus lets the viewer fill in parts of strange color fields with their own story. My inspiration from nature and the narratives I like to weave around the strange beasts in my paintings lets me tell soundless stories to those who wish to explore them. In my paintings, bears covered in moss and trailing mushrooms emerge from the mist, gryphons dive from heights unknown with jewelry trailing them, and sphinxes ask questions unheard from behind blank masks. Where they come from, and what they want to say is left for those who watch them to determine. I hope through my work people can find a bit of mystery, of that wonder you have as a child making shapes in clouds, imagining what monster is in the closet, and making each walk in the woods a journey that may take them to Narnia, to Middle Earth, or a world of their own making

http://www.fairytaleswithtails.com

www.ingramcontent.com/pod-product-compliance
Lightning Source LLC
Chambersburg PA
CBHW051518260626
47170CB00003B/677